THE SERPENT'S DISCIPLE

THE SERPENT'S DISCIPLE

A NOVEL

BY DEBORAH STEVENS

Stevens

Gina
Warmest
Wishes!

Contact information: Deborah Stevens, The Serpent's Disciple
E-mail: request@deborahstevensauthor.com
Web site: www.deborahstevensauthor.com

Published By: Smith House Press
P.O. Box 13545
Roseville, MN 55113

E-mail: publisher@SmithHousePress.com
Web site: SmithHousePressPublishingConsultants.com

Editors: Richard Broderick
Cass Erickson, www.greengrantwriter.com
Cover and Interior Design: Nicholas McDougal, www.nicmcd.com

Author photograph by Mark Triplett

ISBN: 978-0-9894702-1-6

Printed in the United States of America

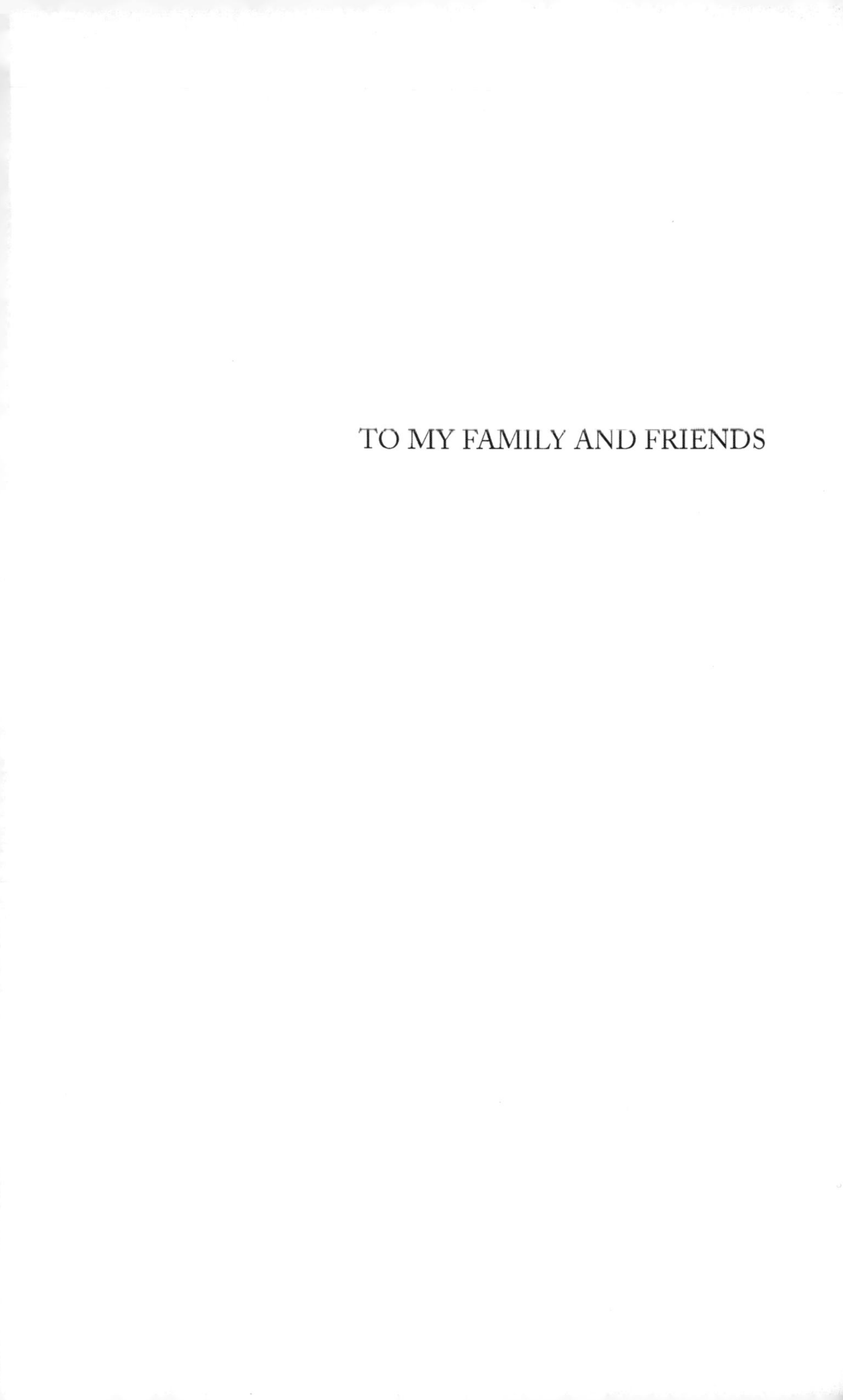

TO MY FAMILY AND FRIENDS

ACKNOWLEDGEMENTS

In producing my first novel, I, like every other author, have learned that a book doesn't reach the public without the assistance of many people. Creating a story and writing it down is only half the process. In helping me complete the other half, I have been lucky in finding talented people, people I now consider friends, who showed me what was needed to be done in order to get The Serpent's Disciple from my imagination to the printed page.

Thank you Sybil Smith, my publisher, who steered me in the right direction showing me the steps I needed to take to achieve an e-book conversion. And thanks to Richard Broderick, my writing coach who went over and above what was asked of him. And to Cass Erickson who did the final editing of the manuscript—any mistakes or typographical errors that have found their way into the finished book fall entirely on my shoulders. Celia Wirth who helped me with the endless issues I encountered with the computer and to the talented Nicholas McDougal who designed the cover and book trailer for The Serpent's Disciple and also did the book's interior design.

To family and friends who supported me and were excited for me, please accept my gratitude. Last, but not least, to my husband Larry who listened to me day after day and encouraged me not to give up.

To all of you, I thank you for helping me achieve the opportunity to make my dream come true.

THE SERPENT'S DISCIPLE

In Rome there are gathering forces of evil
They have entered into the highest places of the Church

Beware of the one who calls himself 'the angel of light'
Do not be deceived by the rank and position

Evil will never admit defeat
It will regroup and arise again under a new disguise

–Deb Stevens

FACT:

Propaganda Due or P2:
"Propaganda" was originally founded as "Propaganda Massonica" in 1877, in Turin, Italy. The name was changed to "Propaganda Due" following World War II, but by the 1960s the Lodge was all but moribund, holding few meetings. Licio Gelli became a Freemason in 1964 and was assigned the task of reorganizing the Lodge, but in 1976 its charter was withdrawn.

Without anyone's knowledge, however, Licio Gelli had secretly created a "shadow government," a pseudo-Masonic, "black," or "covert" Lodge from a list of inactive members and from 1976 to 1981, as Grand Master, P2 was implicated in numerous Italian crimes and mysteries.

Legions of Christ or L.O.C:
A Roman Catholic congregation of pontifical rights, made up of priests and seminarians studying for the priesthood, was founded in Mexico in 1941 by Marcial Maciel.

According to *The Wall Street Journal* (David Gibson, 5/6/2011), "The Legion of Christ ... became a global phenomenon in Catholicism by joining a devotion to orthodoxy and secrecy with an equal fidelity to the Legion's charismatic founder, but complaints of the Legion's cult-like aspects forced the elderly priest from ministry and launched an investigation."

N.B.: All descriptions of artwork, architecture, and secret rituals in this novel are accurate

CHAPTER ONE

Pesaro, Italy 1220 A.D.

Father Anthony, born Fernado Martins de Bulhoes, had just finished with his nightly prayers. Tomorrow, he and the young Giovanni, would prepare the church for people to come and hear the Bishop from Rome speak about the Crusades.

The Bishop was Pope Honorius III' s special envoy. Because of the troubling state of affairs in Italy, the threatening attitude of the Tatars, and the fear of a schism, he was being sent to villages like theirs to inspire and recruit people to join the fight. In 1215 The Pope had issued the Papal Bull "Ad Liberaindam" calling all Christendom to join the crusade. His wish was to reacquire the Holy Land and Jerusalem.

Anthony heard a light rap on the door to his room and someone softly whispering.

"Are you still awake Father Anthony?"

"Giovanni is that you? Yes, come in my son."

Giovanni's father and mother had brought him to the monastery when he was 12 years old. Since then he had grown to be a tall lad, slender with dark wavy hair and warm dark brown eyes.

During the last six years the monks became his family and in exchange for helping around the monastery, he was taught to read and write, turning out to be an excellent student.

"I'm sorry if I disturbed you father but I couldn't sleep. I keep thinking about the Bishop coming the day after tomorrow. Do you think the war will end soon?"

"Only our Heavenly Father knows the answer to that

question. We can only pray on it and ask for the strength to follow the Lord' s will."

The priest could tell Giovanni had something else on his mind.

"There's something I wanted to give to you Father. I have been working on it for months and I finished it a few nights ago." Father Anthony watched as Giovanni brought something wrapped in a brown piece of cloth tied with a string, from behind his back. As he untied the string, the fabric fell away and he held in his hands a beautiful wooden box.

"I made it to thank you for teaching me to read and write. I hope you like it." The priest held the box in his hands and saw that it was quite unique in design.

"Giovanni, I don't know what to say. We've been blessed having you here at the Abbey. When you found the time to make such a beautiful box I will never know but I will always treasure it. One with such devotion is surely one of God's chosen one's. You will be a good servant to those who want to learn the faith."

Giovanni was fidgeting as the Father spoke.

"Please Father Anthony, may I have it. There' s something very special about the box I want to show you."

Curious to see what Giovanni meant the priest handed the box back to him.

"First, the key to lock the box is inside, see."

Then he continued to explain to Father Anthony the secrets of the box.

"Giovanni what a genius you are. I must pass your gifts of artistry on to the Bishop. Perhaps they will have need of someone with such a gift in Rome."

"My only wish was to please you Father Anthony. I am so happy you like the box. Whatever God has planned for me, I will work to please Him the best way I know how but I must tell you a story about the box," excited he continued.

"I was working in the fields a few months back and was trying to think of something I could do to thank you for teaching me to read and write. A monk I had never seen before was also working in the fields that day. When it came time to stop for the midday meal he came over to me and offered to share his.

He had packed more than he could eat, and a young lad like me, he was sure, would be able to eat more than what was in the small pouch I carried. As we ate, I told him I was trying to come up with an idea for a gift to thank you for all you have done for me.

He said he knew of you and was sent to tell me to make a box that could keep a secret safe from others eyes. I did not understand why it must hide a secret but he was so kind and wise of a holy man I promised to create something special. I thanked him for the meal and went out to the field to finish my work. At the end of the day when I looked for him he was gone. I've never seen him again. I said a prayer that night and thanked God for sending me the messenger and that I would fulfill my promise both to Him and to the monk I met in the field that day."

Father Anthony did not question God' s ways. He would accept the box from young Giovanni as a gift of kindness and great effort. If there was a purpose for the box he knew that he would be shown it when the time was right.

"Dear Giovanni, though I would like to hear more about that day in the field, we must get our rest. We have much to do tomorrow to prepare for the bishop. Bless you Giovanni for your faith, kindness and thank God for the gifts he has honored you with. Let us say a prayer and then we must get our sleep for the morning will be here before we know it."

CHAPTER TWO

September 28, 1978 The Papal Palace

Cardinal Jean Villot, Vatican secretary of state, had gotten hold of the list of appointments, resignations to be asked for, and transfers Pope John Paul I planned on putting into motion the next morning. There was one common denominator that linked each of the men about to be replaced … it was Freemasonry.

Villot was aware of each man's affiliation to the Masons; more important, so was the Pope. It was the reason the Pope would strip these men of their power.

Pope John Paul I had evidence indicating that within the Vatican City State, there were over one hundred Masons ranging from priests to cardinals. The Pope was further preoccupied with an illegal Masonic Lodge called Propaganda Due (P2), which had infiltrated far beyond even the Vatican in its search for wealth and power. The fact that it had penetrated the Vatican walls and had converted priests, bishops, and even cardinals made P2 anathema, a formal ecclesiastical curse accompanied by excommunication.

The changes the Pope was intending on making would create, by any standards a dramatic reshuffle within the Vatican. It would set the church in a new direction, directions that Villot and others on the list considered dangerous for their movement.

On the morning of September 29, 1978 at 4:45 a.m., Sister Vicenza entered the papal apartments to bring the Holy Father his morning tea, only to find the lifeless body of the Pope. Fifteen minutes later at 5:00 a.m. it was reported that Cardinal Villot confirmed the death of the Pope. Only thirty-three days after his election, Pope John Paul I was dead.

Sister Vicenza gave two conflicting reports concerning the state in which she first found Pope John Paul I. According to a group of French priests that same morning, it was "in his bathroom" that she found the Holy Father dead, still in his papal robes. Later, after Cardinal Villot was present, she reported that upon entering the room she found the Pope sitting up in bed "with an expression of agony" before he died.

This small detail is significant. If it was true that Sister Vicenza found the Holy Father dead in the bathroom still in his papal robes, it could be construed that he died shortly after his "toast" with Cardinal Villot, the night of September 28, 1978.

That evening Villot hastily arranged for the embalming to be performed, a procedure as unusual as it was illegal, Villot also insisted that no blood was to be drained from the body, and neither were any of the organs to be removed. No official death certificate has ever been issued. No autopsy ever performed. Cause of death: Unknown.

CHAPTER THREE

Present Day

Peter caught a glimpse of the man's reflection in the glass. Recognizing the face he stopped and stared at the image. The person looking back at him had been dead for more than twenty years. A long time ago, Peter decided that if the man were naive enough to believe the world was a just and righteous place if only we followed God's commandments, he was a fool and deserved what he got. That was another lifetime, and he was a man of power and wealth now, not the person he saw in the glass. The events leading up to his death had been buried along with the man.

Peter made the mistake of giving himself permission to remember thinking, that maybe it had all been a fabrication of his imagination. But now in a moment of weakness, he allowed the same thought to cross his mind. By opening that door to the past, he fell victim to the painful memories that came flooding back. The past was now the present and he started reliving it all over again.

Standing in front of his wife and Father Damian, Peter prayed they would tell him it was all a lie. It wasn't enough she was pregnant with Damian's child; they also had been embezzling from his company. A bank account had been set up under the guise that it was for the church, where the pair had been depositing the money that they were stealing.

Peter would never forget the expression on their faces when he presented them with the incriminating evidence. They appeared shocked and stared at him like he was crazy. Could he be wrong? Had he somehow dreamed all of it up? He watched in slow motion as the two most important people in his life stole a glance from each other, then turned and faced him. What Peter saw sent a chill through him. It was as if he were looking into the eyes of the devil himself.

Losing both his mother and father only two months earlier and now, being made a fool of by his wife and the priest was more than he could handle. His world spun out of control. Time seemed to stop as he tried to figure out why this was happening to him. Then he felt a sense of calmness, which puzzled him; he suddenly had no feelings one way or the other about what had just happened. His breathing slowed and his heart stopped pounding. No longer caring, he became aware of the sound of something beeping. Trying to figure out where it was coming from, all at once he remembered setting his watch alarm.

As he checked the time he was back in the present. The past slipped into the dark hole it came from, never to be revisited again. Peter had learned well and would be the ruler of his own soul.

CHAPTER FOUR

Pesaro, Italy 1220 A.D.

"Goodnight Father Anthony, I will see you at morning prayer. I'm so happy you are pleased with my gift."

Giovanni agreed with the Father that they must rest now. There were still a few things to do in the morning before the bishop arrived. Giovanni loved the church and God, but he desired to marry one day and, hopefully, God would bless him with a son or daughter. Until that time, he was happy at the abbey.

As Father Anthony sat on the edge of his bed, he blew out the candle on the side table. Closing his eyes he silently prayed, "I ask for your blessings Lord to do your work here on earth and that I may be worthy of the task."

Opening his eyes, he looked out the window at the full moon. It was extremely bright this evening, its light covering the earth like a warm blanket. He marveled at its beauty and the mystery of God's creations. A moonbeam slowly made its way toward his window. The small room filled with a beautiful white light and an angel took form before his eyes. Anthony blessed himself with the sign of the cross and bowed his head in reverence. Then the angel spoke.

"Anthony, Our Father has sent me to tell you that he has chosen you to be His messenger. I will come to you at sunrise for three days where the olive grove ends and the waters begin. You must come alone. There you will write down the words I speak. After the third day you will become the Guardian of the book. It must be kept in a safe place for the Chosen One."

Anthony now knew the purpose of the gift he had received from Giovanni. The light that had filled the room slowly withdrew and Anthony was alone again in the darkness, except for a soft glow, that came from the cross that hung from his neck. He held the cross with both hands and thanked God for finding him worthy.

CHAPTER FIVE

Day One

Anthony woke early. He had prepared a small breakfast the night before. Eating it quickly he quietly left the abbey while it was still dark. When he first came to the abbey, during one of his many walks, he had discovered the spot the angel spoke of. He often went there to be alone and pray; now silently waiting as the sun slowly rose in the east. A small ball of light broke away from the sun and slowly grew larger as it traveled directly toward him, rays of light shooting from all sides of the sphere. He fell to his knees, afraid, but a voice softly said, "Do not be afraid, Anthony, Our Father is pleased you have obeyed his command. Have you brought paper and pen?"

"Yes, I have it here."

"Then we will begin."

The angel began to speak as Anthony wrote down the words.

"Blessed is the one who reads aloud the words of the prophecy, and blessed are those who hear and keep what is written, for a great battle is near."

"Evil is being accepted broadly when human beings who are temples of God are being desecrated by their own wickedness."

"The spirit of truth came with the knowledge to man that the day would come when a great delusion shall descend upon mankind and cover the earth in a blanket of spiritual darkness. The forces of six sixty-six will enter the

> ***Holy City of Rome. Keep, my children, a constant vigilance of prayer. There will be a war of spirits, the forces of darkness against the forces of light seeking to set upon the Chair of Peter."***

"Now go, Anthony, and write what you have been told today into a book for safekeeping. Then return here tomorrow at sunrise." Anthony did as he was told.

Seventh day of the fourth month of the year 1220 A.D. of Our Lord

Day Two

Quickly changing clothes Anthony slipped out again while it was still dark. He waited for the sunrise and the angel to appear. He was not afraid this time as the ball of light grew larger and the angel appeared.

"Again, Our Lord is pleased you have obeyed His command. Now write down the words I speak."

Anthony took pen and paper and began to write.

> ***"Listen! I am standing at the door, knocking; if you hear my voice and open the door I will come in to you. Many Shepherds have fallen asleep. Awaken from your slumber, O Pastors. Many have come posing as angels of light, but with darkness of heart and dark secrets."***

> ***"Pray for all men of sin and above all pray for the children."***

> ***"Let anyone who has an ear listen to what the Spirit is saying to the churches."***

"Now go and write what you have been told into the book. Return one more day to hear the words of Our Lord."

Eighth day of the fourth month of the year 1220 A.D. of Our Lord

Day Three

Anthony awoke even earlier than the previous two mornings.

He knew this would be the last day he would be visited by the angel. Arriving early to the spot where the angel would appear, he wondered if this was nothing more than a dream that he would awake from and find himself lying in his bed.

Anthony sat quietly as he watched dawn approaching. It was his favorite part of the day. The sun slowly rose in the sky and he watched as the ball of light descended down to earth. Then he heard the now familiar voice of the angel.

"God is pleased with you, Anthony. You have proven your love for Him. This will be the last day for you to hear the words of Our Lord and write them down as you have been told.

"You were given a gift. Place the book in it so no other eyes can read what you were witness to. When the time comes, you will be shown what to do. Now write down what I say, and Anthony began to write down the words for the last time.

> ***"I, your God and your Judge eternal give you in command the direction to turn back and restore My House while there is still time."***
>
> ***"Beware the snake has risen its head again."***
>
> ***"The battle will separate the wheat from the chaff. All that is rotten shall fall."***
>
> ***"Take the knowledge My Son has taught you."***
>
> ***"I spoke through My disciple Daniel who wrote down My words. Study them well."***
>
> ***"I am the Alpha and the Omega. I am the beginning and the end. No one came before me and no one will come after me."***

As the angel finished, Anthony felt a sharp pain in his hand. He dropped the pen he had been writing with and looked to see the reason for the stabbing pain.

"You have received one of the five wounds that Our Lord had to endure when he was placed on the Cross. You will know that what you have witnessed these last three days was not a dream. Now go Anthony and serve the Lord."

CHAPTER SIX

Present Day

He was born Anthony Alberto Andruccioli 82 years ago. Even though he was christened Anthony, after his patron saint, most people knew him by his middle name, Alberto. Few people were aware that Alberto's bloodline could be traced back to a young boy by the name of Giovanni from the thirteenth century who was an apprentice to the future Saint Anthony.

God's plan for Giovanni was not to become a priest. As the monk was near death, Giovanni, now a young man, learned that the gift he had made for his friend and teacher was a sanctuary to sacred scripture. The Chosen One was the only one able to unlock the secret of the box, of which Giovanni would be the first.

As Alberto's final hours approached, his daughter Antonella sat by his bedside. Sad to leave his two children behind, he was happy to be going home. When his own father was dying, Alberto had been the one chosen to receive the cross that now hung around his daughter's neck.

It had not been needed during his lifetime, so one more time it was passed down from parent to child. As the Chosen One Antonella now possessed the secret to unlocking the gift a young boy had made for his teacher hundreds of years ago.

Antonella listened as her father explained what she had been chosen for and the magnitude of what she now possessed.

"You must have faith, my dear Antonella, if it is your destiny to seek out the gift given by the young Giovanni. You will be guided and protected. Never be afraid, I will be right there with you," he said, smiling lovingly at her.

Alberto's breathing was becoming more labored now. "Dad, is there anything I can get for you?"

"No dear, I'm just so tired."

"Just rest, Dad, I'll be right here while you sleep."

It is so hard to know what to do or what to say when a parent is disappearing before your eyes. Antonella could feel her father's hand was cooler than it should be and there was a slightly bluish tint to his skin. She knew his body was no longer fighting to live. She remembered experiencing the same thing when her mother died. They are more in the next world than they are in this world. She wanted him to wake up and be better but she knew it wasn't possible.

Leaning over, she whispered, "Dad, it's okay if you want to go; we'll be okay, Anthony and I, we'll be okay."

Holding his hand, she was looking at him lying there when suddenly his eyes opened and they were so clear and alert it startled her.

"Remember dear the secret lies within. I love you, Antonella, and tell Anthony I am very proud of him." Then he gently squeezed her hand, closed his eyes, and took one last breath. His soul departed. Her father was no longer of this world.

CHAPTER SEVEN

Anthony and Antonella hadn't spent much time together over the last ten years. Anthony went to the University of Michigan and received a degree in architecture and later a doctorate in religion. Professor Digornia, the dean of the College of Architecture, saw great potential in Anthony and became his mentor and friend. He strongly urged Anthony to enter some of his work into two international design contests; Anthony ended up taking first place in one and honorable mention in the other. After graduation the professor recommended him to a large firm that did work all over the world.

Anthony had been with the firm for more than ten years. The last couple years, he had been traveling to Europe quite often to consult on the restoration of historic buildings. Besides becoming fluent in Italian, Anthony also worked on achieving a black belt in the last two years.

Antonella, on the other hand, attended Michigan State University (MSU) and graduated with a Ph.D. in history. After graduation she was offered a position to teach at MSU, which she accepted. This semester her courses focused on the Renaissance.

Unlike her brother, Antonella had only traveled to Europe through books and surfing the Web. For fun, she liked to wander through antique stores looking for small unique boxes. It had become her newest passion. The latest find was a small wooden prayer box thought to be quite old. On the inside of the lid was an inscription and the walls of the box were carved with intricate carvings. It was believed to be a replica of a box from the thirteenth century.

When lecturing to her students, she would notice sometimes in old paintings one of these small treasures, sitting on a table or being held by someone. Insignificant in the overall artwork, but someone had to craft the boxes and maybe they had even been commissioned by the person in the painting. It reminded her of the Russian Fabergé jeweled eggs, and how they are sought after by collectors around the world.

Neither Anthony nor Antonella had married although Anthony had been in a serious relationship, and everyone thought he and Mary Ellen would get married after she received her law degree from Harvard. They were perfect for each other, or that's what everyone thought, but they parted ways. No one in the family knew why; everyone wanted to ask but never did. Not long after that Antonella met Larry and things were going well between them.

Since their mother had passed away a few years ago and now their father had just died, the two of them talked about taking a trip to their father's birthplace of Pesaro, Italy, a small town on the Adriatic Sea.

Antonella had just gotten off the phone with Larry and saw that Anthony had tried to call. She called him back and he picked up on the second ring.

"About time Nelli," his nickname for his sister, "So are we all set? Did you finish covering the course outlines with your replacement?"

"Yes, everything is taken care of. I'm starting to wonder if they're even going to miss me."

"Right, that's why they just made you head of the department," said Anthony.

"It just seems strange," responded Nelli, "I can't remember the last time I took off in the middle of a semester."

"Well, it's the only time that worked for both of us and it should be fun to see where our father grew up."

Larry was very supportive of Nelli taking the trip and thought it was a wonderful idea. It would be an opportunity for Nelli and Anthony to spend time together and reconnect.

It was the strangest thing though, once she and Anthony made the decision to take this trip Nelli swore she felt the presence of her father sometimes.

She'd talked to colleagues who said that was not uncommon when someone close to you died, but lately she was having dreams about him too.

CHAPTER EIGHT

Rome

Mary Ellen O'Farrell had done it! She accomplished the first hurdle. In her newly appointed position she'd broken through hundreds of years of tradition. Now the highest-ranking woman and many consider the highest-ranking female adviser in the Catholic Church. Pope John Paul II had appointed her president of the Pontifical Academy of Social Sciences. The group studies economics, sociology, law, and political science to help the pontiff develop the church's social Doctrines. As a member of the Pontifical Council of the Laity, she was also a papal advisor on some of the most sensitive issues facing the Catholic Church, one of them being the continuing sexual scandal involving clergy.

She made a promise to herself and to her brother to restore his reputation. Laying out a plan she finally felt she had the means available to accomplish her goal.

Both sides of the family being good Irish Catholics had produced priests. Father Patrick O'Farrell on her father's side, now in his seventies, is retired and enjoys filling in on weekends, to serve mass for priests who are either ill or on vacation. Parishioners love it when he visits their church.

Then there is Uncle Clancy McFarland or Father Clancy on her mother's side. He is a slim man; his hair is not as full and not as white as Uncle Pat's. He has warm hazel eyes that radiate a gentle soul ready to comfort anyone in need.

The two uncles are very different; though when they are together at a family gathering they rib and tease each other nonstop.

Devlin and Mary Ellen were born identical twins, Mary Ellen being the oldest by six minutes. Of course, she always had to remind her brother of that. Devlin had followed in his uncle's footsteps, but then false accusations were made by parents of his parish of inappropriate behavior by Devlin with their child. Ever since the day he made his first communion, he wanted to become a priest; the day the Church excommunicated him both his and Mary Ellen's worlds' collapsed.

Devlin somehow came to terms with all of it, putting his life back together again, but Mary Ellen never forgot the look on his face, when she picked her brother up that day, and he walked out of the church no longer wearing the familiar Collarino shirt and clerical collar.

She promised herself then and there that she would prove the sexual allegations against her brother were a lie. So far, Mary Ellen had been unsuccessful in clearing her brother's name. Now that she was at the Vatican in a position of strength, she hoped she would have access to information not available to her before. She would find out who and why someone had done this and take the proof to the Archbishop of the Apostolic Penitentiary at the Vatican.

The Apostolic Penitentiary has jurisdiction only over matters in the internal forum, one of them being the absolution of excommunications, latæ sententiæ, reserved to the Holy See. After proving Devlin's innocence she would then make an appeal to have them reinstate Devlin to the priesthood. But because of her allegiance to her brother, she had sacrificed her relationship with Anthony.

CHAPTER NINE

Present Day

The initiation ceremony was about to begin. P2's Grand Master sits on his throne waiting for the pagan to enter. To everyone present Peter Romanus, Grand Master of Propaganda Due, will be referred to as Naj Hannah, translated means King Cobra.

His dark hair is sprinkled with gray at the temples but he still has the body of a much younger man and did not lack a handsome face to go with everything else. Heads turn when he enters a room. Now perched upon his throne he was an imposing figure.

Across the room in black leather chairs around a red marble conference table, sit twelve members of an elite group known as the Wolf Pack, Naj Hannah's disciples, some even say his execution squad. They are dressed in black satin ceremonial robes and wearing hoods reminiscent of those worn by members of the Ku Klux Klan. Embroidered upon each is the insignia of a cobra head, the symbol of their order. None of the disciples know the identity of any of his eleven brothers.

Two more Masons stand post at the entrance to the meeting room, their faces also covered. They are Peter's personal bodyguards whose job is to protect the Grand Master and kill any disciple who betray the cause "Il Momento di Passare all." Like the twelve disciples, each bodyguard is armed with an ax and automatic weapon. The ax is a reminder to anyone who betrays the oath, "to kill the serpent you must chop off its head."

There is an uneven series of knocks at the door, "Your Worshipful," a disciple announces, "a pagan wishes to enter." Peter Romanus strikes the table with one blow from his ax. The massive door swings open slamming against the inner wall. Two guards escort the initiate to the center of the room where he faces the twelve hooded disciples with his back to the Grand Masters throne.

The pagan is wearing a plain black hood and is blindfolded. His identity is known only to the Grand Master and to no one else. He is asked one question by each of the twelve disciples but the pagan does not answer, instead one of the guards speaks for him. Once all the ritual questions are asked, the pagan is turned to face the Naj Hannah.

Peter had been looking forward to today. With the initiation of Cardinal Cavallari to the brotherhood, the final piece of his plan would be in place.

So he begins, "Pagan, are you prepared to die in order to preserve the secrets of Propaganda Due?"

The initiate now answers for himself.

"I am."

"Do you have the necessary quality of contempt for danger?"

"I do."

"Do you have the necessary quality of courage?"

"I am courageous."

"Are you prepared to fight and perhaps face shame, even death, so that we who may become your Brothers can destroy the forces that want to kill us?"

"I am."

The blindfold is removed. It takes a moment for the cardinal's eyes to adjust. This is the first time since entering the compound that he has been allowed to see light. It represents the power of P2, "Without membership one is blind, with the help of the order, however, the way is clear."

Peter Romanus smiles to himself. In less than two weeks, with the help of the cardinal, he would take his rightful place as Bishop of Rome, taking the name Peter II and the next Ruler of the New World Order (NWO). The world would soon realize that his power would reach far beyond Vatican City. The battle between good and evil would finally be won. Those who did not accept the mark of loyalty would be put to death. He would reign supreme over all the earth.

CHAPTER TEN

As Peter Romanus looked out the window from his country estate in Arezzo, onto the vine-covered hills outside his private office, five men were gathering in a secret location outside of Pesaro. They were not to be told the Grand Master would be watching and listening on closed circuit TV.

Each of them was flying in this morning. They had been contacted only two weeks ago by Thomas, the Grand Master's right-hand man, informing them of the meeting and to rearrange their calendars. Two weeks was short notice for men in their position, but the request had come directly from Peter. They knew better than not to attend.

Angelo Acciaiolio, owner and CEO of Mediaset, the commercial television empire in Italy had just arrived at the location given to him by Thomas. He was a handsome man in his early fifties. The navy Armani pinstripe suit he wore was tailor-made to fit his toned body perfectly.

"Silvio, I didn't expect to see you here." Silvio Berlusconi had been going through some documents and had not noticed Angelo enter the room.

"Buon giorno Angelo, I landed about an hour ago and was driven straight here."

"I didn't know if anyone else would be coming. Good to see you my friend," said Angelo as he placed his hand on Silvio's shoulder. "Or should I call you prime minister? I hope you were happy with our coverage of your campaign?"

They gave each other a knowing glance, implying a secret.

There was no question, that his TV networks would not be favorable towards Silvio and his run for office. P2 was pulling the strings.

The next Prime Minister was also in his fifties. He was a nice looking man, tall and slim and very charismatic, an excellent trait for the role of the next leader of Italy. His wife Sophia was an elegant, self-assured, and beautiful woman. They were the perfect power couple.

Angelo continued, "Do you think anyone else will be attending?"

Before Silvio could respond, in walked General Orazio D'Amoto, Head of the Military Intelligence Service (SISMI). Orazio nodded to both men and headed in their direction.

Angelo and Silvio looked at each other concerned by the general's attendance. Silvio whispered under his breath, "What's he doing here?"

Miles away seated comfortably at his desk, Peter smiled to himself. He could hear every word being said.

"It's good to see both of you," said Orazio, not meaning a word of it.

General D'Amoto was not a large man but the men under his command did not question his authority. He spent most of his time listening and observing the people around him. He sensed that Angelo and Silvio were questioning his presence at the meeting.

More voices could be heard entering the room. They turned to see who else was attending the meeting.

In walked Vingenzo Parocchi, director-general of Banca Nazionale del Lavoro, the largest bank in Italy. Vingenzo was instrumental in all three of their lives. His financial backing was critical to their careers. Walking next to Vingenzo was Thomas. The two men were engaged in a heated discussion. A third man dressed in the unmistakable black cassock, with a red silk sash and the pectoral cross-suspended from a cord of scarlet and gold silk hung from his neck, listened in but said nothing. It was the newest initiate, Cardinal Franco Cavallari from the Vatican.

Cardinal Cavallari was head of the department at the Vatican that oversees religious congregations of men and women. The department was investigating the Legion of Christ and the sexual allegations and charges of the misuse of funds, by the founder of the order.

There were also allegations being directed against Pope Benedict XVI; that he knew of some of the wrongdoings and had done nothing about it. The scandal was seriously affecting the worldview of the Vatican, if it was corrupt beyond repair.

Whatever Thomas and Vingenzo had been discussing had come to an end. They were now standing in front of the other three men who were already present in the room. Thomas now spoke to all five men.

"Gentlemen, thank you for rearranging your schedules. Everyone invited is now present, if you would please show me your proof of membership."

Each man wore the same ring given to him upon becoming a member of P2. When rotated on the finger, it revealed what might be mistaken for a scar. At the end of each initiation ceremony and after the swearing of the oath, each new inductee received a tattoo of the head of a cobra.

"Thank you. Please take a seat and we will begin the meeting shortly. I must make one call before we start."

He disappeared into the next room and closed the door quietly behind him.

Hundreds of miles away Peter's phone rang, the screen showed it was Thomas.

"I see everyone has arrived. Have they each brought the materials I requested?"

"Yes, they have each presented me with a disk and hard copy as requested. The disks have already been put in the vault and an electronic copy has been sent to you. The hard copies will be used during the meeting then shredded afterwards," added Thomas.

Peter continued, "Before the meeting commences remind them; although they are each in powerful positions, they are not to forget who placed them there."

Thomas had been with Peter from the beginning as his propaganda minister and he knew not to disobey Peter Romanus. He had seen what happens to those who had over the years. He would not make the same mistake.

"They are all fully aware of the consequences if they break their oath, but I will remind them again of how they got where they are today. Everything is set on this end, are you receiving a clear satellite feed on your end?" asked Thomas.

"Yes, all the systems are running as planned. I am most

interested in Cardinal Cavallari at this meeting. Please continue to monitor all the devices carefully."

There was not an inch of the room that was hidden from view. The most advanced devices available had been installed. There were cameras even installed under the conference table and under each chair so the guests' hands, legs, and feet could be viewed. Nothing would go unnoticed. There were sensors in each chair that would monitor the individual's respiratory and cardiovascular responses. All the information would be sent directly to computer screens in Peter's office to watch and be analyzed.

If they twitched Peter wanted to know how many times and for how long.

CHAPTER ELEVEN

The paternity test came back positive! Cardinal Donovan McKenna read, and then reread the slip of paper in front of him. Leaning back in his chair in disbelief, he glanced around at the beautifully decorated office he spent his days in. He never grew tired of standing at the window looking out at the Sistine Chapel and St. Peter's Square.

What a blessed path God had chosen for him to journey down, becoming the Prefect of the Congregation for the Doctrine of the Faith (CDF), the oldest of the nine congregations of the Roman Curia. Among the most active of the congregations, it oversees Catholic Church doctrine. Its offices are housed at the Palace of the Holy Office at the Vatican. As Prefect he receives all information first then discerns its level of importance and directs it to the appropriate person.

His ambition had never been to end up at the Vatican. He had become a priest at a later age than most. After graduation from Harvard Law School, he was lucky enough to get a job in the office of the Governor of New York. It was an exciting time in his life but something was missing for him. Unable to ignore it any longer he accepted that his true calling in life was to become a priest. He joined the seminary, one thing led to another and here he was Cardinal Donovan McKenna working for Pope Benedict XVI.

The last five years had not been easy with the ever-growing reports of sexual abuse by priests. He instinctively reached for the cross, which hung from a gold chain around his neck for comfort. Now with this morning's latest information, once the news media got wind of it, who knows what the repercussions would be. The Catholic religion is not the only faith that has confronted such issues. That said, the cover up had been handled badly with no thought of the consequences if it ever got exposed.

Settlements of money were made to individuals and families. The offending priests were transferred out of the churches and many times moved to another with no disclosure to the new parish. This final revelation a Father Marcial Maciel, the founder of the Legion of Christ Order and the Regnum Christi movement, could cause many to question if the Vatican had lost its way.

During Pope John Paul II's reign Father Maciel was a very prominent figure in the church, appointed to various positions such as the Chancellor of the Pontifical Athenaeum Regina Apostolorum based in Rome and to the Ordinary Assembly of the Synod of Bishops on the formation of Candidates for the Priesthood in Actual Circumstances. He was a member of the Interdicasterial Commission for a Just Distribution of Clergy, the IV General Conference of Latin American Bishops (CELAM), the Synod of Bishops on Consecrated Life and their Mission in the Church and the World, the Synod of Bishops' Special Assembly for America and since 1994 a permanent consultant to the Congregation for the Clergy.

The allegations were said to be false, but with this proof that he had fathered a child and other charges surfacing that he had acquired real estate and accumulated large sums of money, the lies were starting to unravel. Sadly, it was becoming evident that evil had slithered its way into all corners of the Church.

So lost in thought, Cardinal McKenna became aware of the increasingly loud knocking at the door by his assistant.

"Come in Robert."

"I'm sorry to interrupt you Cardinal McKenna but your meeting with his Holiness is in thirty minutes. I thought I would remind you in case you needed to prepare."

"Yes, thank you Robert. It was good you did. I lost track of the time."

"Will you need me to get anything for you before your meeting?"

"No, I have everything prepared. Are there any calls I need to return before my meeting?"

"No, nothing more since this morning, are you expecting

one? I can look into it if you wish."

"No, thank you again Robert." Donovan watched as Robert turned and quietly closed the door behind him.

Getting up from his desk, Donovan walked over to the window and looked out onto St. Peter's Square. Millions of the faithful have gathered in this holy square over the centuries. Now millions of the faithful were questioning the actions of the church and its leaders. He silently prayed for God's guidance and blessings for the Pope and His Church.

In less than thirty minutes he would need to inform the Holy Father of the latest information. Would a single word on a sheet of white paper create a tidal wave that could destroy the papacy? He stared out the window and wondered what the future held.

CHAPTER TWELVE

Nelli wanted to finish up what she was working on but was struggling to keep her eyes open. Resting her elbow on the arm of the chair and using her hand to support her head, she thought she'd rest her eyes for just a few seconds. Without warning her head flopped forward, she had fallen asleep and then realized her phone was ringing. Grabbing her purse and rummaging through it, not finding it she stopped to listen but there was only silence. Grabbing the landline, she called her cell phone and following the sound, found it underneath a pile of mail. As she was about to see who called, her home phone rang.

"Hey, I just tried calling you on your cell," said Anthony.

"Sorry it was hidden under a stack of mail," replied Nelli still ticked at herself for falling asleep.

"Just thought I'd check in with you, have everything pretty much taken care of on my end how about you?"

"Just working up some lesson plans, then was going to jump into bed. I haven't been sleeping well."

"We'll only be gone a couple weeks Nelli. Your department will survive without Professor Andruccioli for two weeks."

"You're probably right. I just talked to Larry and he said the same thing. Well dear brother, I think I will read a little about Dad's birthplace before I go to sleep. See what we shouldn't miss when we visit. I'll talk to you tomorrow."

"Okay Nelli, try and get a good night's sleep."

Nelli put the phone back into its cradle and got into bed. She started reading about what to see while in Pesaro. One thing not to miss was the altarpiece by Giovanni Bellini housed in the art gallery of the Museo Civico in Piazza Toschi Mosca just off Via Rossini in the adjoining Pinacoteca.

Between 1471 and 1474 Pesaro's ruling Lord Costanzo Sforza had commissioned the picture from the Venetian artist. The masterpiece called The Coronation of the Virgin was to be painted for the church now known as Madonna delle Grazie in Via San Francesco. The altarpiece situates the coronation not in some starry heaven but in the countryside around Pesaro dominated by the castle of Gradara.

Portraits of saints flank the central scene, ranging from the hesitant Saint Lawrence to the dreamy Saint Anthony. Below, scenes from the lives of the saints occupy the compartments across the base of the painting.

As Nelli continued to read she thought she heard someone say her name.

"That's ridiculous, I'm the only one here," she thought to herself.

Then she heard her name again.

"Antonella, come closer my dear."

A man was waving her forward with his hand. He had the strangest garments on. His clothes and hands were splattered with paint and he was standing next to a painting.

"I signorina, am Giovanni Bellini."

As she looked at the painting it was the one she had just read about in the guidebook depicting the crowning of the Blessed Virgin Mary.

"You can't be Giovanni Bellini; he lived in the fifteenth century!"

"That is very true Antonella, but I've been sent to help you on your journey. My painting holds answers to your questions."

"But, I have no questions. I don't know what you are talking about."

"But you will Antonella. Study the painting carefully. It will guide you along the path you seek. Remember to look within, there you will find the answer."

"My father said the same words to me before he died."

Giovanni looked at Antonella and nodded his head, acknowledging he knew of what she spoke. She looked away as her eyes began filling with tears remembering the day her father died. Composing herself, she turned back to ask him to explain what he meant but no one was there.

There was a loud crash and Nelli sat straight up in bed. Her heart was racing and the light next to the bed was still on. She frantically looked around for the man but the room was empty. Then searching for the painting, which was there just a minute ago, now there was no evidence of either.

Noticing the book on Italy lying on the floor, she realized she must have fallen asleep and dropped it while reading. It was just a dream nothing more, Nelli told herself, but she couldn't shake the feeling that it was more than a dream.

Reaching over and turning off the light, she lay down and pulled the covers up tight under her chin remembering the last words her father said to her just before he died, "You must be of pure heart Antonella. You will be guided and protected. Do not be afraid."

CHAPTER **THIRTEEN**

Nelli was curled up on the sofa watching today's recap of the news on TV. Later in the broadcast an investigative reporter was going to do a piece on the sexual scandal within the Catholic Church and how some believed it was the work of Satan as foretold in the Book of Revelations.

As the TV station broke away for their advertisers, she thought about some things she still had to do before leaving tomorrow morning on her trip with Anthony, but she was tired from staying up late the night before and wanted to get to bed early. Ready to turn the TV off, she felt something wet trickling down her wrist. Her hand, clinched in a fist, was pressed against her chest. She slowly uncurled her fingers; cradled in the palm of her hand was the cross from the chain that hung from around her neck. Nelli had squeezed it so tightly it punctured the skin. Releasing the cross, she applied pressure to the wound. Getting up to go wash off her hand, she collapsed back onto the sofa in excruciating pain.

It felt as if someone was pounding a spike through her hand. Beginning to panic she prayed for the pain to stop. Suddenly, it dawned on her; this must be what it felt like when the nails were pounded into Christ's hands and feet. Staring at the wound, the word stigmata came to mind and immediately the bleeding stopped. Just as suddenly, so did the piercing pain.

CHAPTER FOURTEEN

Looking to see if the cross was covered in blood, it hung from her neck as if nothing had ever happened, not a drop of blood was evident. Instead the cross appeared to be glowing and the diamond in the middle was shooting off rays of light in all directions.

In the background, she heard the news anchor on TV say they were now going to talk with the investigative reporter on the Catholic Church's handling of the sexual abuse scandal. The next voice Nelli heard was one she recognized but it wasn't coming from the TV. She looked around and saw two figures coming towards her. The closer they got the clearer their faces became.

"How is this possible?" said Nelli to the two people.

Her father and mother now stood in front of her and she felt the presence of hundreds of souls surrounding them.

Not saying a word, her father reached for her hand and gently turned it over. Nodding, he looked at his wife and smiled, and then looking at Nelli he turned his hand over and showed her the same identical mark. Nelli didn't understand what was happening. Her parents were dead.

"Is it really you?" asked Nelli.

"Yes, believe what you see my dear Antonella, your mother and I are here to tell you that it is your destiny to search for a box that has been hidden for centuries. It can only be opened with the key you possess. Inside the box you will find written the words of Our Lord. It will show the path that must be taken by the shepherd of the flock if the Church is to survive this crisis it now faces. As each Keeper of the Key before you, they have been given a Guardian on earth. When he sees the stigmata on the palm of your hand he will know what he must do."

"But how will I find him?" asked Nelli. "Will he show me where to look for this box? Dad, I don't know if I can do this. What if I fail?"

"Do not be afraid. You will be guided and protected by all the past Keepers of the Key. Remember my last words to you on my deathbed, if you are of pure heart you will find what lies within. The knowledge inside the box could change the course of the future, if it is delivered to whom it is meant. But know there will be other forces, who wish the knowledge in the box never to be found. Faith in what's good will triumph, if it hasn't been lost."

As Nelli listened the image of her parents seemed to be fading. She heard new voices, turning to see who was talking; she realized they were coming from the TV.

When she looked back, her parents were gone.

CHAPTER **FIFTEEN**

Aboard the Plane to Rome

"You're sure you don't mind taking the time dropping off the drawings and proposal while we're here? It saves me from scheduling another trip," said Anthony.

"Anthony, I've told you already it's fine," said Nelli. "I'll be able to see the Vatican and meet Bishop Rossini; it's an opportunity of a lifetime."

"It is an interesting project. I will be working with a well-known architectural firm from Italy, plus the Vatican's building projects director."

"I think it's exciting Anthony. Who knows, maybe you'll discover some ancient artifact or treasure during the reconstruction." Nelli hesitated, "I know this is a touchy subject for you, but since we will be right there, I thought it would be nice if we stop by to say hi and congratulate Mary Ellen on her new position at the Vatican. It's quite an accomplishment being the first woman appointed to such a high office by the Pope himself."

Anthony's body stiffened. Waiting for him to reply Nelli realized how much he reminded her of their father. Anthony was a few inches taller and had the same black hair and dark brown eyes. But the thing that stood out the most was she always felt safe when her father was around, and that's how she felt with Anthony. Unfortunately, her brother had also inherited their mother's stubbornness, which she had the pleasure of experiencing much too often.

Nelli, on the other hand, looked just like their mother. She had her auburn hair and light brown eyes. In fact, when she was a young woman, she was stopped more than once and asked if she was Ann Andruccioli's daughter. Luckily, like her father, Nelli was slow to anger, which was helpful when she was experiencing her brother's stubbornness like now. But if you pushed them too far you better be prepared for a battle.

Anthony still hadn't responded to her suggestion about stopping to visit Mary Ellen.

"It's been a long time Anthony; wouldn't it be nice to see her again? You both cared about each other at one time."

Anthony stared out the window, "Let me think about it Nelli."

You could hear the flight attendant informing the passengers that the plane had reached its cruising altitude and the captain had turned off the seat belt sign.

Nelli decided not to tell Anthony that she had already called Mary Ellen last night.

CHAPTER SIXTEEN

They'd been flying for close to three hours, Nelli and Anthony had each gotten a glass of wine. In a little while the flight attendant would be coming around to serve dinner. Nelli was reading a book on Pesaro and the surrounding towns, trying not to think about the dreams she'd been having the last couple weeks, but she was losing the battle. Fidgeting with the cross their father had given to her, she started to shake and felt her heart was racing.

The plane hit some unexpected turbulence and Anthony glanced over at Nelli immediately seeing something was wrong.

"Nelli, are you feeling okay?"

"Um, yes I'm fine, why?"

"You're pale as a ghost, and you're trembling."

Anthony had gotten two blankets before takeoff, grabbing one now from the seat pocket in front of him. Nelli watched as he removed it from the wrapping, her thoughts spinning. She needed to tell Anthony about the dreams she'd been having.

"Here, put this around you," said Anthony.

She leaned forward a little and grabbed one side of the blanket. Anthony abruptly stopped, then quickly recovered and continued to wrap the blanket around her shoulders.

After a few minutes he said in a calm voice, "What did you do to your hand, Nelli?"

She pretended not to hear him, closing her eyes and pulling the blanket tighter around her shoulders, as if it could keep the world out creating a safe place for her to hide. She felt her heart beginning to beat slower and warmth flowed back through her body.

"Good, your color's coming back," said Anthony. "Now tell me what's going on? The last couple weeks I've noticed you have seemed distracted and more tired, but I just attributed it to getting ready for the trip. I figured if anything was wrong you would tell me. I can see that you're struggling with something."

He held her hand and gently gave it a squeeze.

"Anthony, I've wanted to tell you but I didn't know what you would think."

"What are you talking about, Nelli?"

"I haven't been sleeping well and I've been dreaming about people who have died. At first I didn't think anything of it. I figured it was probably due to being excited about the trip."

"Nelli, its fine, tell me about the dreams. We'll talk about them together."

Anthony listened as she described them in detail. He was patient and nonjudgmental, asking a few questions once in a while.

For Nelli, it felt as if her father was sitting next to her, nodding and acknowledging that she was remembering everything correctly. It felt good to tell someone, to tell Anthony. She didn't feel alone anymore.

"I'm glad you told me Nelli. I wish you would have confided in me from the start. I have always felt bad I was not in the room with you when Dad died. I know you two had a special bond."

"We each had our own unique connection with Dad, Anthony. I know he loved us both very much. We each filled different roles in his life."

Anthony couldn't tell Nelli that he was there watching as their father gave her the necklace. The time had come. He needed to alert the others.

CHAPTER **SEVENTEEN**

Outside of Pesaro

The five men waited for Thomas to return and begin the meeting. Each was the head of a cell within Propaganda Due. Although they knew each other, none of them knew the members in each faction. The Naj Hannah was the only one who had the complete list of all P2 members.

Angelo was the first to speak, "I must ask Thomas to thank Naj Hannah for returning us to where it all began."

Everyone nodded in agreement.

General D'Amoto spoke next, "The number of our members has expanded more quickly than I imagined possible since my initiation. From the reports I received, we now have members in every part of the world and we are still growing."

He spoke as if he had an important role in making this happen.

Back in Arezzo, Peter made a mental note to himself to have Thomas remind General D'Amoto of his place within P2. He could easily be replaced if need be.

They all remembered being blindfolded and brought to the compound for initiation into P2. The same precautions were also taken this time. No one knew the exact location of the villa, all they knew was that it was on the Adriatic side and about a three-hour drive from Florence.

Vingenzo and Silvio stiffened as General D'Amoto spoke. Each man had been placed in positions that allowed them much prestige and power. They also knew never to forget who the power was behind them.

"Do not forget my brothers, the oath we each took," snapped Silvio. "We are all brothers and only one person is responsible for our success, the Naj Hannah."

"I agree with Silvio, we are all working for the same purpose," said Vingenzo. Then turning his head, he said, "We have not heard from you yet Cardinal Cavallari."

Before the cardinal could say anything, the double doors to the room opened and in walked Thomas. This time two men followed him and positioned themselves at each of the doors. They were dressed in ceremonial robes and wearing black hoods with the cobra head insignia. Each man carried an ax and automatic weapon. As part of the Wolf Pack neither man knew the identity of the other.

Thomas ignored the concerned looks on the men's faces. He took his seat at the head of the table.

"Gentlemen before we begin, we will start by renewing the oath."

"Are you prepared to …."

From the villa, Peter watched as the monitors registered the physical responses as each man answered the questions.

Then Thomas opened the folder in front of him looking at the first item on the agenda.

Looking up he said, "Shall we begin?"

CHAPTER EIGHTEEN

Mary Ellen looked at her watch; she would reach the northeast entrance in another five minutes. She was lucky to have found an apartment not far from the Vatican. Walking it took her at the most twenty minutes.

Even before accepting the job, the church had always been a large part of her life, especially when you have three priests in the family. She began to walk faster, trying to repress her anger, she thought, "I should have said two priests in the family. I will find out who set my brother up. Someone lied and I'm going to prove it." Becoming self-conscious that someone might have overheard her, Mary Ellen looked around to see if anyone was staring at her.

Her family always knew Mary Ellen did not want a consecrated life like her brother. They assumed though that she would eventually do something that centered around the Church but they never dreamed she would have the position she now held.

So absorbed with her thoughts it surprised Mary Ellen when she found herself standing in front of the entrance into Vatican City.

"Buon giornio signorina O'Farrell. May I please see your I.D.?"

"Buon giorno Raphael, Come stai?"

"Molto bene, grazie." Raphael handed back Mary Ellen's I.D. "Have a good day signorina O'Farrell."

"Grazie Raphael. I hope your day goes well also." Smiling at him, she took back her identification card. After the first couple months of seeing Raphael every morning the two fell into the habit of testing each other's language skills.

Raphael is one of 134 Swiss Guards who protect all entrances and exits in and out of Vatican City, among other responsibilities. All recruits must be Catholic, unmarried males with Swiss citizenship, who have completed their basic training with the Swiss Army and come with certificates of good conduct. They must be between the ages of nineteen and thirty, and be at least 175 cm or 68.90 inches in height. Members are armed with small arms and the traditional halberd, also called the Swiss voulge, and trained in body guarding tactics.

Once Mary Ellen passed through the gates at Porta Sant'Anna, one of the two main entrances into Vatican City, it never failed the feeling that came over her. It was like walking through a time portal into another world. Standing on one side of the entrance, you're in Italy, then stepping over an invisible line you've entered a world of antiquity and the papal residency of the Popes dating back to Peter.

Vatican City is a sovereign state, the smallest one in the world. It's a thriving metropolis with a population of approximately 800 people. Almost all of them either live inside its walls or serve in the Holy See's diplomatic service in embassies called "nunciatures." Most of the 3,000 lay workers reside outside the Vatican and are citizens of Italy, Mary Ellen now being one of them.

"Signorina, signorina O'Farrell!" Mary Ellen looked around to see who was calling her name. It was the young priest, Father Roberto running towards her. She stopped and waited for him to catch up.

"Buon giorno, Father Roberto."

"Buon giorno, I was wondering if I could stop by your office today. I would like to talk to you about some information I have recently uncovered. I sent a file to your office; it should be delivered with your mail this morning. There could be some things in it that you might find interesting."

"Yes, of course. Please call my assistant and tell her we spoke and to schedule an appointment."

Mary Ellen had met Father Roberto a few months ago. She had been down in the Vatican Archives gathering information trying to find evidence to clear her brother's name. Father Roberto was also there and they started talking. During that initial meeting, they discovered some of the same concerns but for different reasons. They quickly formed a special bond.

"Have you seen the latest information about the Order of the Legion of Christ?" asked Father Roberto with a raised eyebrow.

"Yes, unfortunately."

"So sad it is."

"I agree Father but we must remember, the sins of man are not void even within the ecclesiastical world of God's church. We were all born with sin no matter what our position is on earth."

"Well said signorina O'Farrell. Ah, we have reached your building. I will call your assistant to set up an appointment and will be interested to see what you have to say, after you have read the file, arrivederci."

Mary Ellen's office was on the first floor of the Apostolic Palace that is also home to the papal apartments and various government offices of the Roman Catholic Church.

"Good morning Ms. O'Farrell, here is your appointment schedule for today and your messages and mail. The large envelope on top was under the door when I got here this morning. There was a note attached expressing it was important and to make sure you looked at it right away."

"Thank you Mary."

Picking up her mail, Mary Ellen wondered what was inside the envelope. It wasn't the file from Father Roberto that was in a different envelope. Hanging up her jacket she headed over to her desk.

"Okay, let's see what this is all about."

There was no return address, just her name on the front. Not recognizing the handwriting she opened the envelope and the only thing inside was a business card. Reaching in she pulled it out not knowing what to make of it and she didn't know why, but it sent chills through her.

On the front was an embossed drawing of the head of a king cobra snake. Its mouth opened wide as if to attack, the hood fully extended, the fangs dripping with its poisonous venom and it only had one eye. The pupil of the eye was actually a blue lapis stone. It was as if the cobra was looking directly at her. She dropped the card and had the sense of impending danger imagining the snake jumping off the paper and attacking her.

Picking it up off the floor, she looked at it again to see if there was anything written on it. There was nothing on the front. Flipping it over, something was scribbled on the back: "The Time is Near."

CHAPTER **NINETEEN**

Flipping the card over again, Mary Ellen wondered why someone would have sent this to her. It wasn't very amusing. Placing it back in the envelope, she tossed it into the top drawer of her desk. Still rattled, she turned her attention back to the rest of the mail. The file from Father Roberto was on top of the pile. She sat down and was going to see what he had sent, when the desk phone rang. It was her assistant.

"Yes Mary?"

"Ms. O' Farrell you have a call from a Nelli Anduccioli. She said she is an old friend."

The name caught Mary Ellen off guard. She hadn't talked with Nelli since.... since she and Anthony went their separate ways. Why would Nelli be calling her? Could something have happened to Anthony?

"Ms. O'Farrell? Would you like me to say you're in an appointment?"

"I'm sorry Mary, no give me a minute, then put the call through."

First the strange card, then the file from Father Roberto, now a call from Nelli, what else did the morning have in store for her? The phone rang again. She hesitated for a moment and then picked it up.

"Hello Nelli. It's been a long time, how nice to hear your voice."

"I wasn't sure if you would take my call."

"I apologize for not staying in touch Nelli. Is Anthony okay?"

"Yes, why would you ask that?"

"Well, I thought not hearing from you after so long that maybe something happened and you were calling to let me know."

"No, nothing's wrong. Anthony is just fine but he doesn't know I am calling you. I do want to congratulate you on your appointment at the Vatican. My other reason for calling is Anthony and I will be flying to Rome tomorrow. We will be at the Vatican on Wednesday. Anthony has an appointment with Bishop Rossini."

Mary Ellen griped the phone tighter.

"You're coming to Rome?"

"Yes, Anthony is consulting the Vatican on a restoration project. Since we will be in Italy he wanted to meet with the bishop in person and drop off some proposals to him. I told Anthony I thought it would be nice if we could stop and see you."

"What did Anthony say to that?"

"He told me he would think about it."

"And did he?"

Nelli started laughing, "He's actually still thinking. I don't know what took place between the two of you. All I know is neither one of you got married the last I knew." Mary Ellen knew the reason she'd never married, but for Anthony, she had no idea.

"I don't know if you heard that Dad passed away. Anthony and I decided to take a trip and see where he was born and where he spent his early years as a young boy."

Mary Ellen had heard the news and had wanted to call Anthony but couldn't get up the nerve.

"I'm so sorry Nelli. He was a wonderful man. It's a great loss."

"Thank you, we do miss him. If I can get Anthony to agree and you would be willing, we could stop by your office tomorrow."

It would be wonderful to see Nelli and Anthony, Mary Ellen thought to herself. When they parted it wasn't because they didn't have feelings for each other. She had told Anthony that she needed to correct the wrongs that had been done to her brother and what it had done to her family first, before she could move forward with her life, but Anthony got tired of waiting and the distance between them grew. There had been a few attempts at communication but it never led anywhere. They had both grown as individuals and had pursued their careers since then. This is ridiculous Mary Ellen thought to herself, nothing has changed; she still cared about Anthony and Nelli.

"Yes Nelli, I would like that. It would be good to see you and Anthony again. I will look forward to tomorrow. I hope you can persuade your little brother. Let me give you my cell number."

They exchanged numbers and Nelli said she would call later. Glancing at the day's schedule Mary Ellen realized she had a meeting in twenty minutes. There would be no time for lunch today. She needed to set this morning's events aside for now.

CHAPTER TWENTY

At the same time, not far from Mary Ellen's office, Cardinal McKenna clasped his hands behind his back and stared out the window towards the Sistine Chapel. Pope John Paul I had appointed him prefect for the oldest of the nine congregations of the Roman Curia at the Vatican, the Congregation for the Doctrine of the Faith (CDF), Congregatio pro Doctrina Fidei, what used to be the Holy Office of the Inquisition.

The burden of the latest news weighed heavily on his heart. He feared the forces of evil were gathering strength. A few months back he had met a young priest by the name of Father Roberto, who had come to work in the Vatican Archives and had bent the ear of the cardinal one day, asking endless questions. He was particularly interested in what the CDF's investigation into the sexual allegations had found out about the priests accused of pedophilia. McKenna remembered the young priest chuckling and saying that maybe he should have become a private eye instead of a priest. He told the cardinal he'd come across some information in his research that was of great concern and wondered if the CDF had also come across the same information. McKenna was curious to see what the young priest had found out and requested he send his findings for him to read.

McKenna had been gathering his own information on a well-established order within the Church, called the Legion of Christ. There wasn't anything in particular that he could point to but his gut told him to look more closely into the activities of the order and its founder. He had a bad feeling about all of this that he couldn't seem to shake off.

As he continued to look out over St. Peter's Square, his thoughts drifted to the many prophecies throughout scripture, of the Holy Spirit being sent down to earth warning mankind that the day would come, when a great delusion shall descend upon mankind and cover the earth in a blanket of spiritual darkness.

One prophecy in particular seemed to jump to the front of the line; it was that of Saint Anthony. As a young monk he had been visited three times by an angel. Each day he was told to write down in a book the words of Our Lord. At the end of the third day he was to place the book inside a gift that had been given to him. When the time came, the gift would be revealed to the Chosen One. Without this knowledge the church could not fight the forces of darkness, which had gathered to create a one-world religion, which would cast aside His Son.

Cardinal McKenna wondered if that day had arrived. He clasped the cross that hung from his neck and began to pray.

"Cardinal McKenna?"

For the second time that day Donovan had not heard Robert knock. His assistant had the door opened slightly, calling out the cardinal's name yet another time.

"Cardinal McKenna?"

"Come in Robert."

"Cardinal McKenna is everything all right?"

"Yes, everything is fine."

"This was just delivered for you Cardinal McKenna and it's almost time for your appointment with His Holiness."

"Thank you Robert."

Donovan picked up his papers and grabbed the large manila envelope that had just been delivered. Walking down the corridor, he undid the metal clasp. All he could see was a small business card. Pulling it out, he stared at the embossed drawing of the head of a cobra, with a lapis stone for an eye. Every muscle in his body tightened.

CHAPTER TWENTY-ONE

Nelli and Anthony spent the rest of the flight reading, playing cards, and watching a movie. The plane landed at Leonardo da Vinci International Airport on time. As their passports got stamped Nelli turned to Anthony and gave a sigh of relief.

"Going through customs didn't take as long as I thought it would."

"We lucked out," said Anthony.

He was glad the lines were short today. Anxious to get to the hotel, he wanted to have some privacy so he could make calls to the other Guardians. All those years of training would now be put to the test. When he saw the mark on his sister's hand a switch flipped on inside his brain. All his senses became heightened. He started watching people's movements, logging their faces into his mental database. At that moment his life changed, he would be living a dual life and hoped he was prepared to deal with what was ahead.

"The car rental place is this way," said Anthony, directing his sister to follow him.

"Slow down! I can't keep up."

"Sorry," said Anthony not realizing how fast he was walking. "I hope you like the hotel I booked the reservations at. It's a small boutique hotel called The Hotel Raphael. Great location and only a fifteen-minute walk to the Vatican."

"I'm sure you chose something wonderful," said Nelli. "You know I trust your judgment completely."

Anthony's felt his whole body tense up. He felt guilty about keeping the information of the Guardians from Nelli, after she just said she trusted him completely. He continued walking.

"When we get to the hotel let's take some time to unpack and get settled," that would give him a chance to contact the other Guardians. "I'd like to take a shower and make a few calls. Then we can find a nice restaurant for dinner. If you aren't too tired afterwards, we can walk to one of the ancient sites near the hotel. Sound good to you?"

"You read my thoughts," said Nelli.

Once they were relaxing over dinner she would tell him about the phone call she made to Mary Ellen.

They had reached the car rental counter and Anthony was conversing in Italian with the agent. When they decided to travel to Italy, Nelli purchased an introductory language program to try and learn some basic Italian. She was able to pick out a word here and there.

They got the car and found the exit for Autostrada Roma-Fiumicino and headed towards Rome.

"Did you see that motorcycle Anthony? There's another one! They're weaving in and out between cars like maniacs. Aren't they afraid they're going to get hit?"

Anthony started to laugh out loud. "Italians refer to them as mosquitoes, because of the annoying way they buzz in and out between cars and the noise that comes from their little motors. Watch for the Viadotto della Magliana exit, it should be coming up soon. It's only about 19 miles from the airport to Vatican City."

Even as Anthony laughed, he was watching for any cars that seemed out of place or were following too close. He knew they would be at the hotel in a few more minutes and he would be in contact with the others within the hour.

"There's the hotel off to your right." Anthony pointed up ahead.

The doorman got someone to unload their luggage. Nelli followed Anthony, as he walked under an ivory-covered façade into the lobby. It was decorated with antiques that rival the cache in local museums. There was even a Picasso ceramics collection in the lobby of the hotel. As Nelli studied some of the pieces, Anthony headed to the reception desk to check them in.

"Abbiamo prenotato a nome Andruccioli."

"Si," replied Anthony.

"Welcome to the Hotel Raphael signore Anthony, we have

two rooms next to each other on the top floor, with lovely views as you requested.

"Grazie," turning to Nelli, "we're all set; our rooms are next to each other with an interior adjoining door. When you're ready to head out, give a knock and we will go have dinner."

Nelli's room was beautiful. It had hardwood floors and had been refurbished with a Florentine touch and luxuriously furnished in a classic modern style. It was lined with oak and was equipped with high-tech innovations, including a digital sound system. There was a set of white painted French doors, which led out onto a balcony overlooking a series of beautiful gardens. As she stood on the small balcony and looked out past the gardens, in the distance she could see the top of St. Peter's Cathedral.

Being here in Italy, where Dad was born, made the last dream she had seem even more real, or was it all just her imagination? As she moved her hand from the ledge of the balcony, a small object fell to the tiled floor.

Picking it up, she couldn't believe what she held in her hand. It was a small religious medal of Saint Anthony.

CHAPTER TWENTY-TWO

As Anthony unlocked the door to his room, he was already pulling out his cell phone.

Instinctively he scanned the room, looking for anything out of place, anything that would make him suspect. Setting down his luggage, he punched in the numbers from memory and waited as the connection was made and for the phone to begin ringing. His training as a Guardian began before he even knew of the plan his father had for him and the purpose for his life. Starting when he was a young boy, several times a year, they would get together with eleven friends of his father and their sons for long weekends at a lodge. At first they would play games and learn survival skills. As time went on the games became more challenging. There were physical games of strength and endurance and mental games solving complicated riddles. They were trained to make educated guesses, based on the facts presented to them, sometimes on their own or together in teams. Each generation trained by the previous generation.

On their sixteenth birthday each father sits down and divulges to their son, the real reason for their training and the legacy they are now part of. For the next two years they would be trained by masters in their individual fields in the latest techniques of their crafts. Upon turning eighteen, they were expected to continue training on their own with the guidance of their teachers. Twice a year they would meet back where it all began, to update each other on any changes or concerns they might have, the last time just three weeks ago.

After the first ring Anthony began pacing the floor. Finally on the fourth one, the person picked up.

"Cephas, its Tau'ma." There was a deafening silence on the other end.

Tau'ma is Hebrew for Thomas. Very few people knew him as Thomas. His full name was actually Thomas Anthony Andruccioli. When Nelli got to be around ten years old, she started calling him by his middle name. She thought it would be fun if they each had the same name, since Antonella in Italian is the female version of Anthony. It stuck for some reason and since then everyone knew him as Anthony.

The only time the Guardians were to use the Hebrew version of their names to contact each other was when the Keeper of the Key revealed the mark of the stigmata.

Cephas took a slow deep breath, realizing the significance of the call asking, "Where are you calling from?"

"Nelli and I are here in Rome. We are at The Hotel Raphael. Cephas, the time has come to alert the others. The mark was revealed to me."

"Who, when?"

"It's my sister Cephas, it's Nelli."

"I will contact the others immediately. Does she understand what's happening?"

"No, not yet, although the visions have begun, she kept them to herself until yesterday. She told me about the dreams she's been having while we were flying here. She still has not come to the realization they are more than just dreams."

CHAPTER TWENTY-THREE

Anthony heard knocking on the door separating their two rooms. Then he heard Nelli softly calling his name. He had purposely kept the door locked so there would be no chance of her walking in during his call.

"Sorry Nelli," he yelled out. "I forgot to unlock the door from this side."

"I'm ready to go get something to eat, if you are Anthony?"

"Sounds good to me, we can head out. Let me just grab my jacket."

They stopped at the concierge's desk and asked about restaurants in the area.

"They are all excellent signore! Osteria dell'Antiquario is a few blocks down on Via dei Coronari. There is also the Il Convivo; it is one of the most acclaimed restaurants in Rome. You will also pass many small family trattorias with outdoor seating. What we sometimes suggest to our guests is to decide what kind of view you want to look at while you dine and that will be the restaurant for you."

"Grazie."

As they exited the hotel Anthony said, "Left or right, left takes us towards the Piazza Navona, right towards the Pantheon."

"Left," said Nelli, "let's try and find a restaurant near the Piazza Navona that has outdoor seating. I think I read that it is Rome's most famous and most beautiful piazza. We can do some people watching while we eat."

"Left it is."

As they began walking, Nelli was astounded by the beauty everywhere you looked. It was just like she imagined it would be.

"I'm so glad we decided to take this trip," said Nelli.

Anthony just smiled, covering up his apprehension; wondering what was in store for both of them.

They window-shopped and read the menus displayed in front of the restaurants. Their hotel was in one of the most desirable sections of Rome. The area was a maze of narrow streets and alleys dating from the Middle Ages, filled with churches and buildings built during the Renaissance. Nelli stopped to study the display of a small shop.

"Anthony, look what they have in their window," she said as she grabbed his arm. "What an unusual collection of small boxes. We must come back here tomorrow. I would love to buy one to take home with me."

"That's right, you have started collecting them haven't you?" said Anthony. "How did that come about?"

"I was lecturing one day on the Early Renaissance period. We were discussing the different styles of painters and their choices of accessories and background. On that particular day, I had chosen five paintings. A student pointed out that each had an exquisitely crafted box either being held by one of the subjects in the pictures or present somewhere else in the painting. Small handcrafted boxes were used to hold precious artifacts or to give gifts in, not that different from today. It dawned on me, how these small works of art have held many secrets throughout the ages inside their four walls. I got intrigued with the idea and started collecting anything that caught my eye.

"Come to think of it, many of the frescos and reliefs I've studied have examples of that but I never really gave it much thought," added Anthony.

He noticed one of the larger boxes displayed in the window was open and the inside of the lid was covered with a mirror. It caught his eye because the sun was reflecting off of it. The image in the mirror was like a small painting of the street and buildings behind them. In the painting, a man stood who appeared to be watching them. Suddenly, the man nervously looked away—realizing Anthony had caught a glimpse of him in the mirror.

Quickly turning towards Nelli, Anthony said, "I'm getting hungry. Let's find a place to eat." Anthony instinctively moved to the outside of the sidewalk to protect Nelli. He glanced across the street and saw the man disappear around the corner.

"Look Anthony, there's the famous fountain by Bernini. What is it called?"

"The Fontana dei Quattro Fiumi," said Anthony, "Fountain of the Four Rivers."

"And look there's a restaurant across from it with outdoor seating. Let's eat there and we can look at the fountain and people watch too."

Anthony liked the choice. If someone was watching them, it would be hard not to stand out. Anthony would have a commanding view of the street. Most of the tables were full but they were able to get one with a good view of the fountain. You could pick out the Italians from the tourists. The locals were animated and engrossed in conversation, oblivious to their surroundings.

After looking at the menu for a minute Nelli leaned towards Anthony and asked, "Can you hear what that table is talking about next to us?" Nelli tilted her head to the right. "They seem to be arguing about something."

Without looking around Anthony started to chuckle, "Would you believe the price of eggs?"

"You're kidding right?"

"No, actually I'm not. The woman is outraged at the grocer she goes to for raising
the price of eggs last week."

Nelli rolled her eyes at Anthony. "How do they act if it is something serious?"

The waiter came over to the table to take their order. Anthony ordered the house Chianti and a plate of antipasto for starters.

Then Nelli chose a homemade linguine with black truffles for her first course and the roasted salmon in salt crust for her second. Anthony decided on the squash ravioli and the sautéed shellfish, and today's special, mussels and clams. Along with the second course their waiter brought a small platter of vegetables. The concierge was right, the food was excellent. After they were finished, Anthony ordered two café Americanos.

"What did you just order Anthony? I was thinking about ordering cappuccino."

"It's the Italians version of our coffee, stronger than ours but weaker than espresso. Here's your first lesson on how not to look like a tourist when in Italy," said Anthony. "Rule number one: Italians never order a cappuccino after 11:00 a.m.—as anything with that much milk is considered a meal in itself and is the classic Italian breakfast. Rule number two: never order cappuccino after a meal. Italian meals usually consist of pasta followed by the main course and dessert. Italians can't understand why anyone would then order a calorie-rich cappuccino. Rule number three: never sit down at a table with your cappuccino. Italians make their coffee lukewarm so it can be drunk quickly. If you attempt to sit down and drink your cappuccino slowly it will be cold before you are halfway through it. Perhaps, the best reason for not ordering cappuccino after a sit-down meal is it will cost two, three, maybe even four times as much as it would cost at a coffee bar. Break the three cappuccino rules and you will expose yourself as a tourist."

"Okay, okay, I got it. No cappuccino after eleven in the morning while I'm in Italy."

Just as Nelli finished talking, the waiter approached with two cups of coffee. After taking a sip of her coffee she decided that this would be a good time to bring up Mary Ellen.

Setting her cup down, "Well have you thought anymore about what I asked you on the plane?"

"Can you be a little more specific Nelli?"

"Mary Ellen?"

There was no reaction from Anthony. He looked over at the fountain and sipped his coffee.

"Anthony you have had more than enough time to make a decision."

At the same moment the waiter came by to leave the check. Anthony smiled and took the piece of paper.

"I might as well tell you, I called Mary Ellen."

Anthony placed his cup down abruptly.

"We had a very nice conversation Anthony. She sounds good, a little lonely I thought, but good. I told her we were coming to Rome. She was surprised of course. Then I told her we were actually going to be at the Vatican tomorrow for a meeting with Bishop Rossini. She was even more surprised. I told her I made the suggestion to you, that it would be nice if we stopped and saw her after our appointment with the bishop. There was silence on the other end for a moment but then she said it would be nice to see me. There was a gentleness and sincerity in her voice Anthony. Then she said to tell you that it would be nice to see you again too."

Nelli sat back in her chair and gave Anthony a chance to mull over what she had just told him.

CHAPTER TWENTY-FOUR

Nelli noticed when she told Anthony Mary Ellen said it would be nice to see him again, Anthony's demeanor changed slightly. He leaned into the table and rested his hands around his cup of coffee.

"Nelli, when you brought up the idea on the plane, I had already thought about the possibility that we could run into Mary Ellen at the Vatican. I never really explained why we separated to anyone. Mary Ellen and her family were devastated, as you know, by the sexual abuse accusations made against Devlin and the Church's decision to excommunicate him. He swore it was not true. She became obsessed with clearing his name. She would get leads and then hit a dead end. This happened over and over. Time kept ticking by and we were growing more and more distant. I threw myself into my work as you know.

"I'm so sorry Anthony, everyone always wondered what happened. We figured when you wanted to talk about it you would."

"Time does heal. I guess it's time to be a grown-up. Mary Ellen was never able to clear her brother's name. I'm sure that has been difficult for her to accept."

Nelli rested her hand on Anthony's, "Are you saying I can call Mary Ellen and tell her we would like to stop by her office tomorrow?"

"Yes Nelli, you can call and tell her we will stop by after our meeting with Cardinal Rossini."

Nelli squeezed his hand, "I know you won't regret it."

As Anthony looked down he visualized the mark of the stigmata beneath the hand that was now resting on his.

CHAPTER TWENTY-FIVE

Mary Ellen could do without another morning like today, first that disturbing card and then the surprise phone call from Nelli. She decided to walk home after work to unwind and clear her head. It was a perfect evening for a walk along the beautiful tree-lined avenue—Lungotevere Tor di Nona, which ran along the Tiber River.

She had been lucky finding the apartment at Lungotevere Tor di Nona 3. The owner had just finished making the upper floor into an apartment when Mary Ellen was searching for a place to live. The timing couldn't have been better and a week later she moved in. Located right in the heart of the eternal city, it was just around the corner from Piazza Navona. Also close by were the Museo Napoleonico, the Pantheon, and it was only fifty meters from Castel Sant' Angelo, and of course in walking distance to Vatican City.

After getting home, she changed clothes and warmed up some leftovers from the night before. Then she sat down with the file Father Roberto had sent on her brother's case and started reading.

A boat going by on the Tiber blew its whistle and startled her. Glancing at the clock, she couldn't believe the time, she had been reading for almost two hours. Reading through the police reports and the witness statements, red flags were popping up everywhere. None of the evidence gathered pertaining to the allegations had been substantiated. There was no objective evidence. Leads had not been followed up on. The whole case was based on hearsay.

The investigator, a Father Gallo, seemed to be leading the

witnesses against her brother with his questions. She was noticing a pattern, it was subtle but it was there.

An order called the Legion of Christ was mentioned in some of the statements. She would look into that more.

Tomorrow she would request files of other cases against priests and compare the evidence. Something was terribly wrong and she intended to get some answers. Everything in the file was too precise, too organized. It was as if a checklist had been made up, of what was needed to bring a judgment of excommunication against her brother, and then someone gathered the necessary documents. Her thoughts were running wild. She had to call Devlin.

"Where the hell is it?" She rummaged through her purse. Then she remembered she'd put the phone in the pocket of her jacket.

"Devlin pick up, please be home."

"Hello Mary, how is my dear sister tonight?"

"Thank goodness you answered."

"Is something wrong? Are you all right Mary Ellen?"

"Devlin, I know you have tried to put this behind you."

"Mary Ellen, let's not go there."

"Devlin, I have to talk to you about this. I just received information I've never seen before."

"Mary Ellen please, the accusations made about me were hard enough, especially since I was innocent, but I was still excommunicated by the Church."

"I know Devlin but this file has reports and testimonies that I hadn't seen before. Something is not right Devlin. It's very subtle but it's as if you were set up. Before the archbishop called you into his office, to inform you that a charge of sexual misconduct had been reported against you to the Italian police, you were hearing and seeing things that were concerning you. I need you to write down what you heard and saw that made you uneasy. Would you please do that for me?"

"I don't know Mary Ellen. I don't know if I can go through all that again."

"Just think about it overnight. We can talk more about it tomorrow. You'll never believe who I got a call from today, Nelli Andruccioli, Anthony's sister."

"You're kidding! How did it go?"

"It brought back a lot of feelings I have tried to put behind me, not unlike you dear brother. I told you that I had heard Anthony's father Alberto had died not too long ago. They decided to visit Pesaro, where he was born, but first they plan to stop in Rome.

Anthony has an appointment tomorrow at the Vatican. His firm has been hired to consult on a project. Nelli asked if they could stop by my office."

"So will they be stopping by to see you?"

"He doesn't know Nelli contacted me. She is supposed to call me tonight and let me know if Anthony will agree to it."

"So how would you feel about seeing Anthony again?"

"It's been a long time but I decided it's time to put the past behind."

"I'll talk with you tomorrow and find out what happened," said Devlin. "I'll say a prayer for you tonight."

"Thank you Devlin but remember to think about the other matter we spoke about too."

"I will Mary Ellen. Goodnight, remember I love you."

"I love you too."

Mary Ellen had forgotten to tell him about the strange card she received. She must remember to tell him tomorrow. It was getting late and Nelli had not called yet. Mary Ellen came to the conclusion that Nelli couldn't get Anthony to agree to stop by her office. Oh well, she would try and contact Nelli in a few weeks and see how their visit to Pesaro went.

Getting into bed she jotted down a few notes concerning her brother's file and questions she wanted answers to. Her cell phone rang. No name or number was showing up.

"Hello?"

"Mary Ellen, its Nelli. Have I called too late?"

"No, it's fine Nelli. I was just writing down some things I needed to do tomorrow." Her heart started to beat faster in anticipation of what Nelli would say next.

"Anthony and I would like to stop by tomorrow. His appointment with Bishop Rossini is at ten o'clock. Would eleven-thirty work for you?"

Mary Ellen was speechless. Had she heard Nelli correctly?

"Mary Ellen? Are you still there?"

"Yes Nelli, I'm sorry, that would be just fine. I will alert my assistant that you will be stopping by. I'm looking forward to seeing you Nelli and please tell Anthony it will be nice to see him again too."

"I'm excited to see you too, Mary Ellen. Goodnight."

"Goodnight Nelli."

CHAPTER TWENTY-SIX

Thomas looked around the table. Each man here enjoyed great power and with that came a life of luxury and prestige. They had been asked to do unspeakable acts along the way to get to this point within the P2 organization. They were all in too deep now to turn back. If they had second thoughts, they knew the consequences of what would happen to them, but could they live with what their loved ones would go through because of a moment of weakness.

The decision to add Cardinal Cavallari this late in the plan was done on purpose. Thirty years ago P2 had almost been destroyed by Pope John Paul I. The Grand Master had gotten close to achieving his dream of a one-world religion but a list of names the Pope was going to expose of all the P2 members in the Vatican made the elimination of Pope John Paul I necessary. The newest Grand Master was not going to allow any chance of that happening again. This time nothing would go wrong. Like the symbol of their secret society, the cobra silently and slowly seeks out its victim, and then waits patiently until the time is right to strike.

Thomas cleared his throat to get the men's attention.

"You're all aware gentlemen of how close we are to our final goal. What happens in the next week will change the course of the world, as we know it. Everything is in place. You have been given a specific time to call in. At that time you will be given your final series of instructions. After executing those instructions, you will return here as the final transfer of power takes place. In the first weeks of transition you are to set up your new departments worldwide. Within six months the New World Order will be in full operation with our leader at its helm."

The sixty-five-year-old Cardinal Cavallari spoke for the first time.

"As the newest member here today I want to thank you for your warm acceptance."

Vingenzo broke in, "We are honored to have you as part of the group. Together we will have a hand in reshaping the world. The Vatican and Banca Nazionale del Lavoro have a long history and we look forward to the continuation of that relationship." Vingenzo leaned back in his chair and crossed his hands on his lap.

"Thank you, Vingenzo. I have no reason to think the relationship will not be a rewarding one. With our help, may I add, the time is right to fulfill the dream of P2 and the Grand Master. The Catholic Church is in uncertain times. I believe it is the right time to initiate the plan for one worldwide religion."

Sitting across the table from the cardinal, Silvio spoke next.

"Each of our roles is essential to bring about this historic event. I have worked with other world leaders and most of them realize that a global government is the way of the future. There are a few that have not accepted this idea but when the time comes, they will not have a choice except to come on board. If they refuse to join us, they will be replaced.

"Even though we will have the privately signed pledges of all the major world government leaders, religion is the underlying factor that creates unrest throughout the world.

"A perfect example is what we are witnessing in the Middle East. Once those governments are under the Naj Hannah's control he will institute the new world religion.

"With the Vatican becoming the seat of power for both religion and government combined, the future holds unimaginable possibilities! Under our new leader the world will be unrecognizable as we know it now."

The four others silently nodded their heads in agreement.

Thomas also knew this would be the last time he would ever see these men again. After they had fulfilled their roles they would no longer be of use to P2. A drawing had already taken place among the inner circle of which five disciples would get the honor of eliminating the five men that sat before him this afternoon.

Thomas remained quiet letting the men exchange thoughts and settling in before they got down to the serious business of today's final meeting. He wondered how Peter was feeling seeing his dream being so close to completion.

Miles away Peter Romanus listened and observed the men in the room. He had been able to bribe someone in the U.S. Department of Defense to get the prototype of a new device they were working on that monitors vital signs of an individual at distances up to one hundred feet. The scancorder, devices no larger than a PDA had been installed in each chair and were working superbly.

CHAPTER **TWENTY-SEVEN**

Mary Ellen woke up before her alarm went off. It was still dark outside. She laid there going over yesterday's events. This was ridiculous, she knew she wouldn't go back to sleep. She might as well get up. After making coffee she went out on the patio.

There was a slight breeze and the air felt cool against her skin. Dawn approached as the sun was beginning to rise over the horizon. Glancing at the skyline she could make out the top of St. Peter's Basilica slowly taking shape. It was a beautiful view, one she never grew tired of. Everything was so peaceful at this time of the day. It almost seemed as if yesterday was all a dream and when she got to her office today, it would be just a regular day of appointments, meetings, and phone calls.

She watched as a large barge was slowly making its way down the Tiber. Lights in a few windows were starting to come on, people getting up to start a new day. She got a little more coffee and headed into the bathroom to take a shower.

Across the river Cardinal McKenna had also awoken early. His meeting yesterday with Pope Benedict had been quite disturbing. As is always the case, there are Swiss Guards stationed at the entrance to the Pope's apartment twenty-four hours a day when he is in residency.

When Cardinal McKenna had arrived at the door to the papal apartment, one of the guards unexpectedly stepped in front of him, "I am sorry cardinal but I must ask to see your identification. It will then be necessary for me to search you."

McKenna was surprised by the request but nodded that he

understood. Finishing, the guard stepped to the side and knocked twice on the door. It was opened from inside by another Swiss guard. Upon entering, the door closed silently behind him.

McKenna had thought the meeting was going to be just between himself and Pope Benedict, but Bishop Moretti from the Synod of Bishops, Cardinal Conti from the Tribunals, and Commander Crevelli of the Swiss Guard were also present. They were all seated except for Commander Crevelli who stood at attention next to the Pope. Pope Benedict smiled warmly at Cardinal McKenna.

"Please be seated, Donovan."

Crevelli then handed the cardinal a folder saying, "Open it please. Have you ever seen this before, Cardinal McKenna?"

As McKenna looked inside he was horrified by what he saw. Closing the folder, he quickly handed it back to the Commander.

Rifling through the papers on his lap, he found the envelope he had received a short while ago. As he pulled out the card, his hand began to shake.

"This was delivered to my office this morning. What does it mean? Do you know who sent them?" The folder he was handed contained an identical card to the one he had received.

"I regret to have to tell you this but it was found lying next to the body of Father Roberto."

Donovan suddenly felt sick to his stomach.

"What are you saying?"

"Early this morning Father Roberto's body, what was left of it, was discovered in the archives by another priest."

This can't be happening thought McKenna, Father Roberto can't be dead; he had just received the file from him this morning. Donovan's head was spinning.

"Who would do this and why?" looking at the commander for answers.

"That's what we are going to find out. Whoever did this wanted to send a warning. Now with you having received the same card, we must find out what you and Father Roberto accidently uncovered that someone does not want known."

CHAPTER **TWENTY-EIGHT**

Father Roberto had come to Vatican City two years earlier. Ever since he was twelve years old he wanted to be a priest but he also had an interest in science, especially the study of epistemology or the theory of knowledge. He felt very blessed, ordained eight years ago; he had also been able to get a doctorate in science and was brought to Rome to work in the Pontifical Academy of Sciences under the Prefect of the Vatican Secret Archives, Sergio Pagano. It was a dream that came true for him.

He had taken a personal interest in the development of the crippling affect the allegations of sexual misconduct by clergy was having on the Church. On his own time, he had been investigating the evidence on the accusations, the history of the victims, backgrounds of the clergy accused, and actions the Church had taken.

Every religion has dealt with some of the same issues. The sins of man can be found everywhere and unfortunately that includes the Catholic Church. There's always a pattern if you look deep enough and Father Roberto was starting to see one that worried him.

The scope of the allegations was growing faster and wider than could be justified by a rational explanation. He felt in his bones that there was some kind of outside force that was feeding on these events. He had always struggled between the study of epistemology and critical thinking, which occurs whenever one must figure out what to believe or what to do.

The Vatican faced some very serious issues and no one knew where it all might lead. Maybe if he very carefully pieced together all the information he was gathering he could find some answers to explain the evil that was taking place within the Church. He wasn't unwilling to consider that there could be a conspiracy to bring down the Church. Could Satan's disciples be behind this destructive path that so many of his fellow brethren had risked going down?

There was something about the order of the Legion of Christ that troubled him. The founder of the order, a Father Marcel, was of great interest to him. Roberto had been looking into his circle of friends and the obscure events that followed many of their meetings. He started inquiring and requesting documents on the background of a few of the individuals, which always seemed to be present at the gatherings. He was told that whatever he needed to know about them could be found through public records or press releases. Responding that he had already done that, he was then told his request would be passed on and someone would get back to him. Funny thing was no one ever got back to him. It seemed these individuals were being protected from prying eyes.

Then there was the personal request from Ms. O'Farrell, for any information he came across that might give some insight into her brother's case, since she knew he was doing research on the sexual scandal that was tearing the Church apart.

Father Roberto was surprised at the judgment by the tribunal to excommunicate Devlin O'Farrell, based on the information he was uncovering. There was no solid evidence against him and there was again a connection to the Legion of Christ.

He had prepared a file for Ms. O'Farrell, with all the information he had gathered and was hoping she could shed some light on his concerns pertaining to her brother's case. Something wasn't adding up. It was the way the facts had been laid out. At first reading, it seemed an open and shut case, but reading through it again, he noticed odd statements and facts that didn't seem relevant to the case.

It was getting late. He had gotten to the archives at nine in the morning and it was almost midnight. He had just finished placing all the information he'd gathered into two large manila envelopes, one for Cardinal McKenna and the other for Ms. O'Farrell, and had taken it to the mailroom for the morning's mail clerk to deliver to their offices. Gathering up the rest of his things, before heading back to his residence for the night, he thought he heard a door open at the other end of the room.

He looked up and caught a glimpse of someone dressed in black disappear behind a row of shelves. Awfully late for someone to be coming in, he thought to himself, but the archives were open twenty-four hours a day. He had come late at night himself a few times.

Roberto was ready to leave and thought he would peek down the row of shelves to see if he might know who had come in to work. He didn't see anyone. That's strange; he didn't hear the door open again if they went back out."

Then Roberto thought he heard a noise come from behind him. It startled him and he turned to see what it was.

There stood a person dressed in black but it wasn't another priest wearing a cassock, it was some kind of ritualistic robe. A black hood covered its head except for two holes for the eyes. It was like looking into the eyes of pure evil, the devil himself. Where the mouth would be was an intricately embroidered cobra's head with its mouth open ready to attack. In his hand he held an ax.

As Roberto felt the cold metal blade enter his body he prayed that God would forgive this poor soul for his sins. Then he watched as a bright light at the end of a tunnel slowly seemed to be moving closer to him.

CHAPTER TWENTY-NINE

The appointment with Bishop Rossini was over and Anthony and Nelli were now standing in front of the door to Mary Ellen's office.

"Well, we're here, Anthony. Shall we go in and see an old friend?"

Nelli grabbed the doorknob and opened the door to the office.

Anthony knew it was the right thing to do but he was still having second thoughts as he followed Nelli into the office. Carlotta, Mary Ellen's assistant, looked at the visitors entering and immediately knew this must be who Ms. O'Farrell was expecting.

"You must be Nelli and Anthony Andruccioli; Ms. O'Farrell told me you would be stopping around eleven-thirty. Please be seated, I will let her know you have arrived."

Nelli and Anthony nodded their heads and smiled, taking a seat.

Ever since eleven, Mary Ellen had been watching the clock. Her level of anxiety had increased as it got closer to eleven-thirty. She had a habit of twitching her cheek when she was nervous. She tried rubbing it to make it stop, and then remembered how Anthony would always kid her about it.

Mary Ellen heard Carlotta talking to someone in the outer office. Nelli and Anthony must have arrived.

"Please dear Lord, grant me the courage to face my past with grace," she whispered softly.

The phone on her desk rang.

"Ms. O'Farrell, your visitors have arrived."

"Thank you, Carlotta. I will be right out to greet them."

She took a deep breath, stood up, and walked towards the door. As she opened it the familiar scent of a man's cologne filled the air. It was the one Anthony had always worn. It took her back to when she and Anthony were planning a future together.

Nelli sensed the awkwardness of the moment and quickly got up from her chair to greet Mary Ellen.

"It's wonderful to see you again," she said, walking over to give Mary Ellen a hug. "It's been much too long."

Mary Ellen was thankful to Nelli for sensing the awkwardness of the moment.

Anthony stood at the same time, "Nelli's right Mary Ellen; it's been much too long."

"Thank you Anthony, it's wonderful to see both of you. Please, come into the office. Let's sit down over by the windows and you can look out on to some of the beautiful gardens we have here at Vatican. I would like to hear all about your meeting with the bishop."

Mary Ellen closed the door and followed them over to the seating area.

"What project will you be working on here at the Vatican?" asked Mary Ellen.

"I've been brought in to assist with the continuation of the restoration project to restore some of the halls in the Apostolic Palace that were subdivided into smaller rooms during the last century. Many of the corridors are in urgent need of repair. I am sure you must be familiar with the project, now that you're working here in the administrative offices."

"Wasn't there a discovery of more pagan carvings along the walls when they overhauled the Appartamento Borgia?" said Mary Ellen.

"Yes, it's quite exciting. I'm going to be able to combine my expertise in architecture and ancient religion, which doesn't happen often.

"That must be thrilling for you. They picked the right person for the job."

As she smiled at both Anthony and Nelli, she felt the barriers coming down between her and Anthony.

"I was so sorry to hear about your father. He was a wonderful man, who will be greatly missed by many. I wanted to call but …."

Nelli touched the cross that hung from the chain around her neck that their father had given to her, "Thank you, Mary Ellen. We do miss him very much. How is your brother doing? I know you had hoped to get the judgment against him reversed."

"That's true, Nelli. He is doing much better. He has moved on with his life. We talk almost every other day."

Mary Ellen didn't know if she should bring up yesterday's events but she wanted to tell someone. There wasn't anyone in her life right now that she felt she could confide in. The issue with her brother is what tore her and Anthony apart, but that part of their lives was now in the past. Maybe she would just mention the file from Father Roberto but ask Anthony what he might know about the card with that awful embossed cobra head on it.

"The strangest things happened yesterday. I received some documents containing information I had never seen before, pertaining to my brother's case. I always said there was no solid proof for the judgment that was rendered against Devlin. These new documents seem to support that premise. Then an envelope was dropped off at my office yesterday morning. I wouldn't mind running something past you, Anthony, if you don't mind? Do you know anything about the significance of the symbol of a cobra's head with one blue eye?"

Anthony had trouble keeping his composure, the same way when he saw the stigmata on Nelli's hand. Remembering the prophecy of Saint Anthony that warned of the rise of the serpent, it was becoming clear it truly had begun and Mary Ellen was part of whatever was happening. He had to find out what the reason was for her question.

"There is a prophecy that warns of the return of the serpent," said Anthony.

"What does the prophecy say?" asked Mary Ellen.

"After I tell you, will you explain why you would ask about that particular symbol?"

"Yes, please tell me about this prophecy."

"There was a monk by the name of Fernando Martins de Bulhoes, who later, upon admission into the Franciscan order would take the name Antonio. He lived in the thirteenth century and was canonized to Sainthood, who we now know as Saint Anthony. He is commonly referred to as the 'finder of lost articles,' but most important is his prophecy. It is said that an angel visited him on three consecutive days. He was to write the words spoken to him in a book. A time was coming when the serpent that was described as having the head of a cobra and having one eye would rise again. If the faithful repented and heeded the words of God that were written in the book, they would win the battle against the serpent and be saved from the gates of Hell. Many believe this is what the final chapter in the Bible talks about in Revelations."

Mary Ellen sat quietly. Anthony noticed the subtle twitching of her cheek. "Mary Ellen have you seen a picture of this somewhere?"

Anthony tried not to show his concern over the question.

Walking over to her desk Mary Ellen opened the top drawer and pulled out a small card of some kind then walked back and sat down and handed it to Anthony.

"I received this yesterday in an envelope with only my name written on the front.

It seemed quite ominous. I feel like it is some kind of warning but I don't know why someone would send it to me. Do you have any idea what it could mean?"

Nelli leaned in to look at the card. She could tell Mary Ellen was disturbed by it.

"It's actually a beautiful drawing," said Nelli, "but the way its mouth is open, as if it is ready to attack, makes it seem threatening, doesn't it? Do you know what it could mean Anthony?"

Anthony didn't want to say much more. His mind was spinning from this newest discovery.

"Can you have your assistant make a copy of this for me and I'll do a little research?"

"I will make the copy. I don't want Carlotta to know anything about this," Mary Ellen got up and walked over to the printer in her office.

Anthony had intended to talk with the other Guardians about the protection for Nelli but now it would be necessary to include Mary Ellen in the plan, and he would need to have it begin immediately. Time was running out.

"Nelli, while I look into this, you could go back to the shop with the boxes," said Anthony, "then later we could all meet for dinner and I can hopefully tell you something about this card you received Mary Ellen."

"Where are you staying?" asked Mary Ellen.

"The Hotel Raphael."

"That's actually very close to my apartment. That will work out nicely. We could stop by the shop you want to go to first, and then I know a lovely little restaurant not far from your hotel."

"That sounds good," said Anthony. "You have Nelli's cell number. Give us a call if you're running late."

CHAPTER THIRTY

The meeting so far had gone smoothly. Thomas was meticulously going through the final responsibilities with each of the five men seated around the table. Every detail of the operation was covered not once but twice, nothing would be left to chance. He knew Peter Romanus was watching and listening to everything from his villa in Arezzo. There would be zero tolerance for error.

It was getting late. The setup for this evening's entertainment was taking place in the grand ballroom in another part of the compound, but Thomas knew he still had a couple more hours of details to go over with the men.

In a calm voice Thomas asked, "Before we continue with the final part of our meeting, does anyone have any questions?" He sat back in his chair relaxing slightly. He looked around the table and waited for the first question.

Back in Arezzo Peter leaned forward in his chair with his elbows resting on his knees clasping his hands. He was curious to see who would be the first to ask a question. Although he was confident, he knew who it would be and what it would be about. He had personally chosen these five men. He knew them better than they knew themselves.

With his backing, the five men before him had achieved their life's dreams. Along the way they had picked up some indulgences that Peter used to his advantage. He always wondered what they feared most, the loss of the power and wealth, or was having their secrets exposed to the entire world the greater threat? It didn't make a difference to Peter. He used them equally to demand obedience. General D'Amoto was the first to speak.

"As you heard today, I have all my troops set up and in place ready for the final execution of the plan. The officers I have in charge are men I have personally handpicked. I have no concern about their loyalty to me." General D'Amoto continued, "Thomas I would like you to clarify one more time exactly how the transfer of money to each of us will be handled for the final stage of the operation."

Peter smiled as he listened to the general, "I should have made a bet with Thomas," chuckling out loud. "I knew the general would be the one making sure he would get his money." He continued to watch the screens for any unusual ticks on the monitors that were outside of the normal readings on each man.

Thomas turned and looked at Vingenzo.

"Perhaps you would be so kind to go over that one more time for everyone."

"I would be happy to Thomas. There have been five separate Swiss numbered bank accounts set up at the Union Bank of Switzerland in Lugano, one for each of the men seated at this table.

"When you return home, a courier will deliver an envelope to you, which will contain a list of numbers. Listen carefully; the first seven numbers will be an account registered in your name, which will be broken up into two separate installments. The next eleven numbers will be the phone number you will call; they will require identification and an electronic signature to access the first sum of money. You will use those funds to pay off all services and products you deemed were necessary to complete your part of the plan. The second account will need two signatures to access the funds, yours of course, and Thomas's. Perhaps you would want to explain this part Thomas?"

"Yes, thank you Vingenzo. After receiving the call, to initiate the final commands to your teams, you will then return here to await the announcement, which will be telecast worldwide, of the newly formed world government, headed by Peter Romanus II.

The statement has already been recorded by Angelo and the feeds to all the networks will go out on cue. Once everything is in place and the transfer of power has begun, I will enter the code and my signature that will allow you to access the second account. It will be the agreed upon amount we discussed with each of you at the onset of this plan. Are there any more questions on this?"

The five men remained silent.

"Good," said Thomas. "There is a small matter the Grand Master feels you should be made aware of. It has been handled and we are confident it will not affect the final plans in any way."

As he glanced around the table, his eyes rested on the newest member, "It will affect you most directly Cardinal Cavallari. A member of P2 made us aware of a priest, one Father Roberto, who was asking questions about the LC. Of course, that was one of the groups we used to accomplish our objective. He was eliminated and a warning was left with him. There have been no news releases, so it appears the Vatican has wisely decided to keep it quiet."

Glancing at Angelo, "You will keep us abreast of any news reports that might be leaked. With all the other problems the Church is facing, we don't think they'll want to have this made public." Turning his attention back to Cardinal Cavallari, "Perhaps you will be so kind, to call your office after the meeting and see if you are informed of any unusual activity at the Vatican we should be aware of."

"Do we know if this priest passed information on to anyone else?" asked Cavallari, showing indifference to the latest development.

"We know a Ms. O'Farrell requested information from him on her brother," said Thomas, "she has been trying to exonerate her brother for years but to no avail. We also know this Father Roberto cornered Cardinal McKenna one day last month and was asking him a series of questions. We have no way of knowing what their conversation covered, but we feel it might have touched on areas that could bring up questions we would rather not have asked."

Thomas continued, "Cardinal McKenna is head of the CDF, who is in charge of looking into the sexual allegations against clergy. We will continue to monitor both Ms. O'Farrell and Cardinal McKenna very closely. I am confident that the Vatican will attribute the death of Father Roberto to natural causes. The papacy cannot handle another scandal at this time. If this priest passed on information to anyone, his death should send a warning not to pursue any further questioning for fear of his or her own life.

"Being a matter of only a few days before the New World government will be in place, there won't be enough time for anyone to stop it from happening," said Thomas with complete confidence.

Even though the cardinal was troubled by the murder he appeared calm to everyone. He was thankful one's thoughts were still private. He could put himself into a state of relaxation with mediation through prayer and control his heart and pulse rate even under adverse situations.

Being the newest addition to the group, he hadn't been exposed, as the other four seated at the table, to the consequences of disobeying the Grand Master. Cardinal Cavallari was aware of the suspected involvement of P2 surrounding the death of Pope John Paul I and the scandal connected to the bank that Vingenzo now controlled. This newest twist with Father Roberto's death put him in a precarious spot. One he was not too happy about. He had to be careful; tomorrow he would be back at the Vatican living a lie.

CHAPTER **THIRTY-ONE**

The last two hours had gone by very quickly. Closing the file in front of him, Thomas rested his hands on top of the cover.

"Our meeting is now concluded."

He nodded to one of the guards at the door who walked over and stood next to him.

"My assistant here will come around and collect any and all papers to be shredded. Please do not attempt to leave this room with anything except your person."

The hooded disciple started with Silvio and worked his way around the table. Whatever they needed to remember would have to be from memory.

Suddenly Thomas's demeanor changed from deadly serious to almost lighthearted.

"It's been a long day, gentlemen," he said. Peter Romanus has planned an exceptional evening of delights for you to enjoy and part take in. After this evening, the next time we see each other, we will be witnesses to the new regime with our own Grand Master as head of the New World Order. It is now six o'clock. We will all meet back on the veranda at nine sharp for drinks and the start of an evening I'm sure each of you will never forget.

"Please take the next few hours to rest and refresh yourselves. You will each find a set of evening clothes made especially for you by the Grand Master's own personal tailor. A masseuse has been arranged on your behalf and if I might say, each one was handpicked for your specific preferences."

Thomas continued, "The next time I see you I am sure

none of the young women in the room will be able to resist the gentlemen that I will have the pleasure of spending the evening with. Peter Romanus himself participated in the planning of the festivities. Anything you might desire will be available; nothing has been left to the imagination. Enjoy the evening gentlemen; it will be your first taste of what life will have to offer from this point on. Anything you desire will be available for your taking."

Thomas pushed back his chair and stood up. The hooded disciple was at his side, one hand resting on the ax and the other holding an automatic weapon. If his eyes could be considered a weapon, they would be knives that could cut out your heart before you even realize what had happened.

"Until nine o'clock gentlemen," said Thomas.

CHAPTER THIRTY-TWO

Anthony and Nelli decided to walk back to the hotel.

"It was good to see Mary Ellen wasn't it, Anthony?"

"Yes, I have to admit it was. It was awkward at first but then it was as if the last eight years never happened, except we both are a few years older. Actually, I think the years have made her more beautiful and she seems more at peace with herself and the world."

"I thought the same thing. I would say the same is true about you too, Anthony. God has a plan for all of us, you know."

Anthony thought to himself, you my dear sister are not yet totally aware of the undertaking that has been chosen for you, and he had no clue of what God's plan was for Mary Ellen.

As they were about to turn a corner and walk down one of the side streets, Anthony pointed out to Nelli a wrought iron railing that enclosed an opening in the street.

"Let me show you something interesting," said Anthony.

He led her over to the walled off area. They looked into the gaping hole that dropped down for at least fifteen feet below the street.

"What's down there?" Nelli asked peering into the opening. "Why do they have this hole fenced off in the street?" Half way down a soft light revealed what looked like nothing more than a dirt floor.

"What you are looking at are the ancient streets of Rome," Anthony said, "there is a subterranean Rome not many people know exists, which is artistically and architecturally equal to that of the monuments above the ground—some of it going down as deep as thirty-six feet below the city. Where we are standing is the culmination of hundreds of years of civilizations that built their cities over those original streets.

"At lunch yesterday, if it had been 96 A.D., we would have been sitting inside the Stadium of Domitian with 30,000 other spectators watching the birth of sports and athletic competitions. Not far away would have been the Odeon, a theater where artistic and literary events happened. These were the so-called "Agon Capitolinus" or Contest at the Capitoline, all conceived by the Emperor Domitian."

Anthony added, "Many of these underground archaeological sites are now open to the public to tour. I've seen pictures but I have never taken one of the excursions. Someday I'd like to do that."

"That's incredible," said Nelli. "It's hard to imagine we're actually looking at the streets that people walked on thousands of years ago."

Nelli suddenly realized she was exhausted and could feel a headache coming on.

"Is it much farther to the hotel Anthony?" Nelli asked.

"No, it's up ahead just around the corner. Why?"

"I'm not feeling that well. I'm messed up with the time difference."

"I'm sorry; I should have paid more attention. Just a few more minutes and we'll be at the hotel, and then you can lie down and take a nap."

Anthony actually felt more comfortable knowing that Nelli would be in the next room resting, instead of going back to the little shop to look for a box. Although he knew that there would always be a Guardian not far away.

CHAPTER THIRTY-THREE

Nelli saw a man walking towards her. He looked familiar but she couldn't quite place the face. He didn't frighten her; in fact she felt a calmness that was hard to explain.

"I've waited a long time to meet my namesake," said the man.

"I don't understand," said Nelli.

"Your father named you after me, Antonella. He chose you to carry on the sacred task of the Keeper of the Key as all those before you. You are the only one who can unlock the box, which holds the book of the words of our Lord. It has been hidden, until the time came, when it needed to be found and that time has arrived."

"How do you know about that?" asked Nelli, shocked by what he had just told her.

"You found a small religious medal in your room when you arrived, do you remember?"

"You mean the Saint Anthony's medal I found on the balcony?"

"Yes, that's right. I left it there for you to find."

"Are you saying that you are who the medal was made for?"

"Yes, Antonella, I am Saint Anthony. Let me explain why I have appeared to you. After receiving a gift from young Giovanni, who was under my care at the abbey, I was visited by an angel who instructed me to write down what I was told and place it in the box I was given. The Lord would decide when the time came for his words to be revealed. I did as I was commanded.

Upon my death, I needed to pass on the box to someone born with a pure heart and who loved our Lord. Since Giovanni made the box for me and had these qualities, I gave him the box for safekeeping. He became the first Keeper of the Key.

Growing into manhood he married, and had a family, naming his first child Anthony. From that time on one child from each generation would be named after me and become the Chosen One.

As Nelli listened, she remembered her father's words to her. Then she asked Saint Anthony, "My father came to me and said it was my destiny to locate the box, but how am I supposed to find it?"

"You have already been given a clue where to look Antonella. You must believe in the souls that come to visit you. We are all around you. We will guide you and protect you along your journey. Temptation cannot win against the pure of heart. I will visit with you again my child. Now rest, for tomorrow your quest begins," and the image of Saint Anthony slowly began to fade.

Nelli called out to Saint Anthony not to leave her, she still had questions to ask him but as silently as he came, he was gone, and she was alone again.

The door separating the two hotel rooms was slightly ajar and Anthony thought he heard Nelli calling him. He got up and headed over to the door.

Lightly tapping on the door he whispered, "Nelli are you awake?"

Peeking around the door it looked like she was still sleeping but Nelli called out his name again. Then Anthony realized she was calling Saint Anthony, not Anthony. He walked over and sat down on the edge of her bed.

"Nelli, its Anthony, wake up, you were having a dream."

Slowly opening her eyes, it took Nelli a minute to register where she was. Then a peaceful look came over her face and she smiled at her brother.

"I just talked to him, Anthony. I just talked with Saint Anthony."

He was no longer surprised by Nelli's visions asking, "What did he say to you?"

After she told him about finding the medal and her conversation, he suggested that she try to remember as much as she could of all the visits and write down every detail even if it did not seem important right now. She agreed that was a good idea.

He checked his watch. "Mary Ellen will be here in a half hour. Let's go get you that box to add to your collection."

CHAPTER THIRTY-FOUR

Everywhere you looked were artifacts from past civilizations.

"Buona sera, benvenuto."

"Buona sera," replied Anthony.

"Ah, le capiscei l'italiano?" asked the proprietor of the shop.

"Si, io capiscei l'italiano, ma no la sorella non capiscei l'italiano," said Anthony nodding at his sister.

"Si, si signore, I will speak English," he seemed happy to have visitors

The man looked as old as some of the treasures in his shop but his eyes held the wonder of a young child. He moved slowly as he walked. His shoulders slouched forward as he leaned on a cane for support but it was obvious he loved being among his possessions.

Nelli had already spotted a large wall case that held even more boxes. She stood in front of the glass doors peering inside. They were more beautiful than the ones that were in the window.

"I see your sister has interest in one of my collections. Each box in front of you has a story to tell signorina."

"They are all so beautiful and each one is so unique," said Nelli not able to hide her excitement. "I recently started collecting these small treasures and have read how they were given as gifts throughout the centuries. Where did you get all of them from?"

"Ah, I see you have done your homework signorina. My life has been blessed and I have lived a long time but sadly everyone I know has gone to be with our Father. I've been waiting to join the others and I think perhaps that the time might be near."

Nelli was listening as the shopkeeper spoke but her eyes were locked on one of the small boxes behind the glass door.

The old man couldn't help but notice and came closer to where she was standing. Anthony and Mary Ellen followed close behind.

"Which box calls to you signorina?"

Nelli pointed to the wooden one with an intricately engraved cross on top.

"There's something special about this one don't you think," turning to look at Anthony and Mary Ellen, Nelli quickly looked back at the box.

The old man smiled and said, "You have chosen a very special one and it has a special story behind it. The person that sold it to me many years ago told me it had been part of his family's estate in Pesaro."

Nelli was startled by the old man's statement.

"That's where we're headed tomorrow to visit the birthplace of our father."

The old man didn't seem too surprised. He just looked up towards heaven and made the sign of the cross.

"The Holy Spirit must have had a purpose for bringing you to my humble shop."

"You spoke of a story with regard to this box?" asked Mary Ellen.

"Si signorina, I was told that it is an identical reproduction of a box given to a monk who lived in the monastery outside of Pesaro in the thirteenth century. It is said the original box held a secret."

Nelli couldn't breathe. Her dreams were coming true. She remembered her father telling her she would be guided on her journey.

Anthony sensed the change in Nelli's demeanor. Moving next to her he put his arm around her shoulder hoping his sister would snap out of the daze she seemed to be in.

CHAPTER THIRTY-FIVE

They were finally on their way to Pesaro. Nelli held the box in her hands, examining it carefully. As Anthony drove, he mentally went over the plans discussed with the other Guardians the night before. Two Guardians would stay behind in Rome to protect Mary Ellen. Two were already in Pesaro, two were close behind in a car following them, and the others to predetermined locations.

"So what do you make of this box Anthony?"

"I believe you were meant to find it."

Anthony had been waiting for the right moment to talk to Nelli about the mark of the stigmata; this seemed as good as any.

"Nelli you never told me what you did to your hand. I noticed it on the plane flying over here," he asked, keeping his eyes on the road.

Nelli moved her hand away from the box looking down at the marking on it and then quickly placed it back.

"What happened?"

"It was after I had the dream I told you about when father came to visit me."

Nelli was fighting back tears trying not to cry. Anthony was struggling with the memory of that day too, as he watched from the other room, where Nelli sat next to their dying father.

"I miss him too Nelli."

"I know," she said in a whisper.

"Go on Nelli."

"I was watching the evening news on TV. The next thing

I remember I felt a sharp pain in my hand. When I looked down I noticed blood dripping down my arm. Then I realized I was holding on to the cross father gave me and immediately let go of it. I thought I must have held it so tightly that it cut into my skin and it never healed."

"You know I have studied religion. What I am about to say to you might be difficult to accept. The marking you now have is the mark of the stigmata. Their existence is so well established historically, that unbelievers now seek only to explain them naturally and no longer dispute them.

"It happens only to the Chosen Ones. They will have visions as are written about in the stories that have been recorded over time. I believe the dreams you are having are not dreams but visions. I would like to explore your dreams a little more Nelli if you are up to it."

As Anthony was talking she grabbed a notebook from her bag.

"I did what you suggested Anthony. I tried to write down everything as accurately as I could remember."

"That's great Nelli.

"Okay, then your next vision was when you spoke with Dad, right?"

"Yes, he told me, *search for the knowledge found in a box that has been hidden for centuries. The box can only be opened with the key you possess. In the box you will find a book. Within the book is written the words of Our Lord that will show the path that must be taken by the shepherd of the flock if the Church is to survive.* He said I would be given a Guardian on earth and when he sees the stigmata on your hand he will know the time has come to be your protector."

Nelli abruptly stopped, looked up from her notebook, turned her head and looked at Anthony, shocked at realizing what she had just said.

"It's you, isn't it?"

Anthony continued to look at the road ahead, then calmly replied, "Yes Nelli."

Neither of them said a word.

Nelli was the first to speak, "I'm glad it's you Anthony."

"There's something else you must know, I am not the only Guardian," replied Anthony. "There are eleven others who will help us on this journey. I can tell you more later."

Nelli now realized that she would be surrounded by many souls, here on earth and by others that had gone before her. She would stop questioning and accept her fate.

"Let's keep going Nelli. Tell me about the one involving Saint Anthony. Did he say anything about the box?"

"Yes, he spoke about the young boy Giovanni and the gift of the box. Being visited three times by an angel who told him to write down the words of Our Lord in a book and place it in the box he had received as a gift.

"Upon his death Saint Anthony entrusted the box to Giovanni. The young apprentice became the first Keeper of the Key. Giovanni married and named his first child after his friend and mentor. Upon Giovanni's death the child named after Saint Anthony became the Chosen One and so on and so on and we know where this ends."

"Now your vision with the artist Bellini, if I remember correctly you said something about a painting that held a clue?"

"Yes, he was at the foot of my bed standing next to a painting and he told me to study the painting carefully. When I fell asleep that night, I was reading from the Frommer's guidebook on Italy and it suggested things to see while in Pesaro. The most significant relic of Renaissance Pesaro is a painting by Giovanni Bellini housed in the art gallery of the Museo Civico in Piazza Toschi Moca called Coronation of the Virgin.

"Here's what I wrote down. He said, *Study the painting carefully, it will guide you along the path you seek. Remember to look within, there you will find a clue.*

"Do you think this could be the painting the artist meant?" asked Anthony.

"At the moment it's our only lead."

CHAPTER THIRTY-SIX

Mary Ellen got to her office earlier than normal. She knew Anthony and Nelli were already on their way to Pesaro. They said they would call her when they arrived at the villa they had rented outside of town.

She checked her e-mails. As she scanned through the messages, there was one from her brother. He had decided to write down everything he could remember, like she had asked.

She began reading and half way through the e-mail Devlin made a reference to an order called the Legion of Christ.

"There's that name again," muttering under her breath, reading more slowly now.

There was something he had noticed with one of the priests from the LC. It didn't seem very important at the time. He assumed it was a nervous habit that people sometimes develop. He noticed upon greeting some of the other clergy he would start to nervously spin the ring on his left finger before shaking hands. But then he observed others and not all of them priests, exhibiting the same idiosyncrasy. He thought it was odd to see the same behavior among that many individuals.

Sitting back in her chair, Mary Ellen thought about what Devlin had observed. It could be nothing or maybe it was some kind of secret sign? She heard the outer office door open, then footsteps. Barely breathing she watched the door slowly being pushed open and then she heard her name.

"Ms. O'Farrell?"

Mary Ellen relaxed when she heard the voice of her assistant Carlotta but was shocked to realize she had the letter opener clutched tightly in her hand. She had received it as a gift her first day at the Vatican. Mary Ellen set it back down on the desk before Carlotta could see.

"Yes, good morning Carlotta."

Her assistant stood in front of her but seemed unusually quiet.

"I was hoping to be here before you."

"I didn't finish some things yesterday before leaving to meet with my friends, so I decided to come in early."

"Have you heard the news?" Carlotta asked nervously.

"From the look on your face, I'm sure I haven't heard what you're about to tell me."

"I hate to be the one to tell you . . . Father Roberto is dead."

Mary Ellen gasped, "But I just talked to him. There must be some mistake. He can't be dead. Are you sure?"

"Yes Ms. O'Farrell the guard at the front gate just told me."

"How did he die?" Mary Ellen felt sick to her stomach.

"That's the strange thing. They're not saying. When I came in this morning, I noticed an increase in security. He was such a nice young priest. At least we know he is with our Lord now."

Mary Ellen looked down trying to collect her thoughts. Inadvertently her eyes fell upon the file that she grabbed from her mailbox this morning. The handwriting on the envelope was Father Roberto's. She didn't know why but she suddenly felt terrified. She didn't want to show Carlotta she was alarmed.

"Yes Carlotta, to lose such a young soul as Father Roberto is a great loss. Please send my condolences to his family today, would you please, and find out when the funeral will be."

Carlotta nodded and then turned to leave, closing the door silently behind her. Mary Ellen stared at the file. As she started to open it her hands began to shake and the tears began to fall. Could it be because of her he was dead? She should have never asked him to help her.

Trying to gain her composure, she looked at the top sheet of paper. There in front of her was a handwritten outline with names, dates, and reference numbers. Flipping through some of the other materials there were copies of e-mails, photos, documents, and more, much more.

She couldn't believe what she was looking at. It could be

the proof she needed to prove her brother's innocence. Mary Ellen picked up the phone to call Father Roberto to thank him. Her hand froze in midair.

Outside the walls of the Vatican, Shim'on, one of two Guardians that had been sent to protect Mary Ellen, was on the phone with Cephas. The equipment that was set up in Mary Ellen's office was working splendidly. They already knew about Father Roberto from their source inside the Vatican but had listened in as Mary Ellen was told about the priest's death.

"Her assistant just informed her about Father Roberto," said Shim'on. "She was shocked when she heard the news. She also received a file that seems to have upset her."

"We need to see what's in that file, Shim'on," demanded Cephas. "See what you can do about that. Tau'ma should be at his destination by now. I will follow up with you later."

Back in her office, Mary Ellen gently placed the phone down. "Relax, think what your next move should be," she told herself. "You need to figure out a plan." Her thoughts were scattered; she needed to focus. About to send e-mails to Devlin, Cardinal McKenna, and Anthony, she stopped herself. What if someone is watching me or has hacked into my computer? She was becoming paranoid. She didn't even feel safe inside the Vatican. Grabbing a note pad she began writing down a list of things to do.

1. HAVE CARLOTTA MAKE AN APPOINTMENT WITH CARDINAL MCKENNA
2. CALL DEV, MEET SOMEWHERE PRIVATE
3. CALL ANTHONY
4. LOOK INTO THE INVESTIGATION OF SEXUAL ALLEGATIONS BY THE CHURCH AND ANY CONNECTION TO THE LC.

Then she buzzed Carlotta.

"Yes Ms. O'Farrell."

"Please set up an appointment with Cardinal McKenna. Ask if it would be possible to meet with him this morning. Express it is of some urgency."

"Of course, can I say what it's about?"

"Just tell him I have some something of interest to discuss with him."

"I will do that immediately."

Next Mary Ellen called Devlin using her cell phone. It went into voice mail.

"Dev, it's me. Call me ASAP."

Then she opted to send a text message to Anthony thinking he might respond quicker than listening to a voice message. She desperately wanted to talk with someone she could trust. There was one more person she could try, Nelli. She prayed she would answer her phone.

CHAPTER **THIRTY-SEVEN**

The human race works so hard at trying to figure out what life is all about, Peter thought to himself. The answers have always been right in front of them. All they have to do is follow the script; it's not as if it's a hidden secret.

The fact is the Bible has sold more copies than any other book in history, but there was this thing called free will. Peter learned early that temptation was a powerful weapon. The story of Adam and Eve, plus numerous examples throughout the Old Testament further substantiated what he already knew, that if you find a person's weaknesses they were yours to control.

The Lord's Prayer even addresses this: Lead us not into temptation but deliver us from evil. A prayer every Catholic and Christian recites asking for the strength to choose good over evil.

Peter had studied the Bible. He had read it for very different reasons than most people. It was the ultimate training manual of how to build his army of souls and become the final successor to the papal seat and the leader of the New World Order.

There was a fine line between good and evil. In his mind he visualized a person teetering on a fence. On the right side was the Holy Spirit with an outstretched hand saying Come with me and put your trust in the Lord. On the left was the serpent holding out an apple hissing, Come with me and pick from the tree of knowledge; it will give you all you desire. Everyone knows how that ended.

Like the serpent, Peter Romanus was the wolf in sheep's clothing, making false promises to those who followed him. He couldn't believe his good fortune. It was as if destiny, without realizing it had created all this chaos just for his benefit.

Peter, an only child, was raised in a Catholic household and attended parochial schools. After graduating from high school, he continued with his education, receiving several degrees from some of the most prestigious universities in the world. His parents had always hoped he might have a calling to the priesthood but eventually they gave up on that dream. They watched, as their son became this charismatic individual who people turned to for leadership. They came to accept his destiny had already been written.

His parents passed from this earth more than twenty years ago. It was better that way. They would have never been able to live with the man their son had evolved into.

As a young man Peter joined the Masonic Order of Freemasonry in Italy known as the Grande Orient or the GOI. It was recognized by the mainstream Freemasonry UGLE (United Grand Lodge of England) and the U.S. Grand Lodges, but the Lodge's freethinking was being replaced by a leftist approach that worried the Masons.

Peter was assigned the task of reorganizing the Lodge. Being given this responsibility he was able to obtain a list of "sleeping members"—members no longer invited to take part in Masonic rituals.

Within two years Peter conceived the idea of secretly forming a "shadow society" within the Lodge and declared himself the Grand Master whose members reported to him and him alone. Even the freemasons were unaware that this covert organization existed. From the start it was illegal. It was not registered and only Peter knew the names of the members. He gave it the name P2, after the nineteenth century Lodge "Propaganda Due."

Under his leadership P2 became the most powerful, political, and violent secret organization in Italy, with its long arms reaching into Europe, the United States, and South America.

He had become the leader of thousands and controlled, or should one say influenced the lives of many powerful men and women around the world. Peter was aware it had become known as the executive branch of the Illuminati and soon he would occupy the final seat of power in the Vatican. His plan had come together; better than he could have ever dreamt.

Taking control of world governments had been simple but tempting the faithful to turn away from their beliefs had been more difficult. Creating mistrust among them had been his greatest challenge.

Lives meant little to Peter Romanus. They were a means to an end. If he could tempt the Chosen Ones called to become priests, bishops, and cardinals, his power was proving to be as great as God's.

The world will be looking for a new leader. He would promise to bring back peace and security to the world, but he had no intention of keeping those promises. He intended to create a one-world religion and a one-world government with a cashless society.

The New World Order would have sovereign authority over all religion, oversee all governments, and regulate the world's finances. His dream finally realized.

CHAPTER THIRTY-EIGHT

Anthony and Nelli decided to stop for a cup of coffee in a small village just outside of Ancona. Anthony would check in with the other Guardians and get updates on any new developments.

Checking his phone he noticed there were two new messages. The first one was from Cephas: "Must talk call ASAP." The second was from Mary Ellen: "Please call me." He must have shown his concern as he read them because Nelli noticed the change in his facial expression.

"What's wrong Anthony?"

"Nothing, why?"

"You look worried about something."

"Just a couple text messages came through I hadn't noticed; one's actually from Mary Ellen. I wonder why she called. We said we would call her when we got to Pesaro."

Nelli was a little curious too but didn't think too much of it.

"I need to call the one person back first, and then we'll try calling Mary Ellen. Go ahead and order a couple espressos and something to eat. I'm going to stretch my legs a little and make my call."

He wanted to have privacy when he called Cephas but not get too far away from his sister. Cephas picked up on the second ring.

"Tau'ma, finally, Ya'agov called me, a priest was found dead in the stacks of the Vatican library, a Father Roberto. The Vatican is reporting it was from natural causes, but Ya'agov said he was murdered. There is heightened security everywhere inside the Vatican and it is rumored the Pope is leaving to go to an undisclosed location for a few days. He also said there is a video, showing someone wearing the garments of a cardinal in the mail center after hours. But the person deliberately keeps his face hidden from the cameras."

"When was the priest found?" Anthony was trying to piece together a timetable.

"His body was found around five a.m."

"Was anything left behind?"

"I don't know anything else at the moment, but I will find out more as soon as I can without causing suspicion."

Cephas told Anthony that he had also taken pictures of the mail room with his phone and was sending them to all the others to study.

"Let's tighten up the surveillance on Mary Ellen, too. Have the cameras and listening devices been installed in her home and office?"

"Yes, it's all been taken care of. We have live feed 24/7."

"I got a text message from Mary Ellen to call her," continued Anthony. "I wonder if she knows about Father Roberto. Let me know immediately what you find out. We should be in Pesaro by eleven o'clock. Cephas, Nelli knows about us, she made the connection in the car this morning. This vacation has now turned into a search to find a box once belonging to Saint Anthony. Whoever this Antichrist is, believes his power is as great as God's. The battle has begun." Anthony headed back to the table.

"Did you get everything taken care of?" asked Nelli. But she could see he was troubled.

"Yes, now let's make that call to Mary Ellen."

"Anthony," said Nelli, not sure what to say, "While you were on the phone Mary Ellen called me."

Anthony instinctively knew Mary Ellen had told Nelli about Father Roberto.

"You already know don't you Anthony?" said Nelli, "that's what your text message and phone call were about."

"Yes Nelli, what else did Mary Ellen tell you?"

"Not too much. She didn't seem to want to talk about it on the phone. I told her we would call her after we got to Pesaro.

I could tell by her voice she's scared Anthony. Can we get one of the Guardians to protect her?"

He could see Nelli was saddened by the news but he sensed she was not the least concerned about her own welfare, which made him even more determined to protect his sister.

"It's already been taken care of."

"One more thing, there was a file from Father Roberto waiting for her when she got to the office this morning. She said it contains information pertaining to her brother's case. There are copies of bank deposit slips and a list of names and other documents in the file. There's also mention several times of an order called the Legion of Christ. Mary Ellen said she had a feeling this was a harbinger of more to come."

As Anthony listened to what his sister was telling him, he silently asked God to welcome the soul of Father Roberto into his kingdom. Then he asked for the strength and wisdom he would need in this war against man's soul.

Anthony could feel Nelli's eyes on him, waiting for a response.

"We know our enemy has no soul. Father Roberto is the first soldier to die in this battle. Let's get back on the road; we should reach Pesaro in an hour."

As they got in the car, a black Mercedes with tinted windows passed by, going a little too fast. It swerved as Anthony started to open the door on the driver's side. Glancing at the car as it sped past him Anthony made a mental note of the license plate.

CHAPTER THIRTY-NINE

In his office on the second floor of the Papal Palace, Cardinal Donovan McKenna sat at his desk. He was going over the events of the last twenty-four hours in his head.

First the mysterious card delivered to him with the embossed head of a cobra, followed by his meeting with the Holy Father and the other officials of the Vatican. Then learning of the death of Father Roberto and the discovery of yet another card with the same drawing as the one he had received. On top of everything else the Vatican had a new problem on their hands.

This morning Mediaset broadcasting released information leaked to them surrounding a Father Marcial Maciel, the founder of the Legion of Christ Order. McKenna reread the news release from the Internet.

> This morning it was reported that a Father Maciel has fathered at least one child, breaking his vows of celibacy as an ordained priest in the Roman Catholic Church.
>
> There are now other questions concerning the order of the Legion of Christ that he founded in 1942. We have sources reporting that Pope Benedict XVI is aware of these latest developments and with the growing scandal of sexual allegations, we can only wonder if this will be the ruin of the Catholic Church as we know it.
>
> We have also received an unsubstantiated report that a young priest was found dead early this morning inside Vatican City. The name is not being released and not much information is being given concerning his death.
>
> We will continue to look into the latest developments surrounding the Vatican and the Holy See and update the public as soon as we learn more.

It was always known that the TV news network owned by media mogul Angelo Acciaiolio was far left politically. They had a socialist view of the world and what it should be. The Vatican being a Sovereign State was protected from their reporter's eyes and ears but somehow they found out about Father Roberto.

Lately a lot of their featured stories were centered on the opinions of their talking heads spieling socialistic views to world problems that seemed to be escalating daily. One of their solutions was the restructuring of religion and government into one ruling body.

Now this, as he gently ran his hand over his name on the front of the envelope. As he did he said a prayer for Father Roberto's soul. McKenna recognized the handwriting immediately. Were these the last thoughts and words of a young priest so full of life and promise?

Pulling the file from the envelope and flipping it open, a handwritten outline on the first sheet of paper stared up at him. After that were copies of documents, reports, and photos. There were notations, words circled, references, and links to dates and names.

"What did you uncover Roberto?" Donovan whispered under his breath.

As he flipped through the file one of the pages jumped out at him. At the top were the words Legion of Christ (LC). Under that was a breakdown of the organizational structure of the Order with notations and question marks throughout the page. That's the second time in one day. He continued to leaf through more pages and came to the last sheet. He felt flushed and his heart started to race. He slammed the file shut.

"It can't be the same."

McKenna slowly opened the file again to the last page. At the top of the sheet of paper was the drawing of the head of a cobra. Beneath it were the words Antichrist/Naj Hannah. Underneath that, in Father Roberto's handwriting was what looked like a genealogy chart for a family tree. He recognized a few names but the others were unfamiliar to him. He jumped when the phone on his desk rang. It was his assistant Robert calling.

"Yes Robert."

"I'm sorry to disturb you; Ms. O'Farrell from the Pontifical Academy of Social Sciences is requesting an appointment. Her assistant expressed there is some urgency to the meeting and that she must speak to you privately.

"Can we find some time in my schedule this morning?"

"I already checked and the first possible time would be tomorrow morning at nine-thirty. Would like me to set up the appointment?"

"Yes, thank you."

As the prefect of the CDF the present scandals fell under his watch. In the meeting with Pope Benedict, McKenna remembered what the Pope recounted of the prophecy of Saint Anthony to all in the room.

"The beloved Saint Anthony wrote about the return of the serpent. This false prophet would promise to end the chaos and bring peace and security back to the world, promises that would not be kept.

When the time came Our Lord would dispatch His Chosen One, the Keeper of the Key and will be the only one able to unlock the words that the Lord told Saint Anthony to write down in a book. For the time would come when His words would need to be read to rebuild His kingdom on earth."

Right after the Pope finished speaking Bishop Moretti from the Synod spoke next. "We have a spreading cancer within the church that must be cut out before it takes over completely."

The gravity of the situation hit McKenna hard as he listened to the bishop.

Bishop Moretti continued, "Father Roberto, may God welcome him into His kingdom, and you Cardinal McKenna must have touched upon information that could expose this evil we are facing. We have been sent a warning."

Pope Benedict raised his hand for silence.

"In my prayers the Lord has spoken to me. A false prophet is here and has created a large army to do his bidding. Evil needs many souls to wage its war. If we trust in Our Lord evil can never win. Many times throughout the scriptures the church and its followers have been tested. Many times mankind chose to follow the false prophet and many times God struck down the disbelievers and rebuilt his kingdom here on earth. We are entering turbulent times I am afraid."

Pope Benedict then nodded to Bishop Moretti to continue.

"Cardinal McKenna, we are giving you total authority and full access to Vatican City. A private security detail has been assigned to you 24/7. You are the only other person that will have knowledge of what the church is facing at this time. The other would have been Father Roberto, but he is now with our Father in Heaven. We are putting the future of the Vatican in your hands. Find the serpent and where it lives."

CHAPTER **FOURTY**

As they drove Nelli took out the Frommer's travel guidebook and read out loud to Anthony some of the background information on where their father was born.

"It says that Pesaro is located in the region known as Marche. The travel brochures call it the new Tuscany. Did you know that Anthony?"

"Actually I did. The city of Urbino is the star of this region. It's the birthplace of Raffaello Sanzio, better known as the artist Raphael."

Nelli continued reading, "In Medieval times Pesaro formed part of the Pentapolis. It was one of the five major seaports of the Adriatic during that period. So, Dad's birthplace was a pretty important seaport at one time." Nelli kept reading, "It's now a destination for Italians to take their families on vacation and also for tourists."

Nelli studied the terrain as they drove along E 78, "It looks like most of the countryside is made up of farmland and hills."

Anthony pointed out the window to his left.

"Up there are the Apennine Mountains. The villa we'll be staying at is inland a couple miles from the water. I thought it would be nicer to experience the area more as someone living here than with all the vacationers and tourists. We'll stay on A 14 all the way to Pesaro. It's an easier route; otherwise you're winding through mountain roads that can be a little treacherous."

"How long before we get there?"

"Another half hour at the most," answered Anthony.

Nelli quietly watched the scenery pass by trying to picture their father as a young boy traveling the same roads they were now driving on. They passed signs to various small towns. The next one coming up said Arezzo. When Nelli read the name she felt an overwhelming presence of evil being near. As the sign faded in the distance so did the feeling that had come over her. She turned to look at Anthony. He was staring ahead and watching the road as he drove.

Anthony was mentally going through a checklist in his mind. He knew Cephas would be tracking their location on GPS. Two Guardians would be doing a sweep of the villa before they arrived and checking the surveillance security equipment that had been installed.

Upon taking the oath to protect the Keeper of the Key, each Guardian had been implanted with a tracking device. Nelli was unaware of the tracking device that had been placed in the cross she wore around her neck.

"Nelli, keep your eyes open for the exit, Strada Ghetto di Lame," said Anthony.

A marker was coming up. It had a symbol that looked like a castle with an arrow pointing to the west. As they got closer it read Gradara.

"Anthony, look I remember reading about that castle. It belonged to the House of Sforza for a period of time. Lord Sforza was the one that commissioned Bellini to do the painting *Coronation of the Virgin* for his private chapel in the castle …."

"Known as the Madonna delle Grazie," Anthony finished Nelli's sentence.

"That's right. We have to visit the castle while we are here Anthony."

"We will Nelli. First let's find the exit for the villa. Later we will figure out what our next move should be. We need to call Mary Ellen and find out what the latest news is from the Vatican."

They hadn't been paying attention to the road signs. Nelli suddenly pointed out the window at a sign they just passed.

"Isn't that the exit we wanted?"

Anthony slowed down to pull off the road. Looking to see if it was clear to make a U-turn he waited for a car to pass. Out of the corner of his eye he noticed that it pulled off onto the shoulder further down the road. He memorized the license plate and make and model of the car, and then watched to see if they were being followed. He would call Cephas when they got to the villa and have him trace the car.

Nelli grabbed the map and directions for the villa from in-between the seats.

"We're looking for Via Trebbiantico road. It should be about two miles."

As they drove inland it became more rural and the road curved through hilly terrain. They thought they must have gone too far. They were about ready to turn around when Nelli saw a stone arch just ahead.

"There it is Anthony."

He turned right onto a gravel road lined with cypress trees as far as the eye could see. In the distance a beautiful country home sat all alone at the top of a hill. It was two stories and surrounded by gardens, with fountains, ponds, and stone statues. It looked like a picture from a post card. As Anthony pulled into the crushed stone circle drive in front of the villa, off to the right was a beautiful loggia with a panoramic view of the Adriatic.

The front door of the villa opened and a man came out and waved to them. Anthony knew him as Mattithyahu (Hebrew for Matthew), but to Nelli he would be Matthew the rental agent here in Pesaro.

"Ciao, welcome to Pesaro and your home for the next couple weeks. You must be Signorina Andruccioli and you must be Anthony who I spoke with on the phone. I hope the directions were clear for you. I'll grab your luggage, then give you a tour of the villa and introduce you to your housekeeper and cook Franco."

Anthony knew Franco was handpicked by Mattihyahu and told that Anthony and Nelli were relatives of a cardinal from the Vatican and were here on holiday.

Nelli followed Matthew through the front door. The interior was as lovely as the outside with terra-cotta tiles on the floor and beamed ceilings. The walls were sandstone done in neutral tones of beige and off white. They took a quick walk through and placed their luggage upstairs in the bedrooms.

Franco had prepared a light lunch for them on the loggia. Nelli asked Matthew to join them. For the next hour they relaxed and enjoyed the food and conversation.

"Well I must be on my way." Matthew pushed his chair

back and stood up, giving them the keys and said to call if they had any questions. He also reinforced Franco would be a good source of information.

Anthony and Nelli decided to unpack and meet back on the loggia at six o'clock. They would call Mary Ellen and then go into town for dinner.

CHAPTER FOURTY-ONE

Devlin O'Farrell began running to deal with the stress after the Church took away his right to be a priest. Before heading out this morning he did a little work on the computer and sent out some e-mails. During his run he thought about his conversation with his sister. He started to run faster thinking, I should have just left things as they were.

He had finally come to terms with everything that had happened, and now Mary Ellen wanted to reopen that door again.

When she asked him to consider her request he was just going to let it drop and not respond. He hoped she would get the message to let that door stay closed but what was this new information she said she had received?

Did she have proof showing that he had not done what they had accused him of? His mind replayed that day when the letter from the Vatican came of the decision to excommunicate him. His world had shattered around him. It had taken a long time for him to rebuild his life and now Nelli wanted him to go back and relive it all over again.

He didn't want to revisit the past but he wondered was there something he'd missed that could have proved his innocence. Thinking back to just before the accusations against him took place, he tried to remember anything that might now seem strange.

Back at the apartment, after a five-mile run, he headed to the fridge to get some water and glanced at his cell phone. There were a couple messages from Mary Ellen.

"Well, Devlin, she must have received your e-mail."

About to call Mary Ellen back he stopped himself, "What have you started?" Realizing it was too late now, he had reopened the door to the past. He hit call, begging for it to go into voice mail.

"Devlin, where have you been?"

"Hello to you too Mary Ellen, you must have gotten my e-mail."

"Yes, thanks for sending me that address."

He was taken back with her comment. What was she talking about?

Mary Ellen kept talking not giving her brother any time to reply.

"Can you meet me for dinner around six o'clock? I thought we could meet at the place where I knocked that glass of red wine all over that new skirt I had just bought."

What in the world was going on? This wasn't like Mary Ellen. She sounded okay, but he sensed fear in her voice; he played along.

"Sure, you were really ticked if I remember correctly. I'll see you at six."

"Remember six o'clock and don't be late Devlin."

Devlin realized there was nothing he could do at the moment to find out what was going on with his sister. He would just have to wait until tonight.

CHAPTER **FOURTY-TWO**

Nelli was looking forward to finally getting settled in one location and not feeling like she was living out of her suitcase. Her bedroom was beautifully done in earth tones similar to the downstairs foyer. It was spacious with a magnificent Tuscan style four-poster bed made out of carved olive wood. The floor was covered with a large tapestry area rug done in beiges, burgundies, and dark greens. Her hotel room in Rome had a balcony; here she had a terrace all to herself.

She started unpacking; as she did she wondered what Larry was doing right now. It would be evening back in Michigan. After she got most of her things put away she looked for her purse and pulled out her cell phone. Walking out onto the terrace she punched in Larry's number. As she waited for the connection her eye caught something off to her left. In the corner sitting on the ledge was a statue of an angel with her hands folded in prayer. It almost felt like it was going to speak to her.

The phone began ringing. On the fourth ring she was ready to leave a message but then an out of breath Larry answered.

"Nelli, finally I was going to call you in another hour if you hadn't called. Where are you? Are you in Pesaro yet?"

"We're at the villa. We got here a few hours ago. It's beautiful. I just finished unpacking and I'm standing out on the terrace outside my bedroom overlooking a small garden with a fountain. The villa is inland up in the hills of Pesaro a mile or two from the Adriatic. You would love it here Larry."

"Sounds beautiful, your own terrace, hey, now if I was there

I could stand outside your balcony and serenade you."

"With your voice, that could be interesting." Nelli started to laugh.

"Are you saying I can't sing? Seriously, how are you?"

She hesitated, "I'm fine Larry." She didn't want to get into the events of the last couple days especially over the phone.

"You sound a little unsure about that Nelli."

"No really, I'm fine. By the way, going to see Mary Ellen went really well."

"That's great. I'm happy to hear that."

"I think I'm going to try and take a little nap before Anthony and I go into Pesaro. We thought we'd look around the area and find a place to eat for dinner."

"Okay, I miss you Nelli."

"I miss you too. I'll talk to you tomorrow. Have a good sleep."

"You too, bye."

Nelli set the phone down and took a moment to enjoy the view from the terrace. She was glad that for the next couple weeks, they would be tucked away up in the hills of Pesaro, away from the activity of staying at a hotel in town.

A small gust of wind caused her to push back a few strands of hair that had fallen across her face, as she did she thought she detected the scent of a man's aftershave cologne. Not any aftershave but the one her father always wore. She turned around to see if ....

"Dad?"

"Yes, Antonella, I've been waiting for you. Much has happened since our last visit. You now know Anthony is your Guardian and I see you have accepted your destiny.

"Yes, a lot has happened and I'm happy it's Anthony."

"You sensed the presence of evil today, do not fear it but use it to guide you. Keep nothing from your brother. Trust your instincts and stay strong in your beliefs. It is when we start to question our faith that evil will tempt the soul to turn away from its beliefs and follow the false prophet. You are the Chosen One my dear Antonella and the false prophet will not want you to succeed in your quest. Remember you are not alone on this journey. All that have gone before are around you. Evil cannot win the pure of heart. The Holy Spirit will guide you. Believe in the true prophet. Only in that can we defeat evil. Bless you, my daughter.

I will always be right here beside you."

Then it felt as if the wings of an angel brushed against her cheek and the scent from her father's aftershave was no longer present. As she stood there, she realized the visits no longer frightened her. Everything had changed. She wasn't alone any longer; she had an invisible wall of all the souls of the past Keepers of the Key surrounding her.

As she started to head back into the bedroom she glanced at the little angel sitting there looking at her, "Well my new friend, I think I'll get a quick shower and put some fresh clothes on before its time for me to meet up with Anthony."

CHAPTER **FOURTY-THREE**

The Diovan had worked perfectly. Cardinal Franco Cavallari's induced vertigo attack happened as planned but had Thomas and the others believed it.

He knew P2 had done their homework on him. A history of vertigo had been slipped into his medical records, along with newly diagnosed high blood pressure. Neither was life threatening but the severity of the vertigo attack could put someone out of commission for days. Unfortunately there was no magical pill for it.

He had done extensive reading on vertigo and talked with others on the pretense he also had the condition, learning the terms people used and how they described their attacks. He researched side effects of medicines that could cause the same symptoms. One in particular met his needs. When taken in the right dosage it would create a controlled attack. No one would be suspicious of the pills he took assuming they were for his high blood pressure.

Towards the end of the meeting he refilled his glass with more water and pulled out his pillbox. The others glanced at him. He raised the pill between his fingers and mouthed "blood pressure pill" and smiled. Now he just needed to wait. Having tested his reaction time, he knew within an hour to an hour and a half he would feel the effects from the medicine. He didn't look forward to it but it would get him out of the evening's activities and hopefully back to the Vatican. In a short while he would start to feel dizzy and nauseated. Even though the side effects from the medicine wouldn't last long, he would continue to act out the symptoms.

The meeting had finally ended and Thomas had left the room.

General D'Amoto stood abruptly, "Well men I don't know about you but after a long day discussing the takeover of the world, I plan to enjoy the evening to the fullest. I will see everyone back here at nine." He headed towards the door. The other four stood up. Silvio and Angelo were in a deep discussion.

The cardinal started to feel nauseated. He noticed Silvio and Angelo were heading over in his direction.

"The meeting went well, don't you think?" Silvio said to all the others. They all acknowledged their agreement.

Peter Romanus was still watching from his villa in Arezzo. Even though the multiparameter monitoring screens were no longer tracking each of the men's vital signs, Peter continued to observe and listen to their conversations. Automated numeric readouts were being printed out and would be looked at for any subtle increases in heart and pulse rate.

Taking a sip of cognac Peter watched as the men walked towards the stairs. Suddenly Cardinal Cavallari grabbed the baluster.

"Are you feeling all right Franco?" Vingenzo asked looking a little concerned.

"I'm fine Vingenzo. I just felt a little light headed for a moment."

Cavallari knew that very shortly he would have what would look like to the others an attack of vertigo. As he reached the door to his bedroom he noticed a slip of paper sticking out from beneath the door. He bent down to pick it up. His world spun out of control. His hands found the wall and his body fell against it as he slid down and hit the floor.

Vingenzo had just turned at the end of the hallway and was almost to his room when he heard the crash. Walking back to look down the hallway he saw the cardinal slumped against the wall.

"Franco!"

Rushing over to help, he reached down to help Cardinal Cavallari up but Franco raised his hand signaling Vingenzo to stop.

"Are you all right? Do you want me to call an ambulance?" asked Vingenzo.

Cavallari was whispering something. Vingenzo leaned closer.

"Going to be sick, get me to the bathroom, vertigo."

Vingenzo pushed the door open and assisted the cardinal up. It was like trying to help someone who was drunk. Once in the bathroom Cavallari motioned for Vingenzo to leave him alone.

"I'll be right here if you need me," Vingenzo said, closing the door after him but leaving it slightly open. Grabbing the phone next to the bed, a voice on the other end asked, "How may I assist you Cardinal Cavallari?"

"This is Vingenzo Parocchi. Cardinal Cavallari is ill. Get Thomas up here." The voice on the other end remained calm and polite.

"I will inform Thomas of the situation and ask him to come to the cardinal's room. Do you require assistance?"

"No, but get me a doctor on the phone to talk to." I will attend to that immediately director-general."

Walking over to the bathroom Vingenzo was going to ask Franco how he was doing. He didn't need to; he could hear it for himself.

Thomas burst into the room. "What's going on?"

"The cardinal has had a vertigo attack." The phone rang at the same time. "That must be the doctor."

Thomas hadn't given permission to make the call; he'd need to address the matter later. Right now he'd take control. "I'll take that director-general. Prego, ah si, thank you for calling. A friend has had a vertigo attack.

Thomas listened silently, thanking the doctor before setting the phone down.

"It appears Cardinal Cavallari will be out of commission for this evening's festivities. The spinning and nausea should stabilize after a few hours. If it doesn't then he needs to be taken to the nearest hospital. I will get one of the guards up here to assist the cardinal."

Franco listened to the conversation going on in the next room. His symptoms were already diminishing but he needed to pretend they had not gotten any better. He would request to be returned to the Vatican where his personal doctor could attend to him. He continued to listen to Thomas talk.

"When the cardinal's symptoms lessen, if he wishes, I will have a car take him to the airstrip and fly him back to the Vatican. Please remain with the cardinal 'til one of the guards get here; otherwise, I will see you at nine o'clock on the terrace for drinks."

Franco smiled, his plan was working. Around eleven o'clock he informed the guard he would like to return to the Vatican. The guard called down to arrange for a car. Fifteen minutes later they exited through a back door of the compound. As the ceremonial blindfold was placed over his eyes to keep the location a secret, Franco could hear music and people laughing.

CHAPTER **FOURTY-FOUR**

Two Swiss Guards were positioned at the door, the same as last night. Cardinal McKenna had spent most of the evening in the Vatican Secret Archives. He pulled out a copy of the last page from the file Father Roberto sent him, God rest his soul. From it, he made a short list of items to research:

1. Naj Hannah
2. LC
3. Saint Anthony and Prophecy
4. Keeper of the Key

He was frightened the world might be on a path of self-destruction. The presence of evil was everywhere. Countries were gathering weapons of mass destruction. The world seemed to be moving away from God. The Vatican, the central governing body of the Catholic Church, was self-destructing from within. He needed to find the connection that would expose the Antichrist among them.

That was six hours ago. It was the next morning. Now, he regretted making the appointment with Ms. O'Farrell guessing it had something to do with her brother's excommunication by the Church. He didn't have time to listen to her conspiracy theories or that the allegations against her brother were lies. The light on his phone lit up. It was his assistant.

"Yes?"

"Your nine-thirty appointment is here Cardinal McKenna."

"Thank you. Tell Ms. O'Farrell I will see her shortly." He looked at the clock. It was nine thirty-five. He'd end their meeting at ten and get back to finding a way to stop who or whatever was happening before it was too late.

In the outer office Mary Ellen's mind was spinning, her hands guarding the file and envelope on her lap as if they might walk away. How much should she divulge to Cardinal McKenna? Could she trust him? Would he be willing to help her with Devlin's case? What would her brother do when he saw what was in the file? How much should she tell Anthony? The questions kept coming.

Inside the office McKenna leaned back in his chair and closed his eyes, he didn't want to appear rattled when he met with Ms. O'Farrell. He took a minute to calm himself. "Just listen to what she has to say. Tell her you will look into his case again and if anything new comes to my attention I will definitely get back to her. All right, Donovan let's get this over with as quickly as possible." He buzzed Robert, "Please show Ms. O'Farrell in."

Robert stood and motioned for Mary Ellen to follow him.

"Cardinal McKenna is ready to see you."

As she entered the office the cardinal was seated at his desk.

"Please come in Ms. O'Farrell."

"Cardinal McKenna, thank you for seeing me on such short notice."

"Please have a seat. How may I help you this morning?"

"I am grateful you could fit me into your schedule, so I will not waste your time and get straight to why I needed to see you. The CDF has the daunting task of handling the sexual allegations that are sending shock waves throughout the Catholic Church."

He was right on his assessment of what this meeting would be about. "That's correct. It is a difficult period for the Church. Pope Benedict is deeply distressed, as you know, by these allegations."

"You are aware my brother was one of the casualties. I have come across evidence that could prove his innocence."

This was something he had not expected.

"What kind of evidence Ms. O'Farrell and where did you get it from?"

"At the moment I would prefer not to discuss that. I have

prepared a petition to present on my brother's behalf that I would like to have his case reopened and ask for a hearing to present the facts."

Mary Ellen pulled out the document and handed it to the cardinal, as she did something dropped on the floor. When she looked down she gasped.

Cardinal McKenna looked down to see what had caused such a reaction. He was alarmed at what he saw.

Mary Ellen quickly picked up the card and placed it back in the envelope. An awkward silence took place between them. The cardinal was the first to speak.

"It's Mary Ellen isn't it?"

"Yes, that is correct."

"Mary Ellen, I am a servant of God and believe that Christ came and died for our sins and that he will come again. We are in troubled times unless we can correct the path we are on. His return could be near. I believe there is an Antichrist among us winning over the souls of many of the faithful. I believe the time is growing short. I must trust my instincts; therefore, there is something I would like to show you. Opening his desk drawer he removed a small item from it and placed it in front of Mary Ellen. Starring at it in disbelief she slowly reached down, grabbing the envelope from her lap. Opening the flap, she removed the card inside and placed it next to the one Cardinal McKenna had just placed in front of her. It was an exact match.

CHAPTER FOURTY-FIVE

Cardinal McKenna picked up his card and put it back into the desk drawer.

"Ms. O'Farrell it's such a lovely morning perhaps you would be so kind to join me on my morning walk."

Mary Ellen wasn't expecting that to be the next words out of the cardinal's mouth. Quickly grabbing her card, she placed it back into the envelope.

Although confused, she agreed to join him. "I would enjoy that, thank you for asking," smiling at Cardinal McKenna.

The cardinal chatted about the weather and asked how her job was going, keeping the conversation light. They reached the museum on the western side of the palace and the door out to the gardens. Taking a left he headed towards the English Gardens. They walked past the palma grande, the tallest palm in Rome that grows under a protecting roof, and then took the path to the right. Cardinal McKenna continued to walk at the same leisurely pace but Mary Ellen sensed a change in his demeanor. As they got a little further away from the palace, the conversation abruptly took a different direction.

"If you could Ms. O'Farrell, please try to appear relaxed and smile once in a while in case anyone is observing us. Now, I must ask how you came by that card."

Mary Ellen didn't answer right away. She had the same burning question to ask the cardinal.

"Before I answer that Cardinal McKenna, I must ask, how do I know if I can put my trust in you?"

"I understand your concern Mary Ellen. As I see it, if we have both received the same warning, whoever sent it must feel we are a threat to them. I would say that places both of us on the same side. Now please tell me how is it you have the card in your possession?"

Mary Ellen had to agree; they must both have, without knowing, uncovered something they weren't supposed to.

"Yesterday morning an envelope was left for me with only my name on the front and no other markings. Inside was the card. I must tell you it frightened me. I don't know why but I took it as a warning of some kind."

"Do you have any reason to believe that someone you know could be threatened by the questions you have been asking?" She stopped and turned, staring at the cardinal.

"Please Mary Ellen I would like it if we kept walking," as he pretended to be asked a question and pointed to one of the flowers to his left.

"I'm sorry. If I may be so bold to remind you Cardinal McKenna, God will be your final judge if you misplace my trust in you. You know I believe my brother is innocent of the charges against him. I was never able to get access to information that could have proven it. I now have photos that show members of the LC in clandestine meetings with people outside the Vatican that there should be no reason for them to be associating with. There's something strange going on, but I can't put my finger on it."

McKenna glanced at Mary Ellen. Had she said these things to see if she could get a reaction from him? No, she was looking straight ahead, absorbed in telling him what she had uncovered.

"I have documents showing deposits in bank accounts, payments on real estate, and much more. Some of it can be traced back to Father Marcial Maciel and the dual life that is now known he led. The question becomes what did he do in return to support his other life? Was my brother collateral damage?"

Mary Ellen looked at the cardinal, forcing a smile, as she waited to hear his response to what she had just told him. They were walking by the Fontana di Paolo Quinto, which is fed by water from the Lago di Bracciano. Cardinal McKenna stopped to listen to the soothing sounds of the cascading water. Standing next to him it seemed as if the weight of the world had suddenly been placed on his shoulders.

"What is it Cardinal McKenna? You seem troubled by what I have told you."

"How did you come by these documents, Mary Ellen?"

Staring at the ground now, "They were sent to me by a priest. His name … his name was Father Roberto."

McKenna continued to gaze at the water now, appearing to be a million miles away.

The silence was becoming awkward. Mary Ellen was about to say something when the cardinal said, "Well Ms. O'Farrell, I guess I must also put my trust in you. It seems we are headed down the same path. I believe a false prophet among us has even won over souls of the men of the cloth to join his army. How deeply the poison from the serpent's fangs has spread we may never completely know. We can only try and save those souls not yet lost. Concerning the LC, I have my suspicions as well. I believe we are at war with the devil. The warnings we each received can only mean we have gotten too close to information they do not want us to know about."

"You do believe me then that I can prove my brother is innocent?"

"If you have the proof, we will correct the wrong, but the stakes are much higher Mary Ellen. The world and the Church are imploding. We must find the key so we can send the serpent back from where he came. Will you help me?"

He turned and looked directly into Mary Ellen's eyes. McKenna could sense Mary Ellen was struggling to grasp the gravity of the situation and come to terms with what he had just asked of her.

"I know it's difficult to think that the world is on the verge of following a false prophet. The Old Testament shows us that evil has waged war against God many times; each time corrupting civilizations to the point He has had to step in. Pope Benedict himself fears we could be in apocalyptic times. When Father Roberto's body was found, the same card as the ones we received was lying next to it. Craved into his chest was the drawing of a snake and beneath it two markings ר and כ, which if I am correct, stand for the letters R and K in Hebrew.

Let me tell you about a prophecy attributed to Saint Malachy. In 1139, as the Archbishop of Armagh, he went to Rome to give an account of the affairs of his diocese to the Pope Innocent II. While there he received a vision and was shown the identity of the last 112 Popes. This document remained unknown for 400 years until it was discovered in 1590 in the Vatican Archives. The list of prophetic predictions consists of a brief Latin phrase or motto for each Pope.

The titles for each Pope have all come to be applicable including Pope Benedict XVI's, who was given the title of Gloria Olivae, Glory of the Olives. He chose his name in honor of Pope Benedict XV, a man of peace and reconciliation. Benedict XV was said to have prophesied that before the end of the world, a member of his order would lead the Church in a battle against evil. But the last part of the prophecy concerns the end of the world and it is as follows: "In the final persecution of the Holy Roman Church, Peter the Roman will reign and will feed his flock amid many tribulations, after which the seven-hilled Church will be destroyed and the dreadful Judge will judge the people." According to Saint Malachy, the last Pope on his list is Peter Romanus.

Now stay with me here, one must remember Hebrew is written right to left so when we see letters it is the reverse of what we are used to reading.

Mary Ellen immediately suspected Cardinal McKenna was referring to the markings carved into the flesh of Father Roberto. Her mind reeling, "But you said the letters were R and K?"

"In Hebrew the name for Peter is Kephas," waiting for Mary Ellen to realize what he was telling her.

Then it hit Mary Ellen: "'K' for Kephas or Peter and 'R' for Romanus!"

Cardinal McKenna smiled when he saw Mary Ellen had made the connection.

"Although some believe we are entering the end times, there is another prophecy by Saint Anthony who lived in the thirteenth century where he described being visited by an angel and was told to write down the words of the Lord. When the time came the Chosen One, the Keeper of the Key, would be sent to find the book and give it to the shepherd of the flock. It would contain the knowledge that could save God's people if there were still enough faithful left in the world."

Mary Ellen's first thought on hearing of the prophecy was thinking that Anthony had been named after the Saint. "That's a coincidence, my friend that was named after the same Saint."

Cardinal McKenna locked her comment away for future reference.

Mary Ellen continued, "I will not question the path that has been put before me Cardinal McKenna; I will do whatever is needed."

"Then may God protect both of us on our journey. Let us head back and we will discuss the next steps to be taken. I am going to place you under the protection of the Swiss Guard from this point on. Whatever you need, I will get you the necessary clearance."

CHAPTER FOURTY-SIX

During the phone conversation with Mary Ellen last night they all decided she should come to Pesaro this weekend. Anthony and Nelli wondered if the events surrounding Mary Ellen could have any bearing on their search for the sacred scriptures. Having her there would make it easier to find out what else she knew.

Returning to the villa after having dinner in town, Nelli went straight to bed. Anthony stayed up talking into the early hours of the morning getting the latest updates and going over plans with the other Guardians.

Cephas informed Anthony that they had found nothing unusual about the morning's delivery of mail to all the offices of the Vatican. They were viewing the photos and video from the mail room; perhaps there was something that was missed that could give them a clue.

After finishing the last phone call, Anthony closed his eyes and rested his head against the back of the chair. He needed to piece together everything he knew so far. Was there anything he'd forgotten to cover?

His cell phone rang and startled him. Snapping open his eyes he was blinded by a bright light. It took him a second to figure out where it was coming from. He realized it was the morning's sun coming in through his bedroom window. He grabbed the phone, "Hello?"

"To'mas, it's Mattithyahu." Without missing a beat Anthony asked, "Were you able to get any information on the license plate?"

"The plate off the car that passed you in Jesi belongs to a privately owned limousine company out of Florence," replied Mattithyahu. "We're still trying to find out who owns the company. Also, I talked with Franco and he said that a woman at the market was inquiring about who was renting the villa. Franco didn't recognize her."

"What did Franco tell her?"

"The only thing he could say Anthony was that you and Nelli were relatives of a cardinal from Rome who were here on holiday."

"Anything on the car that followed us to the villa?"

"It belongs to a family named Bernarducci from Rimini. Perhaps that was just a coincidence." Anthony bristled at the answer.

"Never use the word coincidence again with me," fired back Anthony.

He was angry that Mattithyahu had taken such a nonchalant attitude to the occurrence.

"I'm sorry To'mas. You're right. It won't happen again. I will look into the family and what that car was doing at that spot at that particular moment."

"Have the rest of the surveillance cameras been positioned further out on the grounds of the villa?" Anthony snapped.

"Yes, the last of them were connected early this morning and we are getting live feed from all of them. Again To'mas, I'm sorry. I will look into the above matters and report back with anything I find out immediately."

"Good, thank you. Nelli and I are headed to the Musei Civici after breakfast. I will contact you later."

A couple doors down Nelli awoke from the smell of fresh coffee drifting upstairs. As she got dressed she remembered having a dream about the box she bought in Rome at the little shop. It was the same box but the one in her dream had unusual letters engraved in the wood. She remembered in the dream she was trying to figure out what they stood for. She finished dressing and went down to the loggia where Anthony was already with a cup of coffee in his hand.

"Good morning Nelli. Franco has prepared a plate of Italian pastries and fruit for us."

Nelli walked over to a table that was displayed with a

beautiful presentation of sweetbreads. Franco had prepared a selection of cornettos, biscotti, and brioches with jam and some soft mascarpone to spread on them. He also had a small plate of sliced hard cheeses, Parmigiano-Reggiano and Parmesan and a lovely selection of some freshly cut fruit. As Nelli was deciding what to have she heard Franco's voice.

"Buon giorno signorina Nelli. I hope you slept well. Would you like regular coffee or espresso?"

"Since I am in your country I will have a cup of espresso please."

Franco smiled, "Bravo! Bravo!"

Nelli took a seat across from Anthony, "I don't know about you but I wouldn't mind staying on in Italy for a while if everything turns out, God willing."

"I can't say I am shocked. What about your work and Larry?"

"Perhaps I can take a sabbatical from the university, and Larry has talked about living in Europe for a year or two."

Before Anthony could respond Franco returned with a French press of fresh espresso and was carrying something tucked under his arm.

"I took the privilege of circling on a map some of the sites you should not miss seeing in and around Pesaro." After pouring the coffee, he laid out the map on the table.

"At the heart of the city lies the main square, Piazza del Popolo, where you can admire the sea horses and tritons that decorate the fountain. Across from it is the Palazzo Ducale, built in the middle of the fifteenth century by the ruling Sforza family. It now houses local government offices and an exhibition space open to the public. You must take a few minutes and walk into the grand courtyard.

"Heading towards the sea along Via Rossini you'll pass by the modest house where Italy's great opera composer Gioachino Rossini was born. The annual Rossini Opera Festival in August has earned a worldwide reputation. After that you will come to the town's cattedrale where you must go inside to see the mosaic floor that was uncovered in 2000. It dates from the sixth century and can be seen through glass panels set in the suspended floor. In some parts you can get a glimpse at an even earlier mosaic floor dating from as early as the fourth century.

"Pesaro was also noted for its ceramic workshops that turned out the brightly painted earthenware known as majolica. In the Musei Civici in Piazza Toschi Mosca, you can see one of Italy's finest collections of Renaissance and Baroque pottery. Here you will also find Giovanni Bellini's masterpiece, *Coronation of the Virgin* in the adjoining Pinacoteca. This large painting with a series of smaller panels was originally created as an altarpiece."

Nelli turned to look at Anthony when Franco pointed this out.

Franco didn't notice and continued talking. "The castle in the background of Bellini's painting is the Sforza family fortress at Gradara; it was Pesaro's ruling lord, Costanzo Sforza, who commissioned the picture from the Venetian artist.

"There is a legend that the Lord Sforza had other reasons for commissioning the painting. He had a son whose first name was Lawrence. Most paintings during the Renaissance period centered on figures from the Bible and his father wanted to honor his son. As many Italians, children are named after a saint. You will see that the painting is surrounded with the drawings of eight saints, Saint Lawrence being one, and remarkably Saint Lawrence has an uncanny resemblance to Lord Sforza's son."

Again, Nelli looked over at Anthony.

"Ah, but I ramble on and you must want to see our lovely Pesaro first hand. I will go to the market and prepare a surprise for dinner tonight. Please call me with any questions. Ciao." He headed towards the kitchen.

"It looks like Matthew chose well for us." Nelli grinned. "Franco will be a good source of information a book could never tell us."

CHAPTER **FOURTY-SEVEN**

It looked like he had pulled it off. Even the pilot came out of the cockpit as he was getting off the plane to say goodbye and hoped the cardinal would feel better soon. The pilot explained that his mother had experienced episodes of vertigo and he remembered how debilitating it was for her when she had a severe attack.

Cavallari thanked him for his concern and continued down the stairs from the plane. A man was waiting at the bottom standing next to an open door to a limousine.

"Welcome back Cardinal Cavallari. Thomas informed me of your circumstances and I am to take you back to the Vatican and assist in any way I can."

"Thank you, I just want to return to my apartment and rest. My personal aid will help me with anything I might need."

"Si. I should have you back at the Vatican within twenty minutes."

Cavallari was glad to be back in Rome. He knew how his actions and duties over the next few days could affect the final outcome of P2's plan if he did not succeed. It was going to be a delicate balancing act but he would be instrumental in Peter Romanus becoming the next Pope.

The years had passed by so quickly and for more than half of them he had spent as a priest. The world was about to change and last night's festivities he could do without. That would all come later after his new position within the New World Order.

He had slept better than expected. Even though a pill artificially brought on the vertigo attack, it still had taken a toll on him physically. So last night's sleep was welcomed.

Today he planned on finding out who knew and what was being done about the death of Father Roberto but he had to be careful and not arouse suspicion of himself. A couple things had already aroused his attention. There seemed to be a heavier presence of the Swiss Guard than usual.

Then at this morning's mandatory prayer service for the cardinals, everyone attending is asked to sign in next to their name before entering the chapel. Cardinal McKenna was not present and his name had been removed from the list. Cavallari probably wouldn't have even noticed it if he hadn't heard a couple of cardinals ahead of him say something about it. Why would his name have been removed from the roster?

He had noticed a change in McKenna's behavior recently. Being the prefect of the CDF and a major component in the handling of the ever-growing sexual allegations against clergy, Cavallari was particularly interested in his activities. P2 had done an excellent job on propagation of the scandal that was destroying the credibility of the Holy See and its authority because of the way it had been dealt with.

Peter Romanus had taken advantage of this crack in the wall by corrupting the LC and conveniently having Father Marcial Maciel's secret life exposed had been ingenious. It seemed to be the final straw. In combination with the other organizations P2 had infiltrated, everything was now in place. The Pope's position was in jeopardy. The media reported that Pope Benedict who had been prefect for the CDF at the time had covered up what the Church knew concerning the Legion of Christ and the allegations against Father Maciel. They were asking that the Pope step down. Satan would finally win his battle with God, occupying the seat of Peter and rule God's kingdom on earth leading his sheep to slaughter. That is why the Grand Master had chosen the name Peter Romanus.

Cavallari needed to get the Pope's schedule. It would be crucial for executing the final stage of the plan. A meeting with His Holiness was already on his calendar. He buzzed for his assistant Carlo.

"Yes, Cardinal Cavallari?"

"Please call Prime Minister Reni's office and ask for the itinerary on his visit to the Vatican on Tuesday. Also contact

Cardinal McKenna and tell him I would like a word with him today."

"Of course, I have made the copies you asked for of the latest news articles from around the world covering the sexual allegations against priests and the Vatican's responses. There is one article in particular that you should look at first. It is from an investigative reporter from the United States. He has exposed that there was something called the "apostolic boys" within the LC. It was made up of young boys handpicked by the LC's founder who are now saying they were sexually abused by him. What would you like me to do with them?"

"Bring those in to me first before you make the calls."

Cavallari pulled off his glasses and rubbed his eyes. By next week at this time the world would be a different place and none of this would matter any longer.

CHAPTER **FOURTY-EIGHT**

Heading out the front door to go into town Nelli looked over at Anthony, "I know Dad never returned to Italy after he came to America, but it would be interesting to hear what he remembered of his childhood here. It's hard for me to visualize him as a little boy running around Pesaro with Uncle Ray."

"I'm sure it looks a lot different now," said Anthony.

Before getting into the car Nelli stopped and looked up at the sky. A few puffy white clouds slowly drifted by.

"Franco said there was a chance of rain later this afternoon. It doesn't look like it to me but he's the one that lives here. I think I'll run up and get an umbrella just in case. I'll be right back."

In the car, Anthony could feel the muscles in his neck and shoulders tightening up. Unconsciously he scanned the surrounding land around the villa but saw nothing suspicious. The villa had been a good choice. It sat on top of a hill and you could see clearly in all directions. There were only a few places someone might be able to go unnoticed for a short time.

On the Adriatic side, behind the loggia there were vine-covered terraces with a few large bushes. In the gardens behind the villa there were two small buildings that store equipment where someone could take cover if they got past all the cameras and motion detectors without being seen.

The car door open, it was Nelli back with the umbrella. "Okay, got it, let's go."

They headed down the driveway past the line of cypress

trees and under the stone archway onto Via Trebbiantico.

"Let's drive by the Piazza del Popolo where we ate dinner last night on our way to the Musei Civici, if that's okay with you Nelli?" said Anthony, at the same time checking the rearview mirror.

He wanted to get a better look at it during the day. Last night the conditions were not favorable for him to study the side streets and roads that led in and out of the piazza.

"That's fine Anthony. I'm anxious to see the painting by Bellini. I told you about the night I fell asleep when I was reading about it in the Frommer's travel guidebook, do you remember? How Bellini came to me in a dream. He told me, the answer to the question would be found within the painting."

"Try to remember everything he said to you Nelli. Did he say anything that would be a clue to what you should look for?"

"No, only that it will guide me along the path I seek. That's all Anthony, and then he was gone."

"Well, when we get to the museum, I'm sure they will have information and books in the museum store on Bellini and the painting. We will pick up some of the materials so we can study it in more detail back at the villa," said Anthony.

Nelli decided to change the subject. "How do you really feel about Mary Ellen coming for the weekend Anthony?"

Anthony remained calm and continued to concentrate on the road, checking the rearview mirror and side mirrors on a continuous basis.

"It's fine Nelli, I told you the past is the past. It's good to be able to have Mary Ellen as a friend again. It appears her continuing to look into the case against Devlin seems to be a concern for someone. I don't know if it has any relevance to the journey we are on, but not knowing where to look for this lost book, perhaps Mary Ellen has stumbled across something that could lead us to information that could help us."

"Do you think she is in danger Anthony? You never did tell me what you found out about that card with the cobra symbol on it."

"I don't know why she would be Nelli. Wanting to clear her brother's name wouldn't seem that unusual to most people. But it seems without her knowing it she's stumbled upon something someone doesn't want to have exposed. Hopefully we might gain some insight into what it is when she is here."

Anthony realized that Nelli no longer seemed afraid for herself. She had reached a place of complete trust that God would protect her, but she was worried for the people around her. He had assigned a Guardian to follow Mary Ellen. The last report he got was that after the meeting with Cardinal McKenna, a gendarme was never far from Mary Ellen's side. He needed to find out what had transpired in that meeting between the cardinal and Mary Ellen.

"What about the cobra symbol?" Nelli asked again. "Why is the symbol of a serpent all of a sudden showing up when I have been told to look for a book containing the words of Our Lord?"

Anthony was hoping she wouldn't ask the question again. He'd decided to give her the background on where the symbol originated and the group that was associated with it.

He wasn't going to hide that this group's ultimate goal was to create a New World Order, but he did not plan on telling her about the murders the group was suspected of and the way they were carried out.

"What I know is the symbol of the cobra was created for a group that called themselves Propanganda Due. It's been said that they were the executive branch of the Illuminati. In the 1960s a man by the name of Licio Gelli joined the freemason's largest Lodge in Italy, the Grand Masonic Lodge. Then he got himself assigned to reorganizing the membership. There he was able to get a list of sleeping members, members no longer invited to take part in the rituals of the Lodge. Within two years Licio conceived the idea of a shadow society within the Lodge and its members reported to him alone. Even the freemasons were unaware that his covert organization existed.

"From the start it was illegal. Gelli took the name from the nineteenth century Lodge 'Propaganda.' Propaganda Due or P2, as its members called it, was born. They had 2,400 members in Italy alone and membership spread worldwide throughout Europe and South America and even to the United States. It is said that they infiltrated every sector of society and were even in bed with the Mafia."

"Are you saying they infiltrated the Vatican as well?"

"Yes," Anthony continued. "Gelli's goal was to form a New World Order but as far as anyone knows P2 no longer exists. So the card Mary Ellen received could only be a person or group that decided to use the symbol as a scare tactic to get her to stop asking questions."

They were now nearing the piazza and Anthony shifted his attention to surveying the town center.

"Looks different during the day doesn't it?" Anthony said, changing the direction of the conversation. "On our way home if we come back this way we can stop and walk around a little more. We can go into the Palazzo Ducale and take a look at the courtyard Franco talked about.

"First things first, let's find the museum. Before we go in we will give Mary Ellen a call and get the details on the plans for tomorrow. Why don't you text her that we will give her a call shortly."

"That's probably a good idea. Then we won't play telephone tag all day."

Nelli sent the message as Anthony got back on Via Rossini heading north looking for signs to the museum. The skies were starting to look like rain. She was glad she had brought the umbrella. Her cell phone alerted her to an incoming text message.

"That was quick. Mary Ellen texted she won't be able to answer her cell phone for most of the afternoon and her plane lands at three o'clock tomorrow. She will call us when she's at the airport."

"Well, then let's go see a painting."

CHAPTER **FOURTY-NINE**

Now the next day and back in his office, McKenna waited for a copy of the file Mary Ellen had received from the now deceased Father Roberto. He wanted to study the contents of both files from the priest. He was anxiously waiting to hear if the research assistant found any evidence of a private diary kept by Saint Anthony.

He spent the previous evening down in the archives reading everything he could on the life of the young monk Anthony. He had hoped to discover something that might shed some light on the list Father Roberto had written down beneath Saint Anthony on a separate sheet of paper. Pulling it out again, he reread the list of words.

Private Diaries
Burial places Giovanni /Saint Anthony
Gradara Castle
Altar
Catacombs
Shrine
Monastery
Box

What was the importance of the list? The priest had underlined two words, Private Diaries and Burial places Giovanni/ Saint Anthony. How did it relate to what was happening in the Church? Was Father Roberto killed because of what he was looking into?

The contents of the archives cover more than fifty miles of shelves, some of the information on Saint Anthony and the prophecy had been easily obtained by Cardinal McKenna. What surprised him was how many different versions there were of the saint's life. There were details no one else would consider important but to him they could be a clue.

McKenna got up from his desk chair, walked across the antique burgundy and blue Oriental carpet that he had acquired upon taking over the office he now occupied and headed across the room to a leaded glass door that opened out onto a small balcony. Overlooking one of the many gardens inside the walls of Vatican City, there was a sudden shift in the wind and the sky filled with dark menacing clouds. But the winds shifted again and in a matter of seconds there were only blue skies as far as one could see. Dismissing the strange weather he wondered what significance each of the words on the list held. "What is it you stumbled upon?" said McKenna. Asking the question out loud as if he thought Father Roberto might answer.

Could any of this have relevance to the case against Devlin O'Farrell? McKenna remembered Mary Ellen mentioning something about a paper trail that would prove her brother's innocence. He met Devlin once and recalled thinking how fortunate the Church was to have this young priest accept his calling and to be a servant to the faithful. It was a great shock when he heard the priest had given in to temptation. Walking back to his desk he buzzed for Robert.

"Yes, Cardinal McKenna?"

"Has anything been delivered for me?"

"No. Would you like me to check into to it?"

"No, just let me know as soon as anything is delivered."

Something kept nagging at him, something he'd read about the LC. What was it? If only he could remember. His suspicions about the order were growing. He had questions about its founder. Rumors had been floating around for years but they had been dismissed as nothing more than rumors until now.

The scandal of Father Maciel's secret life was the last straw. Catholics around the world wanted the Vatican and more specifically the Pope to acknowledge the corruption and cover-up that had taken place by high-ranking authorities within the Church. People were angry and struggling with the decision to stay or leave the Catholic Church. Lawsuits were being brought against not just parish priests but against bishops and cardinals.

The media was having a heyday with the latest developments, circling like sharks waiting for the kill, unrelenting with their attacks against the Vatican and the Pope. They were getting bold with their opinions for the need for new leadership and even suggested restructuring the Vatican. They even seemed to be hinting they had someone in mind to replace Pope Benedict.

Looking to the heavens Cardinal McKenna asked God for the strength to complete the task His Holiness had asked of him. Whatever God's plan was he prayed that he would be shown how to stop Satan before it was too late. His thoughts were interrupted by the phone ringing.

"Yes Robert, has the file arrived?"

"Not exactly Cardinal McKenna, Ms. O'Farrell is here and adamant she speaks to you. She has something important she must show you."

He hadn't expected Mary Ellen to personally show up at his office. She was just supposed to send the file. "That's fine, please show her into my office."

Mary Ellen waited until Robert closed the door. Then she walked over to the desk, set down the file, and flipped open the cover.

"There's something very strange here. I asked Devlin to tell me everything he could remember even if it felt trivial. One of the things he talked about was seeing Vingenzo Parocchi from the Banca Nazionale del Lavoro meeting with Father Maciel on a regular basis. It seemed strange Parocchi himself would personally handle the banking issues with Father Maciel and the LC."

McKenna was also surprised. "Mr. Parocchi is the director-general of the largest bank in Italy and also a shareholder in the Vatican Bank. As director of Banca Nazionale, he has a close relationship with the Secretary of State for the Vatican. I don't understand why a man in his position would personally consult with Father Maciel."

Mary Ellen continued, "There's more. Parocchi has traveled to Switzerland four times over the last year, each time making a visit to the Union Bank of Switzerland in Lugano."

She spread out photos taken of him entering the bank on the four separate occasions. On a sheet of paper, she had written the dates of each visit and set it next to the photos.

"Then there's this," Mary Ellen said.

She pulled out another sheet of paper with four dates written on it and placed it next to the first sheet of paper.

"So what am I supposed to be seeing here?"

"Cardinal McKenna, look at the dates on both sheets of paper. What stands out?"

McKenna leaned closer and adjusted his reading glasses.

"The dates on the second sheet of paper are each within a few days of the first sheet. So what do you make of it?" asked McKenna.

"The second sheet shows the dates when Mr. Parrochi visited Father Maciel at the LC offices. Is there any way to get the financial records for the LC for the last ten years? I have a feeling we are going to see more similarities. Where was the money coming from for him to support the secret life he had hidden for so many years?"

McKenna's mind was reeling. Could it be happening again! It had been more than twenty-five years since Roberto Calvi, the president of the Banco Ambrosiano, was found dead hanging from the end of a rope under Blackfriars Bridge. The official record was suicide. But in 1990, new forensic methods reinforced the suspicion he was murdered. With the collapse of Banco Ambrosiano, owned in part by the Vatican Bank, and the murder of Calvi, it was suspected that some of the plundered funds had gone to P2 or its members.

McKenna was in his twenties back then. It was believed Pope John Paul I was going to expose the names of clergy who were members of P2 that were plotting against the Church. The day Pope John Paul I was going to announce changes he was found dead. The talk was he was murdered before he could expose the names.

"Cardinal McKenna, did you hear my question?"

All the color drained from his face and he collapsed into his chair.

"Are you feeling okay? You look white as a ghost!"

He looked up with a blank stare. What she saw was pure fear in his eyes.

"What is it? Do you want me to get medical help?" She was ready to pick up the phone when McKenna raised his hand to stop her.

"I'm fine my child, sit down. You've questioned if there could be a link between the LC and the Banca Nazionale del Lavoro, which brought back memories of 1981. You might not have even been born yet, or you were just a small child at the time.

"I'm sure you are familiar with some history on the succession of the Popes. You may or may not know in 1978 Pope John Paul I reigned for only thirty-three days."

"Yes, I recall reading about that. What does that have to do with any of this?"

"I don't know if it does. I was a young man at that time, just ordained. I remember watching the news coverage on TV as the conclave to elect the next Pope was taking place, waiting to see the white smoke announcing that a new Pope had been elected."

"When Pope John Paul I was chosen, I was very happy. He would be perfect for the Church for those times, a beacon of light. Then a month later he was dead."

"Are you saying you believe his death was not natural?" she was a little surprised the cardinal would actually consider the possibility.

"Many things were never reported after the Pope's death."

He went on to tell her the full story. When he finished she now understood why he might be afraid that something similar could be happening again. If there was evidence of questionable transactions in the bank's records, could history be repeating itself? If Devlin was set up to look like he was guilty of the allegations, then how many others could be innocent?

She really hadn't thought of it in that context before. She just assumed that someone had it in for Devlin. Her focus had been on finding the person that might have felt her brother had wronged them somehow. It had never accrued to her that this could be a much larger plan by someone to destroy the image of the Church for millions of people around the world. Outside it had started to rain.

"Do you think we could have accidentally stumbled upon a plan by someone to take control of the Catholic Church and possibly more?"

As the rain fell harder, the skies darkened, and day turned to night. The sky lit up with bolts of lighting and clashes of thunder shook the windows. The cardinal clicked on his desk lamp. The warmth of the burgundy walls and the thick plush

Oriental carpet created a feeling of being wrapped in a favorite blanket. You felt safe and protected against the world and you felt nothing could harm you, but if you looked out the window it was dark and menacing, as if something evil was trying to get in.

"Evil exists Mary Ellen. Satan feeds on the weaknesses of man. All you have to do is look around. Jesus warns us of false prophets. When Michael the Archangel cast Lucifer out of heaven, it became Satan's one and only goal to reign as king of his own world. The battle between good and evil began. He would use God's gift of free will against him. False prophets would gather souls to build their army. If the conspiracy theory surrounding Pope John Paul I is true, we could be witnesses to another well-orchestrated plan of what God warns us of in the last chapter of the New Testament."

"If what you are saying is true cardinal, then it is out of our hands. There is little the two of us can do to alter the course the whole world."

The storm seemed to be worsening if that was possible. Between the light show and the cracks of thunder it almost seemed like the heavens were being ripped open.

Mary Ellen had never been one to ever back away from a problem. This was different. Leaning back in her chair, she closed her eyes and asked for God's blessings.

Cardinal McKenna cleared his throat and spoke in a soft, calm voice. "Actually the answer is quite simple. All God has ever asked of us is to believe in Him. That is what we must do now more than we have ever done before."

Mary Ellen opened her eyes. "We lose sight of that so often, don't we?"

"Yes, unfortunately Mary Ellen, we do. That is the one weapon evil has no power over, but that does not release us from our duties here on earth."

"Cardinal McKenna, I mentioned that I had two friends that were named after Saint Anthony when we were walking in the gardens yesterday."

"Yes, I remember."

"Sadly, Alberto their father, passed away not too long ago. He was a wonderful man. He gave Nelli the most beautiful necklace before he died. I'm sorry, that's nothing you would need to know. Anyway, he was born in Pesaro and they decided to come to Italy and visit the place where their father was born. They have invited me to spend the weekend with them. I was planning on leaving around noon tomorrow and coming back on Sunday. If you could get me the records we just talked about and anything else you think might be of interest, I will take them with me. Actually Anthony is an expert on religious history. If it's okay with you, I will pick his brain a little without raising any red flags."

McKenna logged the newest information away about Mary Ellen's friends.

"I will assume your friends will be picking you up on the other end?" McKenna asked.

"Yes." She knew that he was concerned about her safety. She felt silly telling him that Anthony had also gotten a bodyguard for her.

The worst of the storm had passed and the skies were beginning to lighten. McKenna clicked off his desk lamp.

"Perhaps God is pleased that we understand the only thing He asks of us is to trust in Him. We should never forget the story of Adam and Eve. Then as now the serpent is using the gift of free will to gather his souls."

Mary Ellen placed a copy of the file on Cardinal McKenna's desk.

"Here is a copy of everything I received from Father Roberto that morning. This weekend I will speak more with my brother and see what I can learn from Anthony, then study whatever information you can get for me on the financial records of the LC."

McKenna stood up now, "Thank you Mary Ellen. Please call me on my private number if you have any questions or come across anything you think I should know. I plan on spending most of the weekend in the Vatican Archives."

After Mary Ellen left, McKenna remembered what Pope Benedict said to him at the end of their meeting. He would have access to anything he needed. So he made a call and requested all the information on the banking scandal in 1981 surrounding Banco Ambrosiano and the IOR, more commonly known as the Vatican Bank.

Besides the other information, he also requested financial records for both the IOR and the LC for the last ten years.

He was told he would have the information by the end of today.

CHAPTER FIFTY

The guests had been arriving for the last hour. Everyone attending was being helicoptered in from a small airport approximately thirty miles from the villa, none of the guests knew the actual location of the estate, and Peter wanted it that way.

As one helicopter landed with guests, another helicopter was in the air, headed back to the airport to pick up more of the evening's attendees. Airspace surrounding both the airstrip and estate had been secured for the next twenty-four hours. The weather forecast had turned out to be ideal conditions for flying, and the forecast was the same for the evening. There had not been a single cloud visible all afternoon. The evening sky would create a dome of stars as a backdrop for the fireworks at the end of the night. Plans for the evening's festivities out in the gardens and on the terrace would not have to be changed.

The guests were made up of members of P2 in powerful positions from around the world. Also on the list: the Grand Master of the United Grand Lodge of England (UGLE) as well as orders that were not recognized by the UGLE, appendant bodies such as female-only orders and Co-Freemasonry or mixed orders. There were also a handful of newly initiated P2 members. They were the fortunate ones. They would be the last brought into the order before the world changed forever.

Peter watched his guests from his office on the closed circuit TVs. He saw that everyone had arrived. Shortly he would join his guests. He smiled, thinking about how easy it was to tempt the soul of Eve. Since that day countless souls had followed Satan.

Many times God stepped in and punished man for breaking the covenant, but the battle of good versus evil continued. This time Peter was about to achieve his ultimate goal to occupy the throne of Saint Peter and possess the keys to heaven. The sounds of music and laugher drifted up from the floor below. It was time for him to join the party. He buzzed for Thomas. Thomas heard the signal in his earpiece, excused himself from the guests he was talking to, and headed to the Grand Master's study. Touching his earpiece to open the two-way radio transceiver he said, "I am on my way Naj Hannah."

Peter laid the pen he'd been using into the handcrafted box made especially for it. In his travels many years back, a friend introduced him to a man who had a private collection of some very unusual pieces. One in particular had captured his attention. He had never seen anything like it before. The collector believed he owned the only one that existed in the world. It was a handmade pen that depicted "the Creation" like the famous painting between God and Adam. Both figures were rendered in a silver and gold overlay that surrounded the full length of the pen.

Peter became obsessed with having his own one of a kind pen but his would be designed with the first description given to him found in the book of Genesis, depicting a serpent when he became Grand Master of Propaganda Due. He commissioned Paul DuClos, the designer of the pen from the private collection, to make one to his specifications. It was the only pen he would use to sign his name on important documents.

The barrel of the pen was made from the rarest wood in the world, Piratinera Guianensis. It was a hardwood, reddish brown in color with irregular black speckles also called snakewood. How fitting he thought.

He chose the king cobra for the symbol of the serpent and had it made out of solid gold. The detailing of the skin was superb. Throughout the body were randomly placed red diamonds, the rarest of gemstones. First the artist coiled the tail of the snake around the section part of the pen then flawlessly joined it to the body of the snake mounted onto the barrel. The third and final part, the head of the king cobra with its iconic hoods fully extended, was mounted on the cap and again flawlessly joined to the body of the snake. The mouth was open wide with its fangs exposed, as if ready to attack its prey. The finishing touch was the distinctive blue lapis eye.

There was a secret about the pen that only one other person knew and if he ever divulged the secret he would meet an unpleasant death. The secret was in the reservoir of the pen. At the same time Peter commissioned the pen he also hired a chemist to create special ink for it. It was to contain the venom and blood from the king cobra snake. He loved the thrill of knowing that a touch from the nib of the pen could kill a person within seconds, and he had the pleasure of witnessing it only a few times. The last appraisal valued it at five million dollars.

There was an abrupt knock and a hooded disciple opened the door to announce Thomas. As he entered, Thomas greeted the Grand Master.

"You look well Naj Hannah. All of the guests have arrived."

"It sounds as if they are already getting into the spirit of the evening."

Walking over to a large black lacquered armoire Peter opened the doors; inside hung his dinner jacket for the evening. Removing it from the hanger he turned and faced the mirror. Placing one arm into a sleeve he imagined himself standing in the Room of Tears donning the white papal cassock of the newly elected Pope.

As he caught the reflection of Thomas looking at him he said, "The next time you see me in formal attire, I will be wearing all white," then he smiled with self-satisfaction. Giving a last check to his appearance, he ran his fingers through his hair and he was ready to attend the party.

"The guests have been anxiously awaiting your appearance Grand Master."

"Well then we must not keep them waiting."

As Thomas and Peter exited the study and headed down the hallway, one disciple walked in front of the two men, and a second followed a short distance behind.

The voices were getting louder as they got closer to the dining hall where the guests were mingling amongst themselves. Arriving at a double set of glass doors, the first disciple pushed open both doors into the room and stepped aside. The people closest to the doors turned to see who was entering. They saw Thomas and behind him, the Grand Master, followed by his two personal henchmen in their ceremonial robes and hoods. There was a ripple effect as heads continued to turn as their leader entered the room.

A gentleman from the UGLE who happened to be the closest to the doors immediately greeted Peter.

"Grand Master it's wonderful to see you. What a magnificent evening you have planned. I look forward to hearing you speak later."

"It's good to see you my friend." Peter shook his hand. "I think you will be very pleased with what I have to say, but first enjoy the festivities and food. We will talk again later on in the evening."

The four individuals from this afternoon's meeting minus Cardinal Cavallari were scattered around the room. Peter had already spotted them and acknowledged them with a slight nod of the head.

"How is the roster being received by our guests?" Peter quietly asked Thomas without looking at him.

"As you might expect Naj Hannah and the UGLE are suspicious of being in the same room with the Orders of the Eastern Star, Amarath, and the Grand Lodge Droit Humain to name three."

Peter had to smile, "It is an interesting gathering don't you agree Thomas?"

"Without question."

"It needed to be done this way Thomas. They will learn that in a few short days the world as they know it will no longer exist. They will each need to decide their future by the end of the evening."

The "worthy matron" from the Grand Lodge Droit Humain was headed straight towards Peter. She was a stunning woman, dressed in a simple red dress that followed the curves of her body like a glove. The color of her hair was the blackest black he'd ever seen and her eyes were like two black coals. They would make quite a striking couple he thought to himself.

"Good evening Grand Master. I saw that you had arrived and wanted to personally thank you for including me on tonight's guest list. I'm hoping this evening will be the beginning of a closer relationship with many of the others present tonight." Besides being beautiful she was also driven.

Her Lodge allowed political and religious discussion, which was against the laws of the UGLE. When Peter created P2, unbeknownst to the Grand Orient Lodge, he built his empire by including the political and religious powers of the world. So he felt a close alliance to this order.

"As always you are direct and to the point. If I may also say Catherine you look bewitching this evening. You put some of my artwork in the room to shame. Don't you agree Thomas?"

Smiling politely, Thomas acknowledged the compliment, then turned back to face Peter, "I will leave you to visit with your guests. I must attend to some arrangements for this evening."

"Of course Thomas, I will meet up with you later."

Thomas gave a nod to Catherine, then to Peter and left. Peter never took his eyes off of Catherine.

Waiting 'til Thomas was gone, Catherine said with a self-assured grin, "Your appreciation of the arts has always been one of the qualities I have admired in you Grand Master."

"Then I believe you will find the evening most interesting. Now if you will excuse my rudeness, I must go and greet some of my other guests."

Reaching for her hand he gently kissed the top of it, "Until we talk again."

CHAPTER FIFTY-ONE

Peter stood off to the side of the stage that had been built especially for this evening. He watched as his guests returned to their seats after the performance and they talked quietly amongst themselves. Four of the five lieutenants present at the party waited in silence for Peter to address the crowd. The fifth sat in front of a closed circuit TV in the comfort of his apartment.

"Is Cardinal Cavallari set up on his end?" Peter asked Thomas.

"Yes, he is receiving the live feed as we speak."

"Good. Then it is time."

Peter turned and slowly walked to the center of the stage. He surveyed the crowd while waiting for everyone to stop talking. After a few minutes the room became quiet. All eyes were now on Peter.

"First, let me start by welcoming all of you to my home. Having all of you here together has been a dream of mine for a very long time and tonight it has finally become a reality. Many of you have traveled a great distance and I thank you for that. Each of us started out at one point, with the same basic concern about the future. Having free will to make our own decisions, each one of you chose to become part of a fraternal organization known as the Freemasons. As you know, not every Lodge recognizes the other based upon adherence to landmarks but I hope to change that this evening.

"The world as we know it is a world divided by religion and politics but controlled by the financial institutions of the world. I believe each of us here tonight sees the need for a one-world government. A world, more important, run by an elite group of individuals with a globalist agenda or a New World Order. It is the only way to bring an end to the international power struggles between countries.

"Please take a look around the room; you see what could be the future "Council of Guardians." A council appointed by a supreme leader, to put into effect the laws of the New World Order."

Peter remained silent, letting what he said sink in. A few of the guests looked nervously around, others were excitingly talking to the person next to them, and others waiting to hear more.

The evening was proceeding exactly as planned, even better. He had spent a small fortune but the cost was of no importance. The stage was being set for the powers of darkness to take the reins. The desire for power and fortune had to be compelling enough that every person in the room wanted their piece of the pie.

Peter felt something brush against the back of his neck as a sudden gust of air blew in through the open terrace doors carrying in with it an army of kindred spirits. He watched as they snaked their way through the guests seated in the room.

Clearing his throat to get everyone's attention again he continued, "The various rites of the different Lodges represented tonight create barriers that need to be revised for a greater purpose. Together as one ruling body, imagine what we could accomplish. I've written a manifesto that is being handed out to each of you as I speak."

Hooded men in ceremonial robes appeared and circulated the pamphlets to everyone in the audience. Then they stationed themselves at designated locations.

"We all want the same thing. Without realizing it, you have each been an intricate part of moving that dream forward and with that comes wealth and power for each person present here tonight. You each have enjoyed the benefits and the pleasures those two things bring, but divided as you presently are, your final goals can never be realized. I'm asking you tonight to put aside these differences and join me as one. We can rule the world together and you will each live a life only dreamt about in fairy tales." Peter paused letting his guests digest what he had just proposed to them.

"The New World Order will be a reality within a few short days with or without you. Reject the old ways and join with me and be part of a world where religions and governments will be ruled by one governing body."

Angelo, Vingenzo, Silvio, and Orazio scanned the room to try and get a read on tonight's attendees. Each of the men knew the consequences for those who chose not to join the New World Order.

Cardinal Cavallari, watching back at the Vatican, only had a view of the stage and couldn't see the reaction of the guests. Closing his eyes he thought, "It's finally happening." Terrified he'd said it out loud and someone might have overheard. Opening his eyes, he was alone except for the portrait of Pope Benedict. It was only a photograph but it seemed as if His Holiness was looking straight at him and could hear everything Cavallari was thinking.

Peter began speaking again and Cavallari turned his attention back to the monitor.

"I now ask each of you to open your envelopes. On the last page you will find a place to sign and pledge your loyalty to the New World Order. After signing, please hand the sheet to Thomas before heading into the garden."

In an instant Peter's face changed from being grim and foreboding to warm and gregarious.

"Now my dear friends at the end of the evening I have planned a magnificent fireworks show, choreographed to music with dancing like nothing you have ever seen before. Please enjoy the rest of the evening."

Smiling at everyone, Peter turned and walked off the stage.

CHAPTER **FIFTY-TWO**

The sky was already clouding over as they reached Palazzo Toschi-Mosca that housed the Ceramics Museum and the Art Gallery containing Coronation of the Virgin.

"Looks like Franco was right about the rain," said Nelli, pointing to the sky. "I'll take the umbrella in case it's raining when we get out."

"Sounds good," replied Anthony.

Inside they purchased two passes for eight euros and grabbed a map to find where the different exhibits were located in the museum.

"Wow, there are six display rooms for ceramics. I didn't think it would be that large of a collection. It states here that a man by the name of Domenico Mazza from Pesaro began the historical collection of ceramics, and today there are more than 3,400 pieces."

"Nelli, we are limited on time; our main focus is finding the painting. If you want, we can come back and go through more of the rooms another day."

"You're right. Can we at least walk through this first room with the majolica pottery display?"

"Yes, then we need to find the painting."

As they began walking, Nelli read out loud from the brochure.

"In the 1200s Italy imported clay and ceramics from Moorish Spain. It was shipped through Majorca thus getting its name majolica. Local styles developed throughout Italy so certain areas became known for specific colors and patterns, deep blue being one of the oldest and the pink rose for the symbol of Pesaro."

Nelli stopped and turned to face Anthony. "That was always the color of roses Dad would bring home for mother, remember Anthony?"

"Yes, now that you mention it."

Nelli starting walking again continuing to read from the pamphlet, "Around the 1500s tin enamel, an opaque white finish, was introduced in Pesaro and it became the birthplace for ceramic art in Italy. I never imagined Pesaro would be so rich in history." Looking up they had reached the first display room.

As they walked around viewing the first collection, for just a moment Anthony felt like a tourist on vacation, but as he watched his sister lean forward to get a closer look at the details on a vase, the lights from the glass case reflected off the cross dangling from the chain around her neck. It quickly brought him back to the seriousness of the situation.

Shifting gears he began applying the years of training and assessing their surroundings. He mentally went down a checklist in his head. One, study the layout of the room, look for possible escape routes. Two, what could be used for a weapon or protection against an attack? Three, study each person for unusual behavior, and four and most important, listen to your instincts.

"Which piece is your favorite Anthony? I think this one is absolutely gorgeous. The blue coloring and the detailing on this plate are beautiful!"

Anthony realized Nelli had asked him a question.

"I'm sorry Nelli, did you just ask me which piece is my favorite?" Anthony took a quick survey of the collection and pointed out one he had noticed when they first entered the room. "I guess I would have to say that one. Nelli, I think we should find out where the painting is located in the museum before it gets any later."

"I agree but it was nice being distracted for a while. Let's go see if we can find the clue that I was told could be found within the painting."

Stopping at the information desk, Anthony asked if they were headed in the right direction.

"Si, si signore, follow the signs to the Pinacoteca," pointing to his right.

"Grazie."

"I'm going to stop in the restroom first Anthony. I'll just leave the umbrella out here," resting it against the wall.

Anthony knew the museum closed at twelve-thirty like everything in Italy. Looking at his watch, they had another hour and a half. He studied the people in the lobby as he waited for Nelli, making mental notes of faces. The man that just entered the museum, something about the way he moved seemed familiar to Anthony.

"Anthony … Anthony," Nelli said a second time tugging at his sleeve. "What were you thinking about? You were a million miles away."

"Oh, nothing just people watching. Let's go. Remember the museum closes in an hour and a half."

CHAPTER **FIFTY-THREE**

The man was average in his appearance in every way. People didn't pay much attention to him and he liked it like that. Trailing behind a group of tourists from England, he watched the brother and sister head up the stairs.

"This isn't what I expected at all, did you Anthony?" said Nelli. "It's so different than what you think of when you go to a museum in a large city."

"Many local museums are renovated homes," said Anthony. "A good local museum will add to your understanding of the region much better than any large national museum ever could."

On the left hung several pieces of art and a door in the middle of the wall that led to another room. On the opposite wall from where they entered there were three evenly spaced windows covered with white fabric shades. Between two of the windows was a painting of Saint Terence, the patron saint of Pesaro.

To their right there was an altarpiece by Jacobello del Fiore, a complex work that combined the elements of painting and sculpture. A rich ornate frame surrounded six panels each painted with the figures of Saint Jerome, Saint James the Greater, Peter, Paul, Anthony, and Nicholas of Bari, and in the center, a beautiful wooden statue of the Blessed Michelina.

Nelli looked up from the brochure; to the right of that piece was another doorway. On the other side of the door there it was: the altarpiece by Giovanni Bellini of Coronation of the Virgin.

"Look Anthony, there it is."

Anthony had already spotted the piece and was walking in that direction. It filled the entire corner of the room. A braided rope hung on posts keeping visitors at arm's length from the polyptych.

It was approximately eight and a half feet wide and eight feet high and it dominated the room. The typology of the painting looked more like a piece of architecture. The painting was framed on each side by pilasters that each contained paintings of four saints. The bottom of the frame, the predella, depicted seven religious scenes. The top of the frame looked like a crown molding or mantel of a fireplace. On top of the crown molding sat another smaller frame called a cusp, identical to the frame on the lower portion of the painting. Inside the cusp was a painting of the *Pieta.*

Nelli was hypnotized by it. "It's quite amazing, isn't it? I didn't expect it to be so large. Look, in the painting behind the throne where Jesus is crowning Mary is another painting framed the same way! It states here that it's a painting within a painting, a new perspective in the art world."

Anthony was also impressed by its size.

"The representation of the fortress of Gradara in the background of the Coronation seems out of place, don't you think Anthony?" said Nelli.

Anthony was reading about the piece when he stopped and reread the last sentence over again.

"Listen to this Nelli. There are eight saints that border the painting, four on each pilaster."

"Yes, I see that."

"Do you know who any of them are?"

"Anthony I have no idea! Enough with the guessing game, read me the names."

"Look at the second from the bottom on the right."

"Okay, now who is he?"

"It's Saint Anthony."

The color drained from Nelli's face. "Why would Bellini include the fortress of Gradara and Saint Anthony in the altarpiece?" she said, asking as if she expected the painting to answer her question. "Look Anthony, he's holding something in his hand. It ... it looks just like the box we bought in Rome!" She turned and stared at her brother. "Is this the first clue?"

Without thinking, Anthony glanced around the room to

see if anyone had overheard their conversation. Luckily they were the only ones in the room at the moment.

He felt Nelli grab his arm. She was pointing to the floor in front of the right pilaster of the altarpiece just under the rope by her foot, her voice no louder than a whisper, "Look Anthony."

It was a small medal of some kind. Nelli crouched down to pick it up. It was a religious medal of Saint Anthony.

"It's just like the one I found in my bedroom. He's guiding us, Anthony. We are on the right path. We need to figure out what the painting is telling us." Wrapping her fingers around the medal, she placed it in one of her pockets.

"On our way out I'll ask at the front desk where the library is located in town," said Anthony. "If I remember correctly it is housed in the Palazzo Almerici. They should have literature on Gradara Castle. It's almost twelve-thirty; Nelli, the museum will be closing soon."

The man from downstairs watched from the doorway as his two prey continued to study the painting. The museum guards would be directing visitors towards the exit in a few minutes.

Anthony heard someone coming up behind him. He spun around only to be met by the uncompromising stare from museum guards.

"Scusi signore, signorina museum closes in fifteen minutes," pointing to his watch.

"Si, grazie," Anthony nodded to the guard.

The guard smiled and walked away. Anthony took a deep breath realizing there was no danger. They were the last to follow the other visitors down the stairs. On the first floor they had to walk through the museum's small store to exit the building.

"Anthony, remember we were going to get a book and some materials on Bellini's altarpiece to take back with us."

Nelli could see the girl behind the register was getting ready to close up. "I'll run and ask if she would wait a few more minutes, go grab some books."

Anthony had already spotted the section on Bellini and rushed over to it while Nelli talked with the young woman at the counter. After a few minutes, Nelli turned, trying to locate Anthony, catching his eye, she nodded yes and waved for him to hurry.

The rain had stopped. Walking to the car Nelli jabbed

Anthony in the ribs. "The girl at the register wasn't too happy with me."

As they got into the car and closed the doors, Mattithyahu was watching them from a distance. He noticed a man following Anthony's and Nelli's movements a little too closely. He snapped a few photos and sent it plus a text message to Anthony's iPhone. "Shoot, I left my umbrella leaning up against the wall by the women's restroom in the museum," said Nelli. "I'll run back and get it. It will just take me a few minutes."

"I'll drive you up to the front entrance. It will be faster." Running in Nelli saw her umbrella was still where she had left it. The young man at the front desk had his back to her and was talking on the phone and didn't hear her approaching.

"Si, si Americanos, signore, signorina asked directions to the library."

Hearing someone, he turned to see who it was. When he saw Nelli he reacted as if he had been caught stealing. Regaining his composure, he ended the phone conversation abruptly.

"Scusi signorina, the museum is closed."

"I left my umbrella." Nelli pointed to it leaning against the wall.

"Ah! Si, si capire."

CHAPTER **FIFTY-FOUR**

Anthony got the photo from Mattithyahu while Nelli was inside getting the umbrella. He stared at the picture on his cell phone. It was the same man from inside the museum. He'd seen him somewhere before. But where? Anthony thought he heard his father's voice, of course that was impossible. He looked around quickly to see who was talking. There was no one there but then he heard the voice again.

"Remember what you were taught Anthony, the mind can function as a camera. It takes a picture of everything we see and logs it away for future reference. Think of your brain as a library. How would you go about researching information you needed? What are you looking for? People, places, or things?" Definitely a person, Anthony thought to himself. "His father continued, how far back do you need to go—days, weeks, or years? He only needed to go back a few days.

Suddenly it hit Anthony. It was as if he flipped the page in a book and there it was: a photograph of Nelli and him looking in the store window at a display of small boxes. Then everything around him faded away and he was staring into a mirror, that's when he realized where he had seen the man before.

When the man knew Anthony had spotted him, he headed for the nearest side street. Just before he disappeared Anthony noticed the man had a slight limp. That's what he noticed about the man in the museum. It was the same man. He called Mattithyahu.

"Anthony, did you get the pic….."

"Mattithyahu, what do you know about the family of the man driving the car that was following Nelli and me?"

"The family name goes back many generations in this area and believed to be connected to the Cosa Nostra. The father has been mayor of Rimini and is also a long-time member of the local Masonic Lodge. The chapter is one not recognized by the UGLE. The son was initiated a few years ago into the same chapter."

"I'll call you back," Anthony said abruptly, the car door opened and his sister got in.

"What's wrong Nelli? You look worried?"

"The strangest thing just happened. When I went back into the museum the young man at the front desk was on the phone. I overheard him telling the person on the other end that the two Americans asked for directions to the library. When he saw me, he got rattled and ended the call."

Anthony had no doubt now that his sister was on someone's radar.

"Someone out there is very interested in you. I must assume they suspect you could be the Chosen One, and I must also assume that that same someone is aware of the Chosen One's role in fulfilling the prophecy of Saint Anthony. If the person knows we are looking for a book . . . ." Anthony hesitated before making the next statement. "Nelli, do you understand what I am suggesting?"

Nelli sat there quietly. She was remembering what her father had told her: if you are pure of heart you have nothing to fear. Turning her head towards Anthony, she reached over and rested her hand on his arm.

"We suspected it might not be easy, but evil will never win against those that believe and put their trust in God."

"I believe that too, Nelli. Although I was chosen to be your Guardian and with that duty, the other Guardians and I must protect you against the dark forces that do not want you to succeed. Unfortunately, evil has already taken its first victim, Father Roberto. When Mary Ellen gets here tomorrow we must find out what the priest told her. Before the day is over, I want to get into the library's archives to see if we can find a link between Saint Anthony and Gradara Castle."

"Anthony, someone knows we've asked directions on how to get to the library."

"I know. I'll make a few inquiries but first let's get away

from here." He drove in the opposite direction of the library.

"Why don't we head back to the Piazza del Popolo? We can stop and get a light snack so we don't spoil our appetites for the meal Franco is preparing for us tonight. You can start to study some of the materials I got from the museum store while I make a few calls."

"Whatever you think is best but aren't you worried about us being followed?"

"We have our own personal security team Nelli. Little does our assailant know he has someone following him."

Nelli smiled and decided to look through one of the books on the altarpiece. Her brother made some calls but spoke in Italian, so she had no idea what was being discussed.

She scanned through the history on Bellini, how he was essential to the development of the Italian Renaissance art and his use of "disguised symbolism" in his paintings. That's interesting, she thought to herself and continued reading.

Commissioned by the Sforza family, Bellini created the great altarpiece, Coronation of the Virgin, which seemed to be his earliest effort in a form of art previously almost monopolized in Venice by the rival school of the Vivarini. Many times the likenesses of the benefactor's family members were represented as religious figures in the paintings.

In *Coronation of the Virgin*, some believe Saint Lawrence had an uncanny resemblance to Lord Sforza's son. She flipped through more pages and stopped on the page titled "Artist's Inspiration." Art historians discussed the reasons of some of the choices for Bellini's works. The artist had kept notes on each of his paintings and what inspired him. Unfortunately, many of his notes that were retrieved were damaged or faded with age. A notebook recently discovered is believed to be on the altarpiece now hanging in a museum in Pesaro. It corresponds to the dates and location when he would have worked on this particular piece.

In it he writes, "It was as if the Holy Spirit came down and guided my hand. Normally it takes much thinking to decide what to put into my paintings but with this painting, I knew immediately what I should include. I believe the divine hand of God directed me to create this work."

Nelli saw that Anthony was finished making calls. "Anthony listen to this," as she read out loud the last few paragraphs from the book.

She turned and faced her brother, "We need to get into the library and find out everything we can about Gradara Castle. I believe it could be the clue we're looking for."

"It's all taken care of; everything is set up for later this evening."

CHAPTER FIFTY-FIVE

The wall clock softy chimed on the hour. Donovan looked up to see if it was really three o'clock already. It was Patrick McKenna's wish that his son get the clock after his death. It was a ritual for the cardinal to wind the clock and say goodnight to his father as he left his office each evening. He always smiled when taking down the key, remembering his father, telling him ad infinitum, "Now don't wind it too tightly son, or you will break the spring."

You never knew what to expect from his father. McKenna would often see his mother shake her head with frustration but laughing at the same time when her husband would pull one of his legendary practical jokes. His father loved his family, life, and his church. Donovan remembered how proud his father was when he announced he wanted to become a priest one day. From that day on his father always introduced him as, this is my son the future Father McKenna.

There was a knock at his door. It had to be Robert telling him he was leaving for the day.

"Come in, Robert."

He was carrying a banker's box in his arms.

"This just came for you Cardinal McKenna. Would you like it in your office?"

"Yes please, place it here on my desk."

"Is there anything else you would like me to do before I leave for the day?"

"Maybe you could make sure our two new friends out in

the hallway aren't sleeping on the job," winking at Robert. Since His Holiness had assigned the two Swiss Guards for protection, he was never alone.

"That I don't think we need to worry about Cardinal McKenna," he said laughing.

"Then I will see you on Monday. Please leave my door open. Goodnight Robert."

Robert turned off the lights as he left except for the small lamp in the corner of the seating area. On the wall next to it hung a painting by Alessandro Botticelli, Madonna del Libro. It was a beautiful painting of the baby Jesus looking up at his mother Mary lovingly as she teaches him to read. When Cardinal McKenna was alone in the office, he liked to have his door left open so he could look at the painting from his desk. Botticelli had captured in the child's face the essence of his love for his mother so exquisitely you could almost feel the emotion radiating from the painting.

Many of the great artists did more than just paint pictures, they told stories. Some even have left clues to mysteries yet unsolved in their works, but that was for another day. His attention was now drawn to the box on his desk.

What, if anything, would he uncover that others hadn't from the stack of financial records and documents of a scandal that happened almost thirty years ago?

He glanced up at his father's clock, "Well, Dad, looks like we have a few more hours of work before we can call it a day." He lifted the lid and pulled out the first file.

Late afternoon had turned to evening and the drapes on the windows now framed black holes in the walls. He didn't remember turning on the desk lamp. Massaging the back of his neck he removed his reading glasses and checked the time. Had he read the clock right? Quarter to ten?

Picking up the legal pad, he looked over the information he had written down. He had divided a sheet of paper into three columns. He wrote the word DATE at the top of the first one. At the top of the second column he wrote NAME and the third column, EVENT.

The meetings between Parocchi and Father Maciel appeared to be just the tip of the iceberg. Glancing at the sheet of paper in front of him, a pattern was developing that he couldn't ignore. Something unholy was taking place. He could feel it.

Where was the money coming from to make all these transfers? The pictures that Mary Ellen had shown him were of Parocchi going into the same bank, a Swiss bank located in Lugano, which was named in the Banco Ambrosiano scandal in the early 1980s.

Swiss banks are known to be safe havens for offshore bank accounts. The main advantage is the bank account owned by the customer, a nonresident in a foreign country, is one hundred percent private and confidential where bank secrecy laws apply. Friends, spouses, tax authorities, personal enemies, and governments can never get access to a person's financial records.

Flipping through the yellow sheets of paper, he read through the notes he had made about the conspiracy theory around the death of Pope John Paul I. It was speculated that P2 had the banker Roberto Calvi killed, and his clothing stuffed with bricks and $15,000 worth of cash in three different currencies. Many considered it to be a masonic warning because of the symbolism associated with the word "Blackfriars." Although it was initially ruled a suicide, it was later prosecuted as a murder.

Mary Ellen's suspicions, plus his own findings, were beginning to frighten him. What was the goal of the P2 leader back then? Had P2 been resurrected with a new leader? Evil is always present even when we think it isn't, that's actually when we need to be the most vigilant.

As he looked at the portrait of His Holiness that hung next to his father's clock, the prophecy of Saint Malachy haunted him. According to the Abbé Cucherat, Saint Malachy while in Rome to give an account of the affairs of his diocese to the Pope, Innocent II, received the strange vision of the future where it was revealed to him the long list of illustrious pontiffs who were to rule the Church until the end of time. The second to the last name on the list was symbolized by an olive branch. Pope Benedict was becoming recognized as the Pope who wanted to extend the olive branch to create world peace.

The next name on that list, which was also the last name on the list, is what caused fear in McKenna. Some say it will be the name the Antichrist takes before the end, with the coming of Christ, as described in the Book of Revelations.

Then there was the prophecy of Saint Anthony and his visit by the angel, who told him to write the words of the Lord down in a book. When the time came, the Chosen One would deliver it to the one who would be known by the symbol of the olive branch.

Donovan's mind was reeling; you need to get some sleep, he told himself. Your imagination is working overtime. You're trying to find a link between the LC, a secret society that no longer exists, and a 600-year-old prophecy. I'd better keep those thoughts to myself, otherwise someone might think I've lost my grasp on reality but the transfers of money to the LC over the last five years were not his imagination. That was fact. He needed to make copies of his findings and give them to Mary Ellen before she left in the morning, so she could read them over the weekend.

He was slow getting up from his chair, his legs stiff from sitting for so long. There was also a message on his cell phone. It was from the archivist from the Vatican library. His heart started racing. Could the researcher have found evidence of the private diary of Saint Anthony?

He replied to the message but it was almost an hour since it had been sent. McKenna decided it would be morning before he would know what it was the researcher had found out.

Removing the key from the top of the clock's mantel he wound the gear, gently turning the key, but not too much. It was all in the touch. One too many turns and you could break the spring.

"Good night, Dad."

Placing the key back on the mantel of the clock, he whispered, "Watch over your son."

CHAPTER **FIFTY-SIX**

Anthony and Nelli found a little trattoria across from the Palazzo Ducale. They decided to split a plate of antipasto and share a bottle of the house Chianti. After placing the order, the waiter stood there waiting for the other menu choices. Anthony smiled and told him that completed their order.

The waiter looked at them like they had just committed a mortal sin. The young man acknowledged he understood, shrugged his shoulders, and walked away.

"What was that all about?" Nelli asked.

"Remember the afternoon meal is a major affair here. Businesses close up and everyone goes to a restaurant or home for a leisurely two to three hour seven-course meal. In Italy, antipasto is equivalent to hors d'oeuvres in America."

Nelli glanced at the tables around them. She assumed most of them were occupied by the residents of the town. She couldn't help notice that almost everyone smoked.

"Italians do like their cigarettes, don't they?"

"Yes, that's an understatement to say the least."

Their waiter returned with a large platter containing cured meats, olives, pepperoni, mushrooms, artichoke hearts, cheeses, and roasted garlic. A second young man placed a bottle of Chianti and two glasses on the table. Nelli was shocked by the huge platter of food.

Their server poured the wine and said, "Mangia, mangia" then grinned from ear to ear, set the bottle down and was off to another table.

Anthony laughed, "I guess he made his point." There is enough here to make up for a couple more courses."

While they ate Anthony filled Nelli in on the evening plans. The afternoon went by very quickly. They took a walk through the gardens at the Palazzo Ducale and on the way back to the villa located the exit for Gradara Castle. They decided to tour the castle after Mary Ellen arrived tomorrow.

Back at the villa Nelli wanted to freshen up a little and make a couple calls. She would check in at the office and then see if she could catch Larry. After she headed upstairs, Anthony took a stroll on the grounds and checked in with some of the other Guardians for updates.

As he walked by the kitchen section of the villa, he could hear Franco singing along to an Italian opera. The smells coming from the window were heavenly. For a second, he allowed himself the pleasure of enjoying the beauty of the countryside and the aromas drifting from the kitchen window. His phone buzzed.

"I'm here, fill me in."

"I just completed the last of the arrangements," said Mattithyahu, "everything's been arranged. I will pick you up at eight o'clock and bring you to a building owned by a friend of the family's. I've invited a small group of friends for drinks and dessert. Anyone watching will assume you are attending my little get-together for the evening."

"Then we will see you at eight." Anthony put the phone in his pocket and headed towards the loggia for what he was sure would be an adventure for his taste buds.

Nelli was already downstairs and talking with Franco. She saw Anthony pass by the kitchen window and ran over and yelled out to him.

"Anthony come inside. I'm in the kitchen helping Franco."

As he entered the room Nelli was wearing an apron and stirring a pot of sauce on the stove.

"Let's eat in here Anthony, it reminds me of when we were young, and we would go to Grandmother Andruccioli's house for Sunday dinner, remember? She'd be in the kitchen watching over all the pots on the stove and the freshly made pasta would be drying on the wooden rack on the counter. Then Grandfather would go downstairs and get a jug of his homemade wine."

Anthony had to smile; it did bring back good memories.

"Nelli, do you remember when we were little, we were allowed two fingers of wine in a juice glass on special occasions?" Nelli started to laugh and so did Franco.

"Ah, the two fingers of wine, an old Italian custom. Remember my new friends, to pass on the traditions to your own children."

Anthony thought to himself, "I hope we can, Franco. I truly hope we can."

Franco had spent the entire day preparing and cooking the food for his two new friends from America.

"Now you must sit here at the counter and I will serve you. I've made some of the specialties of our region for you to sample. The great composer Rossini created more than operas. He was also famous in culinary circles. There is actually a Rossinian cuisine. He loved to cook with mushrooms, goose livers, beef fillet, oysters, and above all, truffles. I've made two of his specialties: one is a woodcock soup and the other his Tournedos alla Rossini, a beef fillet browned in butter and garnished with foie gras and truffles."

While the three of them ate and talked, Rossini's "The Barber of Seville" played in the background. Glancing at his watch, Anthony realized Mattithyahu would be arriving at the villa soon. He caught Nelli's eye and tapped his watch. She instantly understood the message.

"Franco, the dinner was superb! Nelli exclaimed. "Thank you, you have made us feel like family."

"Please signorina Nelli, your father was one of us, am I not correct? You are family!"

"Grazie Franco, but now you must excuse me. I would like to change before Matthew picks us up."

"Si, avanti, avanti," Franco waved his arms at her. Nelli smiled and headed upstairs.

"You must excuse me also, Franco," said Anthony as he pushed his chair back from the counter.

"Si, avanti signore Anthony. It's time anyway for me to change the CD. I like to listen to someone you know well in America when I clean up after cooking." His father was actually from the Abruzzo region that borders Marche.

Looking like the cat that had just swallowed the canary, he had baited the hook and waited for Anthony to ask the question.

"Okay Franco, give me a clue."

With a mischievous grin he said, "His birth name was Dino Paul Crocetti."

It took Anthony a minute but then it registered.

"The lustrous Dean Martin, am I right?"

"Si signore Anthony eccellentissimo!"

Anthony went to wait for Mattithyahu, and from the other room he could hear Franco singing along with Dino to Volare.

CHAPTER FIFTY-SEVEN

Matthew had arrived exactly at eight. The offices he was taking them to weren't far from the library. They pulled in front of what looked like a series of townhomes that had been converted to businesses. A valet was waiting to park the car.

Standing in the small foyer they could hear voices coming from a room off to the left. Matthew put his finger up to his lips and motioned for Anthony and Nelli to follow. He turned right and led them to a closed door at the end of the hallway. Pulling out a key, he unlocked the door and waited until everyone was in the room, then locked the door behind him.

He flipped on the wall switch and a soft light from a floor lamp filled the room. All the walls were covered with built-in bookcases made of mahogany. There were no windows, but the ceiling was one large skylight with an exquisite stained glass panel suspended beneath it. Since it was late evening, there was no natural light to illuminate it but slowly it came alive with color. Recessed lights had been installed all around the edges to create the same effect as daylight, illuminating the rich colors in the stained glass panel.

In one corner was a leather chair and side table. On the other side of the room were two winged backed chairs on either side of a burgundy suede sofa. Covering the floor was a magnificent Persian Oriental rug that sat on top a wood parquet floor.

It was an impressive room but Matthew had something else on his mind. Upon entering he turned immediately to his left, walking to the second set of bookcases. Running his hand along some books, he stopped at one titled *Does Evil Exist in Today's World.*

Pulling out the book he stuck his hand into the bookcase feeling around for something. Then Anthony thought he heard a soft click. Matthew stepped back as one side of the bookcase moved away from the wall a few inches. Grabbing the edge he pulled on what turned out to be a door into another room.

Motioning Anthony and Nelli to follow him, they stepped into a passageway that must have been there for centuries. Switching on a lantern as he closed the door behind them, he finally spoke.

"This will lead us to an exit behind the offices where I have a van waiting to take you to the library," said Matthew.

As they walked, Mathew explained the plan.

"My cousin has arranged to get you into the library's archives through an underground delivery entrance. You will have four hours to find what you are looking for. You must be back here by one o'clock exactly. That's when my guests will begin to depart.

"For anyone that might be watching, it will look like you spent the evening here with me. After you have returned, I will drive you back to the villa."

It was approximately a ten-minute ride and the next thing Anthony and Nelli knew they were inside the library.

"Well, Nelli" said Anthony, "let's see if we can find a connection between Saint Anthony and Gradara Castle."

After about thirty minutes trying to figure out the cataloging system and the layout of the room, Anthony was ready to go hunting.

"We need to look for section fourteen, row seven and any books numbered 245.00 through 245.87."

Anthony was already headed down an aisle he hoped would take him to section fourteen. Nelli followed Anthony as they passed endless shelves filled with countless volumes of books and documents.

"Anthony look to your left, down two aisles, section fourteen," she said pointing with her finger.

Reaching the end of the aisle of shelving, they took a right and found row seven about a third of the way down. They started looking for books with the number 200 and there in the middle, on the edge of one of the shelves was a label with the words "Fortress of Gradara." At the far end of the aisle was a table with chairs.

They each grabbed an armful of books and headed to the table.

The time was going by quickly. A couple of hours had already elapsed, and they were getting concerned about the time they had left before they would have to leave.

Anthony was the first to speak. "Have you found anything, Nelli?"

"Not sure, could be nothing," she said.

"What is it? We're running out of time."

"Okay. I'll read you something I found written in Lord Sforza's diary, *he was laid to rest beside the Holy Ones in a private chamber few had access to*. If the Bellini painting holds a clue, what seems out of place when you look at it? It is a religious painting of Jesus crowning the Blessed Virgin Mary. They are surrounded by saints on each side of the throne and in the left and right-hand pilasters of the altarpiece. After that, what do you notice?" she continued. There is a painting within a painting and the second painting is of the fortress of Gradara and may I add—it is smack dab in the center of the piece. It almost seems to dominate it. I also remember reading one of the eight saints in the altarpiece, the one of Saint Lawrence is said to resemble Lord Sforza's one and only son who died in battle. Do you think it could mean his son was buried next to the seven saints in the painting and he's showing us where by having Gradara painted into the altarpiece?"

Anthony grabbed a book on the architecture of Gradara Castle.

"What is it Anthony?" said Nelli.

"In those times cemeteries were often underground. A perfect example is the Vatican. In 1939, excavators uncovered a second century cemetery beneath the basilica where they found bones now displayed in a wall next to a shrine to Saint Peter, which many believe to be the apostle's. Saint Anthony is one of the eight saints in the painting, right? If he's buried under Gradara Castle perhaps the book we are looking for could be buried with him."

Nelli couldn't believe what she was hearing.

"Do you really think we might have found the location of where the book is buried?"

Anthony didn't hear what she said; he was trying to find the most recent floor plan of Gradara Castle and what were believed to be the drawings of the original plans for the castle.

"Scusi signore Anthony and signorina Nelli," said

Matthew's cousin, "we must think about departing soon if you are to get back to Matthew's office on time."

Without looking at the man Anthony replied, "Si, grazie, a couple more minutes and we'll be ready," as he continued to rifle through prints of floor plans in front of him.

Anthony found the ones he wanted but there wasn't time to study any of the drawings.

"Help me replace the books Nelli, then we need to get back."

"But Anthony, we need more time to study the maps!"

"Don't worry, just grab some books."

They replaced the books quickly except for two that Anthony concealed under his coat. "They'll never miss them, at least for a little while anyway," he said winking at Nelli.

They were back at the villa by two. It was already Friday and Mary Ellen would be there in twelve hours. Exhaustion finally hit both of them; they decided to try and get some sleep but Anthony knew sleep was still hours away for him. He wanted to study the architectural drawings of the fortress. Was it possible they could have found the location of the book?

CHAPTER **FIFTY-EIGHT**

Awakened by the pigeons flapping their wings outside the window, McKenna was shocked to see the sun. Looking at the clock, it read six forty-five. It was a little after midnight when he had gotten back to the apartment, and he remembered sitting on the edge of the bed, removing his shoes and after that it was a complete blank.

Sitting up he realized he was still wearing his clothes from yesterday. If it was really almost seven he needed to take a quick shower, get into some fresh clothes and make copies of the documents before Mary Ellen left to see her friends for the weekend.

As the water from the shower engulfed him into a world of silence, he tried to process what he had uncovered last night. The sense of fear returned and with it the ominous feeling that evil was all around him. He felt like he couldn't breathe.

As he got dressed he prioritized what he needed to do. First, he needed to make copies of everything from last night and get them over to Mary Ellen, and then look deeper into this secret society known as P2. He had to find out if there was any evidence that it still existed.

He also wanted to look deeper into the transactions between the bank and the Legion of Christ. Gathering up his papers, he decided to call over to the Vatican Library to see what the archivist had found out. Locating his phone he saw he had a message. Figuring it must be from Mary Ellen or the archivist, he was surprised when he saw who it was from.

Cardinal Cavallari has requested an appointment with you this morning at ten-thirty. Please be prompt. Call to confirm as soon as you receive this message.

He was furious he had to change plans. He still had enough time to make copies for Mary Ellen but the rest would have to wait. What did the Secretary of State want with him? He couldn't decline. Calling he confirmed the appointment.

In another part of the Apostolic Palace, Carlo tapped lightly on the door.

"Entrare."

"Here are those articles you asked for Cardinal Cavallari. I didn't know if you heard the latest news about the plane crash? I put this morning's newspaper about it on top."

"No, where did it happen?"

"A small Learjet went down in the Appenine Mountains outside of Arezzo early Thursday morning," replied Carlo.

Cavallari felt like he'd just been hit with a baseball bat.

"Is there anything else you would like me to do before I return to my work, Cardinal Cavallari?" Cavallari was trying to remain calm after what Carlo had just told him.

"No, Carlo that will be all."

As the door closed he gasped for air. Grabbing the newspaper he began reading.

AP
The Associated Press
9:32 a.m. Friday

Italy . . . Seven people were killed early Thursday morning over the Appenine Mountains in the Marche region of Italy. It is believed the flight originated outside of Arezzo. A Dassault Falcon 50 EX Learjet exploded upon crashing, said Guiseppe Gabetta, a spokesperson for the Italian air force. The plane crashed about 4:30 a.m. local time. Besides the pilot, copilot, and flight attendant, there is said to have been two dignitaries with high-ranking positions and two heads of large European companies aboard. Their names are not being released until DNA samples can be gathered to make positive identification. Names are being withheld until next of kin have been notified. There is an investigation underway to find out the reason for the crash.

Cavallari was very familiar with the make of the plane. It was the same one P2 uses and what he had flown on. He knew it couldn't have been any of the disciples, or the Grand Master on board, or he would have heard from someone by now but he didn't dismiss the possibility that the four passengers had been guests of P2. He also questioned if the crash was an accident.

Don't concern yourself with these latest developments, stay focused, or you could jeopardize everything, he instructed himself. Timing was crucial if the plan was to succeed. Pope Benedict was wrapping up his visit to the UK and would return to the Vatican on Sunday. It was only the second visit by a head of the Catholic Church since Henry VIII declared himself head of the Church of England more than 500 years ago. The Pope's visit was to create a more open relationship with the Anglican Church and acknowledge the Church's failure to act responsibility concerning the child abuse scandal that rocked the Church.

Cavallari was anxious for his meeting with Cardinal McKenna. As prefect of the CDF he must have consulted with Pope Benedict before the trip and been aware of what the Pope would say on the child abuse issue.

The Catholic Church was rich in assets but unfortunately cash poor. With the number of lawsuits growing against the Church, it felt like a tsunami was gaining strength and would soon hit land, taking everything in its path.

The time was right for a new representative of God on earth. He would restore strength, peace, and security to the church. He would create new relationships with other religions and work to unite with world governments and banks to correct the wrongs of the past. Cavallari needed to find out what McKenna knew that could affect the Grand Master's plan.

The phone on the desk rang, interrupting his thoughts. Checking the time he figured it must be Carlo telling him his appointment had arrived.

"Cardinal Cavallari, Cardinal McKenna is here to see you."

"Thank you, give me a few minutes."

"Of course."

Placing the receiver back into its base, Carlo looked over at Cardinal McKenna, "Cardinal Cavallari will be with you shortly."

Donavan was puzzled why Cavallari had requested this meeting. He was not happy about having to rearrange his morning for the appointment. He was anxious to get down to the archives to see what the researcher had found out.

Glancing at his watch, it had been ten minutes since the secretary had informed Cavallari he was here. How long is he going to keep me waiting? Closing his eyes, he silently said, "Dear Lord, bless this lowly servant with patience, which he seems very short of at the moment."

As he sat there he sensed a growing presence of something evil approaching. Looking around there was only the assistant and himself in the room, but he couldn't shake the feeling. McKenna heard the sound of a door opening, and when he looked up, he stared into the eyes of a monster.

"Cardinal McKenna, thank you so much for meeting with me on such short notice. Come in."

McKenna quickly gained his composure and followed Cavallari into his office.

"Please sit down," said the Secretary of State, motioning to a chair.

As McKenna took his seat he said, "I overheard you were not feeling well, someone mentioned a vertigo attack? I hope it has subsided."

"Yes it is much better, thank you."

McKenna was trying to give the appearance of being relaxed. How could he be sensing the presence of evil from a man of the cloth?

"I noticed you were not at the Morning Prayer," asked Cavallari.

McKenna was surprised that the cardinal had noticed his absence.

"Something came up that I had to attend to," responded McKenna.

Cavallari could see that Donovan would not freely divulge information on his own.

"I, like everyone, am aware of the comments made by his Holiness during his trip to the UK concerning the sexual scandal within the priesthood. It is unfortunate how the Church chose to handle this matter."

Pausing, he waited to see if McKenna would make a comment but he was met with silence. So he continued, "You, more than anyone, must realize the toll it is taking on the Catholic Church being the prefect of the CDF.

McKenna closed his eyes and slowly shook his head.

"Yes, sadly there has been much suffering instilled upon the innocent, I am afraid."

Then looking directly at Cavallari, McKenna continued, "Being called to preach the words of Our Lord has not made us without sin. We can give in to temptation the same as any of God's children. We are no more worthy of His love or absolved from His judgment than any other soul. As priests, we are given, by the grace of God, to give absolution of sins at confession. Now we must ask those same penitents to forgive us our sins."

Cavallari was getting nowhere with his colleague so he decided to up the ante a little.

"I fear for the Church with the religious and political unrest in the world that is taking place. The media is reporting that the Pope should step down. There is even a subtle insinuation that they might have a candidate in mind."

McKenna didn't respond right away. It was almost as if Cavallari was baiting him. There was a coldness about him that he had never noticed before.

"Cardinal Cavallari, the media needs to fill space in newspapers and time on the networks. I realized the other day something that I often tend to forget. God asks only one thing of us, to trust in Him. If we obey his laws and seek no other false prophets, we will never go without want."

Cavallari grew more and more impatient. The world was about to change and this man in front of him had no idea of the inescapable future that awaited him.

"It is good and well Cardinal McKenna, but the present souls are demanding financial retribution for the wrongs perpetrated against them. I don't think the world and the victims will be appeased by a response from the Church to believe in God and his teachings on forgiveness. They did put their trust in God and His representatives on earth betrayed them. His Holiness can go around the world and speak the words of reconciliation but I must deal with reality. How do you suggest we deal with the here and now? The Church is asset rich but cash poor."

McKenna was shocked by the outburst. He was sure he hadn't been able to disguise his reaction to Cavallari's words. He remained quiet, and then in a calm voice replied, "We were all made in the image of God. We have been tested many times by evil forces. Perhaps this is one of those times we are again being tested by the Lord."

Cavallari had a habit of rubbing the palm of his hand

when he became agitated with someone. McKenna noticed that Cavallari's ring had twisted slightly. There appeared to be some kind of ink mark or tattoo beneath where the head of the ring sat on his finger. Odd place for a tattoo, McKenna thought to himself. Cavallari just stared at the cardinal. He had no use for this priest, but he was keenly aware of how McKenna was studying him. He would have to watch this one carefully.

"I am sorry to see we have such a difference of opinion. I was hoping we could join forces on how to address the present issues facing the Church," said Cavallari.

Standing up, "You will now need to excuse me Cardinal McKenna. I have things I need to attend to."

"Of course," said McKenna, as he got up from his chair.

It was an awkward moment as they both stood there looking at each other. Cardinal McKenna decided to speak first, "I will say a prayer today that God will give us the wisdom to see the path we must take."

Expressionless, Cavallari replied, "You do that Cardinal McKenna. You do that." McKenna turned to exit. He couldn't get out of there fast enough.

CHAPTER **FIFTY-NINE**

Nelli no longer heard Anthony's muffled voice coming from the room next door. She needed to get some sleep but she couldn't stop thinking about everything that had taken place since their father's death.

Laying there in the darkness, except for the dim light from a small lamp, she pulled the comforter up to her chin. It felt like a protective armor against the world. Rolling over onto her side she could see the little angel standing guard out on the balcony. There was a gentle breeze and the slightest hint of jasmine in the air.

Reaching over to turn off the light Nelli's eyes rested on the box they had purchased at the little shop in Rome. While unpacking, she put it on the nightstand next to the bed. Picking it up Nelli set it down on top of the comforter next to her. What secrets do you hold, she wondered?

With her fingertips, she studied the box like a blind person would read braille. She felt the intricate details of the cross on the lid and the carving of scrolls in the wood. Out of the corner of her eye she became aware of a bright white light. Turning her head she expected to see the beams from a full moon shining through the window. She quickly realized the light wasn't coming from the moon. She shifted her eyes slightly to the left. It was coming from the corner of the room.

What she saw was a globe of pulsating light. As she watched, an outline of a person formed inside the globe. Then the image spoke but its mouth never moved.

"You've had a very eventful day my child."

Nelli thought she recognized the image but it was impossible. It couldn't be.

"Saint Anthony?"

"Yes Antonella, I was pleased when you found the medal I left for you in the museum today. You are very astute and are asking all the right questions."

"Saint Anthony, my brother and I think we might have found the location of the book. Can you tell me if we are on the right track?" asked Nelli.

Even though the spirit of Saint Anthony had taken a human form, the globe still pulsated and rays of light shot out from all sides of the sphere.

"The words that Our Lord told me to write down will be found when the time is right. You have now come to realize there are evil forces at work that do not want you to succeed but they also want to possess the book."

"Saint Anthony, I am not afraid for myself, but I do fear for the others that are on this quest with me."

The image continued talking but his lips never moved.

"God is aware of your concerns. Be strengthened by knowing that each of them has freely chosen to accept their calling in life. When the time comes to depart from this earth all will have a place in heaven. So do not worry about their souls.

You will be surrounded and protected by all the past Keepers of the Key if you remain pure of heart then no harm will come to you and the forces working against you know this."

Nelli watched as the image began to fade in and out.

"Saint Anthony, I have many questions."

"You must rest my child; the morning will be here soon. Remember to trust in Him."

The next thing Nelli heard was a different voice calling her name. Opening her eyes she was shocked to see it was morning.

"Nelli, are you awake?" Anthony opened the bedroom door and peaked around the corner. "Hey you, you told me to wake you if you weren't up by seven-thirty. I've been studying the maps and think I might have found something."

Nelli listened as her brother spoke but she was trying to figure out how the sun could be out when a minute ago it had been pitch black outside. Looking over at the corner of the room she was expecting to see Saint Anthony but no one was there.

Anthony could see Nelli must have been in a deep sleep and was having a hard time waking up.

"Come on Nelli, time to get moving. I'll meet you downstairs in thirty minutes."

It became clear to Nelli now that she had another visitor last night. This time it was from Saint Anthony.

"I'll be down as soon as I can," said Nelli, still half asleep.

Anthony headed downstairs. He could smell fresh coffee. As he reached the loggia he saw that Franco had already put out pastries and fruit. Although he hadn't slept much, his mind was racing a hundred miles an hour.

The conversation with Cephas last night concerned him. The man from Rimini that was driving the car and the man spotted in Rome and the museum had been seen going into a building rumored to be a meeting place for the hierarchy of Masonic Lodges from around Europe.

Anthony ruled out it being a coincidence. He told Cephas to get inside the building and find out anything he could and report back to him. He was still waiting to hear what he had found out.

"Buon giorno, signore Anthony."

"Did you and signorina Nelli enjoy your evening?" asked Franco.

"Yes, it was a very nice gathering of Matthew's friends," answered Anthony hoping Franco wouldn't see he was lying.

"Will the signorina be joining you for breakfast?"

"Yes, she will be down shortly," said Anthony.

Anthony sat down facing the side that overlooked the Adriatic. Picking up one of the books he confiscated from the library, he opened it up to the chapter on when the Sforza family occupied the fortress of Gradara. There was mention of a family chapel next to the residential quarters. It was a small chapel but the description of the interior caught his attention.

He had also found what was considered to be the first known drawings of the fortress, which included the castle with some odd markings scribbled on the pages.

"Good morning my dear brother," said Nelli coming over and sitting down next to Anthony.

He hadn't heard his sister come in and it startled him,

getting angry with himself for not being more alert to his surroundings.

"Looks like you were having a hard time waking up," said Anthony.

"Actually …." Nelli stopped when she saw Franco.

"Buon giorno, signorina Nelli. Would you like your usual," winking at her.

"Yes, grazie." Nelli smiled and winked back.

She waited for Franco to leave the room, then looking at her brother in a low voice she said, "I had another vision last night. Saint Anthony came to me."

Anthony wasn't surprised, in fact, he waited for Nelli to continue.

"I told him we thought we had found the location of the book. He said evil forces did not want us to succeed."

Nelli stopped talking. Franco was back with her coffee.

"Espresso for the signorina," placing the cup down in front of her. "Your friend will arrive this afternoon, sí?"

"Yes, her plane should land about noon."

"I have everything ready for her. She will have the room next to you signorina Nelli. Ah, I see you must be looking at visiting the medieval fortress, Gradara Castle. It has been voted one of the most beautiful villages in all of Italy."

Then Franco slapped his hands together as if in prayer looking up towards the sky, "And the place where the doomed and tragic love affair between Paolo and Francesca took place. It is recounted in Canto V of *Dante's Inferno.*

Nelli looked surprised at what he had just told them.

"You have not heard the story I see. If you wish, I will tell you about the fated lovers?"

"Yes, please do Franco," Nelli was curious to hear the tale.

"The legend goes Giovanni Malatesta, named Giangiotto, was the eldest son of Sigismondo I, Lord of Gradara. He was described as ugly and lame. Francesca was the daughter of Giovanni da Polenta, Lord of Ravenna. Giangiotto, a courageous but exceedingly ugly soldier, obtained Francesca's father's consent to marry her.

"Fearing that she would be repelled by his ugliness, he persuaded his handsome brother Paolo to court her on his behalf. Once the marriage contract was signed the real Giangiotto slipped into the marriage bed, to the understandable horror of the young bride. But, more tragic still, Paolo and Francesca had fallen in love.

"Giangiotto was Podesta, magistrate, in the town of Pesaro and could not bring his family with him because of a law at that time, so he left his wife and daughter Concordia in the Castle of Gradara.

"His brother Paolo became a frequent caller at the castle but Giangiotto knew of the visits. He caught his wife and brother alone in Francesca's bedroom. Giangiotto rushed upon his brother to kill him but Francesca sheltered him with her body and was killed in his place. Paolo followed her soon afterwards. If you tour the castle they will take you to her bedroom to see where the ill-fated lovers lost their lives."

"That is so sad," said Nelli. "It sounds like our story of Romeo and Juliet."

"Per favore mi scusi, I've talked too long. Please call if there is anything you want me to do before your guest arrives." Franco turned and headed back to the kitchen.

Anthony's phone rang.

"It's Mary Ellen," Anthony mouthed to Nelli, as he placed the phone up to his ear.

"Good Morning Anthony. I thought I'd let you and Nelli know I'll be leaving for the airport in a few minutes."

"All right, we will be waiting for you when you land. See you around twelve Mary Ellen."

"Is she headed to the airport?" asked Nelli

"Yup, she's on her way. Now finish telling me more about the visit you had from Saint Anthony."

"There's not too much more to tell you. He said the book would be found when the time is right and that all the past Keepers of the Key would protect me. Now you said you discovered something?" said Nelli as she ate the last piece of fruit from her plate.

"We have some time before we need to leave to pick up Mary Ellen," said Anthony getting up from his chair. "Let me grab my laptop and I will meet you in the reading room and show you."

Finishing her espresso, Nelli barely made it to the reading room before Anthony. He put his laptop on the table next to the chair she was sitting in. Then he opened up one of the books from the library and laid down some papers he had made notes on next to it.

"Look, some of the architectural renderings have strange markings on them," pointing to a drawing. "Right here where the personal residence and a family chapel should be. The other interesting thing was the description of the interior of the family chapel."

Nelli studied the drawings as Anthony read.

"It was a small chapel, rectangular in shape. As you entered it, at the far end was the altar. Along the two long walls of the room were eight niches, four on each side each holding a statue."

"That isn't that unusual Anthony," said Nelli. Not understanding why Anthony would find anything strange about the layout of the chapel.

"Listen to the list of who the statues represent."

He read the eight names ending with the two that were the closest to the altar, "Saint Lawrence, who we know was supposed to resemble Lord Sforza's son and the other is Saint Anthony."

Nelli was shaken when hearing the names. Then it suddenly hit her, "It's the names of the eight saints that were in the painting!"

"Then there's this," continues Anthony, "Lord Sforza had his son's body returned to Gradara where he was buried in the family chapel along with the others."

"Are you thinking the same thing as I am?" Nelli looked wide-eyed at Anthony.

"All I know is . . . we have to get into that chapel."

CHAPTER SIXTY

Mary Ellen was hypnotized as she watched the water flow lazily down the Tiber River from the balcony of her apartment. It looked like a stream of sparkling diamonds as the sun's rays bounced off its surface. How could anything evil exist when she felt such a sense of peace? But the moment was gone and the reality was that there were evil forces at work. Taking another sip of coffee, she replayed the conversation with Cardinal McKenna.

The sun was much higher in the sky and the water had taken on the appearance of a looking glass. The car would be here soon to take her to the airport and she still hadn't heard from Cardinal McKenna.

As if on cue the doorbell rang. She was about to open the door when she stopped. "You need to be more careful," she told herself. "Check and see who it is first."

Ever since receiving that card with the embossed cobra head on it she'd become much more suspicious of everyone. Looking through the peephole she recognized the cardinal's assistant, Robert, and opened the door.

"Buon giorno, Robert. Come stai?"

"Buon giorno, molto bene signorina O'Farrell, Cardinal McKenna asked me to deliver this before you left on your trip." He handed Mary Ellen a large sealed envelope.

"Grazie, please tell Cardinal McKenna I will call him after I have read through all the material."

"Si of course," nodding his head in acknowledgement.

"Have a pleasant trip signorina O'Farrell, arrivederci." He turned and headed back down the hallway.

She was afraid to open the envelope. Reading the cardinal's findings could further substantiate her suspicions that there was a conspiracy taking place. As she pulled out the contents of the envelope, on top was a handwritten note from the cardinal.

Dear Mary Ellen,

I received documents that deepen my concerns and raise even more questions. There is what appears to be laundering of money between the IOR, Bank Ambrosiano, and the LC. Enclosed you will see my notes with the dates and amounts.

Upon my researching of the events surrounding the death of Pope John Paul I, there are similarities between then and now that greatly disturb me. A secret society called Propaganda Due also known as P2, an offshoot of the Freemasons and some have even suggested it being a branch of the Illuminati, was believed to be behind the conspiracy to kill the Pope.

I am frightened by what I am seeing taking place between the three groups I mentioned above. I believe it could be just the tip of the iceberg. I fear that this group by the name of P2 could have gone underground and have been waiting to gain power again. If we believe the prophecy of Saint Anthony, we could be facing a battle with Satan himself.

If we can figure out what they have planned, we might be able to reverse the course of events.

May God protect and guide us on this journey

Your Friend in Christ,
Cardinal McKenna

Someone was actually starting to believe what she had suspected for so long, but with that she hadn't planned on uncovering a sinister plot.

Flipping through the pages of notes and documents she would have to study the information after she got on the plane. Cardinal McKenna had taken care of her transportation to the airport and the car would be picking her up soon.

Thinking about the prophecy of Saint Anthony her thoughts turned to Anthony. Any animosity between them was gone, but she could sense he was preoccupied with something and there was something else she hadn't been able to put her finger on.

She became more and more frightened and now realized that was what she sensed in Anthony. If he were afraid, what would he be afraid of? Whatever it was Nelli was part of it too. She planned on finding out this weekend.

It was getting late and she wanted to call Devlin before she left. Thankfully he picked up after the second ring.

"Hey Mary, are you about ready to leave for Pesaro?"

"Yes, but I wanted to talk to you before I left. You know it's strange Dev, even though it's been a few years since Anthony and I went our separate ways, it feels like it was only yesterday that I spoke to him.

"Mary Ellen, I never did know what happened between you two."

Mary Ellen had never told Devlin the reason why she and Anthony had drifted apart. She wasn't about to now. The past was history. Discussing it wouldn't change anything.

"It was a difficult time for both of us Dev. It doesn't matter now. We both moved forward with our lives."

"Well, have a nice weekend and tell Anthony and Nelli I send them my prayers."

"I will Dev, but I want to ask you a couple questions."

When they met for dinner the other night Mary Ellen told him of her suspicions and showed Devlin the notes and a list of money transactions that corresponded around the same time of the accusations against him. Devlin thought Mary Ellen's imagination was getting the best of her, but he had been accused falsely for something he never did.

Considering for just a second that there might be something to her conspiracy theory, could there really be evidence that might explain the lies against him?

"Devlin did you hear me?"

"What? I'm sorry what did you say?"

"I need you to contact any of the priests that are still your friends over at the LC. The ones you feel you can trust and ask them if they ever noticed any similar behaviors that you mentioned to me. I have seen more documents that further validate my suspicions. When I get back we will discuss everything."

Devlin wondered what new documents she was talking about but he realized Mary Ellen didn't have the time to get into it right now.

"Mary Ellen, I don't know how they will receive my questioning them about things that happened years ago." Mary Ellen could hear the hesitation in her brother's voice.

"They might be suspicious of me digging up the past," said Devlin.

"Please Devlin, it's very important you try."

He never heard his sister sound so serious in his life.

"All right, I will make some calls today."

"Thank you Dev, I need to run now."

Outside Mary Ellen's building Sho'am sat in a car. He was talking on his cell phone when he observed another car pulling up to the front entrance.

"The limo from the Vatican just pulled up," he said to the person on the other end of the phone. "I'm not seeing anything else out of the ordinary."

"Good, follow them to the airport, then Y'hochanan will take over. He's already checking in his luggage. He'll be seated towards the back of the plane so he can observe everyone. Then follow up with our contact in the mail room and go over the video again. See if you can figure out who our mystery person might be. Report in at your usual time."

CHAPTER SIXTY-ONE

Closing the door behind him McKenna took a deep breath. Whatever evil he had just encountered was for the moment on the other side of the door. Glancing down at his watch, Donovan figured Mary Ellen must be on the plane to Pesaro by now. She should have gotten his envelope and was probably reading through his latest findings.

First, he would stop at the office and make sure Robert had delivered the materials to Mary Ellen, and then he would check his messages. He was anxious to see if Commander Crevelli or Carlo had tried to call.

The Holy Father was scheduled to return to the Vatican on Sunday and then on Monday head to his country estate, Castel Gandolfo, for the remainder of the week. It is only fifteen miles from Rome, making it possible for the Pope to return to the Vatican quickly if necessary. At some point he needed to discuss his findings with either Crevelli or the Pope personally.

To his amazement he had already reached his office. The two guards took their positions outside the entrance to the offices. Robert watched as the cardinal walked through the door.

"I hope your meeting went well Cardinal McKenna. While you were out Commander Crevelli and Carlo from the Vatican Archives both called and are anxious to talk to you. I told them you were in a meeting. They each asked if you would please call them as soon as you got back to the office."

"Thank you Robert. Please hold all my calls," said McKenna as he went straight to his office. Closing the door behind him he was glad to be alone. Heading to his desk he placed a call to Carlo, who picked up on the second ring.

Seeing that the call was from McKenna, Carlo wasted no time, "Cardinal McKenna I was just about to call you again. I believe I might have found something that could be important to your search for a diary kept by Saint Anthony."

"I will come as soon as I can," said McKenna. "I must attend to a few things here first but then I plan on spending the remainder of the day in the archives."

"Then I will see you shortly cardinal," said Carlo.

McKenna tried to reach Commander Crevelli next but he was out of the office. He immediately buzzed for Robert.

"Robert, would you please track down the Commander for me. I am headed over to spend the remainder of the day in the Vatican Archives. When you track him down tell him to call me on my cell phone."

"Is there any other message you would like me to give him?" asked Robert.

"No, he'll know what it's about. I will be leaving in a few minutes. If I need you I will call from the cell."

McKenna started gathering everything he wanted to take with him. He had to stay focused. He'd worry about Cardinal Cavallari later.

CHAPTER SIXTY-TWO

Anxious to see what Carlo had discovered, McKenna took a seat across the table from the Vatican archivist.

"What have you found that leads you to believe there might be evidence of a diary belonging to Saint Anthony?"

"Here's the remarkable thing Cardinal McKenna, there is actually a small collection of the old church journals from the monastery that Saint Anthony belonged to preserved in the Vatican library.

"In them Saint Anthony speaks about a loyal and faithful friend at the abbey. For some unknown reason, it became important for me to find out more about this person. Perhaps, it was the work of the Holy Spirit, but I finally came across some information in some of the earlier documents.

"It is well known that at that time in history the monks were among the very few who were educated. Sometimes a family would send their young son to be an apprentice to the monks. The abbeys always needed help, and in return they taught these young boys to read and write, hoping that some would later want to join the Church.

"A boy by the name of Giovanni was placed under the care of Saint Anthony. In the documents Saint Anthony wrote about what an excellent student the young Giovanni was and how he had the same gift of working with wood as his father in the village. He wrote how he encouraged the boy to practice his writing by keeping a journal. I searched through the rest of the documents but there is little else of benefit.

"I tried cross-referencing different things but came up empty. Still I felt like there was something I was missing but I had run out of ideas.

"I was about to give up when I realized I hadn't searched under the name of the young apprentice. It was a long shot but it was worth a try. To my amazement I found a surprisingly large collection of documents, manuscripts, and drawings pertaining to the abbey.

"As I looked through all of it a small leather bound book fell out from among the papers. It was very old and most of the lettering was worn off. I could make out a few letters, and then I realized what I had found. It was the journal of a young boy by the name of Giovanni.

"The dates of the journal entries would have been around the time of Saint Anthony's death. Unfortunately many of the pages had disintegrated but there was enough for me to piece together a limited picture of who this person was and his relationship with Saint Anthony. Some of the writings I believe were descriptions of things that had happened in his earlier years at the monastery.

"One entry talks about when he was working in the fields one day and meeting a holy man. The man offered to share his lunch with Giovanni. While they ate he told the man his desire to make something special for Father Anthony for teaching him to read and write. The holy man had heard he was gifted at making things out of wood. Giovanni did not know how the holy man would know this but it wasn't for him to question God's ways. The monk suggested he make a beautiful wooden box in which Father Anthony could keep something he treasured.

"Another passage talks about keeping a promise to Father Anthony at his deathbed. He promises to pass on the key to one worthy until the day it was needed."

"Does he write what the key is for?" asked McKenna.

"No, I only saw it mentioned that one time. A key could mean many different things than what we commonly associate with the word today."

"So we're not talking about an actual key like one used to unlock a door?"

"Well it could be many things. There were two ways important information was transported during that time in history. A key could be a code used to unlock a message within the written word. Battle plans were often hidden within a letter sent by a courier to army leaders in the field.

"Then you have the Old Masters like Michelangelo, it is said he included secret messages in his paintings. And finally, it could be an actual key that unlocks something."

This newest lead created a realm of possibilities that McKenna couldn't spend any time delving into right now. He had to stay focused on finding the Antichrist and stopping him. He would run this latest information past Mary Ellen, perhaps this friend of hers knew something about the world of secret codes and keys.

"Carlo, I would like you to continue to see what more you can uncover but I need to research a group called P2. I will check back with you later."

McKenna was now headed down Via di Porta Angelica to Porta di S. Anna, the entrance to the archives, which was adjacent to the Vatican Library. The last he heard, the archives are said to hold more than fifty-two miles of shelving.

He'd called ahead and requested anything they could find on Propaganda Due or P2 be pulled and ready for him. Entering the index room, he was met by a priest wearing the black cassock, required dress at the Vatican.

"I am Cardinal McKenna. I called and asked that some materials be pulled for me."

"Si, everything is waiting for you. Please, if I may ask your indulgence, I must ask for identification, it is protocol."

Swiping McKenna's I.D. card into the computer he quickly handed it back to the cardinal.

"Do you have a cell phone, camera, or other electronic devices on your person?"

"I have my cell phone."

"I must ask that you allow us to hold it for safekeeping while you visit with us," his hand open to receive the device.

He put the phone into a tray and placed it in a lock box, then handed the key to Cardinal McKenna.

"Please Cardinal McKenna follow me."

McKenna was led down a hallway to a small reading room. As the priest opened the door McKenna heard what sounded like a balloon deflating. They entered a small space just large enough to accommodate two people. They stood there until the door closed behind them. The priest knew if this were the cardinal's first time to the archives he would be unfamiliar with the process.

"It is climate controlled to preserve the materials," said the priest calmly without turning around.

When the hissing sound finally stopped the priest unlocked the second door. They entered a small room with no windows. The room was well lit and in the center was a long table surrounded by four chairs. An additional library lamp and intercom were in the middle of the table. The requested materials were placed at one end and next to them were a pair of white cotton gloves.

"We require all our visitors to wear gloves while viewing the materials. If you would be so kind," the priest glanced over at the pair lying there.

Walking to the table Donovan sat down and put on the gloves.

"Thank you Cardinal McKenna. I will leave you to your reading. Please buzz me," motioning to the intercom, "if you need anything or when you have finished."

Donovan watched as the priest turned and exited through the first door. Picking up a file that sat on top of the stack of documents, he placed it in front of him. He sat there for a minute staring at the folder.

"Cardinal McKenna," said a man's voice interrupting the silence. "I thought I would just ask one more time if you have everything you need before you begin."

It took McKenna a second to register where the voice was coming from, then he remembered the intercom.

"Yes … thank you. I have everything I need."

Donovan now had to accept the truth. This wasn't a dream. The Bible has long warned mankind they would be deceived by false prophets unless they kept the commandments.

He had to learn everything he could about P2. Checking the time, he put on his glasses and began reading.

CHAPTER **SIXTY-THREE**

Anthony had been keeping an eye on the time. "We should head out, Nelli. It's about a thirty-minute drive from the villa to the airport. I'd like to be there before Mary Ellen's plane lands."

"Gradara Castle is between here and the airport in Rimini. After we pick her up I thought we could stop and tour the fortress and see if the chapel really exists."

"That's a good idea."

"Help me gather up all the information on Gradara and we will take it with us," said Anthony.

Neither of them spoke as they drove away from the villa down the gravel road past the cypress trees that stood guard. When they reached the stone archway, Nelli looked over at Anthony.

"What if our suspicions are right Anthony? What if the private chapel does exist? Do you think the box could be hidden somewhere inside it?"

As he turned left onto Autostrada Adriatica, Anthony had also been wondering the same thing. He would need to contact Mattithyahu and the others. They'd need a plan to sneak the box out and get Nelli somewhere safe.

"Let's take it one step at a time. First we'll see if the chapel even exists, and if it does, does it match up with the drawing we saw in the book."

They both started watching for the signs to the airport, then they saw airport 1 km. Anthony looked for a cell phone area to wait at until Mary Ellen called that her plane had landed.

At the same time the flight attendant was welcoming the

passengers on Alitalia flight 7212 to Rimini and Federico Fellini International Airport. The flight was short but Mary Ellen had managed to read through most of the file Cardinal McKenna had delivered to her this morning.

If you drew a timeline between the money transfers by the Vatican Bank, the travel records of its president, and the reports of the sexual abuse cases against priests, there were a lot of red flags popping up. It wasn't just the last few months either; it now appeared to have been going on for years and it seemed to be escalating. It was becoming more and more evident a well thought out plan was being executed.

Mary Ellen stared out the window as they taxied to the gate. The world seemed to be carrying on as usual. Planes were lined up to take off while others were coming in for a landing. The baggage handlers were loading and unloading bags. While waiting for people to get their luggage down from the overhead bins, she sent a text message to Anthony's phone: The plane just landed. I'll call when I have my bag.

"Is it from Mary Ellen? Has her plane landed?" asked Nelli.

"Yes, she'll call us when she has her bag."

"Do you think she'll sense something's going on Anthony?"

"I don't know why she would. All she knows is we're here to see where Dad was born, and that I am combining it with a little research."

Ten minutes later Anthony's phone rang again.

"Hello, Mary Ellen. That was quick," said Anthony.

"Hi, I know. I have my bag."

"We're pulling out of the cell phone lot now. We'll be there shortly. Which door are you at?"

"Let's see, looks like number four."

Two sets of eyes watched Mary Ellen as she headed outside of the baggage claim area. The first set belonged to a young man from Rimini. Thomas hoped that the warning that had been sent to Ms. O'Farrell would have scared her enough to stop her from looking any further into her brother's innocence. Unfortunately, that did not happen.

Then there was the new development of her relationship with Cardinal McKenna. The positions they both held within the Vatican could create problems for P2, and no problem was too small to ignore.

Before eliminating the problem, Thomas wanted to learn as much as he could, on what this woman might be up to, so he had someone sent to follow her. The terrain in the area she was visiting could be treacherous. It would be unfortunate if she and her friends lost control of their car on one of the curvy roads through the mountains.

The second set of eyes belonged to the Guardian Y'hochanan, Hebrew for John, one of the twelve Guardians. He watched as Anthony and Nelli's car pulled up. Mary Ellen saw them and started walking towards the car.

Simultaneously Y'hochanan noticed a young man moving in on Mary Ellen, grabbing a scarf off a chair, he started running, "Signorina! Signorina! Scusi."

The other man stopped as Mary Ellen turned around to see who was yelling at her.

"You dropped your scarf, signorina." Mary Ellen looked at the scarf, then back at Y'hochanan and smiled.

"Grazie signore, but this doesn't belong to me. Someone else must have dropped it."

Anthony watched what was happening. He jumped out of the car and came around to the other side. "Is there a problem here?" He took a mental picture of the faces of all the people near them.

"No, this man thought I dropped a scarf, but I just told him it didn't belong to me."

Anthony thanked Y'hochanan, not letting on he knew him. Turning to Mary Ellen he said, "We should get going or we could get a ticket. Give me your suitcase." He opened the door for Mary Ellen to get in, then grabbed her suitcase and put it in the trunk.

Y'hochanan immediately starting searching the area for the young man but he was gone. He needed to call Cephas and report what just happened and get instructions.

"Good to see you, Mary Ellen. What was that all about?" asked Nelli.

"Oh, that man thought I dropped my scarf. I wish it was mine, it was beautiful."

The airport was extremely busy. Anthony was trying to find an opening between the cars to pull out. He wanted to get away from the airport as quickly as possible. Y'hochanan must have spotted something suspicious and Anthony needed to find out what it was that had frightened him.

"Thank you again for inviting me for the weekend," said Mary Ellen from the backseat as she buckled her seat belt in. "It will be nice to see where your father was born. I know very little about this part of Italy."

Anthony found an opening and sped away, getting as much distance between him and the airport as possible. Then he checked the rearview mirror to see if anyone was following them.

"Sorry, Mary Ellen, I just wanted to get out of that traffic jam. Did you have any problems with your flight?"

"No, everything went smoothly. What do you two have planned for this afternoon, if you don't mind me asking?

"We thought we could stop at Gradara. It is halfway between the airport and Pesaro."

"Isn't that where the fortress of Gradara is located?" asked Mary Ellen. "I've heard people talk about it and I've seen pictures. I would love to see it. If I remember correctly Dante writes about the tragic story of the two lovers that took place there in his book, Dante's Inferno."

"Mary Ellen," Anthony said, "has anything else happened since we saw you last?" He looked in the rearview mirror to watch her reaction to his question.

Hesitating Mary Ellen looked down at her hands adjusting the watch on her wrist. Looking up she said, "No, nothing."

Then he saw it. Most people would never even notice. It was very subtle but when Mary Ellen was scared or telling a lie, her cheek would twitch ever so slightly.

"I'm glad to hear that," but Anthony knew she was lying.

CHAPTER **SIXTY-FOUR**

Thomas was on the phone talking with the bank in Switzerland as he stood on the balcony overlooking hills that formed a patchwork made up of vineyards, cultivated fields, and valleys as far as the eye could see.

"The five recipients we have set up accounts for have received their access numbers," he said. "The bank should see activity on them if they haven't already. Please inform me when the last one has been activated."

He could see a storm was moving in.

"Yes of course," said an elegantly spoken gentleman on the other end. "How would you like us to contact you on this matter?"

"Please send me a text message on the private cell phone number you have for me," said Thomas.

"We will contact you as soon as we get information," replied the banker. "Will there be anything else we can assist you with today?"

"No, that is all." Thomas ended the call.

It's finally begun, he thought. As he went down the check-list he made, his thoughts turned to the call he received late last night from Cardinal Cavallari. The cardinal relayed in detail his meeting with Cardinal McKenna and was troubled that McKenna was spending so much time in the Vatican Archives. The cardinal was also concerned with a growing relationship between Cardinal McKenna and this O'Farrell woman.

Thomas had expected the warning he had sent to Cardinal McKenna and Ms. O'Farrell would frighten them enough that they would stop asking questions, especially after the news of Father Roberto's death. Anyway, it was too late now for them to stop what was about to take place. In a few days their feeble attempts to `gather information wouldn't matter anymore, that and if they would even be alive.

Thomas decided to contact Catherine the Worthy Matron from the Grand Lodge Droit Humain and requested that she find someone trustworthy to follow Ms. O'Farrell. At this point it was only a minor concern but he couldn't leave any stone unturned. Ms. O'Farrell was in Pesaro, not in Vatican City. She was with friends not conspiring with Cardinal McKenna. What trouble could she cause? Still it was better to cover all his bases.

His private cell phone buzzed alerting him to an incoming message. It was from the bank in Switzerland: *We have just received the request to activate the last of the five accounts. We are sending text message per your instructions.*

Thomas checked one more item off his list. He knew by the end of today each of the five men would be given their final orders. Wait for Peter Romanus to be named Pope, after which General D'Amoto's men would immediately take control of all governments around the world.

The Grand Master would take the name Peter II, fulfilling the prophecy of Saint Malachy where he refers to a Petrus Romanus (Peter the Roman) as the last of the Popes, whose pontificate will end in the destruction of the city of Rome.

After being able to check off two more items on his list, it was time for Thomas to call in and report to the Grand Master.

CHAPTER SIXTY-FIVE

In a secret location outside Pesaro, Peter was at the P2 compound in the Apennines where Thomas would join him later. The estate in Arezzo was too accessible for this stage of the operation. A war room had been set up on the second floor of the compound's main house.

Walking out onto the balcony, he lit a cigarette and waited for Thomas's call. In the distance he could see the outline of the old abbey and cemetery built centuries ago. He had heard that a recluse order of religious monks still occupied the abbey. He felt like a king surveying his kingdom. How many times has he stood here looking out at the rolling hills and mountains of the Apennines and thought about this moment?

It had been much easier than the last time, Peter thought to himself. The Vatican was alarmed at the number of people leaving the Church. The cover-up of the sexual scandals had been their biggest mistake. All Peter did was leak information out through the news media, and Catholics around the world became outraged and lost faith in their religious leaders.

Then there were the jihadists and their hatred of Christianity. Funding various terrorist groups around the world had put their leaders under his control. Religious battles weren't new but the world was much smaller now and the push of a button could annihilate a whole civilization in a matter of minutes. He was the Puppet Master. He controlled the strings and he had everyone exactly where he wanted them.

His mind shifted to more pleasant thoughts. He could

almost feel the triregnum being placed on his head. Pope John Paul I had dispensed with the 1,000-year-old tradition of a papal coronation and the wearing of a papal tiara. Peter intended on resurrecting the ceremony in retaliation for the dead Pope's role in almost destroying his organization.

Next he pictured himself standing in the Crying Room being dressed for his first audience as Pope Peter II. Then he visualized stepping out onto the balcony that overlooked St. Peter's Square to the mass of souls waiting for the new Pope's blessing. The phone rang, interrupting his thoughts. It was Thomas, right on schedule.

"Thomas, punctual as I demand, is everything in order on your end?"

Thomas wondered if he should waste the Grand Master's time with the McKenna and O'Farrell problem; he decided against it. The Naj Hannah expected him to handle the small matters.

"Yes, the last account was activated. I am waiting to receive calls from each of the five that they have completed their task. Then they will wait for your call."

"We are very close now," said Peter. "I do not intend to fail this time. Victory will be mine."

His tone sent a chill through Thomas.

"Call me when you are on your way," said Peter.

The call was over and Thomas wondered if he had made the right decision by not telling the Grand Master.

Peter took another drag off his cigarette and slowly blew the smoke into the air as he went through the final details in his head. Details even Thomas knew nothing about. The orders had already been given to his personal bodyguards or death squad. As he put out the cigarette with his right hand, he could feel the tattoo beneath his ring come alive.

CHAPTER **SIXTY-SIX**

Anthony listened as Mary Ellen and Nelli talked but his attention was focused on watching the road to see if there were any cars following them a little too closely.

There was a letup in the conversation so Nelli checked the map to see how much farther they had to go before they would reach the castle.

"We should start to see signs for the fortress Gradara fairly soon," said Nelli. "After we get inside, should we stop and have a light lunch before we start exploring the castle?"

Stopping for lunch wouldn't be a bad idea, thought Anthony. He could make some calls and find out what Y'hochanan saw at the airport.

"That's a good idea. Does that sound all right with you, Mary Ellen?" Anthony looked in the rearview mirror to see Mary Ellen's response.

"That's fine with me. I could do with a little something to eat."

Nelli glanced over at Anthony, "We can study the map of the fortress while we are eating."

Anthony gave Nelli an understanding nod. They needed to see the chapel to determine if it still existed.

Nelli turned again to talk with Mary Ellen. "We thought it would be nice to explore the castle first if you don't mind."

"I'm open to anything, I'm just happy to be on holiday. I live here now remember. You have to head back home next week so your time is more limited. You must have a list of things you want to see and do before you have to leave."

As Nelli was listening she felt the temperature in the car drop dramatically and she crossed her arms to keep warm. All of a sudden she felt this impending threat as if something evil was in the car with them but just as quickly as the temperature dropped, it rose back to where it was a minute ago and the feeling was gone. Whatever it was, it was unholy and she did not want to experience it again.

Repeating the question Mary Ellen asked, "Have you made a list of things you want to see before you go back home? Whatever you would like to do is fine with me."

Nelli realized she had not responded to Mary Ellen's question.

"I'm sorry, Mary Ellen, I was thinking about something. Yes, there are a few things Anthony and I would like to see before we leave."

Nelli saw that they were approaching a mileage sign. "Look Anthony," Nelli said as she pointed out the window, "Gradara one kilometer, exit on Strada Ferrata. Remember we drove by this yesterday."

The road wound through hills covered with acres of olive tree groves with row after row of neatly tied vines where grapes hung heavy waiting to be picked. As they rounded the next hill they caught their first view of the fortress in the distance.

"Look, there it is," said Mary Ellen. "It's larger then I imagined and that structure at the top must be the castle."

Nelli read from the travel guide, "Casement walls hold twenty-four towers outlining the city that encompasses the entire top half of the mountain. One side overlooks the Adriatic while the other overlooks a valley and the River Tavollo. At 142 meters above sea level the panoramic view is spectacular."

Could the box really be up there, thought Nelli, as she stared at Gradara Castle? Could something written so long ago still exist, just waiting for her to find it?

Anthony was also wondering if the young monk Fernando Martins de Bulfoes did hide a box somewhere inside the castle and where would he have hidden it?

Mary Ellen watched silently as they approached the walled city. She thought about her most recent conversations with Cardinal McKenna. He now believed there was the possibility of a conspiracy to bring down the Church. She wanted to tell Anthony and Nelli, but would they believe her? She had lost him once because of her desire to prove her brother's innocence; she didn't want to lose his friendship this time around. The lies against her brother might only be the tip of an iceberg. What lay beneath the surface could be apocalyptic. They could be looking at what many already believe could be the beginning of the end-times.

They got lucky and found a parking spot not far from the entrance to the medieval village. They entered through the Porta dell'Orologio, the clock door, the only opening into the fortress. Beyond the door was a series of steep steps carrying them up a street that was bordered by buildings and side streets. As they climbed the steps their eyes were directed to the tower or "keep" in the distance, which was also the highest point of the fortress.

Anthony studied the map, looking for a place they could stop to get something to eat. It wasn't as crowded with people as he expected for a Friday. It would make it easier for him to observe if anyone was following them. As they walked Mary Ellen asked about the box Nelli had purchased in Rome. Had she found out any more surrounding the story the shopkeeper had relayed about its history.

As Anthony listened, Nelli told Mary Ellen that they realized the monk the shopkeeper spoke of was actually their namesake before he received sainthood. He observed a sudden change in Mary Ellen's demeanor. She thought no one would notice her surprise at what she had just learned. No one else would have except for Anthony, who knew her too well.

Mary Ellen sensed Anthony was looking at her as she nervously glanced at him and then realized what he was staring at. Raising her hand, she covered her cheek. She knew he had noticed the almost undetectable muscle spasm that occurred whenever she was nervous or scared. Besides members of her family, Anthony was the only other person who ever noticed the twitch. He had always teased her about it.

"Coincidence isn't it?" said Anthony, not taking his eyes off Mary Ellen.

She knew Anthony was suspicious that she was covering up something. Should she forget about what they might think of her and tell them what she had discovered and about her conversation with Cardinal McKenna? Removing her hand from her face she stopped and turned to face Anthony.

"I don't know if I believe in coincidence anymore," she said crossing her arms. She waited for Anthony to respond but he didn't utter a word.

She stuck her hands into her pockets. She'd forgotten how well he knew her. "I believe God has given each of us a special calling in life. If we choose to listen to that inner voice, He will be a guiding hand along the way and lead us to what we seek."

Anthony nodded. Could Mary Ellen know about Nelli and about what they were looking for? Could she be working against them? His mind was exploding with possible scenarios but he became distracted by a family up ahead. Two young children were crying because they didn't want to leave yet. The parents were trying to calm them down.

As Anthony scanned the crowd and took a mental photograph of all the people, one in particular caught his attention. He was average in height, had dark hair, and was a physically fit man. He seemed unusually distracted. You could see he was agitated by the commotion and was trying to make his way around the family.

He now headed directly towards Anthony, at the same time reaching inside his jacket to grab something from an inside pocket. Anthony was trying to anticipate his next move.

A few yards apart they locked eyes. The man found what he was looking for. He nodded to Anthony as he pulled his hand from beneath his jacket. Anthony's eyes darted to the man's hand.

In it he held a white linen handkerchief with a red border. He wiped his forehead and his neck, and then replaced the handkerchief back into his breast pocket. The Guardian was giving a warning signal to be on the alert. Anthony had no idea what the danger might be, but things had just changed. He needed to confront Mary Ellen and see what she knew and the sooner the better. Lunch would have to wait.

Studying the map he looked for a place where they could talk, away from prying eyes and ears. Not far ahead, if he was correct, the medieval church of Saint Giovanni Battista would be on the right. It was a good place to seek some privacy. Hopefully it wouldn't be very crowded.

"If it's all right with both of you, before we stop and get something to eat, I'd like to stop and see a wooden crucifix, by an unknown sculptor that hangs above the altar in the church just ahead," said Anthony. "It is said that Christ's face, bowing on the right shoulder, shows three expressions according to the side you view it from. From the right he looks to be suffering. From the center, in death throes, and from the left, dead. The church should be up there just on the right."

Nelli was surprised by Anthony's request but saw how her brother's demeanor had changed. Something must have happened. She needed to trust he had a good reason, so played along.

"That's fine with me, Anthony."

"Mary Ellen, do you have your Vatican I.D. on you?" asked Anthony.

"Yes, I have it in my purse. Why?" asked Mary Ellen.

"I was thinking perhaps they might allow us access to some of the private areas of the church not open to the general public."

"Well, we can always ask and see what they say," said Mary Ellen.

Upon entering the church they saw a few people sitting in pews praying. A small group of nuns were standing in front of the wooden crucifix examining it from different angles. There were two priests; the younger of the two was placing a chalice into the tabernacle behind the altar while the other one was talking to a woman in the first pew.

"Mary Ellen, why don't you go talk with one of the priests and tell them you work at the Vatican and ask if we could tour the parts of the church off limits to the public," Anthony suggested.

Mary Ellen decided to talk to the older priest who seemed to be finishing his conversation with an elderly woman. The priest placed his hand on the woman's head and closing his eyes said a blessing over her. When he opened his eyes again, he made the sign of the cross and smiled lovingly at the old woman who slowly got up and thanked the priest.

Mary Ellen started walking towards the priest standing in the front of the church. As the priest waved goodbye to the old woman, he sensed Mary Ellen approaching. Turning, he calmly walked to the end of the pew to greet the approaching visitor.

"Welcome to Saint Giovanni. You have a question for me signorina?"

He reminded her of Cardinal McKenna. It seemed inconceivable that something evil could be at work to destroy all this.

"I have a sense you carry a heavy burden," said the priest, breaking the silence, "but that is not what you came to ask me about."

Mary Ellen was caught off guard by his comment, composing herself she asked, "Father if I may be so bold to request a favor?"

"Of course my child, if this humble servant of God is able to assist you, I will do what I can."

"Thank you Father."

Anthony and Nelli watched from the back of the church as Mary Ellen and the priest talked. Turning to Anthony, Nelli asked, "Why are we wasting our time coming here? We should be seeing if the chapel still exists and if it has a statue of Saint Anthony."

"It's evident to me Mary Ellen is hiding something from us," said Anthony. "I also received information we could be in danger."

"What are you talking about? How, when?"

Nelli glanced to see if Mary Ellen was still talking with the priest, and then looked back at Anthony for an explanation.

"I told you the other Guardians are never far away. I wanted to find a place to confront her and see what it is she is concealing. Maybe Mary Ellen is part of a plot to stop you from getting the box. I can't rule anything out."

"You can't be serious Anthony, Mary Ellen! She's the first woman to be appointed to a position of authority in the Vatican."

"What better cover to have access to the inner workings of Vatican City. She's headed back our way. Let me handle this."

"We're very fortunate," said Mary Ellen, "the priest was aware of my appointment and has the honor of knowing a couple of the cardinals that I work with at the Vatican. I also told him Anthony, that you were advising on a restoration project at the Vatican."

"Thank you, Mary Ellen." Anthony motioned for her to lead the way.

"Father Cossa, these are my friends Antonella and Anthony Andruccioli. As I mentioned they are visiting Italy to see the place where their father was born."

"Ah, is your father with you?" asked the priest as he looked around the church to see where he might be sitting.

"No Father, I'm sorry to say he passed away a few months ago," said Anthony.

"I'm so sorry for your loss, but know he is now in heaven with his Father. I will remember to keep him in my prayers. Ms. O'Farrell tells me you are an architect, signore Anthony."

"Yes, that is correct, Father."

Turning his attention to Nelli, the priest asked, "May I inquire what path you have chosen in your life, signorina Andruccioli?"

Nelli was a little surprised by his question.

"I am a professor of history," she answered.

"Eccellente! You both pay honor to your patron saint." Father Cossa saw the surprise in their eyes. "You were both named after Saint Anthony, si?"

"Yes but ...." Nelli began to say.

"Antonella is the Italian female version of the name Anthony, si?" he looked at Nelli with a twinkle in his eye.

"How did you know that?"

"Just a guess, but I see I was right." A smile spread across the priest's face. "Names have always been of interest to me. When a child is named after a saint they will watch over the child throughout their life here on earth.

"Our beloved Saint Anthony is known as the finder of lost items. Both of you are seekers of history befitting to your patron saint. Perhaps you will discover something that is lost! You must visit the statue of Saint Anthony that is in a small chapel inside the castle."

Anthony and Nelli couldn't believe what the priest just said. The chapel did exist! Neither of them spoke but they each gave each other a quick glance. Something more powerful than them was guiding them in the right direction.

"This chapel that you speak of, is it open to the public?" asked Anthony.

"No, but I will make a call and arrange for you to go inside. With Ms. O'Farrell's credentials there should be no problem."

"Grazie, what can we do to show our gratitude for your kindness?" asked Nelli.

"Please, allow this priest the honor of making your trip a memorable one. I have spent much time within these walls and studied the history of this medieval fortress. If you would allow me to be your guide I can pass on what I have learned. Perhaps God, in his infinite wisdom, planned for our paths to cross."

CHAPTER SIXTY-SEVEN

Father Cossa showed the three of them to a private room off the sacristy before going to make his call. Nelli and Mary Ellen sat down and Anthony decided to stand off to the side by the door. There was no other way out except through the door they used to enter the church.

Could he have been fooled by this woman he wanted to marry at one time? Anthony had to consider it a possibility. He could not explain what had just happened with Father Cossa other than divine guidance but time was running out and he needed to know what Mary Ellen's involvement might be in all of this. Does she know about Nelli? Could she be an enemy?

Mary Ellen could feel his eyes on her. The growing tension between them couldn't be ignored much longer. She felt terrible hiding what she knew from both of them. Maybe it was just her imagination that he seemed suspicious of her? She glanced over to where Anthony was standing. He'd been waiting for her to look over at him.

"You're hiding something from us, Mary Ellen. I plan to find out what it is before we leave this room."

She was surprised by the allegation. For a second, time stood still. Her mind raced as she tried to figure out where to begin with what she and Cardinal McKenna had learned so far and what they were afraid could be happening.

"The morning after Father Roberto's death, a file was delivered to my office. It was from him and contained documents pertaining to Devlin's case," she said, relieved to finally be able to confess what she had been hiding from them.

"He knew of my ongoing mission to exonerate my brother. In the file were documents I had never seen before, documents suggesting that something peculiar was going on. I immediately made an appointment with Cardinal McKenna. At that meeting, I learned that the cardinal also had a file delivered to him from Father Roberto that same morning.

"We are both worried that what Father Roberto stumbled on could have possibly gotten him killed. By trying to prove Devlin innocent, I might have accidently uncovered a much more sinister plot. It could be the beginning of a battle for all of our souls."

She waited now to see how they would react. Would they think she had lost her mind?

Nelli leaned forward and grasped Mary Ellen's hands in between hers. Looking into Mary Ellen's eyes she knew everything she needed to know. She could see that she was telling the truth and was terrified.

Of course Nelli already knew what the world was facing. Smiling warmly at Mary Ellen she said, "Don't be afraid, Anthony and I are right here with you."

Nelli looked over at her brother and Guardian. He knew by her look that he no longer needed to doubt Mary Ellen's loyalty.

"I don't know exactly what you have uncovered Mary Ellen, but there isn't time to get into it now before Father Cossa returns," said Anthony.

"You need to know that Cardinal McKenna received the same card with the cobra head on it as I did," blurted out Mary Ellen. "They also found one lying next to the body of Father Roberto."

At that moment Anthony realized that whoever or whatever they were dealing with had no intention of allowing his sister to find the box.

They heard Father Cossa's footsteps coming down the hallway. "Anthony, one last thing," whispered Mary Ellen, "Cardinal McKenna believes we could be looking at a worldwide conspiracy to destroy the Catholic Church."

Anthony concluded Mary Ellen had no idea that Nelli was the Chosen One but she could be a valuable source of information.

"Mary Ellen, Father Cossa will be coming through the door any moment and there's a lot you don't know. I ask that you do everything I tell you without questioning why."

Father Cossa was now just outside the door and they could hear him talking to someone.

"Si, si, grazie. It will be my turn next, arrivederci."

Anthony glared at Mary Ellen for her answer.

In a quiet voice and looking worried, Mary Ellen answered, "Of course Anthony, I've been completely honest with you, and I will do as you ask."

Father Cossa walked through the door.

"Ah, my new friends, it is all arranged. Per favore, please, follow me."

They followed the priest but he was not headed towards the door through which they entered the church.

"Father the exit to the street is that way," Anthony said in Italian.

"You speak Italian, morte bien! I am taking you a way that few people ever have the opportunity to experience. The back wall of the church is actually part of the wall that surrounds the whole fortress and Gradara Castle. I don't know if you are aware of how the walls of a fortress were constructed at that time in history."

"Are you speaking of casement walls?" said Anthony.

"Si, si, very good! Did you know in ancient times many poor and outcasts lived in between the walls?"

"I have read about that," said Anthony. "There is of course the famous story in the Bible of the Battle of Jericho."

"A wonderful example," said Father Cossa. "A prostitute by the name of Rahab lived in the walls of the city and hid the spies that Joshua had sent to learn the best time to attack the city. She agreed to cover for them on condition that she and her family would be spared in the upcoming battle. The spies agree provided, three conditions were met: One, she must distinguish her house from the others so the soldiers will know which one to spare. Second, her family must be inside the house during the battle, and third, she must not later turn on the spies.

"God spoke to Joshua telling him to march around the city once every day for six days with the seven priests carrying ram's horns in front of the ark. On the seventh day, they were to march around the city seven times, and the priests were to blow their ram's horns.

"This Joshua did, and he commanded his people not to

give a war cry until he told them to do so. On the seventh day, after marching around the city the seventh time, the priests sounded their ram's horns, and Joshua ordered the people to shout.

"During the seven days, they distracted their enemies while they snuck soldiers into the walls to wait for the command to attack. The walls of the city collapsed, and the Israelites were able to charge straight into the city.

"Jericho was completely destroyed, and every man, woman, and child in it was killed. Only Rahab and her family were spared because she had hidden the two spies sent by Joshua. After this Joshua burned the remains of the city and cursed any man who would rebuild the city of Jericho would do so at the cost of his firstborn son."

"Today is your lucky day. The walls were also escape routes for the ruling families during their reign. It can be a maze for one that does not know their way around in them, so follow closely."

Entering what appeared to be the storage room of the church, there were tapestries hanging on the walls, boxes of candles, and altar linens everywhere—all the items necessary for offering mass throughout the year.

Waving for them to follow him, Father Cossa walked towards a large tapestry hanging on the wall to his right. He lifted up one side of the wall hanging, directing Anthony to hold it. To everyone's surprise there was a door hidden behind it. Taking out an old key from under his cassock, he unlocked the door and gestured to Mary Ellen, Nelli, and Anthony to pass through.

Grabbing an ancient-looking kerosene lantern that hung from a hook on the wall next to the door, the priest lifted the glass chimney, lit the wick, and adjusted the flame. Closing the door and locking it behind him, the tapestry fell back in place and covered the door—making it look like they had never been there.

"The space between the interior wall and outer wall was called the killing field," Father Cossa explained as he led the small party of guests, "and could be anywhere from eight to twenty feet in width. It was a term that originated in medieval warfare to describe areas within castles specially designed to bunch attackers, who had breached the outer wall, into an area where the defenders could kill them easily through 'arrow loops' and 'murder holes.'"

Father Cossa continued, "You have undoubtedly noticed, we are walking uphill as we make are way to the "keep", which is the highest point of the walled city and forms the heart of the castle. It was the most defended area and usually the main habitat for the noble or lord."

"Is that where the chapel is?" asked Nelli.

"Yes, but before reaching the chapel there are a few interesting details I would like to point out. Just ahead we will pass by a spiral stairwell that took the soldier up to another level to where slits in the walls allowed for arrows to be shot, the arrow loops I mentioned just a minute ago, and where hot oil or boiling water would be dropped through murder holes onto the invading enemy."

"Father Cossa, I remembered reading about something called a trick step," said Anthony.

"Si, ingenious idea," said the priest. "They are usually located halfway up or near the top of the stairwell. They are also called a 'stumble step.' They would make one or two steps with a different rise height or thread depth. Can you imagine running up the steps wearing a suit of armor, then coming upon a trick step? The weight of the armor would throw the enemy off balance giving soldiers at the top of the stairs another advantage over their enemies."

They hadn't gone much further when Father Cossa suddenly stopped and held the lantern out in front of him and said, "We've reached our destination."

The three of them were confused, the only thing around them were dirt floors and stone walls. They watched as the priest walked over to the wall and started looking for something.

Mary Ellen whispered to the others, "What is he doing?"

Anthony was about to say something when they saw Father Cossa stop and remove a loose stone from the wall. He reached inside, they heard something, then a section of the wall moved and behind it was another door.

Surprised at what he saw, Anthony asked, "Where will this take us?"

"It leads into the sitting room off of the sleeping quarters. The chapel is on the other side of the sleeping chamber." Unlocking the door, Father Cossa pushed it open and standing there stood another priest.

"Benvenuto, avanti avanti, I see you remembered your way Father," the second priest began to chuckle. "Welcome to Gradara Castle, you've chosen wisely with this one," nodding his head and raising his eyebrows towards Father Cossa. "He knows the history of this castle better than anyone and still believes there are secrets that have not been discovered within its ancient walls. Isn't that right, Father? Come, I will take you to see the chapel, a beautiful example of the Renaissance period."

CHAPTER SIXTY-EIGHT

Thomas had arrived at P2's compound a few hours ago. After reporting to Peter with the latest developments, he was excused to initiate the next stage of the plan.

As he exited the war room, the Grand Master's two henchmen stood guard at the door; each of them had to be close to seven feet tall. They were dressed in the ceremonial black robes, their heads covered with the all too familiar black hood embroidered with the head of a cobra. They were perfect examples of what the human body could achieve with self-determination and a rigorous exercise program. Thomas had to keep in mind that one of them probably killed Father Roberto. Being in their presence always made you wonder who might be the next name on the list for elimination.

They stood at attention with one hand resting on the handle of the ax that hung from a belt around their waist, and the other hand holding onto a Steyr TMP semi-automatic pistol. Thomas had no idea who the two men were, but knew they had been handpicked by Peter, as were the other ten disciples. He always wanted to know why the Grand Master had chosen twelve disciples to surround him but would never dare ask. He personally believed it was to mimic Christ and the twelve apostles.
The way they were standing there, they could have almost passed for statues. Normally he didn't give them a second thought but today he felt somewhat threatened by their presence.

Thomas thought it had gotten awfully warm as he wiped the perspiration from his forehead with the back of his hand. Glancing over at the two guards, the only thing that moved were their eyes peering out from behind two black holes cut into each hood.

Then he had the feeling something horrible was going to happen. "Don't be so paranoid, you're just exhausted," he told himself. He had no reason to worry. He had been Peter Romanus's right-hand man since the beginning and nothing had changed.

Back in the war room, Peter was on the phone and not happy with the information he just received.

"He asked you to find someone you could trust to follow this woman and report back to him? Is that correct?" said Peter to the person on the other end of the phone.

"Yes, I assumed the order came from you?"

Catherine waited for Peter to reply but there was only silence on the other end of the phone. Then she heard a clock chiming in the background.

Peter ignored her question asking, "Is everything set on your end?"

"Yes, it won't be long now till the world has a new Pope and leader of the NWO."

Catherine was smart and shrewd, two qualities Peter prized in a person. Charming and beautiful on top of it was a deadly combination, a distraction even for Peter, one he could little afford to take, but he definitely needed to reconsider how to use those assets to his advantage. Right now he had to figure out what to do about Thomas.

While Peter mulled over this problem, he knew each of the five men that made up the inner circle were taking care of the last few details they needed to before claiming the reward for carrying out their part of the plan. Shortly, he would arrange access to the money in the second Swiss bank account that had been set up for each of them. He would decide later what he would do with them.

Over the past few years, each of the men had set up companies around the world under fake names. Everything was in place to have the NWO up and running immediately upon the announcement by the new Pope. In the next twenty-four hours all accounts would be settled in cash and any individuals who could tie any of the members of P2 to the companies would be eliminated.

News coverage from around the globe reported almost nonstop of the escalating unrest in the Middle East and growing criticism against the United States and its policies. There continued to be new cases of priests accused of sexual abuse, and the Catholic Church's attempts to deal with the problem. Little did these reporters realize that the stories they were covering were all part of a grand scheme by one man. The five members of P2 each waited in undisclosed locations for the phone call from the Grand Master.

Angelo Acciaiolio as the head of Mediaset quietly had bought up most of the European and Asian markets of commercial broadcasting networks over the last five years. He had also become a major shareholder in other markets including the United States and the Soviet Union. The announcement that would change the course of the world had already been recorded. Angelo was just waiting for the moment he would get the okay to release the statement across the airways.

Silvio Reni, the future Prime Minister of Italy, during the same time period had put together an alliance of individuals with similar views of the direction the world needed to go. They had all sworn a secret oath to support a new requiem with the promise of power and money. A new map of the world and the division of land had already been drawn, each one aware of the territory they would govern. The money Silvio received was used to set up shore accounts for each of these individuals as a thank you for their loyalty.

Vingenzo Parocchi had fulfilled his role by working with Cardinal Cavallari, creating an epidemic out of the sexual abuse scandal in the Church. They were always surprised at the small amount of money it took to buy someone's soul.

Finally General Orazio D'Amoto in many ways had the most difficult job setting up and training secondary armies around the globe. Any resistance to the New World Order, and they had been trained to kill and eliminate the enemy.

These individuals hadn't been driven as much by the money but more by having power. Each of them was now maintaining a low profile. No meetings, not available for calls, pretty much closing themselves off from the world, each waiting for the call.

CHAPTER SIXTY-NINE

The first hour went by way too quickly. Cardinal McKenna read about the history of P2 and its evolution from the Freemasons. It was to be exposed by Pope John Paul I that some clergy had been members of Masonic Lodges. Catholics were forbidden to join a Masonic Lodge in the strongest terms. The Church's position is expressed in its "Declaration on Masonic Associations."

It states in part: "The faithful who enroll in Masonic associations are in a state of grave sin and may not receive Holy Communion." He hadn't even considered it to be an issue any longer but what if P2 had just gone underground?

He continued to read: "The head of this secret society was known by the title Grand Master and had resided in a villa outside of Arezzo. P2 also had a secret location for initiation ceremonies in the Apennine Mountains outside of Pesaro."

Pesaro! That's where Mary Ellen went this weekend to visit her friends. There was a story in the news recently pertaining to the Apennines? What was it? Then he remembered a plane had crashed in a remote section of the Apennine Mountains. The small privately owned jet was believed to have taken off from a small airfield outside of Pesaro carrying a handful of high-ranking dignitaries and heads of some large European companies. Everyone onboard had died.

He couldn't shake the feeling that all of this information could be connected in some bizarre way. Rummaging through the papers, he looked for something he'd read about the initiation ceremony.

"Here it is," pushing the other books aside.

It described the ceremony and the name used to address the Grand Master, "Naj Hannah," when taking the oath. He had never heard the term before. He checked the index to see if it was referenced anywhere else in the book. Turning to page 105, he read every word but didn't find anything useful, then flipped to page 210, underlining each sentence with his finger as he read. He stopped, backed up a few lines. There, Naj Hannah translated means King Cobra! The King Cobra serves as the symbol for P2. The card … the cards Mary Ellen and I received had the embossed head of a king cobra on it! P2 had been resurrected. His blood ran cold. Would he be able to cut off the head of the serpent before it was too late?

Continuing to read, in interviews with two former members they described how they were taken to a compound somewhere in the Apennine Mountains. A twelve-foot wall sealed off the manicured grounds from view. In the center of the main courtyard stands a cobra-like sculpture. Its inflated hood watches over the compound in a protective posture as if ready to strike. The cobra's head is twice the size of a human skull. It has a single eye, which is blue during the day and turns red after nightfall. Inside the cobra's hood and behind its eye is a closed circuit camera.

The camera is controlled from a room within the villa where eight monitors, each with five stations, cover eight guest rooms, a patio, pool, dining room, sitting room, and party room. Approximately ten cameras, including the one inside the cobra, have infrared lenses. Once inside the walls, anything you say or do will be under the watchful eye of the Naj Hannah.

The villa's interior is magnificent. Every room has marble floors and is furnished with antiques. The high ceilings are finely crafted from gold leaf moldings, and portraits of Mussolini, Hitler, and Peron hang on the walls. The visitor experiences a feeling, a sort of living, breathing odor of danger and power that penetrates the soul and cell-by-cell contaminates the mind with fear.

McKenna took off his reading glasses and sat back in his chair. He stared into space, then closed his eyes, "Father, if this is a dream, please wake me from it so your humble servant may continue to preach the words of your Son to those who hunger for His guidance. If this is not a dream, please give me the wisdom and courage to root out the evil forces that would want to destroy your kingdom here on earth."

He knew the answer to his question before he even asked it. Eyes still closed, he quietly recalled the scripture, Mark 13:32: "But of the day and hour no one knows, not even the angels in heaven, nor the Son, but only the Father. Take heed, watch and pray; for you do not know when the time is."

Strangely, he felt an overwhelming sense of peace come over him. If it is God's plan to have him seek out the false prophet then perhaps it is not time yet for God's final return to earth. He would ask the Holy Spirit for guidance.

McKenna now realized it was more than coincidence. He decided to look deeper into this P2.

He now knew what he had to do. Even though he was no longer a young man, he suddenly felt like he did back when he was in his thirties. He was sitting taller in his chair. He felt a renewed strength in his arms and legs, and he had a new awareness of his surroundings. He felt the presence of the Holy Spirit at work.

Reading faster now, he learned that each new disciple of P2 received a mark that would identify him to another member. During the initiation ceremonies they were given a tattoo of a cobra head. It was placed on the top portion of the ring finger of their right hand. Then they were each presented with a gold initial ring that completely covered the tattoo. With a quick twist of the ring they could signal to another member they were one of them.

He remembered noticing some kind of marking on Cardinal Cavallari's ring finger and how he thought that was a strange place for a tattoo.

He needed to contact Mary Ellen. She could be in danger. He also needed to inform the Commander of the Swiss Guard and tell him of his findings, but would the commander believe him?

He pushed the button on the intercom and spoke in a calm voice, "Father I have finished for the day."

The door hissed as it closed behind the Vatican archivist who walked over to the table where McKenna sat. He accounted for each book by checking it off a list on a small handheld device, and then asked Cardinal McKenna for his signature. It struck him that something seemed different about the cardinal but he couldn't put his finger on it. Cardinal McKenna handed the device back to the archivist and stood up.

"Is there anything else?" asked Cardinal McKenna.

"No, that takes care of the paper work," the priest headed to the door.

Reaching the front desk, he turned and faced the cardinal, "If I may have the key Cardinal McKenna, I will retrieve your phone and identification for you."

Handing the cardinal back his things he said, "I hope the materials were helpful."

"Yes, thank you," said McKenna, "I appreciate all your help, grazie."

Upon seeing the cardinal, the two Swiss Guards came to attention. McKenna nodded to them as they filed in behind him. He had to get in touch with Mary Ellen and the commander.

McKenna could hear the flapping of the hem of his cassock as he walked with new determination. He smiled to himself. It had been a long time since he heard that sound. Picturing himself twenty years younger and his passion to serve the Lord, he often remembered thinking the robes slowed him down as he attended to his duties as a young priest.

The guards glanced at each other with an inquisitive look, noting the change in Cardinal McKenna.

CHAPTER **SEVENTY**

"Father Cossa tells me you were both named after our beloved Saint Anthony," said Father Marti with a twinkle in his eye. "This will be a treat for you. Not many people are allowed inside the private chapel. The statue you will see is of a young Saint Anthony.

"Lord Sforza's son, before going off to war, had developed a close relationship with the young monk. After his son's death, Lord Sforza honored that friendship by having a statue made so that they could be together after death. It is believed that there is a relic of Saint Anthony somewhere here in Gradara Castle, but it has never been found."

"As you may or may not already know," interjected Father Cossa, "five years must pass after a person's death before he or she can be considered for declaration of formal sainthood, unless the Pope grants a special dispensation, which Pope Gregory IX did making the canonization of Saint Anthony the quickest in the history of the Catholic Church, just one year after his death.

"In 1263 his body was transferred in the presence of Saint Bonaventure, minister general at the time, to a chapel to be named after him. When the vault in which for thirty years his sacred body had reposed was opened the flesh was found reduced to dust but the tongue uninjured, fresh, and of a lively red color. It is said that Saint Bonaventure, beholding this wonder, took the tongue affectionately in his hands and kissed it, exclaiming: 'O Blessed Tongue that always praised the Lord, and made others bless Him, now it is evident what great merit thou hast before God.' To this day, his tongue is in a reliquary and is incorrupt. The tongue glistens and looks as if it is still alive and moist." Father Cossa shook his head in amazement, "The ways of the Lord never fail to mystify me."

As Nelli, Anthony, and Mary Ellen listened to the priest, they walked through the wardrobe room and were now in the main hall of the castle. Father Cossa continued to expound on what he had learned through his studies. This time it was about the castle itself.

"The early halls inside castles were aisled like a church, with rows of stone pillars supporting the timber and stone roofs. Some of the windows had wooden shutters secured by an iron bar. A few of the windows had 'white (greenish) glass' a new concept at the time. By the fourteenth century glazed windows would be common."

They could tell he was enjoying being able to educate them on the history of Gradara Castle. Up ahead a museum guide was describing the history of a large tapestry hanging on the wall to a group of tourists. Anthony took a mental inventory of the people in the group. There were two older couples that looked as if they were traveling together and a young couple, starry- eyed, probably on their honeymoon. Then there were six young men and women, probably college students backpacking their way across Europe. Behind them were two very attractive women, Anthony guessed somewhere in their thirties. One of the women, who had beautiful long hair black as night and eyes to match, glanced over when Anthony and his small entourage walked by. Indifferent, the woman turned her attention back to the tour guide.

Finally at the tail end of the group were two men Anthony recognized. They pretended not to notice him as they listened intently to the tour guide. Anthony liked knowing another Guardian was never far away.

Since activating the GPS chips that had been implanted in all twelve of the Guardians as young men, they knew everyone's location at all times. Anthony never believed they would ever need to have use for the tracking devices.

"Anthony did you feel that cold blast of air," whispered Nelli, pulling her sweater tighter around her body. It wasn't as much a question as it was a statement. She started looking around to see where the draft might be coming from.

He couldn't figure out what his sister was talking about. It was warm and the air was stagnant inside the castle but he could see Nelli seemed worried. He immediately began canvassing the area.

A woman from another group started to look away before Anthony saw that she had been watching him and Nelli. But, out of the corner of his eye, he caught the last of the woman's long raven hair as it gently fell around her shoulders. He knew she had been watching them.

"Anthony, perhaps you have something to add?" said Father Cossa.

Startled by the question, Anthony hadn't heard anything the priest had said for the last few minutes.

"No, Father you are doing a wonderful job. I am enjoying listening," said Anthony.

So Father Cossa continued to expound on the latest structure they were passing through.

"We are now walking under a covered external passageway called a pentice," he explained. This covered passageway joined the bedchamber to the chapel. This castle is a little more unusual since the Lord and Lady's Chamber was in a separate wing at the dais end of the hall, and the pentice we are now walking through takes us to the chapel."

Just ahead they could see a door. Reaching it Father Cossa stopped and turned around to face his small audience. Smiling he said, "Here we are."

The door looked like one of the wooden window shutters with its hinges made out of the iron bars. The only difference was there was a small wooden cross mounted on the front of the door.

Nelli and Anthony gave each other a quick glance, each speculating if they would find the ancient box on the other side of the door?

CHAPTER SEVENTY-ONE

"As you can see a metal gate now protects the entrance to the chapel," said Father Marti as he pulled out a key to unlock it. "It was added to stop tourists from trying to get inside the church. At certain times of the year the door to the chapel is kept opened so visitors can look through the gate to get a bird's eye view of the inside, and see where Lord Sforza and his wife came every morning for mass. You will have the privilege of going inside and seeing it up close."

As he placed the key into the lock there was the sound of the chamber disengaging, then the grating of metal against metal as he swung open the gate. He paused for a moment, and then slowly opened the ancient door to the chapel with the simple wooden cross on it.

Father Marti was the first to go inside and motioned for the others to follow. As the rest of them entered the chapel, it felt as if they had stepped back in time.

"You will notice it is two stories high, a popular design of the thirteenth century," said Father Cossa. "The Lord and his family sat in the balcony during the prayer service while the staff sat below on wooden benches.

"At the east end of the nave you can see the wooden altar with the crucifix above it, that area of the nave is called the chancel, the holiest part of the chapel. Just before the chancel there is a perpendicular corridor called the 'transept,' so the floor plan, if you looked at it from above, would look like a Latin cross, shaped like a crucifix … I am sure you already know all this Anthony," said Father Cossa smiling, "since architecture is your specialty."

Anthony and Nelli tried to appear interested but their eyes were scanning the room for any resemblance of a box that looked like the one Nelli bought in Rome. Anthony wanted to keep the attention off of him and Nelli so he light heartily said, "Please, Father, it would be a pleasure if I could be the student and you the teacher."

Father Cossa beamed, "Grazie, signore Anthony."

"The chapel was an indispensable feature of every castle at that time. Mass was said every morning and it was usually located close to the bed chamber or 'solar,' as it was called back then, for the convenience of the lord and his family.

"You will notice the walls are thick and made from stone, allowing the Romans to make use of Greek innovations in architectural ideas such as the post-and-lintel construction and then added the load-bearing arch. If you look above you," as he pointed up, "it allowed architects to open up wide spaces channeling all the weight of the stone walls and ceiling across the curves of the arch and down into the ground via the blind arcades, pilasters, or columns attached to the wall.

"Because of the thick walls, windows were small and few. The spaces between the pilasters were perfect for building niches where statues of saints could be placed. As you look around, you will see an example of that in the chapel we now stand in."

"Father Cossa," interrupted Nelli, "It was my understanding we would see the statues of eight saints and I only see six. Is one of them Saint Anthony?"

"Come my child." They followed the priest.

He walked towards the altar and stopped short of it, stretching out both arms, replicating a human version of the cross and at the same time pointing to either side of the transept section to two side altars.

"Plus two makes eight," he said grinning.

"Look," Mary Ellen said. The rest of them turned to see what she was pointing at. There, above the altar in a niche was the statue of a young monk.

"Is that Saint Anthony?" asked Nelli, her heart racing in anticipation of locating the box. But before anyone could respond, Mary Ellen walked over to the statue and read something engraved on a stone.

"There's a name inscribed beneath it, a Fernando Martins de Bulhoes."

"That is correct, signorina," said Father Cossa walking over to Mary Ellen.

Standing there silently, he looked up lovingly at the stone image of a young man. "If you wish, I can tell you a tale about the young Fernando," looking around to see if he should continue.

Nelli and Anthony tried to be patient but if the box was here they needed to find it, perhaps something the priest would say might give them a clue to its location.

"Yes, please, Father," said Anthony.

"Fernando was from a very rich family of nobility and his parents arranged for Fernando to be educated at the local cathedral school. Against their wishes he entered the religious Order of Canons Regular of Saint Augustine, famous for their dedication to scholarly pursuits and sent the youth to the Abbey of the Holy Cross in Coimbra to study theology and Latin. After his ordination to the priesthood he was placed in charge of hospitality for his abbey.

"Then in 1219 he came into contact with five Franciscan friars who were on their way to Morocco to preach the Gospel to the Muslims there. Fernando was strongly attracted to the simple, evangelical lifestyle of the friars. But sadly in 1220 news arrived that the five Franciscans had been martyred in Morocco.

"Seeing their bodies as they were processed back to Assisi, Fernando was inspired by their example and obtained permission to leave the Augustinian Canons and join the new Franciscan Order. Upon his admission to the life of the friars, he took the name Anthony, after the hermit Saint Anthony of the Desert, to whom the Franciscan hermitage was dedicated."

"Then this is the statue of Saint Anthony who we were named after," said Nelli, for the moment forgetting about why they had come.

Anthony thought he heard a noise at the rear of the chapel. It sounded like something scraped against one of the stone walls but when he looked back the door was closed and the nave was empty. Looking up towards the balcony he didn't see any movement there.

Nelli noticed Anthony became distracted by something

behind him. As she started to turn to see what he was looking at, without warning, her hand felt as if it was on fire. As she glanced down she saw that the stigmata had turned bright red and droplets of blood were forming on her hand. Quickly making a fist she glanced over at Mary Ellen and Anthony hoping they hadn't noticed; fortunately Father Cossa and Father Marti had gone up to the altar.

Mary Ellen leaned in close to Nelli and whispered, "What did you do to your hand?" Then she immediately looked over at Anthony.

Sensing time was running out Nelli took it as a warning. There had to be something they overlooked. She studied the walls of the niche thinking maybe there was a hidden panel or something that could hold a box. Then she noticed the strange markings all along the arch. At the bottom, beneath Saint Anthony's feet, was a plaque with more symbols on it. At first she thought it was some kind of decoration but as she examined it more closely she could see some similarities in the symbols.

"Can anyone read what it says on this plaque?" she asked.

"It's not Italian," said Anthony. "It looks like it could be an early form of Latin. I remember reading about a type of bi-directional text called boustrophedon, mostly seen in ancient manuscripts and other inscriptions. It was a common way of writing in stone in those days. I believe, to decipher the writings you need to know something called the Gortyn code. Instead of reading left-to-right as in modern English, or right-to-left as in Hebrew and Arabic, you read alternate lines in boustrophedon. They must be read in opposite directions.

"Also, to confuse matters more, individual characters are reversed or mirrored. The last was a technique used by the famous painter Michelangelo. I would need to make a copy of the plaque and try to locate the rules of the Gortyn code to attempt to translate it."

Mary Ellen was listening but stared at the statue of Saint Anthony in disbelief.

"What is it Mary Ellen?" asked Anthony.

"Look at the cross hanging from Saint Anthony's neck." She pointed at the statue. "It's identical to the one you're wearing, Nelli!"

Anthony saw the two priests walking back to where he was

standing. He grabbed Mary Ellen's arm, "Please don't say another word. Remember our agreement earlier."

She looked at him and nodded.

"I overheard what you were saying, Anthony," said Father Cossa. "You are correct in your analysis of the writing. I've been working on translating this and other manuscripts that were found when they did some repairs in the chapel a year ago. It's always been an interest of mine to study the development of language in civilizations."

"Were you able to translate the words on the plaque?" asked Nelli.

"Yes, I believe so, although words may not always translate well into another language. The closest I came to an accurate translation is *Blessed is the Chosen One, for the Chosen One will deliver the words of the Lord*. I believe the Chosen One refers to Saint Anthony."

While Nelli was listening to the priest translate the words on the plaque, she spotted it. Lying on the floor at the base of the niche was a religious medal of Saint Anthony. One by one the others noticed Nelli's attention was focused on something on the floor.

"How did that get there? It wasn't there a minute ago," said a stunned Father Cossa.

His thoughts turned to the prophecy of Saint Anthony. It spoke of a Chosen One who would deliver the words written down in a book told to him by the Lord. He always took this as a reference to Saint Anthony. Had he been mistaken? Was the Chosen One yet to be revealed? Could that be what the words on the plaque referred to?

There was something different about Nelli; he felt it when he first laid eyes on the young woman; his eyes fell to the chain hanging from her neck. He'd seen that cross before, but where?

Remembering that Saint Anthony is known as the patron saint of lost articles, Father Cossa turned to the statue of Saint Anthony to say a prayer; there it was: the cross he had seen before.

Just as Nelli bent down to pick up the medal, a bullet missed her head by just inches. Grabbing his gun Anthony spun around, shooting in the direction where the shot came from and yelled for everyone to get down. Off to his right, he could see Mattithyahu and Judah running towards them as another shot rang out from the balcony, but this one found a target. Father

Marti collapsed to the floor.

"Go, go!" yelled Judah to Anthony. "We'll handle this."

Anthony was already moving the two women and the priest towards the altar for protection. As they moved past the dying priest, Father Cossa stopped and knelt down to give last rites to this friend. Father Marti was still conscious but knew he was dying, as a pool of blood slowly grew larger beneath his body.

Father Cossa leaned in close to his friend, whispering the prayer, Recommendation of the Departing Soul. Anthony, with his back to Father Cossa, trying to protect him, his gun pointed towards the balcony, yelled to Nelli and Mary Ellen, "Go! Get behind the altar! Then Anthony heard, "Into thy hands, Lord, I commend my spirit. O Lord, Jesus Christ, receive my spirit. Holy Mary, pray for me. Mary Mother of grace, Mother of mercy, do thou protect me from the enemy and receive me at the hour of my death."

"Please Father we have to move."

Anthony watched Mattithyahu head up the spiral staircase to the balcony. With Mary Ellen and Nelli safe for the moment behind the altar, Anthony turned to Father Cossa, "I'm sorry about Father Marti, but I must get my sister to a safe place. Is there another way out of here?" Still in shock, Father Cossa just stared at Anthony.

"Father, please, we can't risk going back the way we came in. We'd be completely exposed. Is there a back exit?" Grabbing the priest they ran to join the others behind the altar.

Mary Ellen couldn't figure out why Anthony had a gun and why would someone want to kill Nelli. She frantically looked for another way out. Peeking out from behind the altar she saw movement at the back of the chapel. She thought she recognized the person. Pulling her head back she grabbed Anthony's sleeve.

"Anthony, I've seen that woman before," she said.

"What woman? What are you talking about?"

"The one out there in the church, she was one of the people in the tour group we passed back by the tapestry."

Taking a look, Anthony caught sight of the last of the woman's raven hair as she disappeared behind the door.

Father Cossa regained his composure and was quietly motioning for the three of them to move back a foot or two. He crawled to the middle section of the altar and was feeling around for something. Stopping, he pushed against the wood. A section of the altar swung open revealing a three-foot by three-foot opening. Inside it was pitch black but at the opening you could make out what looked like steps cut out between rock and hard packed earth.

"It's called a priest's hole," whispered Father Cossa. "It was an escape route for the priest in case the castle was attacked."

Climbing inside, he motioned for the next person to follow him.

"Avanti avanti! Be careful the rock is slippery," he whispered.

Mary Ellen and Nelli looked at Anthony.

"Go, we have no choice. I'll go last," said Anthony.

As he waited for his turn, more shots were heard, and then someone groaned. He prayed it wasn't Mattithyahu or Judah.

Nelli was in and Mary Ellen was now crawling backwards into the priest's hole. Once she was in Anthony quickly followed, pushing the paneled door back into place.

CHAPTER SEVENTY-TWO

As he stood there silently allowing his eyes to adjust to the darkness, Anthony listened for any movement on the other side of the small paneled door. The only thing he heard was his own breathing; they were safe for the moment. The tunnel wasn't much wider than four feet. At six-foot-four, Anthony barely had room to stand up straight.

"Father, where does this tunnel lead to?" he asked, keeping his voice low.

"I was told that at one time this led to an escape exit above ground just outside the walls of the castle," the priest whispered back.

Father Cossa's loss of his friend was almost palpable even in the darkness, but Anthony also heard a renewed sense of conviction in the priest's voice. Calmly and without any hint of fear, Father Cossa said, "Please follow my voice and watch your step. Pray that those who carved this tunnel through clay and rock centuries ago knew that one day we would need the safety of its walls and built it to pass the test of time. We must have faith in the Lord. He will be our light and guide us to safety. I will not question God's plan but if it was meant for me to be here with you today, then I will use the knowledge our Lord has graced me with to help you."

"I have my cell phone," said Mary Ellen through the darkness. "The light from it could help."

"Yes, my child, that could be very useful," replied Father Cossa.

"We all have our cell phones," added Nelli.

"See, the Lord has already answered our prayers. I will use each one sparingly to reserve the battery. It should not be far to the exit but it will be slow moving. The ceiling and walls are cut out of stone, so use your hands to guide you and keep your head low, especially you, signore Anthony. We must remember the people at that time were not as tall as you."

Nelli knew they couldn't go back but had to ask, "Father, do you know if there were any artifacts removed from the niche of Saint Anthony and stored anywhere else in the castle?"

"No, why?"

"Just wondering."

She was comforted knowing the box wasn't up there for someone else to find but she also realized that she didn't know where to look next for it. Nelli was able to make out the outline of Father Cossa, a small thing, but it helped to lessen the anxiety she was experiencing. With no air circulation, the tunnel was damp and musty from decaying roots and rodents that had made it their home for centuries.

Father Cossa used the light from the phone to see what was up ahead, turning it off, he moved forward slowly. Behind him Anthony, Mary Ellen, and Nelli ran their hands along the walls to help them navigate through the tunnel; each one praying the priest was right about it leading to an above ground exit.

They walked a few feet and stopped, walked a few more feet, stopped again, each time the soft glow from the phone could be seen but this time the light from the phone stayed on.

"Is there a problem Father?" asked Anthony. He became concerned, if they couldn't continue they would have to go back.

"It looks as if a section of the wall has collapsed. I think there is still enough space to get by, but it will be tight."

When Father Cossa reached the pile of rocks, he felt a blast of cool air. The light from the phone revealed a hole where there used to be a wall.

"There's an opening in the wall that leads into another room," he said excitedly. "There's a chamber of some kind."

Nelli's heart began to race. Maybe the box had been hidden in this secret chamber.

"What do you see Father?" she asked, trying to stay calm.

"I can't see much from here. I think I can crawl through and get a better look."

He sounded like a little child who had just found a buried treasure. Climbing up on the fallen rocks, he grabbed on to the inside of the opening to get some leverage. That's when he felt a piece of wood sticking out from the wall. As he wrapped his hand around it for support, it came loose. Losing his balance, he fell forward. Everyone heard him moan as he hit the floor.

"Are you all right, Father?" yelled Anthony.

"Si si, I'm fine, I think. It wasn't that far to the ground thankfully."

He had managed to hold on to the phone. Using the light from it he looked to see what had come loose from the wall. It was laying a few feet away from where he fell. Then he realized what it must be and went over to pick it up.

"I found a torch," he shouted.

Mary Ellen had become very quiet, struggling to fight off panic from being underground and in a dark and confined space. When she heard he'd found a torch she was thrilled.

"Does anyone have a lighter?" she yelled and then remembered she did.

"I almost forgot! I do! I have a lighter!" At the same time she said it, she realized she would have to admit she had started smoking again. Smoking had been a sore point between she and Anthony.

"Mary Ellen, you started smoking again didn't you?" Anthony said, disappointed but also thankful.

"No, I thought I would just carry a lighter around in case we came across a torch that needed to be lit!" she snapped. Everyone burst out laughing.

"Okay, for the moment we're all happy you decided to start up again," Anthony responded.

"Here, Father, do you have it?" said Mary Ellen.

"Yes, my child let there be light." They heard a click and a burst of flame took the darkness away.

"What do you see?" all three of them asked at the same time.

"It's a burial chamber or catacomb. In ancient times they created these underground cemeteries. There are hundreds of tunnels cut into the tufa, or porous limestone, beneath all of Italy, leading to catacombs containing thousands of burial niches especially around Rome. It looks like we stumbled upon one."

One by one they crawled through the opening. As they stood in the middle of the room they were surrounded by niches that each held a burial urn. Anthony, Nelli, and Father Cossa went in different directions to get a closer look and examine some of the urns. Mary Ellen stood in the center of the room holding the torch. Controlling the light gave her some comfort and lessened her anxiety. She thanked God for small blessings.

"All the urns I'm looking at have writing on them," said Nelli.

"It should be the name of the person whose remains are in them," said Anthony from across the room.

Nelli believed finding the burial chamber wasn't just a coincidence. It had been meant for her to discover this room. "The box has to be here," she silently said to herself.

"Do you think there might be one with Saint Anthony's name on it?"

"If there is, remember it most likely will not be under the name Saint Anthony. He was a monk at that time so it could be under his birth name or maybe under Antonio," replied Father Cossa.

Nelli closely examined several of the niches. There was one that seemed different. It had something mounted at the top of the curved arch. As she got closer she saw that it was an angel holding something in its hands.

"I think I might have found something."

Everyone walked over to where Nelli was standing.

"What do you think you've found?" asked Anthony.

"Look at the angel, Anthony; it's holding a box between its hands. Can either of you two make out the words on the urn?"

"It's Latin," said Father Cossa, "the same as on the plaque in the chapel. This one I can translate. It's only one short sentence, "Here rests Brother Antonio, c.1195 – 1231."

He couldn't believe what they had just found, but all Nelli could think of is the box must be hidden somewhere inside this room. There had to be a reason for them finding this burial chamber.

"Anthony, the box must be hidden somewhere in this room."

He couldn't help hear the optimism in his sister's voice.

"What box are you talking about?" asked Mary Ellen.

"A box similar to the one I bought in Rome," said Nelli.

"Why would you be looking for a box?" asked Mary Ellen.

Not wanting to reveal too much, Nelli said, "After buying the box I had a dream that I would find one just like it where Saint Anthony was laid to rest. First finding the statue of Saint Anthony and now the urn, I thought maybe my dream was more than just a dream, but that's all it was, a dream."

Father Cossa was listening quietly and analyzing the events of the last several hours. Now there was this mention of a box. Could this be the same box that was spoken of in the prophecy, a box that was made for Saint Anthony to hold the words of Our Lord?

He had sensed a strong presence of the Holy Spirit when this woman walked into his church. He had to ask and there were only two ways for her to respond. She would either look at him like he was crazy or it would be true.

"Signorina Nelli, there's a question I must ask you," said Father Cossa. "Someone back there tried to kill you, my child. Finding the medal, discovering this catacomb, and the dream you spoke of, I must ask: Are you the Chosen One that was told of in Saint Anthony's prophecy? I sensed there was something different about you when you entered our little church, Saint Giovanni Battista."

Completely taken off guard by the question, Nelli stood there staring at the priest not knowing how to respond. Her hesitation told Father Cossa what he already suspected.

"You do not need to say anything more. The Lord brought us together and wanted us to discover this place. We must trust in His infinite wisdom. There must be something here we need to find. We will look more carefully."

Mary Ellen was still looking at Nelli in total disbelief.

"Cardinal McKenna mentioned something about a Chosen One but I dismissed it."

"What did Cardinal McKenna say about the Chosen One?" said Anthony, startled by her statement. "You need to tell me everything you talked about with the cardinal, Mary Ellen."

Anthony was angry with himself for not considering that the cardinal would know about the prophecy and the Chosen One, and that he could have brought it up in conversation with Mary Ellen. Maybe somehow if he had known, the priest wouldn't have had to die.

As he waited for Mary Ellen to answer, he tried to remain calm.

"Mary Ellen, you must tell me everything you discussed and leave nothing out."

"I told you we both received the same card with the cobra head on it. I thought maybe someone wanted to scare me—to stop asking questions about my brother's case, but when I was told there was one found next to Father Robert's body, I knew something more heinous was going on. Cardinal McKenna believes a false prophet has gathered his army to go to battle against the souls of the faithful here on earth. In each of our files, Father Roberto's findings seemed to suggest suspicious behavior and activity between certain groups and individuals inside the Vatican. We both now think he was killed because he was getting too close to the truth."

"Does Cardinal McKenna know who this false prophet might be?" asked Father Cossa.

"No, but he believes there's a connection between an order called The Legion of Christ and a secret society called Propagan da Due or P2, believed by many to have been behind the death of Pope John Paul I. The conspiracy theory is that the Pope's death was not from natural causes and that the Vatican's Secretary of State, who was thought to be a member of P2, poisoned the Pope. The premise was that P2 was planning on taking control of the Vatican and creating a New World Order. He now believes that maybe the same thing is happening again and they are using the sexual scandal as a way to feed upon and destroy the church from within, my brother being one of their victims," she said. "Lastly, Cardinal McKenna believes the prophecy of Saint Anthony predicted this day. That the Chosen One must fulfill the prophecy and stop the false prophet from accomplishing his goal." No one knew what to say next.

Father Cossa decided to break the silence, but instead of addressing what Mary Ellen had just said, he turned towards Nelli, "As the Chosen One, we must help you find out the reason you were brought here."

The light from the torch was growing weaker. Luckily they had found a second one but they wanted to save that one for the tunnel.

"Just a couple more minutes, Father," said Anthony. "We

need to see if the box is here, then we have to find the way out of this tunnel, or we'll have to go back the way we came and take our chances. I need to get Nelli to safety."

Anthony went over to the opening in the wall to listen if anyone might have discovered the priest's hole and were coming after them.

Nelli and Father Cossa examined the walls and floor of the niche with the urn marked Brother Antonio on it, feeling for anything that might reveal a concealed compartment. There had to be something they were missing, but what?

Father Cossa stepped back and stared at the clay pot. Then, he grabbed each side of the urn and gently started to rock it; it moved.

Nelli was stunned, "Father, what are you doing? That's centuries old," said Nelli, frightened that it might crack into hundreds of pieces.

"God intended for us to find this place. We must leave no stone unturned."

The priest was determined to figure out why. Anthony and Mary Ellen watched as Nelli and Father Cossa very carefully lifted the large clay urn and placed it on the floor. It wasn't as heavy as they thought it would be. They both looked inside, expecting it to be sealed but the mouth of the vessel was open.

"Mary Ellen, come over here with the light," said Nelli waving her closer. "There's something inside the urn."

"It looks like a rolled up scroll," said Father Cossa looking at Nelli in disbelief. "I believe this has to be what we were supposed to find."

Across the room Anthony yelled out, "Did you find something?"

"Si," said the priest, barely audible, fearful that if he spoke too loud it might damage the ancient artifact. "There appears to be a scroll of some kind rolled up inside." Then under his breath he said, "Blessed be the Lord."

"Father, please remove it from the urn," shouted Anthony. "I want to get us out of here. We have spent too much time here as it is."

The flame from the torch was almost out and they would soon be in the dark again. Gently grabbing the end of the scroll, Father Cossa lifted it out. It was about twelve inches in length and about two inches thick. It was in remarkably good condition. It appeared to be a sheepskin tied with a thin leather rope.

"Do you have it, Father Cossa?" asked Anthony.

"Si, signore, I have it."

"Anthony," shouted Mary Ellen, "the torch is going to go out any second," starting to panic at the thought of being in the dark again.

"Grab the second torch and let's get out of here."

CHAPTER SEVENTY-THREE

Judah leaned against the wall, his breathing labored; he'd been hit in the shoulder and it hurt like hell. The shooter thought he'd killed Judah. That was a foolish assumption and he revealed himself too quickly. Judah got a clean shot and watched as his attacker's body hit the edge of the balcony, falling to the floor below.

Mattithyahu, in another part of the chapel, had killed the second shooter. He heard a gunshot, then someone groan and then another gunshot. The next sound he heard was a loud thud as something or someone hit the floor below.

"Please, dear Lord, don't let it be Judah."

Hiding behind a column that was not far from the ledge of the balcony, he slowly started to ease his way around the thick wooded structure. Just a little more and he would be able to get a look at what had made the noise. He was in position now. Just a quick glance and he would have his answer. The man lying on the floor of the chapel was dressed in the same black outfit as the man he had just killed. It wasn't Judah, thank God. Both shooters were dead, so where was Judah?

"Judah can you hear me?" talking into his headpiece. "Are you hurt?"

"Look over towards your left," said Judah, waving at him with his gun hand.

As he ran towards Judah he stopped, ripping off the hood and shirt from one of the shooters. Reaching Judah he immediately applied pressure to slow the bleeding, at the same time, tightly wrapping the shoulder with the dead man's shirt.

"Big SOBs, weren't they?" grinned Judah.

"Looks like you lucked out, clean shot through the shoulder but you've lost a lot of blood."

"I'll be okay, just give me a minute," said Judah.

"What do you make of this embossed cobra symbol?" asked Mattithyahu, handing the hood to Judah as he finished wrapping his shoulder.

"I'd guess a cult of some sort," said Judah, "but we need to find To'mas and Nelli."

"They were barricaded behind the altar the last I saw," said Mattithyahu. "Are you able to walk?"

"I'm fine, looks like the bleeding is stopping. Let's go."

Heading down the spiral steps, Judah went to check the other body to make sure he was dead while Mattithyahu ran towards the altar. That's when he saw the priest, off to the side by the statue of Saint Anthony, a pool of blood next to the body.

"Damn, they killed one of the priests, Judah!"

He was afraid they would find To'mas and the others dead too.

Mattithyahu tried to prepare himself for the worst scenario. Reaching the altar he slowly looked behind it.

"Well, are they alive?" yelled Judah, bracing himself to hear the worst.

"There's no one here," said Mattithyahu. "They're gone."

"What do you mean, they're gone? We would have seen them if they tried to exit the chapel, check your GPS."

Judah continued to search the body for anything that could give them a clue on who the two dead men were.

"Nothing ... wait, it's tracking. They've escaped somehow," Mattithyahu said.

CHAPTER SEVENTY-FOUR

Peter was very familiar with the prophecy of Saint Anthony. In fact he had spent millions of dollars on experts to study the life and writings of the monk, but he was troubled by one expert's interpretation of some of the findings. This particular individual believed that when the "son of perdition" or the Antichrist returns, one known as the Chosen One will be shown a book containing the words of God to be delivered to the one who wears the ring of the fisherman.

He had been foolish last time, this time would be different. He would have his own kingdom and no book was going to stop that from happening. With all his money and connections, how would this Chosen One accomplish what he hadn't been able to? Even if it did exist, after this amount of time, the chances it was still intact was slim.

If it was anything like the discovery of the Dead Sea Scrolls, it would take years to piece it together and analyze the writings. It didn't matter anymore. In a few days, the world would be worshipping a new Pope.

If the only threat this time was a book, what did he have to fear, even if they were the words of God? The world had become so depraved he wasn't worried even if they came from the one who had cast him out of heaven.

For all practical purposes the blueprint for his master plan had already been written. He had to smile; the Book of Revelations included everything he needed to know. In it described the three great centers of faith and the description of each.

First is Jerusalem, the most mentioned city in the Bible, the mother of true faith, believed their people to be the Chosen Ones. It will be at the center of the final world conflict.

Then Babylon, the second most mentioned city in the Bible and the present day Iraq, the mother of false religions. It will play a central role. She will be revived and brought onto the end-time, staged to play a leading role (Rev. 14:8; 16:19; 17–18). How many times it had been destroyed because God's people worshipped false idols.

The third one was the one that brought him much pleasure: Rome, mother of the unholy, mixture of the two. This is where he would build his kingdom by defiling the Holy City and taking the seat of the Pope, declaring himself the representative of God on earth. This time he would rewrite the ending to the scriptures by adding another chapter.

He realized his last attempt had failed because he had been too impatient. Since then the number of lost souls had multiplied beyond his expectations, with little help from him. Some of his foot soldiers had become leaders of their own groups around the world. Genocide and the use of terrorism was becoming an everyday headline in the paper.

He would be heading to a secret location outside the Vatican fairly soon. The Council of Guardians knew what to do once the announcement went out over TV and radio. The world would be stunned learning of the Pope's death, but even more shocked by an immediate replacement to the papal seat.

There are three ways a Pope has been elected throughout history: the first is election by scrutiny or by secret ballot with a two-thirds vote, which is the one used most in modern times. The second is per acclamationem seu inspirationem (election by inspiration or acclamation), where electors simultaneously shouted out the name of their preferred candidate. The third is election by compromise (per compromise); a committee of nine to fifteen unanimously chosen cardinals is delegated to make the choice for all.

Peter had already handpicked the fifteen cardinals; all he needed to do now was to sit back and wait. Although there was that one small matter that Thomas had kept from him. Peter was waiting to hear from Christine, if the problem had been taken care of. He wasn't sure of all the details but better to attend to it now and not have any surprises. His cell phone rang; the incoming call was from Christine. In seconds, he would have confirmation that the problem was no longer a concern.

"I've been waiting. I expect you left no trace?" said Peter.

There was silence on the other end and then he heard Christine's voice.

"I don't have good news to report Grand Master."

Peter's rage could be felt through the phone.

"Continue!" he snapped.

"There are three dead and the target got away," replied Christine.

"This was supposed to be a precautionary measure."

He could barely contain his anger.

"I asked you to take care of this!" His voice crackling with rage, "What's the damage?"

"One priest and two ...." she hesitated, knowing what the reaction would be when she told him who the other two bodies belonged to.

"And?"

"The two others were disciples of P2."

Had he heard her correctly? Two of his disciples dead?

"How the hell did this happen?" yelled Peter.

"The man with the two women was carrying a weapon. Then two more men appeared with guns. After it was over, I waited outside the chapel for them to exit. The two men with guns came out and took off running. I continued to wait for the woman and her companions, but they never came out of the chapel. So I went back in and they were gone."

"Did you find the exit they escaped through?" demanded Peter.

"That's what's so bizarre. There wasn't any other way out."

She didn't care that he was the Grand Master. She did what she had been asked to do. It was back in his court now.

Peter could hear the change in Christine's voice. It was the woman he was familiar with, yet something concerned him. He now wondered why Thomas had asked Christine to have this woman followed.

"Did you take care of the bodies?" he demanded.

Catherine noticed the change in Peter's voice. The rage

was replaced by a cold businesslike manner.

"Yes, they were disposed of, Grand Master. There is no evidence they were ever there."

"Don't talk to anyone about this. I will get back to you."

CHAPTER **SEVENTY-FIVE**

Cardinal McKenna checked his phone again, no messages from Mary Ellen. He had to focus. Who should he trust, who could he trust?

First he needed to get a message to the commander and let him know he had to talk to him without creating any suspicion. Phones could be listened in on and computers could be hacked. He'd have his assistant Robert contact Crevelli's office under the pretense of needing to reschedule their meeting about the Pope's upcoming audience with the bishops and cardinals.

Since it wasn't McKenna's responsibility to coordinate the Pope's schedule, he hoped the commander would read between the lines and realize McKenna had information concerning the Pope. Anyone listening in would think it was just the normal everyday communication between different departments within the Vatican. He'd leave a similar meaningless message with Mary Ellen.

As he walked back through the Sistine Chapel, he thought if only the walls could talk, they could tell him what his predecessors had done when they confronted Satan.

He stopped briefly in front of one of his favorite paintings in this section of the Vatican, *The Last Judgment* by Michelangelo. It was a massive work, approximately fifty feet by thirty feet and spanned the entire wall behind the altar of the Sistine Chapel.

Standing there studying the great work, he reflected on the possibility of being witness to this final Biblical event during his lifetime. The painting centers around the dominant figure of Christ captured in the moment just before the verdict of the Last Judgment is uttered, as described in the Book of Matthew 25: 31–46.

Next to Christ is the Virgin, who turns her head in a gesture of resignation, only to await the result of the Judgment. The Saints and the Elect also anxiously await the verdict. The lower half of the painting shows the angels and devils fight over making the damned fall down to hell.

Satan had won many souls over the years but he would never win the final battle against God.

He had been so deep in thought; he realized he was standing in front of the door to his office. Entering he walked over to where Robert sat and told him to put a call in to the commander and leave a message to expect a call from him shortly. Then he headed to his private office.

Upon entering he stopped and listened for the familiar ticking of his father's clock in the background. It gave him solace knowing his father was watching over him. Then he looked at his desk across the room and imagined Mary Ellen sitting there during their meeting the other day and remembering when he discovered that she had received the same mysterious card with the cobra head engraving on it. Everything changed that day; he didn't realize to what extent until today.

The box and all the papers were still on his desk. Sitting down he opened a drawer and retrieved a legal pad of paper to take notes on, but first he needed to make two calls. Pulling up the contact list on his phone, he punched in the number for Ms. O'Farrell.

It showed "connecting," then "call ended." When he tried again the same thing happened. Again he tried and again it showed "call ended." He could feel the muscles in his shoulders tighten.

"No, don't even think it," he told himself.

Trying a fourth time it finally connected. "Thank you, Dear Lord," he said as he looked up towards heaven. It rang only once and went directly into voice mail. In a calm and relaxed voice he said, "Mary Ellen, this is Cardinal McKenna, unfortunately I need to reschedule our appointment. Please call me back at the number you have for me at your convenience."

The number he had given her belonged to a disposable phone; that way their conversations couldn't be traced.

Next he made the call to Commander Crevelli. On the third ring, he was prepared to leave a message when a voice on the other end answered, "Hello, Commander Crevelli here."

"Commander, it's Cardinal McKenna. I hope you received the message from my assistant Robert. I'm sorry but I need to change the time of our meeting. I was hoping to be able to stop by this afternoon instead."

"Yes, Cardinal McKenna I did receive the message from Robert; this afternoon would be fine. Shall we say two-thirty here at my office?"

The tension in McKenna's shoulders began to ease. He was thankful Crevelli had played along.

"Yes, thank you again, Commander Crevelli. I will see you at two-thirty this afternoon."

Finishing the call, he looked at the disposable cell phone sitting on his desk; he mentally commanded it to ring but it just laid there silent. Where are you, Mary Ellen?

He had a few hours before his meeting with the commander, and he needed to read through all the documents in front of him. As he reached to turn on the desk lamp, his eyes fell upon a letter he had been writing to a friend who was struggling with a personal problem. It was open to the second page of his response. On it he had quoted a line from the Scriptures, "Put your trust in the Lord and He will be your guiding light."

It was strange that he stumbled upon that at this moment. It brought back memories of when he turned seven. After making his first communion, sometimes at home, he would set up a table with his parents silver wine glasses. Using a Ritz cracker for the host, he would make his mother sit and watch as he pretended to serve communion. Since that early age, he trusted that God would show him the path he was meant to take and it was no different now.

Pulling his reading glasses off from the top of his head and placing them on the bridge of his nose, he looked at the papers spread across his desk. He needed to connect the dots and figure out who among them could be the false prophet.

He decided to look more closely into the relationship between Vingenzo Parocchi, the director-general of the Banca Nazionale del Lavoro and a shareholder in the Vatican Bank, and Cardinal Cavallari, the Secretary of State for the Vatican. Next, look deeper into the most recent activities of the Union Bank of Switzerland, then try and figure out what the connection was to Father Maciel and the LC. Maybe by following the money trail he would find his answer.

For the next hour he read through all the information, pulling out anything that might confirm his suspicions. Now sitting in front of him was a small stack of documents. The rest of the documents were in the box, which now sat on the floor next to his chair.

"Okay, let's see what we have here."

He began arranging the documents in some kind of order the first being the card with the cobra head laying on top of the envelope it came in. Then next to that he placed the ill-fated file from Father Roberto, with some additional documents he'd pulled out. To the right of that, the copy of Mary Ellen's file she received from the priest, again with some additional information he thought relevant. The next small group of papers was the list of the money transactions and photos taken in Switzerland with the ledgers from the LC and Banca Nazionale. Last, the notes from his visits to the Vatican Library on Propaganda Due aka P2.

On the top sheet of a memo pad he wrote, *meeting with Pope*, on another *meeting with Crevelli* and stuck them in the appropriate locations of the timetable he had laid out on his desk. Then beneath all of it, on a third piece of paper, he wrote the words *prophecy of Saint Anthony*.

He wanted to provide as clear a picture as possible to the commander, showing him how he believed his findings and the sequence of events taking place seemed to be pointing to the possible return of an Antichrist and of a Chosen One spoken of in the prophecy of Saint Anthony.

Crevelli needed to realize this could be the battle God spoke of in the end times. It was written in the Book of Revelations 1: 3, "Blessed is the one who reads the words of this prophecy, and blessed are those who hear it and take to heart what is written in it, because the time is near."

Satan was building his army for battle. When and where was the question and would they be too late? It all seemed to rest on finding a book. A book with words God told to a young monk centuries ago. The prophecy speaks of the Chosen One who would have the key to unlocking it.

The cardinal remembered Mary Ellen telling him how her friend was named after Saint Anthony. Could there be a connection, he wondered?

CHAPTER SEVENTY-SIX

The light from the torch made all the difference in the world. They were making up for lost time.

"Father, do you know if it's much farther?" asked Mary Ellen. The only thing keeping her from losing it was thinking about having a cigarette when they got out.

"We're almost there," said Father Cossa. "I can see where the tunnel gets wider up ahead. If I'm right, the exit should be somewhere around there."

"Father," said Anthony from the back, "when you see it let me go first. I don't know what or who might be waiting for us."

Above ground Judah and Mattithyahu were at a loss, their GPS' showed they should be within a few feet of Anthony and Nelli, but they were nowhere to be seen. Judah's wound had stopped bleeding for the time being, but he knew he would have to get medical treatment. He was thankful there weren't more men in black hoods chasing them. He'd lost more blood than he would have liked and was feeling a little shaky.

"I don't see them," said Mattithyahu. "They should be right around here. We're practically on top of them."

Frantically surveying the surrounding area, they both looked at each other confused on what to do next.

"Look they're moving again."

"No, they've stopped," said Judah. "Unless they've suddenly become invisible we should be looking right at them."

They felt fairly certain they had not been followed but they decided to take cover behind some trees. The area was heavily wooded, which would give them some protection but would also give cover to their enemy.

As they were running, Judah's arm caught on a broken branch and he could feel something warm soaking through the shirt used to wrap his shoulder. Once hidden behind the trees, Mattithyahu shook his GPS to see if it would get the signals moving.

"I don't get it, if this isn't broken where the hell are they?"

"Well I'm getting the same reading," said Judah, "so it must be working. They could be hurt and lying on the ground and we just can't see them. Look for anything unusual or something they could be barricaded behind or hiding inside of."

"The only thing around is that old crumbled down well over there to the left," whispered Mattithyahu. "There's not much else around here. Do you think who ever those guys were back there know about our tracking system and jammed the satellite frequencies we're using?"

Anthony could see on his GPS that the two Guardians above ground were no longer on the move. They were either trying to figure out why they couldn't get a visual on him and Nelli or, God forbid, they'd been killed.

"Anthony," whispered Nelli, "we have to bring Father Cossa with us. I don't think he would be safe if he went back to his church now."

"I know Nelli, I've already considered that."

"I see steps," shouted Father Cossa.

"Father, stay there, I'm coming up front."

Anthony had no idea what could be waiting for them when they escaped from the tunnel and he had the only gun. Squeezing pass Nelli and Mary Ellen, he said, "You're doing great, I will get all of us out of here."

Standing next to Father Cossa now, he looked to see what the priest had found. There in front of them was a spiral staircase that disappeared inside a small shaft of some kind.

"What is this?" asked Anthony.

"From the surface it should appear to be an old well," said the priest, "but in reality it's the exit out of the tunnel. Ingenious don't you think, but I worry what condition the stairs are in."

"What's up there once we climb out?" asked Anthony, already inspecting the stairs.

"There's a small clearing around the well. On one side will be the west wall of the castle. On the other side you will be surrounded by woods," explained the priest.

"Well, we have two choices," said Anthony. "One, we can take our chances and go back, or, two, pray these stairs were built to pass the test of time. I opt for the second. When I get to the top wait till I give a signal to begin climbing up, but if you hear gun-shots take Nelli and Mary Ellen and work your way back to the chapel. Wait there and someone will come and take you to safety."

"But how will they know where we are?" asked Father Cossa.

"They will. You must trust me on this Father."

"All right, my son, I will also ask Saint Anthony to watch over you."

"You do that, Father. I will take all the help I can get."

"Be careful, Anthony. We haven't been brought you this far to fail now."

Anthony tested the first step. It gave a little under his weight but seemed stable. The three others watched as he slowly made his way up the spiral stairs and disappeared.

Up above Mattithyahu whispered to Judah, "How's your shoulder?"

"Well, it would feel a lot better if I didn't have a bullet in it," looking at Mattithyahu as if to say, you're kidding right!

"Just thought I'd ask!"

The signal for Anthony began pulsating telling them he was operational, but it wasn't tracking movement.

"What do you make of that?" Mattithyahu, pointed to his GPS. There are only two directions he can go … unless … all at once it hit both of them, "The well! Cover me."

Taking one last look around, Mattithyahu made a run for it. Reaching the well he dropped to the ground leaning up against what was left of its crumbling stone wall.

"Judah," speaking into his headpiece Mattithyahu asked, "Is it clear?"

"Clear," replied Judah.

Anthony methodically made his way up the ancient stair-well. A few of the wooden trestles in the structure were badly deteriorated. Grabbing onto roots of trees that had snaked their way through the hard earth, he tried to lessen the weight he placed on each step. One side of each winder was anchored into the wall of the shaft but the outside edge, towards the center of the staircase, was completely open. One mistake and it would be all over for him. Then he saw them just a few feet ahead, two steps were almost completely rotted away. It was too dangerous to try and jump to the step above them. If he missed, the fall could kill him.

The only other way out would be back through the tunnel. He wasn't sure if that was even an option anymore. After they had all made their way out of the burial chamber where they found the scroll, he heard a strange rumbling sound and felt a small vibration. He suspected another section of wall had collapsed.

"Think, Anthony!" He scanned the wooden supports and looked at the crumbling stone wall and then had an idea. If he only had a rope he could rig up a version of top roping used in rock climbing. Using one of the wooden beams up ahead to anchor off of, he would then use the stones in the wall of the shaft and climb up to the next step, but he needed a rope.

His mind flashed back to all those summers with his father and the other eleven boys and how they were trained to use the resources one had at hand. In almost all cases nature could provide whatever one needed. So what could he use for a rope? The tree roots, the ones he had been using for support, they were all around him, but he would need something to cut them with. Praying it hadn't fallen out, he reached into the pocket of his cargo pants, and his fingers felt the rounded corners of the Swiss Army knife Nelli had given him. The knife was small, but it would do the job.

Spotting what he was looking for, he carefully descended back down the last two steps. Protruding out from the wall was a mass of long sinewy tree roots. It took some doing, but it worked.

He was almost to the top of the stairwell shaft when the steps ended. There was still about twelve feet to go. It didn't make sense, this was an escape route. Maybe the rest of it had rotted away over time, but it appeared to him the steps were supposed to end here.

"Now what?"

Looking around, that's when he saw them. Steps had been cut into the stone to climb the rest of the way up. Of course, from above it had to give the appearance of a well.

As he placed his foot onto the first ledge he thought he heard someone talking. Pulling out his gun, he continued slowly climbing with the gun in one hand pointed at the opening.

"Anthony?" called out Mattithyahu.

"Is that you Anthony?" he said a little louder this time.

"Mattithyahu?" whispered Anthony.

"Yes, thank God. We found you."

"Is Judah with you," asked Anthony, afraid of what the answer might be.

"A couple hundred yards off to our west, ready to do some target shooting if necessary. He's got a nasty hole in his shoulder that will have to be looked at by a doctor. Still, could fight off a grizzly bear though."

"Is it safe for me to come out?" Anthony asked.

"Best I can tell, yes."

Grabbing the edge of the well Anthony flipped himself over and almost landed on top of Mattithyahu.

"I'm not even going to ask how you got here," said Mattithyahu. "Is Nelli with you?"

"Yes, once I give them the signal it's safe to climb up, but we'll need to rig up some kind of pulley to help get them all out. There's a section where the steps are completely gone. Give me your flashlight, and I'll signal to start climbing up. You look for something we can secure a cable to."

"Them?" repeated Mattithyahu.

"Nelli, Mary Ellen, and a Father Cossa," answered Anthony.

"Was the other priest …." Mattithyahu didn't have the chance to finish the sentence. Anthony finished it for him.

"Yes, he was a good friend of Father Cossa's," said Anthony as he signaled with the flashlight to the others below.

As they lowered the makeshift hoist down the well, Mattithyahu said, "You should know Anthony that Cephas has been trying to contact you. We followed the two men who tried to kill you and they were seen going into a building rumored to be owned by members of the local Masonic Lodge. We were able to get inside without being seen and found them talking to a third man. He was extremely angry with them and was yelling that the Grand Master would not be happy they had failed."

Anthony stopped what he was doing. "What did you just say?"

CHAPTER SEVENTY-SEVEN

"Do you see anything?" said Mary Ellen.

"No," answered Nelli, wondering if something had gone wrong.

"Wait, do you see that?" said Father Cossa. "There … that small beam of light swaying back and forth. It must be the signal."

The cell phone he'd been using for a flashlight rang. Anthony explained the conditions of the stairs and what they needed to do when they climbed up. Father Cossa repeated the information to Nelli and Mary Ellen.

"Okay Nelli you go first, and then Mary Ellen you follow right behind. I'll go last and remember, go slow and don't look down."

Mary Ellen wanted to go first. She was trying everything she could think of, not to panic. If only she had a cigarette it would help calm her nerves. Just then Nelli turned and smiled at her. As they locked eyes, Mary Ellen had this overwhelming feeling of peacefulness come over her. There was a change in Nelli since that day in her office, nothing anyone else would necessarily notice, only those close to her. She watched as her friend had slowly grown more introspective and seemed to have no fear.

Nelli turned and placed her foot on the first step, testing each stair as she climbed. On the third step her foot slipped and she fell down on her knee, scraping her face.

"Hug the wall, Nelli. Stay to the inside of the steps," shouted Father Cossa. "I'm right here and Anthony's waiting for you at the top. Just take your time."

Anthony and Mattithyahu rigged up a temporary pulley system that had lowered the rope with a body strap down to the area where the steps were missing.

"Nelli, can you hear me?" yelled Anthony.

"Yes, I can hear you."

"When you reach the place where the steps are missing put the strap around your waist and we'll pull you up. Don't be afraid. It's just a short distance from there."

"We? Who else is up there Anthony?" asked Nelli. Had the men who tried to kill her in the chapel found them after all?

"Mattithyahu and Judah," Anthony shouted down.

Nelli and Mary Ellen were pulled up and now it was Father Cossa's turn. As they sat on the ground with their backs against the wall, Nelli leaned over and whispered to Mary Ellen, "I know you must be trying to comprehend everything that's happened," she said, resting her hand gently on top of Mary Ellen's. She waited as Mary Ellen put out her cigarette in the dirt.

"Have you and Anthony always known?" asked Mary Ellen.

"No, when Dad was dying he told me I would become the Keeper of the Key that would unlock a secret."

"What secret? Did he give you a key?"

"The only thing he gave me was the cross he always wore around his neck just before he died."

Remembering that day, Nelli's eyes filled with tears. Now Mary Ellen was the one to gently squeeze Nelli's hand.

"He was a good man, Nelli, and he had a rich and full life. Did he tell you what the secret was?"

"No …." Nelli hesitated.

"What is it Nelli?"

Nelli looked at Anthony who had overheard most of the conversation. He looked at his sister, silently telling her, it's up to you.

"I've had visions that are guiding me, showing me the way," said Nelli.

She waited to see Mary Ellen's reaction. Remarkably she didn't seem surprised.

"Then you must be the Chosen One that was spoken of in the prophecy of Saint Anthony," responded Mary Ellen. "We will need to find the key that unlocks this secret your father spoke of."

Mattithyahu was helping Father Cossa over the edge of the wall. Protected now by the darkness, one by one they ran to where Judah was waiting.

"Good to see you Judah," said Anthony smiling, "heard you had a run-in with some bad guys."

"Sure did, but they won't be causing anyone any more trouble," grinned Judah.

"Did you find out who they were or what group they belong to?"

"They were dressed in strange clothing. Looked like the Klu Klux Klan except they wore black hoods with an embossed head of a snake on it." Judah pointed to the one on the blood-soaked shirt used to wrap his shoulder.

Anthony froze. There it was again, the cobra head.

"Is the villa secure?" asked Anthony.

"Yes, additional security was put in place. We have a van parked not far from here."

"Who are these two men?" asked a confused Father Cossa.

"They're part of the team of Guardians to protect the Chosen One. You will remain with us now Father. It's not safe for you to return to the church, plus I need you to help me translate the scroll we found."

"Then I will need my notes on the Gortyn code. They're back at the church."

"Is there someone you can trust that can get them for you?" asked Anthony.

"Yes, there's a student from the university that has been working with me. He knows where I keep all my notes."

"Good, then we will help you make the necessary arrangements."

He turned to Mary Ellen, "I am going to need you to contact Cardinal McKenna as soon as we get back to the villa for an update on what he knows."

She was wondering to herself what the cardinal had found out. Glancing at her phone she saw that there was a message from him.

"Anthony, the cardinal called and left a voice mail. There might be enough power left to listen to it."

She immediately tried retrieving the message. Looking at Anthony, she nodded yes as she listened intently until the phone went dead.

"He said he needs to change our appointment and left a number. It's different from his private number, and I don't recognize the area code."

"When was your appointment with him?'

"That's what's strange. He knows I'm here with you this weekend. We have no appointment set up. Something's wrong."

"When we get back to the villa, you call him back after you get the phone on the charger so he sees the call is from you. What's the number he told you to call?"

Listening to the number Mary Ellen repeated, he knew immediately what the cardinal had done.

"If I'm right," said Anthony, "it's a number to a disposable phone. He must be worried about someone listening in on his calls. He didn't want the call he made to you traced."

Judah's shoulder was bleeding again. Turning to Mattithyahu, Anthony asked, "Do you know a doctor you can trust that we can pick up on the way back to the villa?"

"There is one person I know that will help us," said Mattithyahu.

"Then, let's get out of here," said Anthony.

Thankfully, they didn't have to go that far to reach the van. It was right where Mattithyahu and Judah said it would be. Anthony, Nelli, Mary Ellen, and Father Cossa would ride in the back, but first Anthony helped Judah into the passenger seat as Mattithyahu ran to get behind the wheel. Anthony then raced around and got in the back. Before the door closed, the van started moving. Anthony slammed the door shut as they sped off.

Mattithyahu was already on the phone. After a couple of calls he turned and looked at Anthony, "It's done. An uncle of mine, who's like a second father to me, is a retired doctor. He'll be waiting for us to pick him up. If I take a back route to the villa, it will only take us a couple miles out of our way."

"Can you trust him not to say anything?" asked Anthony.

"He said he wouldn't ask any questions. He will help in any way he can."

"We need to do something about Franco," added Anthony. "He'll be at the villa when we get back."

"Already been taken care of," said Judah, trying to make it appear as if the loss of blood had not affected him, but his voice was getting weaker.

"He's been told that you are on a secret assignment for the Vatican, and that Mattithyahu and I are actually your security detail. He wants to be of assistance. If he can help a cardinal from the Vatican, he feels God will bestow special blessings on him and his family. As a Catholic in Italy this would be an honor only given to a few. He would give his life for such an honor."

"All right, first pick up your uncle and then head straight to the villa."

CHAPTER SEVENTY-EIGHT

Franco was told to prepare a room with the list of medical supplies Mattithyahu had given him over the phone. Judah had been wounded and they would be bringing a doctor with them.

When the van pulled up to the villa, Franco was shocked by what he saw. He immediately took Anthony's place assisting the doctor in getting Judah upstairs. Everyone watched as the three men disappeared into a room. When Anthony turned to face the others he could see the uncertainty they were all feeling.

"Franco has kindly prepared a room for each of us, where you will find fresh clothing to change into. I suggest we freshen up and then meet back down in the library, let's say, in an hour."

Franco came rushing down the stairs. "Scusi, signore Anthony, I prepare food for everyone."

"Grazie Franco. I think we would all like to clean up first. Could you please bring it into the library when everyone has come back downstairs?"

"Si, si, of course, I will go now, prepare for you." Franco immediately headed down the hallway towards the kitchen.

Anthony was the first one down. He hadn't concerned himself with shaving, and his hair was still wet but the fresh clothes and shower felt good.

Mattithyahu was the next one to enter the library.

"How is Judah doing?" asked Anthony.

"Weaker than he had let on. Lost a lot of blood but my uncle said he'll be fine. He also said Judah was very lucky; a little lower and the bullet would have hit a major artery."

"Let's pray the past Guardians will continue to watch over us," said Anthony.

Father Cossa saw Franco coming down the hallway with the food and held the door open for him going into the library.

"Smell's wonderful. I could eat a horse, I'm so hungry," said Father Cossa jokingly.

Franco headed to a table to place the tray of food down with Father Cossa right behind him. Anthony and Mattithyahu couldn't help stare at the priest as he walked across the room. Franco had laid out a pair of jeans and a denim shirt for the priest to wear. Father Cossa saw the surprised looks and said, "Been a long time since I've worn street clothes. Feels a little strange, but I think God will forgive me this time."

"Mi perdonare, Father, they were the only clothes I find that fit you. I wash your vestments," said Franco apologetically.

"Don't worry; I'm sure that Our Lord understands the circumstances."

"Grazie," said Franco, rushing off to get the rest of the food.

Nelli and Mary Ellen entered the library right after Franco left.

"Feeling better?" asked Anthony, looking at both women. He could see they were tired as was everyone.

"Yes, it felt good to get a hot shower and put on fresh clothes," said Nelli, trying to be upbeat.

"I couldn't agree with you more," added Mary Ellen, appearing much more relaxed.

Anthony could smell cigarettes when she entered the library and knew she had been smoking again.

"I could go for a cup of coffee and some food," Mary Ellen said, heading straight towards the table where Franco had set the tray.

Mary Ellen wondered if anyone could smell if she had been smoking. She promised herself she would give them up for good when this was all over. Then noticing Father Cossa, she said, "Is this the new dress code for priests off duty?" winking and smiling warmly at him.

"What do you think? You think the Vatican would go for it?" he chuckled.

Anthony hated to ruin the moment but there were serious

matters to attend to.

"We're all here and I know everyone is tired," he said, then looked at Father Cossa, "I've sent someone to pick up your notes on the Gortyn code, Father. He should be here shortly."

Franco came through the door with the last of the food and a thermos of espresso.

"Franco, will you please show Andrew to the library when he arrives."

"Si, of course, signore Anthony, is there anything else I can bring for you?"

"No, grazie, we'll come and get you if we need anything."

"Si, I will go and attend to the laundry." Franco quietly closed the door behind him.

The aroma of coffee drifted through the air as they all stood there looking at one another waiting for someone to speak.

The library was lined with ornate bookcases made out of cypress that stretched from floor to ceiling and held countless volumes. There was a ladder attached to a metal rod that ran along the very top, allowing access to the books on the shelves. Any walls in the room that did not hold shelves were covered in dark green silk fabric. The floor made of tongue and groove planks was also made from cypress. Some historians believe the ark was constructed from the same wood.

In one corner of the room were a green suede Lawson sofa and a green and taupe tapestry upholstered Benton armchair. In another corner were two brown leather Chesterfield chairs and between them a beautiful hand carved round inlaid mahogany and walnut table. On the opposite side of the room was a library table with two chairs.

The scroll lay all alone on the long wooden table. Anthony was about to say something when Father Cossa gasped.

"What is it, Father?" asked Nelli.

Anthony and the other two Guardians went for their guns.

"Signorina Antonella, the cross around your neck, the stone in the middle …."

"What about it?"

"The stone … the stone is glowing," said Father Cossa.

As Nelli glanced down to look at the cross, it was true; the stone in the middle was emitting a white light.

"It's the scroll, I felt it the moment I laid my hand on it," said Father Cossa in a whisper. "Saint Anthony is telling us that we are in the presence of something sacred. May I ask how you came by the cross, signorina Antonella?"

"It was a gift from my father. He gave it to me just before he died."

"The Holy Spirit's presence is strong around you. You must keep the cross close to your heart," said the priest.

Nelli knew it was true. Ever since they discovered the scroll, she felt a renewed sense of purpose and what was being asked of her.

There was a soft knock at the door and in walked Andrew. He held up a black notebook.

"Is this what you wanted?"

"Yes, that's it. Grazie, grazi," said Father Cossa rushing to retrieve his notebook.

"Father, if you please," said Anthony, walking towards the table where the scroll laid. "I think it's time we get to work."

"While you two get started I think this would be a good time for me to return a call to Cardinal McKenna," said Mary Ellen, looking directly at Anthony.

"Yes, I agree," replied Anthony. "Your phone should be charged enough by now to make the call."

"I'm going to have something to eat and each of you should do the same," said Nelli. "Can I make up a plate for anyone?"

"Yes, I could use a little food and a large cup of espresso," replied Anthony. "It's going to be a long night."

"Father, how about you?" asked Nelli.

"Yes, please," but as he walked with Anthony towards the scroll, he was already immersed in his notes.

CHAPTER SEVENTY-NINE

Anyone in Peter's presence would have felt fear seeing the diabolical grin come over his face as he waited for Thomas. There was a single knock at the door. Thomas had arrived. Peter checked his watch, right on time.

"Come in."

Entering, Thomas found Peter standing on the other side of the French doors that opened onto the terrace, starring out into the hilly terrain that surrounded the villa.

"I've been waiting for you," said Peter without turning around.

He was a daunting figure dressed in black linen slacks and a gray cashmere sweater. His black hair was beginning to gray a little at the temples and at six-foot-five, you couldn't miss him in a room. Thomas never really paid attention before but he realized the Grand Master hadn't seemed to age over the years.

Peter turned and faced Thomas.

"Thomas, before I begin I'll give you a chance to explain."

Peter's black eyes pierced him like hot skewers. Thomas immediately knew what this was concerning. He gathered his thoughts together before he began speaking.

"You have always relied on me to handle the small matters, Grand Master, and I have done so, as far as I'm aware, to your satisfaction."

Peter had to agree that Thomas was right, but this time his error in judgment had cost him two of his disciples.

Thomas continued, "I was made aware of a number of

meetings between the woman, Mary Ellen O'Farrell and Cardinal McKenna from our inside contact in the Vatican, and the additional security being placed around them. I made a decision to look into it."

Thomas hesitated for a moment before continuing. He knew he had overstepped his authority by asking the Worthy Matron from the Grand Lodge Droit Humain to assist in the matter. He was sure the Grand Master was now aware of this.

"You dared to contact Catherine under the pretenses that I requested her assistance in this matter!" Peter's rage could not to be contained.

Thomas remembered only one other time he had seen Peter so angry. It was right before he had ordered that Roberto Calvi—the president of Banco Ambrosiano, owned in part by the Vatican Bank—be killed. That time he had not been the cause for Peter's rage.

"I only requested if she could recommend a member of her Lodge she could trust to follow Ms. O'Farrell when she went to Pesaro on vacation to meet friends. I assumed there was little threat from her if she was not at the Vatican. I still figured it would be better to have her followed just to make sure."

"Well, you assumed incorrectly. I made the decision to have them quietly eliminated. I was not going to have anything jeopardize my plan this time. I did not expect to be met with resistance and it has gotten two of my disciples and a priest killed."

Thomas's heart stopped; had he heard correctly? Taking a deep breath he asked, "How? When?" Now Thomas knew why he had sensed fear around the two bodyguards earlier. They must have known two of their brothers had been killed.

In a calm but deadly tone, Peter said, "The priest I could care less about but my two disciples—they will pay for their deaths.

"They?" asked Thomas.

"This O'Farrell woman and her two friends, the brother and sister, and whoever else is protecting them."

"Where did this all happen?" asked Thomas. He was still trying to make sense of it all.

"They were followed to Gradara Castle. Once inside they added two priests to their small entourage and were secretly taken inside a private chapel not open to the public."

"Do we know what's inside the chapel?" said Thomas. He

needed facts to try and piece together a plan. The medieval fortress was the setting for the tragic love story of Paolo and Francesca. Many went there to see the bedroom in which her husband Gianciotto murdered Francesca and his brother with his sword. So why was there interest in the chapel?

"What about the bodies? We must get rid of them before they are discovered," said Thomas.

"Do you think that has not already been taken care of," growled Peter. "I have waited too long for my plan to fail now. I will not have it destroyed due to your stupidity. Due to the quick thinking of Christine, all the bodies have been disposed of."

For the first time Thomas realized the Grand Master no longer had complete trust in him. He knew his authority over the disciples was also in jeopardy. He had to correct this catastrophe.

"Christine must know where to find the others," said Thomas. "With your permission, I will contact the Worthy Matron and send someone to take care of the problem."

With that question Thomas could feel the rage building in the Grand Master. Peter turned his back to Thomas to look out over the vast open land that surrounded P2's initiation compound. At one time it was productive farmland. Cows and sheep roamed the hills, olive trees grew, and acres of grapevines covered the hills that produced wine and olive oil. The monks from the abbey, he could see off in the distance, had attended to the land during that time.

As he stared at the peak of the old abbey, he contemplated why so many would give up everything, all worldly possessions to preach or follow the words of one they had never even seen.

Peter did not turn around but the words Thomas would never forget, "They have disappeared."

CHAPTER EIGHTY

Anthony and Father Cossa stood there for a moment looking at the ancient artifact lying on the table in front of them. They both realized that they were in the presence of something sacred.

"Well Father," said Anthony, "I believe it was God's plan for us to discover this scroll. What we will find inside it I do not know but there is a reason why we now have it in our possession. Since you chose to follow Our Lord's calling to the priesthood as did Saint Anthony, I believe you should have the honors."

Father Cossa looked at Anthony, then at the sacred scroll, then back at Anthony. He didn't feel worthy. The realization that he could soon be looking at the words the Lord spoke to a young monk centuries ago rendered him immobile.

"Father, are you all right?" asked Anthony.

The priest seemed to be in a trance. Then Father Cossa's lips moved.

He spoke so softly Anthony wasn't sure what he said but then he saw the priest's hands begin to move slowly towards the scroll. They were shaking. Anthony hadn't noticed before but they were the hands of a scholar that turned pages of books and lovingly transcribed words onto paper, not hands that had seen manual labor.

All of a sudden Father Cossa grasped his hands, trying to stop them from shaking.

"Just take your time, Father," said Anthony but the priest pulled his hands back towards his body.

"No Anthony, you and Antonella were named after our

beloved Saint Anthony. If your sister is the Chosen One, then she should be the one to open this sacred scroll."

Anthony realized Father Cossa was right. He turned, looking at his sister; Nelli nodded and took the place of Father Cossa.

Taking a deep breath, she leaned closer to the table and gently touched the leather ties wrapped around the scroll. The others watched as Nelli ran her fingers around the knot and the leather strap, letting them guide her.

"Remarkable, after all this time the leather has not dried out," she said speaking to no one in particular. "It's stiff, but not brittle."

Nelli leaned even closer to the scroll and softly massaged the knot working to loosen it. The others in the room barely breathed—worried that might cause the scroll to crumble into a million pieces.

"Let your sense of touch and Saint Anthony guide you Nelli," Anthony said.

After a while the knot began to loosen and the two leather ties gently fell to each side. The rolled sheepskin loosened slightly as if it had taken its first breath after a very long time.

Father Cossa made the sign of the cross. His mouth was moving but no sound came from his lips. The Chosen One seemed to be encircled by the same Holy Presence that surrounded the scroll.

Suddenly, Nelli let go of the scroll, watching as letters of light were being revealed through the sheepskin.

"Do you see them?" Nelli said in awe. "It's the same writing that we saw back in the chapel."

Anthony and Father Cossa looked at each other puzzled. All they saw was a rolled up sheepskin.

Nelli sensed a new presence in the room and then heard her father's voice as if he was standing right next to her.

"Dear Antonella, we are here with you, all the past Keepers of the Key. Remember to be pure of heart. If you are, you have nothing to fear."

Then the letters slowly disappeared and the scroll returned back to normal.

"Did you hear him, Anthony?"

"Hear who, Nelli?"

"Father, he was just here. He was talking to me."

"No, I didn't hear anything."

Nelli looked at Anthony and saw the sadness in his eyes. She knew he would have loved to hear their father's voice and be able to speak with him, but she also knew that he had accepted the roles they had each been chosen for. She turned her attention back to the scroll. The others in the room watched . . . mesmerized.

She slowly began unrolling the sheepskin. The letters became words, words she could not read but that appeared to be alive as if they were a living and breathing entity. They were the words a young monk was commanded to write down 600 years earlier. There was nothing more she could do. It was up to Father Cossa and Anthony now to translate the ancient writing.

Father Cossa had his notebook open and was already working on trying to decode the manuscript. Just before the priest made the decision that Nelli should be the one to open the scroll, Mary Ellen placed a call to Cardinal McKenna. With what the cardinal had told her and what she was witnessing, it was almost more than she could absorb.

Nelli stepped aside so that Anthony and Father Cossa could work on deciphering the letters that lay before them. There were no words to explain what had just happened to her. The only thing she knew was she was exhausted.

Anthony watched Nelli turn and walk over to the sofa. There was something different about her, when she touched the scroll it seemed as if she and the scroll became one. So much has happened in such a short time; the death of their father, coming to Italy, and the discovery of the stigmata on Nelli's hand. And, making the calls to the other Guardians to announce that the Chosen One was among them . . . and Mary Ellen coming back into his life. He worried would he be strong enough to protect his sister against the forces that wanted to stop her?

Nelli sat down and rested her head against one of the pillows on the sofa, her eyes already starting to close. Looking up, Anthony saw Mary Ellen standing off to the side. He could see her mind was somewhere else.

Turning to Father Cossa, he said, "I'll be right back Father," and he walked over to Mary Ellen.

"Mary Ellen," said Anthony, gently touching her arm. She looked at him with a blank stare. He touched her arm again.

"Mary Ellen, did you get hold of Cardinal McKenna?"

Suddenly she realized Anthony had asked her a question.

"Yes, I did Anthony."

"And what did he tell you?"

"It looks as if he might be right about what could be happening. It's no wonder I could never clear Devlin's name. He is only one out of thousands being used as puppets to achieve the goal of someone completely evil."

"What is it he uncovered?" Anthony asked, almost afraid to hear what she had to say.

"Do you remember when you told me about the prophecy of Saint Anthony and a time could come when a serpent with the head of a cobra would rise again?"

"Yes, of course, it was all because of that card with the embossed cobra head on it that you received."

"Cardinal McKenna has discovered that a secret society called P2 is headed by a man they call the Grand Master. During their initiation ceremony he is addressed as the Naj Hannah. Do you know what the name means?"

Anthony could see the fear in Mary Ellen's eyes.

"Translated it means King Cobra. It is believed by some that P2 was behind the short life of Pope John Paul I. P2 members had infiltrated into the Vatican, bishops and even cardinals were believed to be members of this secret society. It was thought that the goal of the Naj Hannah was to proclaim himself Pope, the new representative of God on earth and to create a New World Order, which would rule over all religions and all governments. He would become known as the Antichrist. There's more Anthony. You won't believe what I have to tell you next. The initiation compound is not far from here. It's just outside of Pesaro. The cardinal fears we could be in danger."

"Well, unfortunately, we have already found that out Mary Ellen," said Anthony.

"He believes Cardinal Cavallari in the Vatican belongs to P2 and that each member wears a ring that covers a small tattoo of a cobra's head. By twisting the ring and exposing the tattoo, they affirm to one another their membership in P2. Devlin noticed a similar behavior among certain members of the LC."

"Is Cardinal McKenna worried about his safety?" Anthony inquired.

"He knows he's being watched. He's meeting with the

Commander of the Swiss Guard to present his findings. He believes time is crucial. Whatever is going to happen, is going to happen soon."

"What did you tell him about Nelli?"

"Nothing, but I think he suspects something," she said. "All he said was: I pray that the book is found soon. He will call back after his meeting with the commander."

"We have to find that book," said Anthony with a sense of urgency.

"What can I do to help?" asked Mary Ellen.

"Nothing at the moment, I pray Father Cossa and I can translate what's written in the scroll and that it tells us where the book is hidden," he responded.

"What if it doesn't Anthony?"

"I'll cross that bridge when the time comes. Nelli is being guided by a power greater than all of us. I will do what I can and wait to be shown the next step to take."

"There's got to be something I can do to help," Mary Ellen pleaded.

"I know you want to help but right now Father Cossa and I need to decipher the scroll. You could help me by watching over Nelli and getting some rest."

Mary Ellen looked at Anthony with respect and admiration. Her feelings for him were returning. She had been foolish to push him away because of her preoccupation with clearing her brother's name. She was never able to prove his innocence. Finally, she was learning why with the help of Anthony and Nelli.

CHAPTER EIGHTY-ONE

Grabbing a cup of coffee and some food, Mary Ellen sat down in the chair next to where Nelli was sleeping. Sipping her coffee, she watched Anthony and Father Cossa studying the scroll.

Pulling up the Internet on her phone, she googled Saint Anthony, a long list of websites appeared. Opening the first, she started looking for any reference to a private journal or manuscript kept by the monk. As she was doing that, across the room Anthony was trying to decipher the writing using the boustrophedon algorithm. Father Cossa worked on transposing the letters from Greek to English.

"More coffee, Father?" asked Anthony.

"Si, perhaps you could just bring the thermos over here. We have a long night ahead of us."

As Anthony walked over to get more coffee, he saw that Nelli was still asleep and Mary Ellen's head was now resting on the back of the chair with her eyes closed. It felt good knowing for now that the two most important women in his life were safe. He wondered what would happen once they found the book, or worse, if they didn't find it.

"Don't dwell on what ifs," he told himself. "It wasn't by accident, their meeting Father Cossa and then finding the scroll."

The priest stared at the words in front of him. Turning around looking for Anthony, he frantically motioned for him to return.

Grabbing the thermos, Anthony headed back to the table. "What is it? Did you find where the book is hidden?"

"Saint Anthony was known as the greatest thaumaturgist and teacher of the Scriptures," said Father Cossa. "It was believed that nothing was left of his sermons or lectures, the primitive ones as well as the legendary ones."

"So how does that help us here?" asked Anthony.

"There were three well-known manuscripts scholars have hoped one day to find: *Expositio in Psalmos* written at Montpellier in 1224; *Sermones de tempore*; and *Sermones de Sanctis* written at Padua between 1229 and 1230. I believe this scroll is the first of the three I just mentioned, *Expositio in Psalmos.*

Anthony remembered reading something about these during his research on Saint Anthony and realized what a great discovery it would be if they weren't facing the possible demise of Christianity. Trying to remain calm, he responded, "Father I realize what an archaeological discovery this could be, but we have a much more pressing problem."

Father Cossa was busy writing in his notebook and wasn't listening.

Anthony snapped at the priest, "Have you forgotten what is at stake here, Father? We need to find a book that could save the souls of millions. If this manuscript doesn't tell us where to find it, then it is irrelevant."

Father Cossa looked up and saw the indignation in Anthony's face. He smiled.

"Do not despair, my son, I believe Saint Anthony has hidden within this manuscript what the Chosen One needs to know."

For a moment, Anthony had allowed his anger to cloud his judgment. He had jumped to a conclusion without having all the information. He flashed back to the summers when he and the eleven other boys were taught that anger serves no purpose; it only prevents one from moving forward.

More calmly this time, Anthony asked, "Have you found something that can show us where to look?"

"I believe so. Cryptology has been a passion of mine. The originator of an encrypted document shared the decoding technique only with intended recipients, thereby preventing unwanted persons from being able to read the message they are sending without having the secret knowledge of the code.

"The boustrophedon text that we see here is taken from the Greek language. It is a type of bi-directional text, which you spoke of back in the chapel. What is unique is there were additional twists, which were used to confuse the decoder even more. A boustrophedonic script called Rongorongo has remained undeciphered to this day. I have been trying to break the code but never had an example of writings to work with until today.

"It is used in combination with the bi-directional text, an upside down and a reverse boustrophedon. In addition there were no spaces between words and it was written, albeit irregularly: reading from top to bottom, lines 1, 3, 5, 7, 9, 11, 12, 14, 16 run from right to left; lines 2, 4, 6, 8, 10, 13, and 15, from left to right; 8, 9 and 16 are upside down.

"Please write down exactly what I tell you. When we are finished, I believe the message Saint Anthony cleverly hid within this manuscript will be revealed to us."

CHAPTER EIGHTY-TWO

Nelli opened her eyes and saw her brother and Father Cossa across the room in deep conversation. To her left, Mary Ellen was asleep and Andrew and Mattithyahu were stationed on opposite sides of the library, standing guard. There was a new person in the room standing off to the right. He must have come in while she was asleep.

"Ah, you are awake," said the stranger walking towards her, "You needed to sleep."

He was dressed in an old fashion monk's cassock. Because of the brown color of his vestments she wondered what religious order he was from. Still not completely awake, she watched the monk sit down next to her. There was something familiar about him. Then her eyes grew wide.

"Yes, Antonella it is me," said Saint Anthony, smiling at her. "The end of your journey is drawing near. Anthony and the Guardians will keep you safe. You possess everything you need to unlock a gift I was given a long time ago. When you find it, deliver it to the one who waits for you."

"How will I know where to look?" asked Nelli.

"When the time comes, those who trust in the Lord will be shown the way. I must depart now, but know I am always right here beside you."

Out of the corner of his eye Anthony saw that Nelli was waking up.

"I'm glad you were able to get some rest," he said.

"What are you talking about? I was talking to …." she

turned her head to look at Saint Anthony, but no one was there.

"No, Nelli you just woke up."

"How long was I asleep?"

"Almost two hours," Anthony responded, guessing she'd had another vision.

Looking over at him, Nelli confirmed what he had already surmised.

Hearing Nelli, Mary Ellen woke up, knocking the plate of food off the table. "Did something happen?"

"I believe Nelli might have something to tell everyone," said Anthony.

Nelli sat quietly for a moment and then in a calm and steady voice relayed her conversation with Saint Anthony word-for-word. No one in the room even questioned that it wasn't the truth.

"While you were asleep, I believe Father Cossa and I have deciphered a passage from the scroll."

All eyes in the room now converged on Anthony.

"We believe we've found a hidden message concealed within the writings."

Words can often change in meaning," said Father Cossa, "but I will read what I believe to be as close to the translation as I could come."

Picking up a sheet of paper, he began reading.

Blessed is the Keeper of the Key
For they shall cut off the head of the serpent.
The Ark of the Testament
holds the gift that you seek.
A statue in my honor will
point you to the peak.
Find the final resting place and
remember the words of your father
Be Pure of Heart.
There is where you will find the key

"It's a riddle," said Nelli. "It talks about the Ark of the Testament. Mankind has been searching for that for centuries, and there are hundreds of statues of Saint Anthony." For the first time, she wondered if they would find the book in time.

Father Cossa saw the disappointment in Nelli's face.

Anthony had also hoped for more. He had counted on learning the exact location of the book.

Nelli sat holding onto the cross her father had given her.

"Would you please read the message again, Father?" she asked.

Father Cossa read it again, this time more slowly.

Nelli realized she heard what she wanted to hear the first time it was read. She was mad at herself. There were other ways to interpret the message. What she has been told over and over again appeared here in the passage from the scroll: "Be pure of heart and you will be shown the way."

"Please forgive me," said Nelli, "I allowed myself to question God's plan and whether he had chosen the wrong person for this mission. I will not question His plan again."

"My child, even the apostles questioned our Lord of the things he asked of them," replied Father Cossa. "Do not be disheartened by a moment of weakness. When asked, you chose to accept the responsibility that you were given. Your faith won, that's what's important." He smiled as a loving parent would to a child."

"It's telling us where to look," said Nelli. "At first, I thought it was telling us we're supposed to find the final resting place of the Ark of the Covenant, the Holy Grail, but what if we're supposed to look for the final resting place of Saint Anthony, and that will point us to this Ark of the Testament that holds a gift we seek?"

Mary Ellen gasped, remembering something she had read about Saint Anthony and of the testament's reference she'd come across while searching the Web just before falling asleep.

"Oh my God!" she shouted.

Andrew and Mattithyahu pulled out their guns, thinking she saw something. Everyone's attention was now on Mary Ellen. Grabbing her phone, she began scrolling through her searches on Saint Anthony.

"Here it is! I came across this doing a Web search just before I fell asleep, the new Pope, Gregory IX, the former Cardinal Ugolino, a friend and sponsor of the young monk Anthony, invited him to preach to the Curia. This was not unusual when a distinguished preacher was available. Preaching from his extensive knowledge of the Scriptures, yet in a way accessible even to the uneducated, the cardinals were impressed and the Pope coined a new title for Anthony, Ark of the Testament."

"Why did the Pope choose this phrase? Certainly it had something to do with Anthony's familiarity with the Old and New Testaments. When Anthony wrote the prologue to his Scriptural Commentaries for Sundays, he began with a text from the Book of Chronicles, which tells how King David gave gold to make the figures of the cherubim that decorated the original ark. The theme of the ark returns several times in Anthony's writings. There are, in fact, two arks mentioned in the Scriptures, that of Moses and that of Noah."

Mary Ellen stopped reading and looked up, "You won't believe what I am going to read next."

"Anthony wrote that an ark was simply a chest or strong-box, in which valuables were kept safe from theft or damage. Now here, listen, later on his tomb was often referred to as the ark."

The room fell silent.

In a quiet voice, Nelli asked, "Father Cossa do you have knowledge of where Saint Anthony's final resting place might be?"

"It is well-known and it's not far from here, about 187 km, or about a two-hour drive. Padua, better known as the city of the saint, the most beloved saint in the world, the one you were named after, my two new friends, Saint Anthony."

There it was again, the guiding hand gently leading them on their journey!

"Do you know the exact location of where his remains are buried in Padua?" asked Anthony.

Chuckling, Father Cossa answered, "Being so loved was Saint Anthony that a magnificent basilica was built to house his remains. It is not easily missed when you visit Padua."

CHAPTER **EIGHTY-THREE**

Time was critical. The meeting with Commander Valentino Crevelli made that clear. After hearing everything McKenna had to say, the head of the Swiss Guards told the cardinal they had been following the activities of the LC for a long time. McKenna listened as the Commander continued.

"After Father Roberto's death, I contacted a longtime friend of mine outside of the Vatican, and asked him to find out everything he could on the cobra symbol that was left next to the body.

"A few years ago the Italian justice reopened the investigation on the defunct Banco Ambrosiano and an organization called P2—learning that the bank had set up branches in Lima and other South American countries. It has been brought to my attention that secret transactions and possible money laundering has been taking place with a bank in Rio de Janeiro.

"The bank is run by the son-in-law of a former deputy chairman of Banco Ambrosiano, Carlo De Benedetti, who was convicted of fraud by a Milan court in connection with its collapse.

"Also, after Pope John Paul I's death, it was believed P2 had been abolished, but the Vatican remained diligent on following up on any leads on members who might still be active. We could not have a repeat of September 1978.

"We've been monitoring the activities of several cardinals within the Vatican as well as other clergy from around the world.

"When Ms. O'Farrell started looking into clearing her brother's name and Father Roberto discovered some aberrant activity associated with the LC, we became concerned. We believe this time there is a threat not only to the Vatican, but also to the world."

Cardinal McKenna was speechless; he relayed his meeting with Cardinal Cavallari.

"He is one of the cardinals we have been watching very closely," replied the Commander.

"Are you aware of the strange marking beneath the ring he wears?" asked McKenna.

"No. Please clarify."

"Ms. O'Farrell told me that her brother mentioned an idiosyncrasy he had observed with a few of the priests when he was with the LC. On occasion, a few of them would appear to spin the ring on their finger when they would gather, but he brushed it off as a nervous tic. In my meeting with Cavallari, I caught a glimpse of some kind of tattoo that was hidden under his ring."

"Continue," said Crevelli.

"I believe it's a tattoo of a cobra's head. That is how they acknowledge to each other they are a member of P2."

The commander picked up the phone and barked orders to the person on the other end.

"Pull up all the video we have with Cardinal Cavallari in them and look for any unusual behavior pertaining to the ring finger. Report back to me immediately." He slammed the phone down.

"Is there anything else you have not told me, cardinal?"

McKenna hesitated. He knew that the commander had been around the spiritual leaders of the Vatican most of his life, but his world was one of gathering information, getting evidence, and profiling people. What he was about to tell the commander was based on faith, prophecy, and personal belief.

"Cardinal McKenna, time is our enemy; you need to tell me everything you know."

"All right, here it goes. Ms. O'Farrell's friends, the brother and sister … I believe … one of them could be the Chosen One spoken of in the prophecy of Saint Anthony," said Cardinal McKenna.

The commander was trying to grasp the ramifications of what Cardinal McKenna had just told him. He had always dealt with facts but could this time be different? Was there more happening here than just the human need for power and money?

"If you are correct Cardinal McKenna, then we could be facing what the Bible speaks of in the Book of Revelations. May God bless all the souls of the faithful."

It seemed as if the commander aged ten years right before McKenna's eyes.

"I must tell you Cardinal McKenna, Pope Benedict has always felt a special connection to Saint Anthony. He believes in the prophecy, that a Chosen One or the Keeper of the Key will deliver the words of Our Lord and have the power to convert all the lost souls on earth. If Saint Malachy's prediction is correct, Pope Benedict is the second to the last Pope on his list to be followed only by one called Peter Romanus, Peter the Roman. Saint Peter being the rock the church was built on, Peter Romanus, with the help of Satan, would be the one to tear down the church."

The phone rang, startling both men.

"Yes, when was the last one noticed and where?" asked Crevelli. All the color drained from the commander's face.

"Bring those to me now and prepare to move the Pope."

"Cardinal McKenna, I need to get in touch with Ms. O'Farrell immediately. If what you believe is correct, the world is in grave danger. I am moving the Pope to a secure location for his safety. We need to know if she is the Chosen One and if this book has been found that Saint Anthony speaks of in his prophecy. We must get it to Pope Benedict. It could be our last hope for the church and all mankind. I have arranged for additional security for you. And once you know the location of Ms. O'Farrell and her friends, they will have protection 24/7. You must excuse me now cardinal."

"Yes of course. I will contact you as soon as I know anything." As he exited, he could already hear Commander Crevelli giving orders over the phone.

Heading back to his office, McKenna passed by colleagues he'd known for years. Now he wondered if any of them had the cobra tattoo. As he got closer to the Apostolic Palace he saw Cardinal Cavallari up ahead talking with two other priests. One of the men looked up when he sensed McKenna approaching. McKenna could tell they did not want their conversation to be overheard. Cavallari turned to see what his companion was looking at. If looks could kill McKenna would now be with Father Roberto. Turning his back, Cavallari said a few words to his companions, and then they dispersed going in separate directions.

Time was running out. It was as if his body knew it before his brain did and was pushing him to walk faster. His heart was pounding and his mind racing. He had to talk to Mary Ellen and find out if her friend was the Chosen One and if she had the book. When he entered his office he found out that his assistant, Robert, had been replaced with an officer from the Swiss Guard.

"Cardinal McKenna my name is Angelo; Commander Crevelli has asked me to be of service to you for the next few days. Robert was asked to help on a project over at the Vatican Archives. While you were out, we took the liberty to sweep your office for any unwanted devices."

"Thank you, Angelo. That is comforting to know."

He missed having Robert there, but he did feel safer with this young officer outside his door. Wanting to contact Mary Ellen immediately, he entered his office, but decided to first stop and wind his father's clock just a few turns.

Reaching for the key, it accidentally slipped off the edge and fell on the floor. As he bent down to pick it up, the window behind his desk suddenly exploded. As he dove to the floor, a bullet missed his head by inches.

Angelo came rushing through the door, his gun pointed, ready to kill the intruder. Not seeing anyone, he immediately looked to find out where the shot came from, at the same time yelling, "Cardinal McKenna have you been hit?"

"No, it missed me."

"Stay down," Angelo shouted, taking a quick glance to make sure the cardinal was telling the truth, then ran to the window to see if he could tell where the shot came from. The two Swiss Guards outside the entrance to the office were now in the room. One of them was on his cell phone, getting instructions.

"Cardinal, if you would please come with us, we must get you to a safe location," said Angelo.

One of the guards helped McKenna up, who stood for a moment staring at his father's clock. It was his usual routine to stop and wind the clock every evening as he left the office but something had told him to wind it this morning.

"Please, Cardinal McKenna, we must go," Angelo said now in a commanding tone.

"I'm sorry, please lead the way," he answered.

Before turning his back on the clock, McKenna silently thanked his father for saving his life.

McKenna was taken through a secret door that led into the tunnels beneath St. Peter's. Angelo seemed to know his way among the catacombs, taking them to a secure location underground that the cardinal didn't even know existed.

Once inside, he was asked to make a list of any materials he wanted from his office and they would be brought to him. He handed the list to a young man that looked too young to be a member of the Swiss Guard.

"Thank you, Cardinal McKenna. What you have requested will be brought to you as quickly as possible. Commander Crevelli would like me to remind you of his request for you to make a call to the person the two of you spoke of at the end of your meeting."

McKenna almost forgot, with what had just happened.

The guard continued, "To your right is a room with a desk and a secured phone line for your use."

"Thank you," replied McKenna. "I will make the call immediately. Please inform the commander and bring me my things as soon as they arrive."

"Of course."

McKenna didn't need to fear a bullet finding him down here, there were no windows. It was some kind of underground bunker. Angelo would return to the office and remain stationed at the desk. He would spend the rest of the day answering calls and rescheduling meetings, telling everyone that Cardinal McKenna had come down with a nasty flu bug.

CHAPTER EIGHTY-FOUR

General D'Amoto understood that there was to be no further communication between the members of the Inner Circle or with Thomas until the announcement by the new Pope establishing the New World Order. So why was he receiving this call?

He was chosen because of his expertise and he had done his job well, if he must say so himself, to perfection. The final stage of the plan was underway and as a military leader he taught his soldiers to follow orders even if it meant death. When he was told there was a call from a man named Thomas, it did not sit well with him.

He stared at the phone trying to decide if he should take the call. On the other end, Thomas waited impatiently.

Finally, D'Amoto reached for the phone.

"This is General D'Amoto."

"It took you long enough to answer," snapped Thomas. "Something has come up. I need you to send someone to pick up a brother and sister and their companions. They've rented a villa outside of Pesaro."

"There was to be no …." but before D'Amoto could finish his sentence, Thomas cut him off.

"Just do it," he said, "and bring them to the compound."

There was a moment of silence.

"I will make the necessary arrangements."

Outside of Pesaro the dark blue Alfa Romeo with the unmistakable white roof and red stripe on the side sped up the cypress-lined gravel road to the circle drive of the Villa Cattani

Stuart. The patrol car carried the captain and one other officer of the Carabinieri police force, followed closely behind by an Iveco VM 90 van holding four more officers. The captain was a longtime friend of General D'Amoto. If called, he would assist his friend, no questions asked. Once his officers had surrounded the villa, the captain pounded on the door.

"Polizia!" Noticing the ring on his finger had shifted slightly, exposing the corner of a tattoo, he pushed it back in place.

Franco never much liked the man that was now knocking at the door but he would give him the respect he demanded as the local police captain.

"Buon giorno. How may I assist you today, captain?" said Franco politely.

"Your guests, the Americans, where are they?"

Franco acted surprised.

"They're no longer here. I'm just finishing the last of cleaning before locking up and heading home. Why, has something happened?"

The captain didn't bother to answer, walking right past Franco.

"If you don't mind, I will take a look for myself." He pointed to his other officer to cover the first floor while he headed upstairs.

"Chiaramente, of course," said Franco, stepping to the side. As he stood waiting he could feel sweat beading up under his shirt. After a few minutes, the captain was back.

"Where are they headed?"

"I'm sorry, I don't know. Although, I overhear signore mention Rome. They asked phone numbers of airlines and car rental agencies, then got into vehicle and left. Perhaps they are taking scenic drive back to Rome." Franco prayed he believed him.

The police officer knew the man's family well. They were devout Catholics, he still wondered if Franco was telling the truth.

"What kind of car were they driving?"

Franco knew the captain was trying to decide if he was lying or not. He needed to appear calm and not allow the captain to see he was scared.

"I so sorry, I do not know the make of car. I can tell you it was dark green. If you're finished here, I need to lock up and get home to my Angelina."

"Si, but do not go far. I may need to have you come down to the station later." The police captain turned and headed to his car.

On the way back to headquarters he started working on locating the car. He had someone call all the rental car companies trying to find out the make, model, and license plate number of the vehicle the Americans were driving. He was determined to hand these Americans over to D'Amoto before evening.

By the time he arrived back at the police station his men had the information he requested. Pulling out a map, he began setting up roadblocks. Once that was done, he decided that he would make his call. He knew the general would not be happy that he did not have the Americans in custody, but when he told him of the steps he was taking perhaps D'Amoto would be appeased for the moment.

Placing the receiver back in its base the captain sat back in his chair. Perspiration stained his shirt collar as he ran his finger along the inside to separate it from his neck. D'Amoto had given him 'til five o'clock to locate the Americans.

He'd heard rumors of what happens to those who disappointed the general. He didn't want to find out for himself if the reports were true. There was a knock at the door.

"Captain, the chopper spotted the car. It was headed to Rome like the caretaker thought."

"Have you seized the car and are the occupants under arrest?"

"Yes and no, captain."

"Either we do or we don't, which is it?" he snapped.

"The car has been secured and we do have the one occupant under arrest."

"What do you mean the one occupant?"

"There was only the driver and he's not American. He's a resident of Pesaro, sir."

"Who are these Americans?" shouted the captain. "They must have thought they'd be followed and set up the decoy."

He'd done what General D'Amoto had asked of him. The general couldn't hold him responsible for the ruse by the Americans.

"What did you find out from the driver?"

"His friend who owns a truck rental company had a man

stop in to rent a truck and asked if they knew of anyone who might want to earn some money driving a car back to Rome. The owner said a friend of his could use the extra cash and contacted him."

"I assume you've talked to the owner?"

"He didn't know much more. The man was an Americano. He was looking for a truck to haul some small items. The owner of the truck rental told the American he had nothing available on such short notice. The customer was persistent. He had seen a truck in the parking lot for a company that processes olive oil and asked if that was available to rent. It would do just fine for what he needed. He would pay well to rent it. The owner was letting his brother-in-law park the truck there for the week. He decided if the man was willing to pay a lot, why not. His brother-in-law would be happy with the extra money."

"Get the license number of that truck and find it," screamed the captain.

CHAPTER EIGHTY-FIVE

They had been driving north on A13 for more than an hour. The rental car Anthony paid a young man to drive to Rome was headed in the opposite direction if they were followed. He hoped the story that they were taking the scenic drive back to Rome would work.

Andrew and Anthony sat up front in the delivery truck while Nelli, Mary Ellen, and Father Cossa rode in the back on a makeshift bench. On the outside of the truck, bold lettering read: **Agricola e Biofattoria Aleandri - Single Estate Organic Olive Oil**. In Italy the highways were littered with trucks from small family owned vineyards delivering their products to restaurants and stores. No one would give it a second look as they passed the truck.

Mattithyahu and Judah, who refused to remain in Pesaro, followed behind in a car. Anthony was on the phone with Cephas who informed him that they now believed the person in the mail room was Cardinal Cavallari.

The missing pieces began to fall into place. Cardinal McKenna believed Cavallari was a member of P2. Anthony updated Cephas on their plans and arranged for the Guardians to meet them in Padua.

Mary Ellen's phone rang. The small window in the panel separating the front cab of the truck to the back was open. Looking at Anthony, Mary Ellen said, "I don't recognize the number. It's not the one Cardinal McKenna told me to call him at. Should I answer it?"

Anthony nodded yes.

Putting the phone up to her ear, Mary Ellen hesitated, "Hello?"

"Mary Ellen, its Cardinal McKenna. Can you talk freely?"

"Yes, but where are you calling from? It's not the number you gave me."

"I'm in a secure location."

"Secure location? What's happened?" Everyone listened intently to the conversation.

"There was an attempt on my life but of course you can hear they failed," said McKenna.

"Who? When?" Mary Ellen asked.

"The who I think you probably can figure out, the rest is not important right now. My meeting with Commander Crevelli was very eye-opening and disturbing. The commander and I will be working together from this point on, but Mary Ellen I must have you tell me everything you've learned. The future of the Church and possibly all of mankind could depend on it."

Mary Ellen covered the phone, "Someone tried to kill the cardinal. He's working with the head of the Swiss Guard. He wants me to tell him everything I know." Mary Ellen looked at Anthony, then Nelli, waiting to see what they wanted her to do.

"Mary Ellen, are you still there?" asked Cardinal McKenna.

"Yes, cardinal, one moment please."

Nelli calmly turned to Mary Ellen, "You need to tell him everything."

Mary Ellen glanced over at Anthony to get a second okay. He nodded his approval. She put the phone back up to her ear.

"Cardinal McKenna, what is it that you want to know?" she asked.

Cardinal McKenna hesitated, taking a deep breath, "You mentioned to me that your friends, the brother and sister, were each named after the beloved Saint Anthony. You call the woman Nelli but you use the name Anthony for the man." Pausing, he said, "Is Anthony the Chosen One spoken of in the prophecy of Saint Anthony?"

Mary Ellen expected the question, but even with the seriousness of the situation she smiled. "No, Cardinal McKenna, Anthony is not the one. Thomas is his given name. Anthony is his middle name."

Everyone knew what the cardinal must have asked Mary Ellen. They could almost see the disappointment on his face, believing all was lost.

"Cardinal McKenna, I believe Nelli might be of some benefit."

The cardinal didn't understand, "Does she know who it might be?" he asked.

Ignoring his question, Mary Ellen said, "Cardinal McKenna, a name can often have two different spellings."

He didn't hear a thing Mary Ellen said after that.

"Nelli … Nelli could be a nickname. What was the female name in Italian for Anthony?" He remembered Antonella!

From the silence on the other end, Mary Ellen knew he had figured it out.

"Is she with you now?" Cardinal McKenna asked with reverence. "Does she have the book?"

"Yes, but no, we do not have the book. We are headed to where we believe it is hidden."

Mary Ellen filled Cardinal McKenna in on everything that had happened in the last twenty-four hours. McKenna took notes. He wanted to be sure he didn't leave anything out when he relayed the information to the commander. Within a short time he knew everything.

"Mary Ellen, please inform your friends that Pope Benedict has been moved to a secret location, although it is made to appear that he is in residence at the Apostolic Palace. But from what you have told me, we could be running out of time. It looks as if the future of the Church rests upon the shoulders of the Chosen One. Is there anything I can do to help?"

"There is one thing, Cardinal McKenna. In the Scriptures, it is written that the Ark of the Covenant holds the Tablets of Stone on which the Ten Commandments were inscribed but are there any other ways the term has been referenced in the Bible?"

"I will do some research and get back to you," replied Cardinal McKenna. "How long before you reach Padua?"

"Anthony estimates we should be there in less than thirty minutes."

"I am going to ask the commander to send one of the Vatican's private jets to the closest airstrip near there. It will be waiting to bring the Chosen One and the book back to Rome. Additional security will be sent as soon as I inform Commander Crevelli of your location. I'll text you with the directions to the airstrip and call as soon as I find out any other reference used for the Ark of the Covenant. Godspeed."

CHAPTER **EIGHTY-SIX**

PADUA

Citta di oldst in Italy Settentrionale

1.6 km

Exit VIA BATTAGLIA

Inside the truck the sense of anticipation about finding the book was palpable.

"There it is—the exit for Padua." said Andrew. "Watch for a sign that shows which way to Prato della Valle Square. We can park the truck down one of the side streets, and then walk from there. A portion of the city's center is closed to traffic except for pedestrians. That way we can blend in and be less conspicuous. Keep your eyes open for an empty parking spot."

"We can't keep driving around," said Anthony, "we're wasting time."

"Let's go down a couple more streets and see if we don't find something, or we'll have to come up with another plan," Andrew replied.

On the next corner there was a small outdoor cafe with people seated at tables, most likely tourists visiting Padua for the day. Andrew turned right on a side street.

"Slow down, back up, there, behind the restaurant," Anthony pointed.

"It's fenced off To'mas," said Andrew, "the sign says: Deliveries Only - Violators will be Towed."

"I know. Pull over and get out. Wait there with the others. I will park the truck and pretend to be making a delivery. I'll leave a note on the window saying I will be back after getting something to eat. No one will question it being parked there with the company signage on the side."

Mattithyahu and Judah were following close behind. They saw Andrew get out with the others and stopped to find out what To'mas was up to. After hearing the plan, they started looking for a place to park. Half way down the street, Nelli saw the taillights of a car come on.

"Look Mattithyahu, that car is leaving," yelled Nelli.

Stepping on the gas, he cut in front of the car that was coming down the street and grabbed the parking spot. As the second car passed, a lively exchange of Italian took place between Mattithyahu and the occupants of the other vehicle.

Waiting for the car to go by, Mattithyahu and Judah got out. At the same time Anthony came up behind them. As the three of them crossed the street, without turning to look at the other two, Anthony said with a completely straight face, "I'm sure they wished you a nice day."

"Astute as always, and we, of course, returned the greeting," smirked Judah.

"I'm going to take Nelli, Mary Ellen, and Father Cossa and try to find a map and then head to the basilica. The three of you split up, but stay within visual contact of each other. Watch for anyone a little too concerned about our whereabouts. The rest of the Guardians should be arriving soon. Once they are here and depending on what we have found, we will figure out our next move."

The Guardians stayed back while Anthony and the others headed towards Prato della Valle Square. Within a few minutes the priest spotted an information booth that had maps of the city.

"The basilica shouldn't be very far from here," said Father Cossa as he opened a map to study.

Anthony listened to the priest, but was also trying to locate Mattithyahu, Judah, and Andrew. He noticed a small group of people passing by, following a male tour guide holding up a blue sign with the words "Basilica di Sant'Antonio" written in large white letters.

Father Cossa and the others also became aware of the small group and watched as they walked a short distance and stopped in front of a store selling Italian-made items. They heard the guide tell the group, "The time is now eleven o'clock. Meet back here under the sign per favore no later than eleven-thirty. The owner of the store behind me allows my agency use of the restrooms and of course hopes you will pick up a little something to take back home. There are also cold drinks to purchase.

"At precisely eleven-thirty, we will head to the last stop on our walking tour, one of the world's most famous religious monuments, Il Santo."

Anthony looked at the others. They all knew what he was thinking. Moving even closer to where the group had stopped, they pretended to be studying the map of the city. At precisely eleven-thirty, they heard "avanti, avanti" and watched as the blue sign began to move down the street. The four of them silently began walking as if they, too, were part of the entourage.

Along the way, the tour guide commented on many of the historical landmarks, walking backwards sometimes, answering questions, and interjecting interesting facts about Padua. Periodically, he stopped to allow people to take pictures.

As they approached the end of the block he turned to address the group, "We will turn right at the next corner and you will get your first glimpse of Il Santo, the basilica built to honor our beloved Saint Anthony. At that time I will spend a few minutes and discuss some of the features you will be seeing once we get closer." Turning, he headed toward the final stop on their walking tour.

Nelli and Anthony, along with Father Cossa and Mary Ellen, watched while the tour group disappeared around the corner. Trailing just a few feet behind, they got their first peek at the church.

"It's huge," said Nelli, "we'll never find the book in time."

Mary Ellen and Father Cossa were thinking the same thing. As they stood there staring at the huge structure, their minds trying to grasp the task ahead of them, the guide began to instruct the group about what to look for once they got closer.

"Saint Anthony's will stated he was to be buried in the small church of Sant Maria Matel Domini. That church was incorporated into the present structure as the Cappella della Madonna Mora or the Chapel of the Dark Madonna.

"Construction on the basilica began around 1235. You will observe that it is a giant edifice without a precise architectural style. It has eight Byzantine domes and as the result of three different reconstructions, incorporates a variety of different influences as shown by the exterior details of Romanesque and Byzantine elements with Gothic and Islamic features. It was completed in 1310 although several structural modifications took place between the end of the fourteenth and the mid-fifteenth century.

"Once inside you will notice the architecture is Gothic in style and that the church is a single-naved plan with an apsidal chancel, broad transepts, and two square nave bays roofed with hemispherical domes. With more than five million pilgrims visiting the church each year, there will be other groups besides ours, so please stay together, avanti." Ten minutes later they were standing in front of the cathedral.

"Please notice that the brick façade is Romanesque in style," said the tour guide, "it was extended outwards when the aisles were built, acquiring in the process four deep gothic recesses and a balcony that stretches across the entire front of the building." He waited a few moments while people took pictures.

Nelli gasped, "Do you see it?" she whispered to the others. There, above the entrance, in a fifth smaller recess was a statue of Saint Anthony holding something in his hands.

"Yes, Nelli, I do," said Father Cossa.

"Is that a book he's holding?"

Before anyone could answer she looked at the priest, "Father, will you read the line about the statue again?"

"A statue in my honor will point you to the peak," replied the priest.

"Do you think this could be the one alluded to in the message?" Nelli asked no one in particular.

"But he is not pointing to anything," said Mary Ellen.

"If I may," said Father Cossa politely, "I will read the line again. A statue in my honor will point you to the peak."

Nelli realized her error.

"We need to look in the direction the statue is facing, not expect Saint Anthony to literally be pointing."

Turning, all they saw were the buildings and streets of Padua.

"Maybe this isn't the right statue," said Mary Ellen.

Nelli felt someone tap her on the shoulder.

"Scusi signorina," said an older gray-haired woman.

"Can I help you?" asked Nelli.

Anthony watched reaching for his gun.

The woman's right hand slowly started moving, her other hand holding onto the scarf wrapped around her shoulders. Anthony pointed the gun at the woman from inside his jacket pocket with his finger resting on the trigger.

"I think you may have dropped this," she said, smiling at Nelli.

In the palm of her hand lay a medal of Saint Anthony.

Anthony pulled his finger away from the trigger but kept his hand on the gun.

"Yes, thank you so much," said Nelli.

"You must get it blessed my dear, if you haven't already, before you leave Padua."

"Yes, I will do that. Thank you again."

The woman smiled and went back to listening to the tour guide.

"Saint Anthony is showing us we're on the right path," Nelli said to the others. "Look around. We're missing whatever it is we are supposed to be seeing." Closing her eyes, she prayed to Saint Anthony.

"O Holy Saint Anthony, gentlest of saints,
your love for God made you worthy,
when on earth, to possess miraculous powers.
Miracles waited on your word,
which you were ever ready to speak for those in need.
Encouraged by this thought,
I implore of you to obtain for me that which I seek.
The answer to my prayer may require a miracle.
Even so, you are the saint of miracles."

When she opened her eyes, she was looking out past the edge of town to an old structure that sat at the top of a hill. Was this what Saint Anthony wanted her to see? Turning around, Nelli raised her hand to ask a question of the tour guide.

"Yes signorina, you have a question?"

The guide looked a little surprised. He didn't recognize the face from the group but they often picked up people along the way.

"Yes, can you tell me what's up there?" Nelli pointed towards the structure at the top of the hill.

"Ah si, signorina, it's the oldest structure in Padua. It was the abbey where our beloved Saint Anthony spent his last days."

"Is it open to the public?" asked Nelli.

"No signorina, it is still a working monastery, inhabited by a small order of Benedictine monks."

"Grazie," Nelli replied.

The guide then directed his group to follow him, walking towards the entrance to the basilica. Nelli and the others stayed behind.

"What is it, Nelli?" asked Anthony.

"Don't you see? The message says a statue in my honor will point you to the peak!" Saint Anthony's statue is looking past the city to the abbey where he spent the last days of his life. He's keeping watch. That's where we'll find the book."

Not far away, another tour guide was pointing out the features of the basilica to his group. Christine pretended to listen but was keeping a close eye on Anthony. Whispering something to the man standing next to her, he nodded, and then signaled to two other men in the group. The three took off, walking in different directions.

Cephas and Y'hochanan arrived in Pesaro a few hours ago. From a distance they observed the three men separate from the group. At the same time, Cephas heard Judah's voice in his earpiece.

"Check out the blonde woman, two o'clock. She keeps looking over at Anthony. She whispered something to the man standing next to her, and now he's leaving, followed by two men," said Judah. "I'm getting bad vibes about this."

"Got it," said Cephas. "Mattithyahu, Andrew, and I will each take one. You keep an eye on the blonde. Judah, I have to ask, your injury, are you okay? Or should I have one of the other Guardians take over?"

"I'm good to go. A little sore but that won't stop me. There's something familiar about that blonde though."

"Everyone has their targets, let's go," said Cephas.

CHAPTER EIGHTY-SEVEN

Nelli and Anthony walked in front, Father Cossa and Mary Ellen close behind. They didn't want to draw attention to themselves so they tried to act like any tourist visiting Padua that day, pointing to different things and taking a few pictures. They were two blocks from where the truck was parked, but Anthony led them down a different street and through an alley.

"Where are you going?" asked Nelli.

"We're going to switch vehicles," replied Anthony. "Mix things up a little."

Entering their destination into the car's GPS, the next voice they heard was that of a woman's—giving them the first set of directions as the car sped off.

"Anthony, what if they won't let us in?" asked Nelli.

"Don't worry, we'll get in."

Nelli was beginning to see a different side of Anthony. The gentleness was gone, and he was guarded now, and on edge, but she felt safe with him.

From the backseat, Mary Ellen blurted out, "I just got a text message from Cardinal McKenna. A plane will be waiting for us at the Venice Treviso Airport. It's twenty miles north of Padua along SS-515, close to intersection SS-53, and he's still working on the other request. Do you want me to reply back?"

Anthony checked the rearview mirror to see if they were being followed and caught a glimpse of Mary Ellen's face. It crossed his mind that maybe they should try again and wondered if she had considered that possibility too. He couldn't ignore that it felt good to be with her, but this time it was he who was trying to save someone. His thoughts were interrupted by a new set of directions: "In approximately a quarter mile, turn right on Via Cavalleto and then drive 1.9 kilometers to Via Sorio."

"Anthony, should I text the cardinal back?" Mary Ellen asked again.

"No, not right now," he answered.

In the backseat Father Cossa stared out the window thinking how strange it was that at one time he had considered the monastic life. He recalled praying and asking God for guidance. During the discernment process and with the help of a spiritual director, he decided that the ascetic life was not his calling. God had a different plan for him; perhaps the last couple days were the reason for the decision he made so many years ago. Then came another set of directions: "In 500 feet, turn left on Via Sorio, drive .8 kilometers."

"There it is," said Nelli as she tried to picture Saint Anthony walking the grounds of the monastery.

Mary Ellen looked out her window as the ancient walls got closer and closer. "I feel like we are about to set foot onto sacred grounds."

The directions continued: "At the next curve follow it to your right. In .2 kilometers you will arrive at your destination. You have arrived at your destination. Goodbye."

Anthony slowed the car to a crawl as he drove over the gravel road up to the main entrance.

Father Cossa stared at the walls of the monastery. He now knew what God's plan was for him. He had been selected to help fulfill the prophecy of Saint Anthony.

The monastery was perched high on a hill. The land immediately surrounding the structure was made up of flat dry earth and cobblestones. The monastery almost seemed as if it were built in the middle of a desert, except for the trees and hills that stretched as far as the eye could see beyond the cobblestones. There was no chance of anyone sneaking up on the building without being noticed.

Getting out of the car, the four began walking toward massive bronze doors cut into stone that made up the outside walls of the monastery. They were not sure what to do once they reached the doors. Drawing closer, it became clear that the doors consisted of a set of panels with inlaid silver lettering that looked very old. The inscriptions on the doors appeared to show, in detail, the possessions of the monastery and the churches that had depended on it in earlier times. To enter now, as in earlier times, someone inside would have to open the doors. Stepping back, they looked for a way to alert the monks they had visitors.

Stretching into the sky above the set of doors was an ancient bell tower where Anthony thought he saw someone watching from one of the openings.

"Hello!" yelled Anthony, "I saw you looking at us. Please, we must speak to the abbot of the monastery."

Finally, a face shrouded by a hood appeared in the narrow opening.

"No one is allowed inside. This is a cloistered community. Why have you come here?"

Father Cossa stepped back so the monk could see him.

"Please, we have been sent here by the Holy Spirit. It concerns the Book of Revelations and what Our Lord foretold of what was to come."

The monk did not respond and disappeared.

"Now what?" asked Nelli.

Anthony was trying to see if there was another way in.

"Shhhh, listen did you hear that?" whispered Mary Ellen. No one moved or said a word. "There, do you hear it?"

It sounded like wood being dragged across metal. It was followed by a noise like metal scraping against metal. They waited to see what would happen next, but the bronze doors remained closed, guardians against the outside world.

Becoming annoyed, Anthony was about to pound on the doors when he heard the release of a metal bolt. A smaller door concealed within the intricate designs of the panel slowly opened inward. A monk appeared, looking as though he could have been from the twelfth century.

"I am Abbot Giuseppe. My brother told me of what you spoke. We live a monastic life of hermits behind these walls, away from the secular world. He said you spoke of the Holy Spirit guiding you to our monastery. What business is it that you have with us?"

"We are here because of the prophecy of Saint Anthony."

Anthony watched to see if there was any reaction from the monk. The abbot appeared undisturbed and said nothing. He stood in silence waiting for Anthony to continue.

"We are here in search of a gift the monk Antonio received from his young apprentice who served him while at the monastery before he died."

Anthony thought he saw a hint of surprise in the abbot's eyes when he mentioned the gift.

"I'm sorry but we cannot help you," said the abbot as he started to close the door.

Nelli had been quietly standing behind Anthony. When she saw the door closing, she quickly stepped in front of her brother.

"Please, wait Abbot Giuseppe, my given name is Antonella. I was named after and have been visited by Saint Anthony since my father's passing."

The door came to an abrupt stop. The abbot stood still then slowly turned to face the young woman. When he came face to face with her, he noticed the cross that hung from her neck.

"What a beautiful cross. May I ask where you got it from?"

"I have a feeling you might already know the answer to that question Abbot Giuseppe, but I will tell you anyway. On his deathbed, my father removed the cross he had worn his whole life and passed it on to me for safekeeping."

"And what did he say to you when he gave you the cross?"

"That I was now the Keeper of the Key."

"Did he say anything else to you?"

"That the secret lies within and to be pure of heart."

Abbot Giuseppe looked up to heaven and closed his eyes in prayer. When he opened them again he said, "Our order has been preparing for this day, but we did not know when the time would come for the Chosen One to visit us. It appears that time is now. Please, come inside."

After they entered, the monk closed the small door and slid the heavy wooden beam back across the metal brackets. They now stood in a large stone courtyard that was surrounded on three sides by arched walkways. Off to the right, seven monks sat on benches facing each other. They did not look up at the strangers in their monastery. Softly they began chanting.

The abbot saw the visitors' heads turn to observe the monks. In a calm and respectful voice he said, "The monks have scheduled times of prayer. They will chant for twelve minutes then return back to their daily duties. Now if you please, I ask that you follow me." He began walking towards the left set of arches.

Outside, the Guardians watched as Anthony and the others disappeared into the monastery.

CHAPTER **EIGHTY-EIGHT**

Thomas got off the phone with D'Amoto and he was furious. He'd planned to be able to report to the Grand Master that the problem had been eliminated and gain back his trust. Secretly he'd put a trail on Christine. Thankfully it paid off.

D'Amoto was sending a car to drive Thomas to the airstrip where a plane was waiting to take him to Padua. He was banking on the reason why Christine was in Padua: because she had located the two siblings and his only hope was to get to them before she did. If not, he was as good as dead, and it wouldn't be a pleasant death. He knew Peter left earlier in the day to meet secretly with the fifteen cardinals who would vote him in as Pope. In less than twenty-four hours, Peter Romanus would become the 266th Bishop of Rome and the leader of the New World Order.

A new Bombardier light business class Learjet was waiting for him when he got to the airstrip. Once on board he was told the flying time to Padua and realized it would be even shorter than he thought.

The plane cut through some low-hanging clouds, but Thomas's thoughts were on planning out his next moves. He needed to beat Christine at her own game. He would let her lead him to where these two individuals were located and then eliminate them before she had a chance to do it herself. Afterwards, he would inform the newly elected Pope Peter II that the problem had been taken care of and he planned on bringing back a souvenir to prove it.

The pilot came on the intercom announcing they would be

starting their descent shortly, and the aircraft had been cleared for landing.

Thomas could see the city coming into view, making out some buildings and homes as the plane continued its descent. Somewhere down there was Christine.

On the outskirts of the city an old monastery sat on the top of a small mountain. That must be the same one they could see from the terrace at the compound, he thought.

General D'Amoto watched from the ground as the Learjet 40 XR landed and taxied to the hangar. The air steps were ready to be placed as soon as the plane came to a stop. The door on the side of the aircraft opened and there stood Thomas. He locked eyes with D'Amoto. Heading down the steps, he yelled over the noise from the engines, "Do we know their location?"

Most likely the general had not spoken to anyone else, and Thomas wanted to give the appearance that his authority hadn't changed.

"We've followed Christine as you asked," replied D'Amoto. "It appears she is headed to a monastery on the outskirts of Padua. You most likely saw it from the plane when you started your approach for landing."

"I don't like changes at the last minute," said D'Amoto angrily.

Thomas was infuriated that D'Amoto would dare chastise him.

"Just take me to where Christine is," said Thomas.

Knowing he wouldn't get any answers from Thomas, the general turned abruptly, "Of course. If you will follow me please," D'Amoto did not like the feeling he was getting. They walked in silence towards the waiting vehicle.

Thomas decided to deal with Christine after he took care of the problem. It would be easy enough to say she had been caught and killed in an exchange of gunfire. If Christine was on her way to the monastery then that must be where the brother and sister were headed. But why the monastery? What was so important about going there? His biggest concern was whether Christine talked to Peter and, if so, what she had told him.

"Tell the driver to take us immediately to the monastery," Thomas said, climbing into the backseat of the black Cadillac SUV. Settling in, he asked, "Do we have any idea why they would be going there?"

"What we know is that the monastery is inhabited by forty monks who spend their days in prayer and doing tasks associated with maintaining a self-sustaining community. They produce olive oil from their own trees under a private label and sell it in town and through some other sources.

"Once a week, someone from the monastery goes into Padua to fill orders and purchase items they cannot grow or make on their own. It is said their chanting can be heard for miles when the wind conditions are right. It is also where Saint Anthony spent his last days before being canonized, one year after his death.

"There is a folklore that the monks are the Guardians of an artifact that Saint Anthony willed to his order for safekeeping but the Vatican has stated that any relics of the saint have been obtained and are under their dominion. So it is believed that the rumor was made up by the townspeople to create a mystery around the abbey."

All Thomas knew was that he wanted to be the one to tell Peter that the people responsible for killing two of his disciples were no longer a threat; they had been eliminated. Whatever they were up to, it was too late to stop what was about to happen but he would make sure they wouldn't cause him or Peter any future problems.

"Are you certain Christine does not suspect she's being followed?" asked Thomas.

"Yes, I have no evidence to the contrary to believe she is aware of our presence."

"Excellent," smiled Thomas. "Tell your men to be ready to move on my command. Let's see what the Worthy Matron has found for us."

General D'Amoto didn't show his anger but there was no way in hell Thomas was going to tell his men what to do.

Thomas looked at his watch. Peter's meeting with the cardinals would be ending very shortly. Next he would be getting together secretly with his disciples. Thomas was never allowed to be present at these meetings. This was the private world of the Grand Master and no one was allowed in when he met with his henchmen. He wondered if Peter had already replaced the two who had been killed.

A few hours away just outside of Rome, Peter gave the

final orders to his disciples. He watched as they left the room headed to their assigned locations. Everything was in now in place. In a matter of hours the world would be his to rule.

Staring out the window Peter could see his future home. He visualized himself standing on the balcony of the papal apartment overlooking the mass of people there to see the new Pope and to receive his blessing. All he could do now was wait.

His thoughts drifted as he wondered who would be victorious, Thomas or Christine, in eliminating the problem that had gotten two of his men killed. He assumed it had been taken care of. Even if they both failed, the committee of cardinals was already setting in motion the proceedings to have him become the next successor to Saint Peter. The cardinals were made to believe that a scandal surrounding the Pope would be cause for him to step down.

None of the fifteen had been told of Peter's plan to have Pope Benedict killed except for one, Cardinal Cavallari. His reward would be a position within the New World Order that would give him more power than what he ever had at the Vatican under the Pope.

Cavallari had sent a message that the Pope was seen heading to his apartment about an hour ago. It was well-known that when the Pope is in residency, Swiss Guards are posted outside his apartment 24/7, and they were now stationed outside the door. Later that evening, Cavallari would request an emergency audience with the His Holiness.

Cavallari had already received what he needed to carry out his part of the plan. The gold ring had been delivered in a box made especially for it. It was an exact duplicate of the one he'd received during the consistory ceremony in which he received his red zucchetto upon becoming a cardinal and a full member of the Sacred College.

Besides the ring, the box contained a vial of liquid. He had already carefully injected the small amount of venom into the empty chamber of the ring and set the spring.

When he would go to see the Pope later that night and kneeled to kiss his ring, the pressure when he grasped the Pope's hand would be enough to trigger the spring. The prick from the needle would release the venom from the King Cobra into the bloodstream of Pope Benedict XVI.

He would wait long enough for the poison to enter the bloodstream before calling for help, knowing it would be too late to save the life of the Holy Father. During that time he would switch the rings, placing the duplicate one back into the box.

The committee of fifteen cardinals would be immediately informed of the pope's death and would be summoned to convene. Using the procedure of Compromise, they would elect the next pope, Pope Peter Romanus II.

Miles away in Padua, Judah had followed the blonde woman back to a hotel. He now remembered where he'd seen her; it was back at the castle. Those eyes were hard to forget. Across town the other Guardians were pursuing their assigned targets.

As Judah waited for his target to come back out he heard Cephas's voice in his earpiece.

"Judah, the three men have joined back up and got into a black SUV heading out of town. It looks like they are headed in the direction of the monastery. Where's your target?"

"She went inside the Hotel Donatello near the basilica on Via del Santo," said Judah. She picked up a key at the front desk and headed to a room on the fourth floor. I'm outside the hotel now waiting for her to come back out. I remember where I saw her before Judah. It was back at Gradara Castle. She was the one in the chapel and watched the whole thing but her hair was black then."

"Don't let her out of your sight, Judah. She could be in there changing her appearance again, so stay alert."

"The eyes will give her away," said Judah. "I'll never forget those eyes."

"Have all the exits been covered?" Cephas asked.

"Taken care of."

"Okay, looks like we're all headed to the monastery on this end. Report in when you have her in your sight again."

Judah sipped a cup of espresso as he kept an eye on the entrance. A small group of men and women exited and were standing in front of the hotel trying to decide which way to go. The tall, slim man in the group seemed to be the leader. He had a map and was pointing in different directions. Judah noticed one of the young men texting and a woman at the back of the group talking on her cell phone.

The redhead at the back on her phone seemed annoyed by the phone call. She had on a pair of khaki cargo pants and boots.

She wore a white tank top with a denim shirt. She wasn't carrying a purse and wore sunglasses that complemented the color of her hair. Her phone call ended, and she turned her attention to the tall slim man. The group had decided to head north on Via del Santo.

Judah started to turn his attention back to the hotel entrance when out of the corner of his eye, he caught the redhead removing her sunglasses and looking at the man coming out of the hotel. She watched him as he turned south and headed in the opposite direction. That's when Judah saw her eyes. He watched as the woman dropped back from the group and disappeared down a side street.

Speaking softly so no one would overhear, he said, "She's changed her hair color; she's a redhead this time. I'll follow her, one of you follow the man headed south on del Santo, six feet, short black hair, tan slacks, and navy sweater."

Judah ran across the street, barely avoiding being hit by a young Italian driving a Vespa. He yelled something in Italian at Judah, and Judah returned the greeting. Reaching the side street, he caught sight of a denim shirt as the woman turned right again at the next corner.

Running now, Judah reached the end of the street and stopped. He had to find out if the woman suspected that she was being followed. A man and woman speaking Italian passed by as he stood there deciding his next move. Using the opportunity presented to him, he walked after them requesting help with directions, at the same time giving him a cover, and allowing him to observe the redheaded woman. A couple streets down, coming from the opposite direction he spotted the man in the tan slacks and navy sweater.

Judah pretended to be having trouble understanding the directions the couple was trying to give him as he continued to observe the redhead. She stopped to talk with the man in the tan slacks and then they both headed east at the next corner. Judah thanked the couple and said he understood now. Pulling out his phone, he headed east.

CHAPTER EIGHTY-NINE

Nelli and the others followed the abbot wondering where he was taking them. Up ahead two monks were walking towards them. They wore tunics tied around the waist with a cloth belt. Over each tunic was a scapula. As they passed by, the two men nodded, acknowledging the abbot, and continued on their way in silence.

Picturesque gardens encompassed most of the cloistered courtyard. Off to the right a monk knelt in prayer in front of a statue of the Blessed Virgin Mary, praying the rosary and surrounded by beds of red roses. If he was aware of the visitor's presence, he did not give any indication of it.

"We come here to pray and reflect during the day," said Abbot Giuseppe, breaking the silence, "and to be surrounded by God's many creations."

The abbot never even turned around. It was as if he had read their minds. He continued walking and was now headed towards the arched arcades to the left of the courtyard. As they came near the end of the colonnaded walkway, there was a narrow opening to their left. You could see a large vegetable garden and beyond that a grove of olive trees and fruit trees.

Again reading their thoughts, Abbot Giuseppe said, "As you can see, we grow most of our own food here on the grounds of the monastery. Besides making olive oil for our own use, we produce and sell it under our own private label. It is one way we earn money to purchase items we cannot make on our own.

"We go into town once a week to buy the things we need

and we also deliver the latest production of olive oil. If you look up ahead," he said pointing, "and to your left, you will see the abbey. This is where we gather each morning to celebrate mass and begin our day."

Abbot Giuseppe stopped walking and now turned to face the strangers Saint Anthony sent to him.

"You may or may not know the tomb of the beloved Saint Anthony is often referred to as the ark."

The four of them looked at each other, stunned by what they had just been told.

"If you will please follow me I have something to show you that I believe might be of interest to you. In his will, our brother Antonio asked that a gift he received from a young apprentice, a small wooden box, be kept here at the monastery. It was said that when the time came the Chosen One would come seeking it." He then turned and headed towards the abbey.

When Giuseppe saw the cross hanging from the chain around Nelli's neck, he believed that she could be the Chosen One, but when he saw the stigmata on her hand he no longer questioned it.

Since arriving at the monastery Nelli had the growing presence of the past Keepers of the Key surrounding her and knew this was the end of her journey. She was about to be shown the gift a young boy made for a monk, which had been hidden from the world for 600 hundred years.

CHAPTER NINETY

God knew that mankind would turn away from his teachings and the dark forces would become so powerful that the faithful would be in peril. Nelli didn't know if finding the book would save the world, but she knew what she had to do. She thought about everything that had transpired since that day when her father gave her the necklace just before he died. Now more than ever she needed to have faith that she would be shown the secret of the box. The rest was in God's hands.

Having reached the entrance to the abbey, they were about to walk up the three steps to the door when Nelli asked, "I'm curious, Abbot Giuseppe, have you looked inside the box?"

Giuseppe stopped and faced the young woman.

"No, my child, we do not have the key. Only the Chosen One possesses the secret to unlocking the box."

"But I was never given a key," said Nelli.

"Our Holy Father has not brought you here to us without the necessary tools," the abbot said.

Standing beside Nelli, Father Cossa gently touched her arm. In a reassuring voice he said, "You have been guided to this spot by Saint Anthony. Trust in him that he will show you what you need to know."

Mary Ellen leaned forward and whispered, "We are right here with you, Nelli, and we'll figure this out together. Remember what you were told by your father and Saint Anthony, be pure of heart, there is where you will find the key."

They followed Abbot Giuseppe into the little church where

the monks met every morning for the first of their daily devotions. Once inside, each of them expected to find a statue of Saint Anthony. The space was smaller than they envisioned, and it was devoid of any religious decoration. The walls were stucco and the floor and pews were made of wood. At the far end of the church was a simple altar with a crucifix on the wall behind it.

Nelli was the first to speak. "I don't understand. There's nothing here that has to do with Saint Anthony."

The abbot nodded, acknowledging he had heard the question, but only said, "Please, follow me," and proceeded to walk to the front of the church.

When they reached the altar, their eyes were drawn to the cross. It was not the standard four-pointed Latin crucifix. It consisted of the upright post and single crosspiece but on it was no corpus or representation of Jesus. Instead, a crown of thorns was wrapped around the crossbars and in the center was the most beautiful white stone set inside a halo of gold. One by one each realized where they had seen the cross before. It was identical to the one Nelli wore, except for the crown of thorns.

Nelli held up the cross her father gave her to compare it to the one that hung above the altar. There could be no mistake, it was identical. On top of the altar sat a tabernacle with a small crucifix beside it. The wooden arched doors were exquisitely carved with scenes of a young man's life. Anthony and Father Cossa moved closer to study them.

"I presume that the scenes portrayed on these doors are the life of a young monk named Antonio?" stated Father Cossa.

"Yes, you are correct."

Nelli and Mary Ellen moved closer to examine the doors.

Starting in the lower left hand corner was a scene depicting a privileged young man who wore the clothing of his time. Another one showed him donning a monk's robe. There were scenes of him speaking to large crowds of people. In another scene, a young boy handed a box to the monk. One showed him in a grove of olive trees looking up towards a glowing light in the sky. The story of Saint Anthony's whole life was documented on these doors.

They had been so focused on studying the carvings depicting the life of Saint Anthony that at first they didn't notice the small engraved letters along the edges of the doors. Then, one by one, they recognized the letters.

"Are you familiar with boustrophedon script, Abbot Giuseppe?" said Father Cossa.

"Ah, I see you are aware of the ancient writing. Good. Yes, one of our labors of love here at the monastery is copying old text to preserve it for future generations."

"Then I imagine you have translated the message on these doors," Anthony said.

"Yes, a long time ago." The abbot followed the script using his finger. "When the time comes, the Chosen One must carry the words of God to the one who bears the symbol of the olive branch."

Father Cossa gasped, startling everyone in the room.

"What's wrong Father?" asked Nelli.

"The prophecy of Saint Malachy uses the cryptic phrase 'olive branch' to symbolize Pope Benedict XVI. Saint Anthony is telling the Chosen One to whom she must travel to see."

Abbot Giuseppe reverently opened the intricately carved wooden doors, exposing a second set. This time they were made of gold and in the center was the acronym IHS. Genuflecting first, he slowly opened the doors and removed the chalice of consecrated hosts, placing it on the altar next to the tabernacle. Walking to the end of the altar, he pushed against one of the wooden panels; a small secret compartment was revealed. Inside laid a key.

Returning with it, he reached inside a second time and began searching for something on the back wall. The other four were trying to figure out what he was looking for when they heard a soft click.

They watched as Abbot Giuseppe gently pushed against the wall. It moved, exposing a hidden compartment. Stepping aside, he allowed the others to see what was inside. There it was: a wooden box identical to the one Nelli had purchased in Rome. They couldn't believe their eyes. It was true after all.

A monk silently appeared out of nowhere and whispered something to the abbot.

"It seems you are not the only visitors to our monastery this day," he said.

Anthony didn't like what he was hearing. Checking his GPS, he could see that some of the Guardians had taken positions outside the walls.

"You must not allow anyone else to enter the monastery,"

Anthony said. "There's been an attempt on Nelli's life and two priests have already been killed."

Giuseppe was distressed by what he had just been told, but remained calm. "Brother Remi will wait here with you while I attend to our new visitors."

Before taking leave, the abbot turned to Nelli. "You are the instrument through which God is working. Have faith and believe that God is here with us. Open your heart completely to Our Lord. Only then will He know that His trust in you has been rewarded, revealing to you the secret to unlocking the box. Remember it will be up to mankind to alter the future. You have done your part."

CHAPTER **NINETY-ONE**

Anthony followed Abbot Giuseppe toward the exit, speaking to him so no one else would overhear. After they finished talking, Anthony pulled out his cell phone and placed a call.

A look of concern came over his face. When the call ended, he walked quickly towards the others, his hand resting on the barrel of his gun.

Looking at Father Cossa, he said, "Father, I ask that you help my sister in any way you can to get whatever is inside that box and put it in a safe place. I will emphasize to you if a book exists, the sooner we have our hands on it, the better."

Father Cossa understood. Time was of the essence.

Now Anthony turned to Mary Ellen, "As I remember, when we did target practice out on your Uncle Harry's farm, you were pretty good. I need you to do something for me."

Grabbing her hand, he placed the gun in it. "If you need to use it, remember, shoot to kill. I know you can do this."

Looking into his eyes she saw the man she'd fallen in love with. They were a team again.

"All right, Anthony, but I pray I won't have to do what you ask. Promise me you won't be gone long."

"I won't," he said, squeezing her hand to show he knew he could count on her. He took off running towards the door.

Nelli knew time was running out. She and Father Cossa stared at the ancient artifact inside the tabernacle. It felt reminiscent of when they'd found the urn with the scroll inside. Reaching in and cradling the box between both hands, she slowly removed it, placing it on top of the altar.

"Isn't it remarkable, Father, to think that the scroll and this box have survived after so many centuries and to be in such beautiful condition?"

"Nothing is impossible if you believe in God's omnipotent power." They began examining the box, looking for a way to open it.

"I don't see anything that looks like a place to put a key, do you Father?"

"No. We need to try and think like the young apprentice Giovanni. Now if I was a young lad back then what …."

As Nelli listened, she studied the details of the cross on the lid. She remembered that the box she bought in Rome had the same design. Around all four sides was a beautiful hand carved pattern of an acanthus scroll. It reminded her of the rolled up scroll they found. Perhaps this was a clue?

Closing her eyes as she had done with the scroll, she explored the box with her fingers, letting her sense of touch guide her. She felt for anything that might open the lid. Maybe there was a concealed drawer where the key was hidden, like the one for the tabernacle.

Father Cossa watched her examine the box, but was still trying to figure out what a young boy back then might use instead of a key.

"I wish Anthony would get back," said Mary Ellen. She had never shot a human being before. Could she do it if she had to? She wasn't sure.

Nelli could see Mary Ellen was beginning to panic. In a calm voice, she said, "I need you to be strong Mary Ellen. I trust you with my life. We are almost at the end of the journey." Then she turned her attention back to the box.

"Try applying a light pressure to the lid. Maybe it will pop open," said Father Cossa.

She gently pushed down, but nothing happened. Then she tried again, applying a little more pressure.

"No luck, Father."

Nelli wished her own father was here with her now. She lovingly touched the cross that he had given her and tried to think of what to do next. She could hear his words as if he was standing right beside her. "Be pure of heart, Antonella." Remembering Saint

Anthony was also the patron saint of lost articles, she said a prayer.

Gentle and loving Saint Anthony
my friend and special protector.
I come to you with a pure heart.
Please listen to my humble petition
in spite of my unworthiness and sinfulness.
I implore you to show me the secret to unlock the gift
you were given so long ago,
and I ask that God will keep us safe from harm.
I pray that I might be worthy to fulfill the responsibility
given to me as the Keeper of the Key.

Opening her eyes, Nelli again examined the box.

"Shhhh, did you hear that?" said Mary Ellen.

Father Cossa averted his attention from the box to listen. "I'm sorry. I don't hear anything, Mary Ellen."

Suddenly his eye caught a small flickering of light. Instinctively he looked at the altar, thinking the light came from a burning candle. Then he realized his mistake. He knew where it was coming from. He'd seen it once before.

"Nelli," he said gently, trying to get her attention. She didn't hear

"Nelli," he said again, this time touching her hand.

Looking over at him she watched his eyes fall on the cross her father had given her. Glancing down she became aware of a soft glowing light coming from the stone.

Then it hit her. If she was right, she had been looking at the secret to unlocking the box all this time without even knowing it. Tilting the box to get a better look, she removed her necklace, slipping the cross off the chain, and compared it to the one on top of the box.

Nelli's was smaller but upon closer investigation, she saw that the design of the cross on the box was made up of not one but two crosses, one inside the other. A smaller one lay just below the surface, making it look like part of the design. Father Cossa looked on in amazement as he came to the same realization as Nelli.

"Could I have had the key all along?" said Nelli.

"I believe your prayer to Saint Anthony has been answered, my child."

Nelli tried placing her cross into the one on the box.

"Look, Father, it's the right size but it's sticking up above the two crosses."

She removed it and both she and Father Cossa examined the cross on the lid more carefully.

"Nelli, look at where the cross intersects. It has a recessed area for something round to fit into it. Turn yours over and try placing it back inside the one on the box."

The cross fit better than before, but it still wasn't flush with the edges. The wooden box was old; maybe it just needed a little coaxing. Nelli tried wiggling it with her finger.

"This has to be the key. What are we doing wrong?"

She wasn't expecting an answer, but just thinking out loud. Applying more pressure this time, it moved, surprising her. She immediately pulled her hand back, afraid she might have broken the lock.

But she and Father Cossa watched as the cross fell into place and now appeared to be part of the design of the box. The next thing they heard was a click. The lid separated from the bottom. She'd had the key all along.

"Our Holy Father knows of your devotion to Him," said Father Cossa. "You have proved it by truly believing in your heart that he would show you the way. Look inside the box, Antonella, and fulfill your destiny. It is time to complete the prophecy."

Mary Ellen and Father Cossa watched Nelli slowly lift the lid. On the inside of it was an inscription:

S S ITA:SECRETUS:ISTIC:INSIDEO S S

"This writing is different from the scroll," said Nelli. "Can you read it, Father?"

"Yes. It's written in medieval Latin, a form of Latin used in the Middle Ages primarily as the liturgical language of the Roman Catholic Church. I will translate: And so the secret here in dwells."

"That's what my father said to me before he died!" said Nelli.

CHAPTER NINETY-TWO

Anthony reached the courtyard and hid behind one of the columns. He spotted the abbot on the far side of the garden. When one of the younger monks saw the abbot, he started running towards him. The men exchanged words, and the younger one pointed to the monastery's entrance.

Keeping his eyes on the two monks, Anthony whispered, "Andrew, tell me what's happening out there?"

"I already told you about the two black SUVs. Three men got out of the first car. One of them has a gun pointed at the head of a monk. The other one is pounding on the door."

"What about the second car?"

"Six men dressed in full military gear and heavily armed," replied Andrew.

"Where are your original targets?"

"Now, that's what's strange," said Andrew. "They're watching all this from a distance. What do you want us to do? And where's Nelli? Did you find what you were looking for?"

"Give me a few minutes to figure things out here. Nelli's safe for the moment, and yes, I believe we have."

Anthony did a quick scan of the courtyard, and then took off running, surprising the two monks by his sudden appearance. Directing his question to the young monk, he said, "Tell me everything you just told the abbot word for word."

The postulant hesitated, looking at Abbot Giuseppe for permission to speak, which was quickly granted. The man was clearly terrified but in a low voice said, "The two men at the door said they would kill Brother De Luca if we don't let them in."

"Did they say anything else?"

"That their men are surrounding the monastery and more monks will die if we don't open the door."

"Andrew, did you hear that?" said Anthony.

"Yes To'mas, every word."

"The one pointing the gun at the monk just gave the other men orders and all six of them took off running. They're carrying some serious fire power. A couple of them are armed with the CZW 43 PDWs. Those things will penetrate anything. Two of the others are carrying the CZW 556 assault rifle. And the last two have SAG-30 automatic grenade launchers. Who are these guys?"

"Cephas, are you on this frequency?"

"Yes, To'mas, I heard everything. I'll take care of things out here. You take care of things in there."

Anthony asked the abbot, "Why was this Brother De Luca outside the walls of the monastery?" He was not happy these people had been able to take a hostage.

The abbot calmly replied, "I mentioned that once a week we go into town to purchase supplies. Whoever these people are must have seen him on his way back to the monastery."

Outside Thomas was losing his patience, yelling, "I suggest you open this door now or in a few minutes, or I'll put a bullet in this monk's head!"

Anthony turned to the young postulant and whispered, "If there's somewhere inside the monastery you can hide, round up everyone and do it, now. GO!"

The young man looked wide-eyed at the abbot. Giuseppe nodded his head and the monk took off.

"Try to stall them as long as you possibly can, then let them in." Anthony told the abbot.

"But what if they want me to take them to the Chosen One?" said Giuseppe.

"Just do whatever they ask," said Anthony. "I don't want anyone else to die." Anthony ran back to where Nelli and the others were waiting for him.

The abbot took a long deep breath, and then seemed to metamorphose into a decrepit old man barely able to walk. Shuffling towards the entrance, he addressed the man on the other side of the door.

"I am an old man and the abbot of this monastery. The Lord has been kind to me but I can no longer move as fast as I would like. I beg you not to harm my brother. I will open the door as quickly as I am physically able."

"I won't wait forever, abbot. If you want to see this monk alive you better move quickly," threatened Thomas.

A few minutes went by before Thomas heard the sound of something scraping against the back of the massive doors. He knew D'Amoto's men were in position and ready to move in as soon as they got the order, plus there was no sign of Christine up to this point. Finally, things were going his way.

CHAPTER NINETY-THREE

Nelli was visibly moved by Father Cossa's translation of the inscription. She looked to him for reassurance, both of them afraid to look inside. If the book were there, it meant that the Antichrist was among them.

In a soft voice, Mary Ellen said, "Do you see it?"

Father Cossa watched as Nelli turned to look inside the box. He kept his eyes on Nelli, wanting to get permission from the Chosen One before he gazed upon the Holy Scriptures.

Time seemed to stop; finally, Nelli looked at Father Cossa and Mary Ellen. Looking in the box they couldn't believe what they were seeing. Father Cossa bowed his head and began to pray. Mary Ellen didn't know what to do. Her first thoughts were of what Nelli must be thinking at this moment. The three of them waited for the first one to say something. Finally Mary Ellen couldn't stand the silence any longer.

"I'm so sorry, Nelli, I guess it doesn't really exist after all." Her voice expressing the disappointment she imagined they were all feeling.

Nelli kept staring into the empty box. Its inside walls were covered with squares, each one made from a different type of wood. Inside each square was an ornately carved letter. The bottom of the box was lined with red satin. If the box once did hold a book, it was now gone.

"It's got to be here somewhere," said Nelli. "We weren't brought all this way for nothing. I won't give up that easily. Father Cossa, do these letters mean anything to you?"

"No. It appears to be just a random selection of letters. There's an odd number of them, thirteen. It's anyone's guess what each one might stand for. It could take years to interpret the meaning."

Nelli pointed to one letter in particular. "Look, this one stands out more than the others; it's larger and more ornate."

Father Cossa couldn't believe he hadn't noticed it already.

"It's actually two letters, the first and last letters of the Greek alphabet, alpha and omega. The symbols were first used in early Christianity signifying that God is 'the beginning and the end.' It comes from the phrase 'I am the alpha and the omega,' an appellation of Jesus found in the Book of Revelations. It was often used as the monogram of Christ."

Mary Ellen suddenly had a thought. "So that leaves twelve letters. Father Cossa could the other letters each stand for one of the twelve apostles?"

"You might just have something there," he said. "We have to remember the names of the apostles were of Hebrew, Greek, and Aramaic origin. The names you will most often find for them will be Cephas for Peter, there," he pointed to the letter ***C***. "Shim'on for Simon," again pointing to a square with the letter S in it. "Mary Ellen you could be right."

"There would be four ***Y***'s: Y'hochanan for John, Yehuda for Judas Iscariot, and Ya'aqov for James twice. Remember there were two apostles named James."

They found four squares each containing the letter ***Y***. Each one had its own unique design; so no two looked alike. He continued to work his way around the walls of the box.

"There's the ***M*** for Mattithyahu, or Matthew; ***B*** for Bar-Tolmay, or Bartholomew; ***J*** for Judah, or Jude. Quickly he spotted the remaining letters; ***T*** for Tau'ma, or Thomas; ***A*** for Andrew; and lastly ***P*** for Phillip. They're all here."

It dawned on Nelli that these were the same names used for each of the twelve Guardians. This wasn't just a coincidence.

"It's here and we're not seeing it. Don't you see? Jesus and his twelve apostles are keeping watch over the words spoken to Saint Anthony by the angels."

Nelli lifted the box and studied it again from all sides.

"Wait a minute, something's odd. Look, Father, the height of the box on the outside is around five inches, but when you look inside, it's maybe three inches deep at the most."

Mary Ellen kept constant watch on the door; all she knew was that the box was empty, and Anthony had been gone a long time. She didn't like the feeling she was getting. It was the same one she had with Cardinal McKenna when they came to the realization that something evil was about to happen.

CHAPTER NINETY-FOUR

"Where's Anthony?" said Mary Ellen. "He should have been back by now. Can't we just take the box and go find him?"

Before anyone could respond she heard footsteps. So did Father Cossa since they both turned their heads expecting to see Anthony. Instead it was Abbot Giuseppe followed by two men holding small caliber rifles. Nelli was still focused on the box, not paying attention to the men entering the church.

Mary Ellen knew she had no chance against the two gunmen. She was wearing a loose fitting blouse and slid Anthony's gun inside the waistband of her pants.

"Finally, we meet," said Thomas, with contempt in his voice.

Mary Ellen and Father Cossa turned to shield Nelli with their backs. "Thank you for pointing out who it is I came to kill, but not before she gives me the key. A monk we picked up in town was a wonderful source of information," he smirked, "and told us all about the gift entrusted to the monastery. He told us the Chosen One was the only one who could unlock it."

Anthony was observing everything from the balcony. He watched as Nelli slowly turned around holding the box in her hands.

"Is this what you came for?" she asked.

Thomas's eyes grew wide. "I came for you and your brother. I hadn't planned on the added bonus of you solving the mystery of the prophecy of Saint Anthony. The Grand Master will be pleased when I show him what I found. I am sure you are unaware of the problems you have caused me, but after today that will no longer be an issue. I see the box is still unopened."

Mary Ellen and Father Cossa were praying that Anthony had gotten help and was out there somewhere. They were also confused by the man's last statement. They knew Nelli had figured out how to open the box.

"Where's my brother?" Nelli demanded.

"Let's just say he will no longer be a problem to anyone. But what to do with you?"

Thomas figured lying would be to his advantage at the moment. Her brother had to be close by and his men would find him and then it wouldn't be a lie.

Nelli closed her eyes, devastated by what she had just been told. Could it be true, was Anthony dead?

"I see that got a reaction," said D'Amoto.

Enjoying the pain his words had inflicted, he added, "My men are very good at what they do," a smile spreading across his face.

Mary Ellen's eyes filled with tears.

Father Cossa lowered his head, his lips moving but no sound came out of them.

Anthony wanted to jump out and show them he was alive but that might risk getting them all killed.

"If you would please come with me, we are running out of time," said Thomas. He motioned for Nelli to start walking towards him.

Before doing so, Nelli set the box down, turned to Father Cossa and gave him a hug. Looking at him, she said, "My journey's come to an end Father, yours has just begun. Please pray for me."

Then turning to Mary Ellen, grabbing her hands as her eyes filled with tears, she said, "Anthony never stopped loving you Mary Ellen, always remember that. Stay close to Father. He will need your help." Picking up the box she began walking towards the men.

Abbot Giuseppe was not a violent man, but he couldn't let this happen. He wouldn't allow Satan's forces to win. Without warning, he reached for the general's rifle. As they struggled, shots rang out.

Mary Ellen pulled out the gun Anthony had given her. "Remember, shoot to kill," she kept repeating to herself.

Thomas grabbed Nelli, pulling her in front of him like a

shield and began walking backwards. Anthony watched in horror. Lining up his target, he held his breath, his finger on the trigger, ready to release it as soon as he had a clean shot. He had to be accurate, or he might hit Nelli.

Thomas was amazed at the strength of the old monk. He began rooting for him. If D'Amoto were killed, it wouldn't bother him. He had what he came for and if the general was dead, there would only be his version of what happened. It would be even better if they both died. It would make his life a lot easier.

Anthony was running out of time. The man who had Nelli was almost to the door. At the same time, he was watching the struggle between the second man and Abbot Giuseppe. He made a snap decision. Moving the gun a fraction of an inch to the right, he waited for his chance. There, it was now or never.

Barely breathing, with a slow steady movement, he pulled the trigger back. The man dropped to the floor and didn't move, a clean shot through the head. Anthony already had a line on his original target, but all he could do was watch as Nelli and her captor disappeared out the door.

"Anthony, talk to me. What the hell's going on?"

Cephas's voice could be heard through Anthony's earpiece.

"I killed one of them but the other one's got Nelli. They should be coming out the front any minute."

"What do you … wait I see them. The men from the second SUV have returned and are surrounding the man and Nelli. We can't risk shooting; Nelli could be hit."

The next thing Anthony heard was gunshots coming from outside. "Cephas, anyone, what's going on! Who's shooting?" he yelled.

"The shots came from the blonde and the three men with her. They just killed all six men that were surrounding Nelli and the man holding her hostage. The monk took off running into the woods. Damn good shooting, if I say so myself."

"Was Nelli hit?"

"No, she's alive. The blonde is walking towards them."

Anthony's head was exploding. He hadn't taken his eyes off the events below but he was totally preoccupied with what he heard taking place outside. His brain finally registered what his eyes already knew.

"No!" he screamed.

CHAPTER **NINETY-FIVE**

Four bodies lay on the floor. The man that took Nelli must have seen Mary Ellen pull out the gun and start shooting.

Anthony flew down the stairs, taking two steps at a time. Reaching Mary Ellen, he found that she had been shot in the chest. He leaned in close. She was still alive, but was losing a lot of blood.

"Mary Ellen, stay with me. I'm going to get help."

When she heard Anthony's voice at first she thought she was dreaming but then opened her eyes and saw it really was him. "We thought you were dead!" Mary Ellen exclaimed. Anthony could barely hear her.

"I'm very much alive, Mary Ellen."

The gun was still in her right hand. With her left, she grabbed Anthony's arm. "You have to save Nelli. You can't let them take the box."

Just then Abbot Giuseppe staggered over. He had a large gash on his head and blood was running down his face.

"Go, my son. I'll take care of things here."

"But you …."

"I'll be fine. A little beat-up, but our blessed Lord must have more work for me to do before he takes me home. Go."

Anthony was torn; he didn't want to leave Mary Ellen but the killers had his sister and the box. He looked at the monk. "I'll send help."

Now looking at Mary Ellen, "I'll do what you ask, but only if you promise me you'll be here when I get back."

Mary Ellen smiled and nodded. "Now get going."

Standing up, he ran over to Father Cossa to see where he'd been hit. A stray bullet had found its way into the priest's lower abdomen. When Anthony knelt down, the priest motioned for him to come closer, his other arm was hidden beneath his cassock. He removed it. He was holding a small book.

"Take it Anthony. Nelli must have figured out the second secret to the box. When she gave me a hug she slipped it to me."

Anthony stared at the book. It was difficult to register what he was actually seeing. People had died. Now his sister was next if he didn't get to her before it was too late.

"Take it Anthony; you must take it to Pope Benedict. The future of the Church could depend on it."

"I will do my best, Father."

"I feel the presence of the Holy Spirit, Anthony. Take comfort in knowing He is watching over our souls."

Anthony paused as he glanced over at Mary Ellen and saw Abbot Giuseppe applying pressure to try and stop her bleeding. He looked back down at the priest.

"You must go, my son. It is in God's hands now."

Anthony hesitated. "I will send help, Father, just hang on."

The next voice he heard was Cephas's. "Anthony, tell me what you want us to do!"

"I'm coming! Tell me exactly what you're seeing."

"The blonde woman has a gun pointed at the man, and the man has his gun pointed at Nelli's head. They're talking and it appears as if they know each other. He's very angry about something."

Anthony was now within a few yards of the entrance. He slid up against the wall working his way to the door. Stopping just a few inches before it, he listened in on the conversation.

"If you think you can replace me, you're out of your mind. I know the Grand Master was not happy with me when two of his disciples were killed because of this woman and her brother. But when he sees what I have found because of it, he'll forget all about that.

"He has spent years and millions of dollars trying to find out if this box existed and when it's in his possession, he will see that in the long run, it was a good thing this happened."

"I can't let you do that, Thomas."

"Be smart, Christine. Peter likes you. You could have a prominent position in the New World Order. He'll have his hands full being Pope. He'll need good people around him to run the new government."

Anthony was trying to grasp what he was hearing. He had assumed they were both working together. Maybe he was wrong.

"We could say we worked together on this," Thomas smiled.

Christine said nothing at first. Then calmly, she told him, "We're on different sides, you and I."

Thomas was confused, "What are you talking about? You're the Worthy Matron of one of the largest P2 Lodges we have."

"Yes, and it took a long time to infiltrate your group."

Anthony couldn't figure out what this woman was talking about. Infiltrate? Who was she working for?

"Anthony, can you hear what they're saying?" said Cephas. "Do you want us to take them out?"

"No. I don't think she's one of them, Cephas," Anthony whispered.

"You're nuts. She was the one back in the chapel when they killed the priest."

"But she didn't kill him. She could be working uncover."

He inched closer to the door thinking about his next move when he heard the man say, "Whoever you are, you're too late to stop what is taking place. While we stand here talking, Pope Benedict should be dead and by a special decree fifteen handpicked cardinals will have already named Peter Romanus the next Pope."

Christine appeared to be unaffected by the news, which troubled Thomas. Then, with an air of confidence, she said, "I think you might be mistaken, Thomas. If my men have done their job as I am confident they have, Pope Benedict is alive and in a safe location."

Whoever she was, Anthony was now convinced she was on the side of good.

"Cephas," said Anthony, barely audible, "She's on our side. I'm going out. Cover me."

"You got it. Let's pray you're right."

His gun extended, Anthony began to make his presence known to Christine. He counted on her not giving him away.

Christine caught the movement of someone coming out of the monastery. She knew that Anthony, the other woman, and the priest were still inside. Seeing Anthony, she kept the conversation going with Thomas, raising her voice to hold his attention.

Completely exposed now, Anthony saw that the woman was covering for him. His gun was within a couple of inches of Thomas's head. Christine was talking with Thomas, but she could see everything Anthony was doing.

The Guardians were watching from their different locations, their targets lined up in the crosshairs of their rifles, fingers resting on the triggers.

Anthony now placed the barrel of his gun against the back of Thomas's head. "It's a funny thing, Thomas. Thomas, that's your name, right? Is that I am still alive. I suggest you remove the gun from my sister's head."

"You're supposed to be dead."

"That's unfortunate for you," said Anthony.

"Anthony, you're alive," said Nelli, shocked at hearing her brother's voice. "They told me you were dead." She started to turn to look at Anthony. Thomas was surprised by the movement and jerked back. Realizing the gun was no longer against her head, Nelli slammed her elbow into Thomas's chest. Before he had time to recover, Anthony took Nelli and pushed her behind him, at the same time grabbing Thomas's gun and knocking him to the ground. The next thing he heard was two gunshots.

He looked up to see where they had come from. Next to him stood Christine with her gun pointed down at Thomas. She had shot him once in the shoulder and once in the leg. He wasn't feeling very well, but he was alive.

Anthony stared at the woman. "Thanks. Who are you working for?"

Without taking her eyes off of Thomas, she replied, "You need to get your sister to the plane. It's waiting for you at the airstrip."

He was shocked that she knew about the plane. At the same time Nelli was tugging on his arm.

"Anthony," she whispered, "we have to go back inside. I found the book and secretly gave it to Father Cossa."

He did not want to tell her about what had happened. Facing her he said, "Nelli, Father gave it to me. I have it now. This woman's right. I need to get you to the plane."

"We still need to go back inside Anthony and get Mary Ellen and Father Cossa so they can come with us."

The look on his face gave him away.

"Anthony, what is it?" Nelli could see something was wrong. Nelli … Father Cossa was hit by a stray bullet."

"Is he going to be okay? Mary Ellen, what about Mary Ellen?"

"She was struck too, Nelli. I don't know what to tell you. Abbot Giuseppe said he'd do everything he could."

Swinging his gun around, he pointed it at Thomas, "This bastard shot both of them."

"Anthony stop and think," Christine said, trying to defuse the situation. "I need to question him. He can tell us things we need to know. You can hurt him more by delivering the book to Pope Benedict."

Anthony was using every ounce of control to stop himself from pulling the trigger. What Christine said was true. If he killed this man, then it would be personal. That's not what he was trained for.

"Anthony, I'll have my men attend to the people inside. They're trained combat medics." She motioned for two of them to head inside. "You must get on that plane. The Pope is waiting for you."

"Who are you?" asked Nelli.

The other Guardians were now standing just a few feet away, waiting to hear what the woman had to say.

"I am part of an elite group of men and women. We report to only one individual whose name I cannot divulge to you. Few know of us and it must remain that way. We are similar, you and I, Anthony. We were each chosen to be Guardians. Have your men go with you for protection. Take the SUV that our friend here has so kindly left for our use. I don't think he will have much use for it."

Anthony knew he couldn't do anything more for Mary Ellen and Father Cossa. He had taken a vow to protect the Chosen One. He had not known that person would turn out to be his sister. The words written in this book that he was given offered hope to millions of souls. If they chose to believe and repent perhaps the Church and the world could be saved.

"You're right, Christine, or whoever you are. Perhaps we will meet again."

CHAPTER NINETY-SIX

"I've been trying to reach Mary Ellen, Commander Crevelli, but all I get is her voice mail."

"Let me know the minute you reach her," said Crevelli.

Cardinal McKenna wouldn't allow himself to believe the worst, so he tried to speculate on all the different reasons why she hadn't called. The plane had been sent as promised and was waiting to bring everyone back to Rome.

The last few hours had proven to be devastating for the Vatican. The plot to kill the Pope had been uncovered and the Vatican dubbed the name of the investigation the "Serpent's Disciple."

They were beginning to learn who some of its members were and the extent this group had infiltrated the Church. It was never proved P2 was behind the death of Pope John Paul I but at least this time the Vatican had moved His Holiness to a safe location. If Mary Ellen O'Farrell had not persisted in trying to clear her brother's name, maybe none of this would have ever been brought to light.

One of the ways they were finding out who was a member of the group was to view surveillance video. Cameras were positioned throughout Vatican City, many visible, but others hidden.

They searched the video looking for small groups of people standing around, slowing it down each time to focus on the hands, watching closely for any evidence of anyone nervously twisting the ring on the left hand, exposing a tattoo.

McKenna had been asked to help in viewing the tapes. It

made him sick to his stomach when he saw who some of the individuals were who'd joined this secret society; one of them had even been in the seminary with him. These were devout men, dedicated to Christ, or so he had thought. Cardinal Ruffo in particular was one he had always looked up to as an example to follow because of his unending love for the Church. Where had it gone wrong for these men of God?

He had been faced with temptation many times. Yes, he made some poor choices in his life but never when it came to selling his soul. He wondered why he had been given the grace to choose good over evil, and the next person had not. One day he would know the answer to this and other questions he had wondered about throughout his life, God willing.

His thoughts were interrupted by footsteps headed in his direction. Commander Crevelli came through the door and walked over to where McKenna was working. He looked tired. Crevelli leaned over, placing both hands on top of the desk. "He wants to see you."

McKenna was caught off guard by the request. "Did he say why?"

"You will come with me now, please." Crevelli wasn't about to get into a discussion speculating why his presence had been requested.

"Yes, of course."

Pausing the video and placing his glasses on the desk, he rose more slowly than he planned. His body was stiff from sitting for so long. They had not gone very far when the lights began flickering on and off. Suddenly they were encased in darkness. McKenna's heart began racing and beads of sweat were forming on his forehead. Instinctively, he reached out for the wall to get his bearings, at the same time expecting to feel his attacker's weapon of choice.

What he heard was the calm voice of Commander Crevelli. "Do not be concerned cardinal; we have our own power source down here. It is just switching over to the other generator. It will only take a few seconds."

Before the commander had even finished his sentence, the lights came back on. Ahead, the cardinal could see two gendarmes, holding the traditional halberds, standing at attention. Just past them, the hallway veered to the left. As McKenna followed Commander Crevelli around the corner he saw two more gendarmes standing on each side of a metal door.

Crevelli tapped twice and a pair of eyes appeared from behind a small window. A bolt was released and then Crevelli entered a code into a keypad mounted on the wall, placing his hand against the panel to be scanned. He waited for the small red light to turn green, and then opened the door. Four guards were stationed inside and a fifth man seated in a chair.

"You're here, Cardinal McKenna. Wonderful. I so much wanted to have a chat with you."

The man sitting in the chair sickened McKenna. Surprisingly, Cardinal Cavallari seemed even more arrogant than before, if that was possible, still dressed in his black vestments along with the scarlet sash and skullcap.

"I wanted to see your face when I tell you the news. Sit, please," he said nodding to the chair across from him.

"No thank you. I'll stand," McKenna said.

"Suit yourself," said Cavallari shrugging.

The commander of the Swiss Guard stood opposite McKenna on the other side of the room, one hand resting next to his side, the other wrapped around the handle of his gun.

"The Church is finished as you know it, McKenna," Cavallari began. "It's been so easy to gather souls for the other side, including our own brethren. Temptation combined with free will is a wonderful thing. It was unfortunate for Father Roberto that he had such an inquisitive mind. We couldn't allow him to start connecting the dots and put a wrench in our plans. It was hoped that the warning we left behind would end any further meddling, but we had time on our side."

"It's not the first time we've been able to bring the Church to its knees, but never before was the whole world so easily accessible to us. The faithful around the world are angry at the Church for the cover up of the scandal involving priests and are looking for someone they can believe in again, and Peter Romanus is just that person."

"So what is it you're trying to tell me?" asked McKenna.

"Perhaps you think by uncovering my involvement in this that you can stop what is about to happen."

Cavallari's attention was diverted as a young priest rushed into the room. He headed straight to where Commander Crevelli was standing.

The commander did not take his eyes off of Cardinal Cavallari even as he listened intently to the young priest. When the man finished, Crevelli continued to keep his eyes locked on Cavallari and said something to the young man. Acknowledging that he understood, the commander motioned for one of the Swiss Guards to take his place. Heading for the door, he first stopped to whisper something to McKenna.

McKenna closed his eyes and lowered his head, overcome by the information just relayed to him. Cavallari figured they had just learned that Pope Benedict was dead. Unable to resist, he said, "Looks like you received bad news, McKenna," he smirked. "I told you it was too late to stop it. By this time tomorrow, our new Pope will be the ruler of the New World Order."

McKenna looked at the man in front of him. The only thing he had ever wanted was to become a priest. The calling had been strong in him. He spent his whole adult life praying for the lost souls who turn away from God, that they may discover the errors of their ways before meeting their Maker. Now he couldn't stop himself from thinking evil thoughts; he wanted to see this man suffer. He wanted him dead.

Cavallari started to laugh. "You want to kill me, don't you? The apple the serpent is offering is tempting isn't it, Donovan? You were given free will, what will you choose?"

Cavallari started laughing even harder but McKenna had already made his decision. He feared what the future held for him but he didn't have any choice, allowing the cardinal to enjoy the moment. It would be his last.

"I choose to follow the teachings of the Bible. You will be judged by one greater than any of us. I pray he will be merciful on your soul."

"I'm disappointed in you," said Cavallari. "I thought you were your own man, but I was mistaken."

"Cardinal Cavallari, I will assume you believe you know what the commander told me. Let's see how close you are. I was informed that by this time tomorrow, Pope Benedict XVI will have already addressed the world over Vatican Radio. He will have exposed the conspiracy by a group called P2 against the Catholic Church and the plot to kill him. He will also tell the world of a miracle that has taken place that the prophecy of Saint Anthony has been fulfilled and a book containing the words of Our Lord has been found, which he now has in his possession."

Cavallari couldn't catch his breath. Then the most awful sound came out of him. It sounded like the howling of thousands of souls being cast into hell.

McKenna was not frightened by the sound. In fact it gave him hope. Satan had been defeated once again and this servant of the devil sitting across from him knew it.

"But your reaction a minute ago?"

"I did receive bad news. A friend of mine has been shot and is believed to be dead."

Cavallari realized his life was over. For Peter Romanus, well, he would have to reign another day. He was almost glad he wouldn't be there to see the aftermath of Peter's anger. "May I make a request?"

McKenna had never witnessed the loss of a man's soul in front of his eyes. He hoped he never would again.

"Would it be possible to have my hands released from these restraints enough that I might be able to pray before I am taken away and make an Act of Contrition?"

McKenna had not even realized they had secured Cavallari's arms and legs to the chair, which was bolted to the floor. He didn't see how releasing the restraints would create any risk so he asked the guard to loosen the straps. Cavallari lowered his head and made the sign of the cross, joining his hands as if to pray. The prick from the needle was so negligible he wondered if it had even broken the skin, but the venom of the King Cobra was now surging through his blood.

Feeling lightheaded, his lips and tongue began to swell and he now struggled to breathe. He grabbed his throat, gasping for air. McKenna looked on, confused by the seizure, as Cavallari doubled over, screaming in pain.

"Go get help!" yelled McKenna to the guard. He ran over to where Cardinal Cavallari was sitting but just as he got there the cardinal slumped forward, held in place by his legs, which were still strapped to the chair.

CHAPTER **NINETY-SEVEN**

Anthony could see the plane up ahead. Pushing down on the accelerator, he sped towards it, braking just before reaching the steps to the open cabin door of a Challenger 300, where a young priest from the Vatican stood waiting.

After they were on board and in their seats, the priest secured the door and immediately prepared the cabin for departure. Within minutes the plane began taxiing down the runway for takeoff. Once in the air Nelli and Anthony were handed a phone.

"Someone would like to speak with you," said the priest.

Putting the phone on speaker, they heard someone on the other end say, "Go ahead, the line is secure."

They were stunned when the next voice was Pope Benedict's. They talked for quite a while. During the conversation he told them about a vision he had the first month he became Pope. He relayed to them how one of God's heavenly messengers came to him and revealed that a Chosen One would deliver the words of Our Lord written down in a book.

At the time, he didn't know what it meant. Then a month ago the Holy Father had another vision. The angel told him he must see through the façade and recognize Satan's servants for what they *are*, rather than what they appear to be. These bearers of false promises will cause people to give their allegiance to and worship a false prophet. Even the elect will not be totally immune from the wolf in sheep's clothing. This time the Pope was shown the book and told to preach the words to every ear that would listen.

When the call ended, Nelli and Anthony looked at each

other, not knowing what to say. Thankfully, the plot against the Pope had been discovered in time and the commander of the Swiss Guard had the assassin in custody.

The young priest came and retrieved the phone and then handed headsets to them so they could listen to the Pope who was about to speak to the world on Vatican Radio.

Nelli and Anthony put on the headphones and plugged the cable into the outlet in their armrest and waited for a second time that day to hear the voice of Pope Benedict.

This time he told the entire world about a false prophet who was now among them. Many faithful, including religious leaders, had turned their backs on God and joined the army of Satan. If this was the end-time, then every person created in the image of God needed to examine his or her conscience and repent.

At the close of the broadcast, he asked the world to pray, that he would be given the wisdom and strength to rebuild the Church, as God once asked of Peter. He closed with a verse from Matthew 16: 18: "And I tell you, you are Peter, and on this rock I will build my church, and the gates of hell shall not prevail against it."

A few minutes later, the pilot's voice came on over the intercom, "We have started our descent and should be on the ground in approximately fifteen minutes. The Vatican has sent a car and will be waiting to take you directly to see the Pope."

Nelli and Anthony stared out the window, each lost in their own thoughts. Up here everything seemed so calm and peaceful. Looking out at a clear blue sky, they found it hard to believe that the world could be on the verge of an apocalypse. Would they be awakening to find out that this had been nothing more than a dream? Then someone touched Nelli's arm.

"Signorina, you must fasten your seat belt, per favore."

Forced now to realize it wasn't a dream, she turned and looked at Anthony. She could see the toll all of this had taken on him. Mary Ellen, not to mention others, was dead. As she held onto the box, tears began to run down her cheeks.

Sensing someone staring at her, she looked over to see a man standing in the aisle. Leaning over, he gently pushed back the hair from her cheek. "I'm proud of you Antonella and also of Anthony," said her father.

"I didn't know if I would see you again. I am so glad you're here Dad," she said. "I'm afraid it might be too late. So much has happened."

"Do not be sad. Many souls that were lost are already repenting and once the words of God are revealed, the world will begin to see the wrong of its ways. You must now live your life. You will not see me again, Antonella, but know I am watching over you. Always remember, I love you."

Nelli felt the wheels of the plane touch down. Glancing out the window, she spotted a black limousine. On each side of the front of the vehicle were two small flags carrying the papal emblem flapping in the wind. She turned to speak more with her father, but there was no one there. She saw Anthony looking at her.

"Father is very proud of you, Nelli," he said, smiling warmly at his sister. "So am I."

"Did you get to speak to him this time, Anthony?"

"Yes, Nelli, this time I was able to talk to Father."

They arrived at the hangar where the emissary from the Vatican was already starting to unlock the door so the steps could be pushed up to the plane.

"I would never have made it without you by my side, Anthony."

Nelli looked down at the box resting on her lap and in a quiet voice she said, "It's going to be hard getting over losing Mary Ellen, Father Cossa, and the others that gave up their lives to help us."

"Yes I agree, Nelli, but I cannot allow myself to dwell on what has transpired. As your Guardian, I must continue to do my job as protector of the Chosen One until the book has been delivered to Pope Benedict, and I see it placed in his hands."

Two more members of the Swiss Guard now joined the two that had accompanied Nelli and Anthony on the plane.

"Signorina and signore, if you please Pope Benedict is waiting."

The door of the armored limousine opened, and Nelli and Anthony got inside. The Guardians and the four Swiss Guards were divided up between four patrol cars sent to escort the Chosen One to the Vatican.

As soon as Anthony slid in the backseat next to Nelli, the door closed and the car sped off. The lead car's siren blared, clearing the road in front of them while the other three vehicles followed close behind.

They couldn't have driven for more than ten minutes before reaching Arco delle Campane, the southeast entrance into Vatican City. Barricades had been set up as they watched through tinted windows; they were waved through the heavy security that was everywhere. The car came to a stop, and the door on Nelli's side was opened.

Nelli got out, and came face to face with Commander Crevelli and Cardinal McKenna.

"We finally meet. I wish it could have been under better circumstances. Let me introduce myself. I'm Cardinal Donovan McKenna and this is Commander Valentino Crevelli, the head of the Vatican Swiss Guard." Nelli smiled and nodded her head, acknowledging both men.

Cardinal McKenna glanced down at the article Nelli cradled in her arms seeing for the first time the box that held the book of Holy Scripture.

Then Cardinal McKenna said, "You must be Anthony; I see that your father chose well in picking you to protect the Chosen One. The Church will never be able to show its gratitude for keeping her safe. Please, if you will both come with me now, the Holy Father is very anxious to meet with you."

CHAPTER NINETY-EIGHT

Cardinal McKenna began filling Nelli and Anthony in on some of the things uncovered so far. He understood it would take time to discover the full extent of the conspiracy.

For most of the conversation, McKenna looked straight ahead as he talked. Pausing before making his next statement, he turned to look at Nelli and Anthony.

"Remarkably enough, a small insignificant detail that Devlin O'Farrell noticed is what allowed us to uncover a group of cardinals within the Vatican who were part of the conspiracy to replace the Pope."

Nelli and Anthony glanced at each other at his mention of Mary Ellen's brother.

The cardinal continued, "Luckily, through that information, we were also able to discover and apprehend the individual who was to carry out the assassination. Unfortunately, before we were able to find out what he knew, he took his own life.

"This is not the first time evil has invaded these sacred walls. Some thirty years ago, this same organization attempted to take control of the Church. Of course you can see that they did not succeed. Many believe they were behind the death of our beloved Pope John Paul I. If they had succeeded a second time in killing Pope Benedict ….

"It is not an exaggeration to say the Church is facing some serious issues," he continued. "The Antichrist is among us and, I believe, behind this cancer that has spread throughout the Church. We will have much to atone for within our own walls before we ask others to do the same," his face expressing the gravity of the situation.

"Commander Crevelli, as we speak, is putting together a secret team of select individuals who will fly under the radar, to locate this false prophet and anyone associated with him."

Anthony hesitated at first, but then said, "You could enlist the woman Christine that helped us back at the monastery." Anthony wanted to see if she was connected to the Vatican in some way.

"I do not know this woman Christine that you speak of," said Cardinal McKenna.

"But you knew we were headed for the plane back at the monastery."

"Yes, we were lucky that Abbot Giuseppe sent word ahead to let us know you had found the book and were on your way to the airstrip."

Anthony was baffled by what group Christine could be a member of. After all this was over he planned to find out, but for now decided not to say anymore.

McKenna continued, "If our dear Mary Ellen had not been so stubborn about her quest to clear her brother's name, we would have probably never found out, or found out too late, to save the Pope from being assassinated."

Anthony wasn't sure if he should bring this up right now but decided to anyway. Since the cardinal had brought up Mary Ellen. "If I may inquire Cardinal McKenna, it would be comforting to know that Mary Ellen's belief in her brother's innocence had been rewarded."

McKenna knew, but he would let the Holy Father address that question.

"Might I suggest you ask Pope Benedict about that when you meet with him. I was asked to tell you that he regrets your time with him must be short, but he would like to visit with you again at a later date.

"As you know the last few hours have been unprecedented here at the Vatican. Pope Benedict has declared his intention to convene an Ecumenical Council, only the third time in the history of the Church.

"His Holiness has already begun to gather the College of Bishops. The council will be the first to witness the secret text. But, before that can happen, there will need to be the expulsion of all individuals who chose to go against the Church doctrine. So you see the Holy Father has a heavy burden before him."

Nelli and Anthony could only listen, not knowing what to say.

"Well, we're here," said Cardinal McKenna.

Up ahead were two massive wooden doors, flanked on either side by Swiss Guards in full dress uniform. Through the partial opening could be seen Michelangelo's The Last Judgment, covering the entire back wall of the Sistine Chapel.

The doors opened slowly and a priest dressed in a black cassock with the distinctive red watered-silk sash wrapped around his waist stood in silence, looking at Nelli. It was the camerlengo to the Vatican. Behind him was a sea of red; clergy from around the world were gathering on this austere occasion, divided into small groups and involved in serious discussions.

Anthony turned to face Nelli. "It is time, my dear sister. The prophecy said that the words of Our Lord should be given to the one who is known by the symbol of the olive branch. He's waiting for you in the next room."

Cardinal McKenna waited until Anthony finished talking, and then made the introductions.

"Camerlengo, may I present Antonella Andruccioli and her brother Anthony. As you can see, they have brought something for the Holy Father."

"Si, Pope Benedict has been anxiously waiting for you. Per favore, un momento."

Before going to announce the Chosen One's arrival, the camerlengo bowed, knowing he was in the presence of Holy Scripture. Then he turned silently, disappearing into the crowd.

After several minutes, a few of the priests near the doors of the chapel turned to look at the two strangers who were standing outside in the hallway. As the priests moved aside there stood Pope Benedict, holding the ferula that was often associated with him. Although he used others, this pastoral cross seemed to be his favorite. The camerlengo was standing next to the Pope and motioned for Nelli to come forward.

Nelli turned towards Anthony. "Are you coming?" she asked.

"No, Nelli, you must do this alone. Go, the Holy Father is waiting."

Holding the box tightly, she began to walk toward the entrance to the chapel. Anthony and Cardinal McKenna watched in silence as Nelli and the Pope spoke privately. They continued to watch as she opened the box so the Holy Father could see the book for the first time. One by one, the voices in the room grew silent.

Genuflecting with assistance from the camerlengo, and then making the sign of the cross, Pope Benedict lovingly removed the sacred book. Nelli lowered the lid and handed the box to the camerlengo.

CHAPTER **NINETY-NINE**

Pope Benedict looked at Nelli with admiration. "You have served Our Holy Father well, Antonella. I hope I will be able to do the same. I've been informed that you and your brother have something you wanted to ask me?"

Nelli was taken aback by the question. With all the Pope was facing, she felt it would be inappropriate to inquire about Devlin O'Farrell.

"You have much more urgent matters to attend to, Your Holiness," she said.

"If my information is correct, my child, perhaps I can give you the answer to your question."

In the antechamber Anthony and Cardinal McKenna watched as the camerlengo that stood next to the Pope, turned and disappeared from view. When he returned, there was another priest with him. Anthony immediately recognized the face. You couldn't mistake the resemblance. It was Mary Ellen's brother, wearing the vestments of an ordained priest.

Without looking at Anthony, Cardinal McKenna whispered, "Mary Ellen can rejoice, knowing her brother's name has been cleared, and he is again a priest in good standing."

Back inside Nelli couldn't believe her eyes.

"I believe this answers your question," said Pope Benedict.

Devlin bowed with respect to the Holy Father, and then turned to Nelli. "It's good to see you, Nelli," he said, smiling at her. Turning back to Pope Benedict, he said, "I have brought what you asked, Holy Father."

He handed a small box to the Pope. It was covered in fabric made of red silk. On top was the insignia of the Vatican in gold. He stepped to the side, looked at Nelli and said, "Pope Benedict has something he would like to give to you."

Nelli turned to look at Pope Benedict.

"Come closer, Antonella. You have fulfilled the destiny of the Keeper of the Key as was prophesized by Saint Anthony. The key that your father passed on to you must now remain with the box. Since you can no longer wear the cross to remind you of him, perhaps this will keep his memory alive for you."

Accepting the box, Nelli removed the lid. Inside was a pendant attached to a gold chain. It was in the shape of a rose, a pink rose. It was the flower her father always brought home to their mother. Nelli couldn't take her eyes off it.

Pope Benedict went on, "The symbol of Pesaro is the pink rose where your father was born. Perhaps this will help keep him close to your heart. Please bow your head now so I may give a blessing before you must depart."

Nelli bowed her head and felt the hand of the Pope gently placed on her head. Then he said a prayer.

Nelli watched Pope Benedict walk away. She was now alone with Devlin. Her eyes began to fill with tears.

"Mary Ellen would be so happy to know you are a priest again."

"I'm sure that's true," said Devlin. "Let's join Anthony. There is someone else who would like to talk with both of you before you leave."

As the two of them exited the Sistine Chapel, the Swiss Guards at each door with coordinated robotic movements, began closing out the world to all who remained inside.

One of its main objections of the council would be the execution of a thorough reform of the inner workings of the Church.

Nelli turned her head to see if she could catch one last glimpse of the Holy Father. Just before the massive doors closed, she did get one last look. He was standing as if waiting for her to look back. He smiled at her. Then the doors closed, locking out the rest of the world.

At that moment she knew Satan had lost. The Church would be rebuilt.

EPILOGUE

Nelli and Anthony walked behind Father O'Farrell and Cardinal McKenna as the two men talked quietly so not to be overheard.

Outside again they walked a short distance to another building that had no markings on it. Upon entering, they found a nun sitting behind a desk who nodded when she recognized Cardinal McKenna.

They walked past the front desk and through a set of French doors. Straight ahead was a sitting room that looked out onto a lovely garden with a central fountain surrounded by trees and flowers. Turning right, they headed down a short hallway.

Stopping in front of one of the doors, Cardinal McKenna knocked lightly. Opening it, he turned to Nelli and Anthony.

"Please," he said motioning for them to enter. "Someone has been patiently waiting to see you."

Stepping aside he watched with Father O'Farrell as the two entered the room, anxious to see their reaction.

Stunned, Nelli and Anthony stared at the person in front of them. There, sitting up in bed, was Mary Ellen.

She was still very weak but smiled from ear to ear when she saw them. "So I heard you brought Pope Benedict a gift?" she said.

"She certainly did." The voice came from behind them this time. A nun pushed a wheelchair holding Father Cossa into the room.

"Sister Francis here has been taking very good care of Mary Ellen and me," he said with a twinkle in his eye. "I want to hear everything and don't leave anything out."

As Cardinal McKenna and Father O'Farrell watched, Cardinal McKenna turned to Devlin, "Do you think Anthony will accept a new assignment?"

ABOUT THE AUTHOR

Deborah Stevens lives in the Twin Cities, Minnesota with her husband. A native of Detroit, Michigan, Stevens majored in interior design. Her interest in the arts and to detail is evident in her work: from famous paintings to architectural descriptions to intriguing but little known facts. Deborah has traveled extensively to Europe, Mexico, Hawaii, and the Caribbean, and has a soft spot for her ancestral home of Italy. She is currently working on the sequel to *The Serpent's Disciple.*

Made in the USA
Charleston, SC
06 September 2013